Patricia Elliott writes:

'Names have a huge importance for us. Perhaps you hate your own and long for something cool and glamorous, more or less unusual – something that's right for the *real* you. But what if you didn't have a name at all?

'One of the things *Ambergate* is about is the earning of a name. At the start of the story, a frightened little kitchen maid has only a nickname, "Scuff". In order to grow into and deserve her real name she is forced to embark on a dangerous journey and face trials and temptations, betrayal and despair along the way. Only at the end will she discover who and what she is – if she can survive long enough to find out.'

Also by Patricia Elliott:

WINNER OF THE FIDLER AWARD 2001
SHORTLISTED FOR THE
BRANFORD BOASE AWARD 2003
AND THE WEST SUSSEX AWARD
The Ice Boy

LONGLISTED FOR THE GUARDIAN AWARD 2004
Murkmere

Other titles available from
Hodder Children's Books

The Shamer's Daughter
The Shamer's War
The Serpent Gift
Lene Kaaberbol

Silverwing
Sunwing
Firewing
Airborn
Kenneth Oppel

Otto and the Flying Twins
Otto and the Bird Charmers
Charlotte Haptie

Radmila,
with love,
Patricia Elliott.

Patricia Elliott
AMBERGATE

Hodder
Children's
Books

A division of Hodder Headline Limited

A Catalogue record for this book is available from
the British Library

ISBN 0 340 88246 8

Typeset in Baskerville by Avon DataSet Ltd,
Bidford-on-Avon, Warwickshire

Printed and bound in Great Britain by
Bookmarque Ltd., Croydon, Surrey

The paper and board used in this paperback by
Hodder Children's Books are natural recyclable products
made from wood grown in sustainable forests.
The manufacturing processes conform to the environmental
regulations of the country of origin.

Hodder Children's Books
a division of Hodder Headline Ltd
338 Euston Road
London NW1 3BH

For my husband David – who is definitely
'the meaning of his name'

The superstitions in this novel are largely found in folklore

Part One

The Eastern Edge

MURKMERE

Five years earlier

The little girl was hiding in the long grasses that fringed the mere.

She had never seen so much water before. She had never seen the way it changed as the sky overhead changed. And in this place the sky was huge and filled with birds. She was frightened of birds, though she had been taught that some were more dangerous than others. In the pocket of her pinny was the rosemary she had picked from the kitchen garden to keep her safe.

No one would miss her in the house yet. None of the servants ever came down to the mere. They were fearful of the mud and the deep, weedy water. In the nearest reed bed there was an empty nest, like a huge, upturned pudding bowl, from which grass stuck out untidily.

She was bored now, and beginning to whimper to herself at the thought of braving the kitchens again, when she heard a voice close by.

'Come along, do! I'm taking you home. Can't you walk faster?'

It was a child's voice, impatient, bossy and very clear, coming from over her head. She was too startled to be frightened, and the little girl who had spoken, who looked a few years older than she was and clutched a boy smaller than them both, stared down at her, equally surprised.

'What are you doing here?' the older girl demanded, and at her tightened grip on his hand the tiny boy began to wail. He was wearing only a pair of breeches and a tattered shirt, and his chubby forearms were mottled with cold. She was wearing a velvet coat, laced boots and a bonnet, and her face was pink with heat and the effort of tugging him along.

'Beg pardon,' whispered the little girl in the grass, knowing that she had somehow done wrong by being there.

'The mere belongs to me. No one else must come here.' She glared down. 'My name is Leah. What's your name?'

The little girl pulled back her left sleeve and held out her arm timidly. 'Number 102.'

Frowning, the girl called Leah studied the branded numbers, the scars still red and puckered. There was a long pause.

'A number isn't a name,' she said, finally, dismissively. She nodded down at the little boy. 'You'd better help me. Hold his other hand.'

It sounded like a threat. The little boy's hand was clammy

and soft. As the girl took it, he looked up into her face with a dark, trusting gaze and his wails quietened.

'Where are we taking him?'

'Home, of course,' said Leah.

The three of them began to walk across the hard, sunlit mud. The boy toddled quite willingly now between the two of them. At the water's edge the younger girl halted, the little boy clinging to her hand. She looked over his head at Leah, puzzled but not frightened yet.

'We can't go no further.' She saw the older girl's face and her voice grew uncertain. 'Can we?'

Leah didn't answer. She was looking over at the big untidy nest in the reed bed.

'Is that where he lives?' said the little girl. Anything was possible in this strange, country place. But it didn't seem right that a tiny, tender boy should live there. She saw the gleam of the water and a little shiver of fear came to her in the sunlight.

'I'll take him. You stay here.' Leah was bending down and unlacing her boots, beginning to unroll her white stockings. 'Don't look, it's rude.'

Obediently, she looked away.

Then suddenly there was a sound in the undergrowth behind them: a crashing and scrabbling like a large, bemused animal trying to find its way, then a plaintive female cry. 'Miss Leah! Miss Leah!'

Swiftly, Leah pulled on her stockings again and re-laced her boots. The intent look in her eyes had vanished and her mouth turned down mutinously. 'That's my nurse. She mustn't know I'm here.'

She lifted her skirts and ran away, past clumps of rushes towards the overgrown scrub. The other girl went on holding the little boy's hand, their two palms sticking together. She didn't know what to do with him. In front of her the water glinted and sparked in the sun; the baked black mud was under their feet and over their heads curved the vastness of the sky. It was all too big.

So she led him away from the mere.

The little boy knew his way home, then; he took her to a cottage. It was without a window and filled with smoke. The girl saw a moving mound of clothes by the fire, bright eyes looking at them. She was too frightened to move, although she'd left the door open. But the little boy ran straight across the earth floor, into the old woman's arms.

She kissed and cuddled him, and all the time she was racked by bouts of coughing. When he had wriggled his way into her lap contentedly and her crooning was done, she gazed at the little girl, smiling. Her face had been pitted by the pox, but her eyes were beautiful and still young. The little girl couldn't smile back; she wasn't used to smiling.

She looked away. In the middle of the earth floor was a table, and spread out over it a cloak that shone in the half-light. When she looked closer she saw it wasn't made from cloth, but from long, silver-white feathers, the softness of the feathers lying over the delicate, bony tracery of the barbs. She stared and touched her pocketful of rosemary, frightened yet curious.

The old woman was watching her, the child still in her arms. 'You like the swanskin?' she said hoarsely.

The little girl shook her head, then nodded quickly.

The woman smiled again. 'You will not forget it,' she said. The boy scrambled off her lap and began to play with a long wooden box, opening and shutting the lid. 'Thank you for bringing my grandson back. What is your name?'

The girl shook her head and whispered, 'I don't have a name.'

'Everyone has a name,' said the old woman. 'But some have to find it for themselves.' She coughed again, spitting into the fire.

'You will find yours in the end, but only after a journey. It will take you far from here – far from Murkmere . . .'

1

I am the girl with no name. I have a number branded on my left arm, but no name.

They call me 'Scuff', here at Murkmere. Soon after I was brought here from the Orphans' Home in the Capital, they fixed on it, on account of my big shoes, which made me scuffle when I walked. I have almost forgot what the old woman said to me about a journey, for I never want to leave this place. And so I must be content with the nickname, Scuff.

I have a secret. A secret I must never tell.

Once, when I lived in the Capital, I committed a crime. I did something so wicked I must never speak of it. If I did, they would come after me: the Lord Protector and his men.

I think I did this wicked thing because of the ravens. I remember them, those great black birds, their jarring cries as they shifted the air above my head. I think they made me do it, those Birds of Night.

Ravens. In the Table of Significance *it says they are the birds of Death.*

* * *

One spring day, Jethro, the steward, had to leave us alone at Murkmere to go to a funeral. By then I'd been at Murkmere five years or more, but that day my life changed.

After Jethro had ridden away, Aggie and I couldn't shut the gates. During the winter they had become stuck fast in the ridged earth.

Aggie took her hand away from the rusty iron. She looked pale in the morning light, as if she hadn't slept. 'Leave them, Scuff. They won't budge.'

Overhead a herring gull laughed mockingly, but the rooks were silent in the beeches, where they had new nest-homes. I fingered the amulet of red thread around my neck. 'Jethro would want them shut while he's away,' I said doubtfully. 'Shall we dig them free? I could fetch spades . . .'

Aggie shook her head almost angrily. 'Who's to come bothering us at Murkmere? We're forgotten here.'

I always did everything Aggie asked, because she had been kind to me from the moment we met. So I stopped pushing against the unyielding iron and turned to go back to the house. I'd mixed up sand and lemon the night before and had a day of pot-scouring before me. Scouring is tedious work, but I like to see pots and pans winking from their hooks.

Aggie didn't follow me, so I stopped. She was standing in the gap between the gates, staring wistfully out at the Wasteland road. I thought she followed Jethro in her mind, was missing him already: Jethro, our young steward, who is Aggie's love.

'Don't you ever want to leave Murkmere, Scuff?' she said, surprising me.

I looked out at the long road stretching away into the distance. All you could see was sky and marsh and standing water. The Wasteland was a wild place, and what might lie beyond it? Even standing between the gates of Murkmere, you could feel the thrum of wind in your ears, the thrum of dangerous space.

I shook my head vehemently. 'This is my home. Why should I ever want to leave?' Long-ago memories of the Capital stirred, but I pushed them away.

Aggie sighed. 'Sometimes I long . . .' She didn't finish, but said, 'Do you feel young still, Scuff, truly young still?'

'I've never felt young.'

'I did feel young once,' Aggie said. 'But I don't any more, not nowadays. I feel old, as old as Aunt Jennet.'

'Jethro will be back in three days to help you.'

I didn't know what else to say. We all worked too hard, and Aggie hardest of all. There were too few of us at Murkmere. Not enough villagers had joined us over the last three years, since the old Master had died. They were fearful of leaving their cottages open to vagabonds, fearful that the Lord Protector might suddenly decide to take the estate over and they would find themselves in his employ. Jethro said the Protector could not do such a thing lawfully, but I reckoned that being the most powerful man in the country he could surely do what he wanted.

'I wish I could have ridden with Jethro. I long to see

somewhere else – another place than this,' Aggie said, all at once passionate. 'But he said we shouldn't go together in case anything happened to us. The Master made me official caretaker of the estate before he died and so it's my duty to stay. But I envy Jethro. I do, Scuff!'

'Even with such a sad end to his journey?' I'd lowered my voice, although there was no need. There was no one to hear that the steward of Murkmere was away to attend a certain funeral. But we had our story ready for anyone who should enquire: that Jethro had gone to market early.

Aggie bit her lip. 'You're right. How can I feel envy at such a time? Jethro is devastated by the death of Robert Fane. In truth, Scuff, I don't know what will happen to the cause now.'

It always made me nervous when Aggie talked of the rebels. Secretly I hoped that now their leader had been killed they would cease struggling against the Protectorate, and on the Eastern Edge at least we could all lie easier in our beds.

We began to walk back to the Hall together in silence. Weeds had grown in the spring warmth and tough young grass sprouted from the potholes of the drive. We had to walk on the verges, past the sheep grazing on the rough parkland. Aggie shook her head at the weeds, and at the growth of creeper covering the front of the house.

'Everything's even more overgrown than it was when the Master was alive,' she said, twisting her hands together. 'It's so hard to keep this place going.'

'You do very well,' I said. I didn't like to see her low-spirited, she who was so warm and generous and kind. 'We wouldn't want the old days back again, any of us.' She smiled at that and tucked her arm into mine, and I was happy.

'See, Scuff. You're nearly as tall as I am now and filling out a bit, I declare! You'll never be as fat as I am, though.' She was not fat, but big-boned. 'How old are you, do you think?'

'They reckoned I was ten when Mr Silas bought me at the Home, so may be I'm fifteen now, or thereabouts.'

'Then we should give you a proper name,' Aggie said. 'You can't be Scuff for ever. You need a name to suit a young lady!'

'I shall never be that. Scuff does me very well.'

'Our girl with no name. Orphan Number 102, from the Capital.' She saw my face. 'You need never go back, Scuff. You live here now.' For a moment she looked wistful again. 'If only Leah were here too.'

Jealousy pierced me suddenly. Whenever Aggie talked to me, Leah would somehow come into the conversation. Leah was the late Master's daughter, who had run away from Murkmere the night he died. She had left Aggie with the responsibility of managing the estate. Nothing had been heard of Leah since she disappeared, almost three years ago.

I was glad when she went. I'd always thought her a spiteful, unkind girl; I was frightened of her, too. I never understood why Aggie cared for her so much.

Jethro had left in a spring shower and now another came, a mist of drops too fine to wet us. We began to run the short distance to the Hall. We'd not bothered with hats and cloaks earlier. Aggie was laughing and trying to cover her bright hair, which always curled wild in the damp. A shaft of weak sunlight pierced the mist and touched the house, and we were in a green world.

Murkmere. A safe world.

So I thought, then.

2

Later, on the same day that Aggie and Scuff had struggled in vain to close the gates of Murkmere after Jethro's departure, three figures in travelling capes were riding purposefully along the Wasteland road towards the neighbouring village. Occasionally the wind would tweak aside a cape flap to reveal the dark grey uniform of the Militia beneath, with the distinctive emblem of the Eagle on the jacket pocket.

The leader, a middle-aged man called Mather, with cropped iron-grey hair and cold eyes, was in the Eastern Edge on an important mission, sent from the Capital by the Lord Protector. He had brought the two youths with him to gain experience. One was the Lord Protector's own son, Caleb Grouted. The other was Mather's bodyguard, Chance.

Chance hunched further into his rain-spattered cape and glanced at Mather. Three years ago in the Capital Mather had plucked him from the Highgallow Orphans' Home as being likely material for the Militia. He never showed any emotion, did Mather, yet Chance longed to impress him above everything, to see that stony face lighten with approval. Chance burned to become more than a mere bodyguard: he wanted to be accepted as an officer – as one of Mather's men in the Special Interrogation Branch, of which Mather himself was Chief. All Chance needed was the opportunity to prove himself to Mather, but so far it hadn't happened.

The Wasteland gleamed in the waning light as their horses shied and jittered on the stony road. All Chance could see on either side were pools of still water, yellow-green sedge, wind-bent trees. All he could hear was the wind moaning about his head. How he missed the Capital, with its maze of narrow streets and secret alleyways, its crowds and clamour!

A sudden clattering made his horse start so that he had difficulty in preventing it from bolting. If it hadn't been for Mather's impatient eye looking round on him, he might have been glad to bolt himself. Eerie white shapes had suddenly risen with great commotion from a pool close to the road.

Swans. Chance recognized them from those he had seen on the ornamental lakes in the Capital. He touched his free hand to his amulet, an iron locket at his neck, and tried to remember what it said about swans in the *Table of Significance*.

Swans were an omen, he was sure of that.

* * *

As they neared the Lawman's hut, which stood at the entrance to the village, Chance felt a thrill of anticipation. The Lawman might well hold the information they needed to succeed in their mission; he knew Mather would not hesitate to prise it from him if necessary.

The hut looked deserted, its watch panel shut fast. Clearly the Lawman was not expecting any strangers. Behind it, nondescript cottages straggled away into the mist and rain. On a rough patch of enclosed land, sheep eyed them incuriously, then went back to pulling at the tufty grass.

Mather dismounted and tethered his black horse to a broken fence. 'Rouse him, Lieutenant,' he said curtly to Caleb Grouted.

A grin flickered over Caleb's handsome face. Nipping down from his own horse, he went smartly over to the closed door of the hut and rapped on it with his pistol. 'Open up, Lawman!'

There was the sound of startled movement inside, something heavy knocked over, then a querulous, suspicious voice. 'Who is it?'

'Officers of the Special Interrogation Branch of the Militia!' shouted Caleb, with relish.

There was a shocked silence the other side of the door, then a bolt slid back. An older man stood blinking at them in fright. Behind him Chance could see the Records table, with a bread roll and half-eaten piece of cheese lying on top; a tankard had fallen on its side so that ale dripped darkly to the floor.

'Forgive me, good Sirs. We have so few travellers along this road . . .'

Mather moved smoothly forward. 'It is always best to be on your guard, Lawman – to keep careful watch. No doubt you have heard of the recent death of the rebel leader, Robert Fane?'

The Lawman nodded quickly, his rheumy eyes widening.

Mather came close, keeping his voice low yet heavy with menace, as he looked down on him. 'The rebels may be quiet at the moment, but soon they will appoint a new leader and gather their forces. The Lord Protector will want his loyal subjects to be on their guard. His people look to their Lawmen for security – reassurance. It would be a shame if your retirement had to come early.'

The Lawman wrung his hands together. 'Forgive me . . .' he began again, but Mather cut him short.

'I trust that in other areas you fulfil your duties. You keep the records of persons in this village, alive or dead?' He looked up at the rolls of parchment stacked neatly along the shelves. 'I see you do. I hope they are up to date.'

'Indeed they are, Sir,' said the Lawman tremulously, clutching the withered herb amulet at his neck.

'We need to go back five years. To the household of the Murkmere estate, as it was then – when the late Master of Murkmere was still alive, before his daughter ran off.'

Caleb Grouted swaggered over to the shelves and stared

up. 'These arranged in date order, Lawman? They'd better be.'

The Lawman's hand was trembling as he reached down the correct parchment. 'There has been much coming and going at Murkmere since then, Sirs.'

'And, no doubt, you have recorded all of it.' Mather spoke grimly. He had picked up the Register of Visitors from the Records table and was turning the heavy vellum pages to stare at the Lawman's cramped writing. 'We shall look at that roll first, then we shall investigate the more recent records to see if our quarry has escaped us or is still there to be ensnared.'

Chance could see the glitter in Caleb's eyes as they both crowded the Lawman, breathing hotly down his neck while he split the sealing wax and spread the roll open on the Records table.

'What name should I look for, Sir?' The Lawman fumbled for his spectacles.

'Not a name,' said Mather. 'This girl has no name. You are to look for a number.'

His business successfully completed, Mather strode to the door of the hut. Chance, about to follow Mather out, heard the Lawman let out a moan. He glanced back.

Caleb was slapping his hand along the shelves. Carefully ordered rolls of records toppled down under the onslaught like a house of cards; old parchment curled and cracked as it hit the floor, wax seals split open. As a final gesture

Caleb wrenched a map from the wall. He glanced at it, then crushed it into his cape pocket as he trampled and kicked his way to the door.

Tears ran down the Lawman's face. It had only taken the young officer a moment to ruin the work of centuries.

That's Caleb Grouted, thought Chance. *A quick worker*. He almost admired him.

3

Miss Jennet doesn't love me.

To her I am the little illiterate orphan girl from the Capital, someone to be saved by education. So she does what she considers her duty by me, as former schoolmistress to the village. For the past three years she has taught me to read and write and talk in proper grammar, and I'm truly grateful for it. She's an excellent teacher. It's strange that though she's so impatient in other things – desires the house clean and tidy and well run, and often raps our knuckles if it is not – in her teaching she has infinite patience. She doesn't teach Doggett: Doggett says she'll stick with what she knows already; she's fearful of the blasphemy in book-learning.

I am a little frightened of Miss Jennet, but I long for her praise. Most of all I long for her love, but that is all for Aggie, her niece.

All the same, by the evening of that spring day Miss Jennet was pleased to see the pots shining on the kitchen walls. 'You've done well, Scuff,' she said.

I smiled, and a little glow lit in my heart. A dog lying before the fire wagged his tail at the sound of her voice. They've grown fat and soft with Aggie's spoiling, the guard dogs of Murkmere that were once so fierce and ready to eat any stranger.

'I think that is your job done for today, Scuff,' Miss Jennet said. 'You can rest now.'

Rest! With vegetables to be picked from the kitchen garden before daylight faded, and water to be brought in from the pump in the stable yard and heated, and supper to be cooked. Pease pottage tonight, and all that shelling!

Aunt Jennet was smiling, though: it was a little joke. She knew as well as I, that there was no rest for anyone.

But then her smiled faded. She said, 'I think I will take a little rest also,' and sat down at the table. Her face sagged into little folds about her chin, so that she looked old. Miss Jennet is as thin as a whip and brown as tanned hide, but I don't believe she is an elderly woman. She always refuses to do any less work than we do.

I brought her a cup of water. Her brown face was white. She raised the cup to her lips, then her hand drifted down, the cup tilting, the water spilling; and she was suddenly crumpled on the flags at my feet.

I didn't know what to do. I knelt down. I was trembling, for I remembered a dead woman in a cellar long ago. In the end I'd had to go up into the street by myself, and that was when they'd caught me and put me in the Orphans' Home.

But Miss Jennet opened her eyes, and I was safe in Murkmere again. 'I've not eaten much today,' she murmured. 'There hasn't been time. I was sorting – carrying – Don't tell Aggie.'

'You must get to your bed,' I said, in a fluster. 'I'll help you.'

To my surprise, she did not protest. She leant on me, surprising heavy, and I helped her from the kitchen, upstairs to her chamber, past all the closed doors of those rooms we no longer used. It was beginning to grow dark, and a wind was rising outside; I lit a candle and closed the window.

'It's chill in here,' she said, shivering, as she climbed on her bed.

'I'll light a fire,' I said.

'No, it's too much bother. Bring me an extra coverlet from the linen cupboard. That will warm me.'

The cupboard was vast, lined with shelves that were piled high with sheets, quilts, old pillows, and scented with crumbling sprays of dried lavender tied with wisps of silk. The linen was Doggett's responsibility: she did the washing, ironing and darning. Her stitches were exquisite: she'd been lady's maid to Miss Leah until Miss Leah had disappeared three years ago. She was as eager for Miss Jennet's good word as I was, and a jealous girl. I did not trust her, though Aggie did. Aggie still called her by Leah's name for her – Dog – though with Aggie it was said with affection. She was indeed like a little dog that will nip you when you think you have made friends.

'What are you doing?'

Doggett's voice. Always there when not needed.

'Fetching a quilt for Miss Jennet.' I could feel my heart beating. It was so hard to stand up to Doggett. 'She's not well.'

'Not well?' I was surprised to see that Doggett looked taken aback, shocked even, her little eyes darting here and there as if for reassurance. 'I'll go to her.'

'There's no need. She's comfortable, and sleeping now.'

'I'll take her some supper later, then. Shouldn't you be in the kitchen, preparin' it?'

'I will be soon,' I said meekly, and I went.

When I delivered the quilt to Miss Jennet she said, 'You're a good girl, Scuff.'

'Not good,' I said in a low voice, thinking of my secret crime and suddenly longing to tell it to Miss Jennet this very moment.

'Very good.' She smiled and stretched out her hand. I took it, the palm hard in mine but the fingers surprisingly, disconcertingly, frail. I thought she must be ill indeed to be so soft with me. I left her shortly afterwards, once I'd seen her lie back beneath the warmth and close her eyes; and I hurried back along the passage, through the growing shadows to the back stairs, for I didn't want supper to be late.

Even as I reached the top of the stairs, I heard the noise

funnelled upwards from below: dogs barking, running feet.

It was so strange in the usual quiet of Murkmere that I stood rooted to the spot. And then Aggie was running up the stairs towards me. She was breathing fast, her hair tumbling down.

'Scuff! There are three men – soldiers, I think – riding down the drive!'

I stared at her and caught her fear, and my hand went to my mouth. She pulled me over to the window and we looked out into the fading light. We couldn't see the men's faces, but they were in uniform and they rode high-stepping, black horses. These men were important, and they looked set on important business.

Aggie turned to me, her eyes frightened. 'Why ever can they be coming to Murkmere?'

4

The light was waning when the three soldiers reached Murkmere Hall. The stable yard was deserted; a solitary pony whinnied from one of the dark stalls.

They dismounted in the gathering shadows and tethered their horses to iron hoops in the wall. Mather kicked at the weedy cobbles. Chance watched his lip curl and knew what he was thinking. Mather liked control and order. He was used to immaculate stables, grooms standing to attention, lackeys with flaring torches.

'We've surprised them,' said Caleb Grouted, with satisfaction. 'That's how we want it, isn't it, Chief?'

Mather cocked his grey-stubbled head to the frenzied barking inside the house. 'Not for long, I fear, Lieutenant.' He began to walk over to a back entrance, a plain but imposing wooden door set in the stone. 'It seems the Mistress of Murkmere employs neither ostlers nor groundsmen. One wonders if she runs the whole place with four-legged servants.'

Caleb sniggered, but then he looked up at the blank

façade of the house with its shuttered windows, and some of the swagger left him. He touched the amulet of egg-sized amber beads around his neck. 'We'll demand supper and shelter before we start our questioning, eh, Mather? My father would expect hospitality from Miss Cotter. After all, she's managing this estate for him.'

'Yes, indeed, Sir,' said Mather drily. He nodded at his bodyguard. 'Try some vigorous knocking, Corporal Chance.'

Chance was strong, and his gauntleted hands sounded like hammer blows on the wood. The dogs' barking grew muffled, as if they were being shut away. All the same it took some time before the door was opened, and they saw a girl standing before them, holding a guttering candle in a pewter holder that quivered in her hand.

She was frightened, Chance thought, and a pleasant feeling of power stole through him. She was a little younger than he was, short but stiff-backed and comely, with a startling mass of red-gold hair standing out around her shoulders. He'd never seen hair that colour, not even in the Orphans' Home where he'd been brought up, so he stood and stared while she stared back at the three of them, speechless and biting her lip.

'Corporal!' Mather spoke harshly behind him. Hastily, Chance stepped to one side.

'Forgive the intrusion, Miss Cotter,' said Mather.

'You know my name?' said the girl, in astonishment.

'Special Officer Mather at your service.' He saluted her,

and the girl flinched. 'We didn't mean to alarm you. It's late and we're weary, and we've travelled from the Capital the past few days. May I introduce my junior officer, Lieutenant Grouted? You will know who he is, of course.'

Chance was not introduced.

The girl looked at Caleb, as if dazed. 'You are the Lord Protector's son, Sir?'

Caleb bowed his head, his eyes bright with excitement and anticipation.

Caleb was sure to be the one to question young Mistress Cotter, thought Chance. He would merely get the servants. *If only I could discover the girl who is Number 102 . . .* he thought.

Mistress Cotter was very pale. 'Please, Sirs – forgive me. We're so unused to visitors here now. We only keep a small household, but if you'd care for a simple supper and a bedchamber, then I can offer you both.' She hesitated, and her voice trembled. 'I'm afraid my aunt won't be able to greet you. She's unwell and has taken to her bed.'

'We need not disturb her,' said Mather.

The girl looked beyond them, at the horses. 'We've no ostlers. You'll wish to rub down and feed your mounts, no doubt. There's hay in the storeroom.' She gestured across the twilit yard.

'Chance will tend them,' said Mather.

When Chance had finally finished in the stables, it was almost dark. The lantern Mistress Cotter had brought him flared in the wind as he made his way to the back entrance. He stepped into a passage and wondered which way to go.

'Sir?' A girl, pudding-faced and wearing an apron, stared eagerly at him from a doorway. He recognized her accent at once. How could he not? The Capital was in his very blood. He tried to see if she had a brand mark, but a serge sleeve covered her wrist. 'Let me show you to Miss Leah's old parlour, Sir,' she said.

In the small dank room to which she brought him, he found Mather and Caleb alone, gulping wine and trying to warm themselves before a spitting fire – by the look of it, only recently laid and lit. The bare windows gave them a dismal view of the darkening mere.

'I do not think interrogation is appropriate here,' said Mather in a low voice to his trainees when the girl had left them. His cool, intelligent eyes regarded them. 'When I have the opportunity I shall ask Miss Cotter straight out if she has ever or indeed still employs a girl from the Capital bought from the Gravengate Home. Only then shall we know if we have our prey within our grasp.'

'I believe I've spotted her already, Sir,' said Chance quickly. Out of the corner of his eye he watched Caleb glower. 'Shall I fetch her, Sir?'

'Wait, Chance,' Mather said. 'You are too impetuous. It is best to tread softly through the forest when you are a hunter, then your quarry is all unaware.'

After a long wait and several jugs of the wine, which was watered down and oversweet, they were ushered into a cold, dimly lit dining room by a lanky footman in a wig. The curtains had not been drawn against the black windows, and Miss Cotter, who was already waiting for them at the head of the table, made no move to do so. She had changed into a green silk skirt and her hair was piled on her head in a glowing mass that seemed to drain the colour from her face.

Chance was placed at one end of the table. At the other, Caleb Grouted sat on Miss Cotter's right side and Mather on her left. The footman served them with soup and a cold ham joint accompanied by a mess of peas. 'Thank you, Jukes, you may go now,' said Miss Cotter, with quaint dignity.

The maid, whom Miss Cotter called Doggett, cleared their dishes, and when she went out, Chance heard whispers in the passage: another female voice. His ears were sharp: for years as a child he had listened in fear for the whereabouts of his tormentors, the guardians of the Home in the area of the Capital known as Highgallow. He fingered the broad iron band which he'd had forged to hide the brand mark on his wrist, and waited.

Miss Cotter scarcely touched her food. 'It must be inconvenient for you to leave the Capital and come to such distant parts, Sir,' she said, with an effort, to Mather. 'A contrast, indeed.'

'You have visited the Capital, Miss Cotter?'

She shook her head.

Caleb leant towards her over the table. He had downed

too much wine and his eyes were glassy. 'So you've not heard the news from the Capital? And it concerns Murkmere Hall!'

'No, Sir.' A strange look crossed her face: eager, yet fearful.

'You'll be glad to hear that my cousin, Miss Leah Tunstall, heir to this very property, has been found. Three long years it took, but we've got her!'

She gave a little gasp and seemed to grow paler still.

'But you need not fear for your livelihood, Miss Cotter. I think it will be a long time before Leah Tunstall comes home to her inheritance.'

'Why?' she began, her eyes wide. 'What . . .?'

Caleb sniggered into his wine. 'She's not in her right mind. My father has her under his protection.'

'So she has survived!' breathed the girl. Then she looked at Mather in supplication. 'Surely she should come home?'

'You can be assured that the Lord Protector will do his best for her,' said Mather stiffly. 'He is her uncle by marriage, is he not? I hear he has the best doctors to treat her.'

'She's sick? What's the matter with her, Sir?'

Mather hesitated. His hand brushed the amber at his neck. 'She has delusions, so I gather. Some sort of religious fervour has taken hold of her during her period of privation. She must have been homeless for almost three years. She believes she is one of the avia.'

'The avia . . .' The girl whispered it.

Mather regarded her carefully. 'The doctors think that she may have presented early symptoms at Murkmere. It would certainly explain her extraordinary disappearance from here the night of her father's death.'

A shiver ran through Chance. He'd always been frightened of the old legend of the avia. He'd never known whether it was true or not. In the story a group of men and women had desired to fly like the Gods. As punishment, the greatest of the Gods – the Eagle – made them half human, half bird, forever trapped between two forms.

In the Home, Chance and the other orphan children had been told that what had happened to the avia, would happen to them if they didn't respect authority. For the children, authority meant the Guardians of the Home. All his years there, Chance lived in constant dread of the ultimate punishment.

Caleb Grouted leant forward and brushed Miss Cotter's hand. She withdrew it at once. 'We'll look after Leah, never fear, Miss Cotter. We won't let her go until she's cured of such delusions.' He sniggered again and drained his glass.

Doggett brought in cheese on a china platter. As she offered it to him, Chance held the dish so she could not leave. 'Who's out there?' he whispered, amid the talk at the other end of the table. 'There's another girl in the kitchen, ain't there?'

* * *

When dinner was over, they returned once more to the damp parlour, this time with a decanter of port and a bowl of nero leaf brought in by Doggett. Miss Cotter departed upstairs to oversee the preparation of their chambers.

Doggett set down the tray and bent to poke the fizzling fire. As she turned, her eyes met Chance's. It was a sign, he knew it was. The other female must be out in the kitchen alone, now the footman had been dismissed. He followed Doggett from the parlour, mumbling that he needed the privy.

Two steps along the passage and he'd caught up with Doggett. She turned and beckoned. He knew he'd judged her correctly: there was treachery in her slant-eyed glance. She was less stupid than she looked, and thought there might be reward in it.

With a growing sense of triumph, he followed her.

Through a swinging door and into the kitchen quarters. Doggett disappeared, gesturing towards another door. There was a sound from within: the swilling of water from a bucket.

He pushed open the door and went straight in. There was a single candle burning on the table in the centre of the room and flickering light from the dying fire. At the clip of his boots on the stone floor, the girl in the shadows at the sink turned her head. She was younger than he was, small and slightly built, with long brown hair half hiding her face.

He went up to her without preamble and stood over her.

His shadow was huge on the wall. Her sleeves had been rolled to the elbow for washing the dishes; her hands and forearms were in the water.

'My name is Corporal Chance. We're here by order of the Lord Protector.' Chance spoke clearly, so there would be no likelihood of her misunderstanding, but he knew she'd recognize his accent all too well. 'We've been sent to find a girl who was in the Gravengate Orphans' Home five years ago.'

He could hear her frightened breathing. She didn't move her hands from the water.

'The girl will have a number, a branded number. We know the girl was brought to work at Murkmere and is still here.'

A sound escaped her, an intake of breath.

Chance didn't want to pull her fragile arms from the water, to use physical force. He wanted to savour his triumph and that made it too easy, too quick.

But suddenly the girl seemed to capitulate of her own accord. She stood away from the sink, lifted a trembling, reddened hand to brush the hair from her face and gazed up at him in mute appeal. Her eyes were enormous and shone with fear in her shadowed face.

Chance looked down into her eyes. This was his moment, his victory. He could almost hear Mather's words of praise. This was the girl for whom they were looking, he was absolutely certain. There was about this slight, bedraggled girl a dark, secretive aura that spoke to Chance of his own past: of endless running, stinking hide-holes and then the Orphans' Home, with its pain and misery. He remembered the little boy who had sobbed in the loneliness of the night. She could not hide her past from him, when he'd suffered it all, too.

Chance looked into her eyes and saw his secret self, and was afraid.

5

He was standing so close to me, I thought he must hear my heart banging. I prayed for Mr Jukes to come. I looked up at him, but my eyes weren't working properly: I couldn't focus on his face. He was staring down at me. I caught the sharp smell of his sweat. I waited for him to grab my wet forearms and see the branding.

But he didn't move. He stood stock-still a moment, then he dropped his gaze, muttered something and turned on his heel. The kitchen door banged behind him and I was alone.

I finished washing the dishes, but I couldn't stop trembling. He didn't come back. Neither of the other soldiers came for me. I didn't understand why. All the same I waited until the men had left the parlour before I dared clear the glasses and damp down the fire. I don't know why I still bothered with my duties when I knew I was doomed: out of habit, perhaps. I didn't see Doggett, nor anyone else.

Later I crept up the stairs to my chamber and sat on the

bed in the darkness, without undressing. I knew Aggie would come eventually. By now she would know why the soldiers had come.

It seemed a long time before the soft knock came on my door. There was a whisper of silk over the floorboards and shadows jumped on the walls. She set down the candlestick on the chest and sat on the bed next to me, shivering, pulling her shawl close around her. Her voice was low and urgent.

'Scuff, you're right. They are looking for you. Mather told me as much tonight after supper. He said it casually enough – was sorry to trouble me, but he knew a girl from a certain Home in the Capital had worked here, was still here, according to the village records. He's been sent to find you.'

A chill of terror ran over me. 'What did you say?'

'I said we'd had many kitchen maids at Murkmere in the old days of the Master, but that the Lord Protector had since taken away all but our most loyal servants, and the tenant farmers and shepherds. It wasn't exactly a lie, was it?'

We looked at each other. She was biting her lip. 'But why – why are they looking for you? What have you done? There must be some mistake. I know it can't be so very bad. I know you, Scuff.'

'But you don't,' I said, desperate. 'You don't know me at all.' I shuddered as I thought again of my dark life in the Capital – the cellar, the Orphans' Home, the ravens, the blood. I'd told Aggie so little. 'It was wicked what I did. They track down and punish criminals however young they be. In the end all criminals must face the justice of the Ministration.'

'They dispense no justice! You've told me yourself about those dreadful prison ships and the houses of correction!'

'And I will face worse than that,' I whispered, twisting my icy hands together. 'I will face the death penalty, certain sure.'

She looked shaken. 'I wish you'd tell me what you did.'

I fingered the red thread amulet around my neck. 'It's best you don't know. Then if they question you, you won't have to lie.'

'I suppose I must believe you,' she said uncertainly. 'Mather has shown me a search warrant signed by the Lord Protector himself. He says that because of the recent unrest and rebellion in the country, the Ministration is tracking down all criminal elements for public punishment. You – a criminal element! How can I believe it?'

'It's the truth.'

She thumped the mattress. 'I wish Aunt Jennet wasn't sick! She'd send these men packing without more ado.'

'You mustn't tell her!' I cried out, and Aggie put her hand across my mouth.

'Mather has asked me to give him a list of all those who work here. I'll have to give it to him tomorrow. I won't include you, but they may well search the estate. You should hide until they go.'

I shook my head. 'They'll find me. I must leave tonight.'
I thought of the vast dark space beyond the gates and
shivered: I had never got over my fear of open places.

She read my mind. 'You can't venture into the Wasteland,
it's too dangerous. No, you must stay here.'

'But where can I hide where I won't be found?'

She gave me a quick hug. 'I'll protect you, don't fear. I
always have, haven't I?'

I gazed at her hopelessly. This was not Mistress
Crumplin's bullying or Miss Leah's frightening tempers;
nor was I any longer a small girl who could be sheltered
from mistreatment by an older, more confident ally. In my
spirit, I'd already surrendered to the soldiers; I knew there
was no escape from my fate. It would be a just punishment:
I deserved it. If I did not suffer it now, I would surely
suffer it in the hereafter. I'd prayed often enough for
forgiveness from the Almighty, but clearly He had not
granted it to me.

But Aggie was more robust than I. 'I do know
somewhere you could hide,' she said suddenly. 'But you
must be brave enough to stay there all alone until the
soldiers go.' She looked at me so anxiously that more to
pacify her than anything else, I nodded.

'Quickly, then!' She jumped up from the bed, and lit my
candle with hers. 'Put on warm clothes. I must, too. It will
be cold. I'll return in a moment.'

Then she was gone.

I began to move about in a trance, collecting clothes

from the closet: my cloak, a lined bonnet, boots. When Aggie came back, she carried an unlit lantern in one hand; in the other was a basket in which lay a clay bottle of water, a loaf of bread wrapped in a cloth and spare candles. 'Hurry!' she hissed, giving me the basket. 'The soldiers are dead to the world. Let's go before they wake.'

I blew out my candle and followed her trustingly through the silent house. We knew our way so well down the back stairs to the kitchen quarters, it only needed the occasional fingertip touch to guide us in the darkness.

In the kitchen Aggie lit the lantern from the dying embers of the fire, then she led the way to the door that opened into the vegetable garden. I was too agitated to think clearly, but Aggie was calm. She'd realized that, if we went out through the stable yard, the soldiers' horses, restless in their strange quarters, might whinny and give us away.

I do not like night in the countryside. It is a wild time, a time for animals and birds – those that wake then – to hunt and kill. Only in the city is night for the people, and then, only the very worst of humankind, those that are animals in everything but name. I came to life as we went out through that door into colder, damper air, and I clutched Aggie. 'Do we have to go outside?'

'There is no other way,' she whispered, and she took my arm. I could feel her trembling. *She is as scared as I am*, I thought.

'But the Birds of Night . . . ?' Even as I spoke, I heard an owl hoot far away.

'They'll not harm us. I've walked the night before. Try to think only of good things, Scuff. It will keep evil at bay.'

She has a stronger amulet than I have. It is made of amber and has more power to protect. But when the owl's hoot came again, closer, it sounded not threatening to me, but mournful, the crying of a soul lost in darkness.

The cloud was thick above us, hiding the moon and stars. The black bushes seemed to press closer, always just beyond the lantern light. Then, clinging together, we were beyond the overgrown garden, out into open space where there seemed to be more light, as if the earth had stored it up during the day and still held it.

All this time I hadn't asked where we were going. But now I knew.

The old square watchtower stood at the top of a rise, amongst a knot of black trees. I'd never dared enter it, for I'd always heard such stories of horror from the servants. It was a damned place: it still held the Master's ancient books that should have been destroyed for the blasphemies they contained. Miss Jennet had wanted to use them to teach me to read, but I'd been too frightened: I couldn't add more sins to my great one. So I'd pleaded with Miss Jennet, and she had sighed and given me Aggie's old state-approved readers instead. I knew that Aggie, like Miss Jennet, had turned away from orthodox religion, but she always let me take Devotion with the estate tenants.

In the old days the servants had whispered another story, too: of a worse blasphemy committed by the Master. He had had a flying machine built, which still lay in one of the top rooms.

I hung back, forcing Aggie to stop. 'I can't hide there!'

'You must! They'd never think a servant girl would dare go in. Mather is well aware of its reputation locally. They've told me they plan to search the house tomorrow, and the cottages.'

'But I'll be alone!'

'You want to die?' She grabbed my cloak, and half crying with fear, I let myself be dragged up a boggy path to the edge of the copse.

Beyond the trees the tower loomed darkly. The Master had needed a lift to take him to the top and the old winches still stood at the bottom of one of the square walls. A cold wind tore at the chains that ran up to the black windows, scraping them against the brickwork and making them jangle and groan like live things. Once when I'd first arrived and knew little of the blasphemy the tower contained, I'd escaped from the kitchen to admire the Master's lift system. Now I thought it held his spirit in its tortured movements, and I shuddered.

Aggie led me round one side of the tower to a wooden door. She took a brass key from the pocket in her cloak and fitted it into the keyhole. The door scraped open and she pulled me after her into an empty, windowless place. The air smelled of stone and wood and age.

'You needn't go up,' said Aggie, her voice suddenly too loud. She held her lantern out to show me a flight of wooden stairs that led from one corner to a denser darkness above us. 'You'll be safe enough down here.'

I looked around at the leaping shadows, my heart sinking, while she set down the lantern and the basket. 'I'll come back for you when the soldiers have gone.' She bent and lit a candle at the lantern, and the flame showed her anxious face. 'I'll lock you in, Scuff, and keep the key next to my heart. They'll have to break the door down to get in.'

I swallowed hard. There was nothing I could say. She was risking so much for my sake. Already she was at the door, slipping through the gap to brave the night with her single candle. I heard the wood protest as the door scraped shut, and then the click of the key turning. I stood alone in darkness, my feet in a pool of lantern light.

The air of the tower was thick and warm around me; the darkness pressed on my eyeballs. I could hear nothing from outside, none of the sounds of night. For a moment I was too terrified to move, thinking of the cellar with the dead body beside me. Then I picked the lantern up. The shadows fell away and there were no bodies.

I wanted to creep into a hole to hide, as I had done all my life. At last I crawled into the dusty space under the stairs, pulling the basket after me.

6

Chance had woken early, with tears on his face.

He was lying on a pallet in an unfamiliar passage. Mildewed wallpaper on the walls, faded rugs on floorboards; beyond him, a landing with closed shutters. The door to Mather's bedchamber was still closed, and a draught blew damply beneath it. When Chance tried to bury his cold face in the blanket he'd been given the night before, the wool had the same bitter, salty smell.

When he unfastened the shutters, he saw that yesterday's wind from the sea had brought a mist with it overnight. This morning the mist had settled over the parkland, blurring the outlines of the massive oak trees just coming into leaf and turning the new green world back to grey. *But even in the mist that girl won't escape us*, he thought. *Mather won't let her go like I did.*

It took most of the day for the three of them to search the house and the cottages of the frightened farmers: a cold day, with the mist playing strange tricks on them, furring up their eyeballs so they couldn't see and muffling sounds, indoors and out, so it seemed.

Mather checked the list in his hands for the umpteenth time. Miss Cotter's handwriting was legible and bold. Mather had checked everyone on it in his usual thorough way, questioned each person himself, forced the women to show him that they had no branding scar. The estate workers knew nothing of an orphan girl. The household – if you could call it that – of the Hall itself appeared to consist of Miss Cotter, the young maid Doggett and two older footmen, apart from the aunt and the absent steward. And surely Miss Cotter could not be dissembling. Why should she risk all she had for the sake of a criminal?

'This girl must have left Murkmere,' said Miss Cotter, shaking her head.

Mather was used to interrogating; he revelled in it, the thrill of the chase. In the end he always broke the protesting men and women who claimed innocence. He was too clever for them. But now Miss Cotter held his gaze and her eyes were clear. He could not detect a lie within them.

'What is the girl supposed to have done?' said Miss Cotter.

Mather did not like being questioned; he frowned. 'That is highly confidential, I'm afraid.'

'You may have to extend your search to the Wasteland, Sir. It swallows many a criminal.'

They were standing in the stable yard. It was afternoon

and the mist was beginning to lift, but the clouds were thick overhead and the light gloomy.

'We must leave before the daylight goes,' said Mather. He was weary of investigating damp little hovels. The prospect of hunting through the Wasteland or the squalid little village where he had interrogated the Lawman, was tedious in the extreme.

He beckoned to the two young men. 'Saddle your horses.' Then he clicked his heels and bowed abruptly to Miss Cotter. 'My congratulations,' he said dryly. 'You seem to run your household with remarkably few staff.'

The girl didn't blink. 'We all help each other. It's not me but my aunt who runs the house, in truth.'

'Then I hope your aunt recovers soon.'

'Thank you, Sir, she is much better. Indeed, she is rising for dinner, I believe.'

Mather had heard of the fearsome reputation of the aunt, who at one time had been Chief Elder in the village. It would be the last straw to encounter her at the end of this unsuccessful day. He didn't like women at the best of times. 'I'm glad,' he said stiffly, and made for his own horse with haste.

But he'd return, he thought. He'd return with extra men before the steward was back. He'd take them by surprise, at night. Then he'd know for sure whether the girl, Number 102, was still there.

7

I don't know who she was: the woman with me in the cellar, who died.

I don't believe she was my mother. But it was she who had brought me there, stayed with me in the dark and damp. She fed me and clothed me and wrapped me in blankets, yet I sensed I was a burden to her. Sometimes she took me up into the street in my little hooded cloak, and I would blink at the daylight, at the throngs of people, the tumult. She never let me venture forth by myself: it was too dangerous, she said. In the streets of the Capital there were statues with eyes that would see me; birds that would carry off the tasty morsel of a tiny child; soldiers who would shoot a stray little girl. So I stayed hidden in the cellar until one morning when I awoke and she didn't, and I knew she must be dead.

It was a long time ago. It was before I committed my crime. I was at the Orphans' Home by then.

In the end I must have dozed through the night in the watchtower. When light came eventually from somewhere above me, I had to move out of my hole because of the pain in my arms and legs.

A long day followed the long night. I was back, tucked in beneath the staircase, and dozing again, when I heard the key turn in the lock outside. It wasn't Aggie, but Doggett. She looked all around, then she saw me in the light from the open door and gave a great giggle.

'You look like a mouse in there, Scuff! You can come out. The soldiers have gone. Aggie sent me to fetch you.' She sank down on the bottom step of the stairs and spread her skirts, pretending to catch her breath, as if it was such an effort to come for me.

I didn't come out at once: I could scarce believe I'd escaped.

'Come on, stupid!' she said, impatient. 'Aggie is preparin' the supper tonight. We are to have a feast, she says, but with what, I don't know. And why we should celebrate, I don't know neither.'

It was still daylight: a windy evening, with shreds of grey mist blowing between the trees. As we went down the slope towards the Hall, Doggett looked at me with her sly, sideways glance. 'What was it you did, Scuff?'

I stared back at her, startled.

'Your crime,' she said impatiently. 'Come on, I know those soldiers were lookin' for you. Number 102, they said.' She seized my left arm, dragging the sleeve back to expose my scar. 'You forget I come from the Capital too. I know all Homes brand their orphans. They're too useful to lose.

And I've seen your mark before, though you always try to hide it.'

I couldn't say a word. Eventually she had to give up pestering me with her questions; I thought she sulked.

But as we reached the stable yard, she said, 'Those two young men – they was good-lookin', wasn't they?' I was astonished to see a dreamy look on her plump, sallow face. 'I wish they could have stayed longer. One was the Lord Protector's son – fancy!' She flicked her greasy plait and smiled. 'I'm going to find myself a husband one of these days. I'll leave Murkmere – go back to the Capital!'

'You can't! What will Aggie do?'

'She'll manage.'

'I'm never leaving Murkmere,' I said, and I haven't forgotten the pitying look she gave me then.

'You think you're safe here?'

'Aggie will protect me, I'm sure she will,' I said.

'Aggie pretends we are her friends, that we're all equal here. But we can never be more than servants to them, Scuff. They'd sacrifice us if they had to.'

We were merry at supper: it was the relief, I think. Certainly for me, it was. And Aggie had baked a cheese and leek pie, which we finished between us. 'Better than Miss Jennet's cat's piss soup,' Doggett said to me, in an undertone.

Only Miss Jennet was grave. 'I wish I'd been up and about when the soldiers came,' she kept saying, for Aggie had told her – but not why they had come. 'I can't understand why they should be investigating us after all this time. The Lord Protector sent them, you say. Were they suspicious of Jethro's absence?'

I sang to her after supper to distract her. Since Aggie had taken over the running of Murkmere, I often sang. Tonight I sang 'So Sing Success to the Weaver', for Miss Jennet had been a spinster herself once and it was her favourite song. All the same, her worried frown came back when I'd finished.

We cleared the supper dishes and Aggie went to lock and bolt the outside doors, which was usually Jethro's task at night. I could hear her quick, light footsteps echoing through the darkness of the Great Hall, as she made her way past empty tables and dusty tapestries to the big double front doors.

In the kitchen I bade Doggett and Miss Jennet goodnight, took a tallow candle and went to my chamber. The wind was up, rattling the windows, and when I went to fasten them more securely, I saw the night sky was filled with stars. The wind had blown the mist away. *I must say my prayers*, I thought.

But as I knelt on the hard floorboards by my bed and clasped my hands together in the familiar way, the words wouldn't come. I fingered the red thread amulet around my neck and tried to picture Him – the great Eagle head in the room with me, rearing out of the dim tallow light. But what could I see in the black eyes? Anger.

Blame. Contempt. He would never forgive me for what I'd done.

A knock at the chamber door made Him vanish. Miss Jennet came in as I rose from my knees. She had not yet undressed for bed, and her eyes looked very wide-awake.

She set down her candle on the chest by the door, and said in a low voice, 'Dog has told me why the soldiers came to Murkmere. They came for you, didn't they?'

I nodded dumbly, shocked at Dog's betrayal.

'Don't blame Dog,' said Miss Jennet, as if she knew what I thought. 'I only had to ask in the right way. She's not good at keeping secrets. Both you and my niece are better at that.'

'I'm sorry . . .' I began miserably, but she raised a hand.

'Did you really think you could keep such a thing from me? Haven't I the right to know? We've lived with each other these past three years.' She seemed reproachful, sorrowful, rather than angry.

'What I did was a sin,' I faltered. 'I could never bear to tell it . . .' *I never had the courage*, I thought, and looking at her shadowed face now, my courage failed me again.

'I don't mean that,' she said, sighing. 'I don't want to know what you did. It's safest that none of us knows. I mean not telling me why the soldiers had come here.'

'We didn't want to worry you,' I said. 'You were poorly.'

She twisted her hands together. 'I thought it was Jethro whom they'd come about, Jethro whom they suspected. Never you.'

'But the soldiers have gone. Why does it matter?'

'You think it's over so easily?' She shook her head. 'You poor, foolish child. They'll be back. I've heard of that man, Mather. He's merciless in hunting out his victims. You may have hidden from him this time, but next time he'll find you. Then we'll all be in trouble.'

I sat down on the bed, my hands to my face.

'I've never been to the Capital,' she said quietly, 'and never want to. In such a place committing a crime must be easy enough, though surely your tender age should be considered. But the Lord Protector is ruthless in his efforts to cleanse the country of those he perceives as possessing criminal potential, particularly at the moment with all this unrest.'

'I've not told anyone here of my crime, ever,' I whispered. *Nor of my past before it, for I wanted to forget.* 'You'll all be innocent of the knowledge.'

'That's as may be, but the very fact that we are sheltering you makes us complicit in your guilt. Do you not see that if you stay here, then Aggie is in danger, let alone the rest of us? And Aggie is my responsibility, the only child of my late sister, and I've brought her up as mine own.'

You love her. 'What will they do?'

'Aggie will certainly lose Murkmere,' said Aunt Jennet grimly. 'It's her livelihood, and ours. We'll be destitute. The villagers will never accept us back. They think of us as the enemy now that we manage Ministration land. Why do you think so few joined us when the Master died? They're suspicious and frightened. We have some friends there still, it's true, but there are plenty that will betray us for money.'

She sat down on the bed at a distance from me, and her voice was harsh. 'But that's the very least. Worse could happen if the soldiers return and find you with us. We could be taken to the Capital and imprisoned. We could all die, in the end.'

I had a horrible sick feeling in my stomach, which might have been the meaty stink of tallow in the room, but I knew had been caused by what she said. 'What do you want me to do?'

'Do you always wait for other people to tell you what to do?' she said, in sudden anger.

I hung my head. 'I suppose you want me to leave?' I said, from under my hair.

'I don't want it, but I can't see any alternative.'

A little gasp escaped me. 'But this is my home.'

'You'll find another.' Her voice shook suddenly.

'But where?' I said, desperate. 'Where can I go?'

She put a sealed parchment on my lap. 'Listen, child. Leave at first light. Take food with you, and water. Go to the address I've written on the outside of the letter. Relatives of mine – a cousin and her husband – live in Poorgrass Kayes, at the rivermouth. They will take you in and give you employment. I've written requesting as much, but saying nothing of this matter. I've given you an excellent reference.'

Beneath my hair I stared at the paper, and the seal

caught the candlelight like a drop of blood. 'Is Poorgrass far from here?' I brushed my hair aside and looked up at her pleadingly, hoping for a change of heart. My heart sank as I saw her resolute expression. She had risen from the bed and was pacing about the chamber, her gaunt shadow leaping before her.

'It has to be far from here, don't you understand? You don't want to be arrested, do you?'

I stared back down at the paper, gulping. There was a long silence broken by the sound of her restless footsteps, while I tried to master myself. At last I asked in a tiny voice, 'How do I find this place?'

'Follow the river, don't go by road. There's a causeway through the marshes – the old river road. Follow it all the way to the rivermouth. Pray you find it, and let's hope there's a god somewhere to hear you.'

I touched my amulet, for she wore none. Her eyes met mine, and I thought I saw pity in them. 'You are braver than you think, Scuff. But remember – on your journey – know your friends.'

'Can I say goodbye to Aggie?' I whispered.

Her face froze.

'Please, I beg you.'

She shook her head violently, and wheeled round to the door, jerking her shawl over her shoulders.

My voice cracked. 'Won't you say goodbye to me, Miss Jennet?'

She paused, half turned as if to speak; I saw her eyes

glitter with tears as she took her candle, then she hurried from the room.

I wouldn't let myself cry: it was only the tallow that made my eyes smart. I wouldn't let myself think either, in case I thought of the fearful things that might be waiting for me in the Wasteland, and of my unknown employers in the port, when – and if – I ever reached it. I moved stiffly about the room, collecting my warmest shawl, my cloak and bonnet, and laying them on the foot of the bed ready for first light. In the pocket of the dress I'd made from old curtains, the letter crackled. I wondered whether to undress or not: I couldn't seem to make up my mind.

I was still standing, undecided, when from below the dogs began to bark again.

8

My heart rose in my throat as if it would choke me. *They have come back for me*, I thought. *There is nothing I can do, nothing*; and I did nothing.

It must have been only moments later that Aggie burst in, wild-eyed, fully dressed but dishevelled, as if she'd hastily thrown more clothes on top of those she already wore. 'What are you doing?' She saw my cloak and shawl on the bed. 'Put those on, hurry!'

'Miss Jennet . . .'

Aggie spoke rapidly. 'She's gone down to speak to the soldiers. She's asked Jukes and Pegg to take you to the door in the boundary wall, the door near the tower.' I stood, rigid with fear, as she threw the cloak around me, then the shawl over my head. 'Quick, Scuff! I must get back to Aunt Jennet.'

'What will she say to the soldiers?'

'Nothing about you,' she said sharply. 'She has a speech all ready, and she's taken two dogs with her to protect her.' She tugged hard on my arm, pulling me back into life. 'Come on!'

The soldiers were at the front of the house so we fled down the back stairs, as we had the night before. There were some sconces still left lit. The dogs that slept in the scullery were howling with frustration, clawing at the other side of the old wooden door as we ran past, into the kitchen.

Jukes and Pegg loomed out of the shadows by the dying fire. Jukes, already wrapped in his cape and without the footman's wig he insisted on wearing each day, was a stranger with straggling hair and unsmiling face. Pegg, short and burly, glowered beside him at the interruption to his sleep.

'You have the key?' said Aggie urgently, above the clamour of the dogs.

'Aye, Miss.' I saw it in Jukes's hand, a great rusty piece of iron.

'I hope it turns, Jukes. That door's not been unlocked for years.'

'I'll do my best, Miss,' he said, lugubrious; while Pegg, always a rude, uncouth man, scowled at me as if I was scarce worth the bother of saving. Shaking his head at the folly of it all, he turned to the back door that led out into the stable yard, with a brusque gesture indicating I was to follow.

'Come, girl,' said Jukes, jerking his head at me as he went out after Pegg.

I stared at Aggie, full of fear. 'They've no lantern!'

'The men would see it. They're out by the main gate

as well as at the front. More have come this time.' She saw my hesitation. 'Go, Scuff!' She pushed me out of the door.

I caught her hand. 'Goodbye, Aggie.'

She wrenched her fingers away. 'No time . . .' The door shut behind me, I was out in the stable yard and the black figures of the two men were striding away over the cobbles, the wind lifting Jukes's cape. I thought I'd be left alone in the dark spaces; I fled after them, clutching my amulet. But a thread of red cotton was so frail against the powers of darkness, so easily broken.

After a moment I could see the stars shining in the heavens, like tiny golden beads. The round moon hung above the rise on which the tower stood and filled the night with a soft white light, so that nothing – tree, bush or blade of grass – had shadow. To our left I could see the flare of torches: the other group of soldiers had left the main gates to search the grounds.

'Mr Jukes!' I ran to his side as he quickened his pace up the track to the copse of blowing trees. 'They will see us!'

He made no answer. *He's doing this for Aggie*, I thought, *otherwise he'd leave me to face them on my own. He must hate me for putting the household in such danger*.

Jukes and Pegg skirted the dark ring of trees. Across a patch of rough ground, pitted with night-filled hollows, was the high stone wall that ran around the boundary of the Murkmere estate. It stood in shadow, but they knew the whereabouts of the door and made for it without hesitation. Jukes felt for the keyhole; I could hear him fumbling as he tried to fit in the rusty key.

At last it was in, and he managed to turn it with great effort. Then, with Pegg's help, he struggled to draw back the bolts, top and bottom. They, too, were rusty and wouldn't slide.

'No chance,' Pegg muttered.

A sound made us start round. Across the stretch of moonlit grass Aggie was running towards us, without cloak or hat, her hair streaming in the wind. She held her skirts in both hands and her petticoats fluttered wildly. 'I had to warn you!' she gasped, as she reached us. 'They're putting men at every exit from Murkmere! It won't be long before they're here!'

'We can't move the bolts, Miss Aggie,' Jukes said.

'Can't we lift her over the wall? We must!'

'Too high, Miss.'

I knew he did not want to help, and Aggie knew it too. But what he said was true: even tall Jukes couldn't lift me high enough.

Lights flickered among the distant trees. 'They're here already,' I whispered.

'You must go to the tower!' said Aggie. 'I've the key here.'

'We'll be spotted, Miss,' said Jukes, but he took it.

'Not if you approach it from the other side.' She pressed something warm and round into my hand. 'My amber – take it, Scuff.'

'I can't!'

'Take it – you have more need of it than me.'

Then she was gone. Blindly, I put her amulet around my neck. Pegg grunted, 'Come on, then,' and the three of us began to steal along in the shadow of the wall. The shouts of the searching men carried to us on the wind, the crashing in the undergrowth. Light flared among the trees.

Somehow we made it to the tower unseen, each of us taking it in turns to cross open ground to the doorway. Once there, the noise of the men seemed further away.

Into the tower again, the door open a crack, squeezing through one by one into darkness. Inside, I couldn't hear the wind, only our breathing, my heart pumping. 'Lock the door,' said Pegg.

I heard the scratch of metal in the darkness, the click of the key turning. Above us the darkness was lifted by a softer grey tonight: moonlight shone through an arched window; below it was the black band of the stairs.

'We must go up,' said Jukes.

We reached the landing and I followed the men into a large room. Through a great glass door at the far end, the night sky was spread in its glory; a million stars glittered and danced around the glowing lamp of the moon, so that I thought I'd faint at so much strange expanse of beauty, so much space.

What is this place? What infernal magic did the Master conjure here? But I was too frightened to dwell on my old

Master's certain damnation; my palms were wet with the prospect of my own.

Jukes stood by the glass, staring down. 'See how close the men are?' he said nervously to Pegg.

I went cautiously towards him, past a desk on which dust glowed luminous in the moonlight, past curious cabinets, glass surfaces that gleamed. As I came to the window, I gasped, and for a moment I thought I'd fall straight out, straight down to where the soldiers would soon come. A ragged line of light – torch flames torn by the wind – was moving towards the tower, along the boundary wall.

A clatter made me jump. Behind us, Pegg had opened a drawer in the desk and was examining a small pistol in his hand. 'The Master's gun's still here. Still loaded, too.'

The men were nearly at the tower, as if they knew we sheltered there. 'Are those rifles they're carrying, Mr Jukes?' I said, my voice high and strange.

Jukes nodded briefly. 'Look at that, Pegg.'

Dark shapes slunk low around the soldiers. 'They've brought dogs!' I whispered.

'They've followed our scent. Be sniffing us out next,' muttered Pegg, moving to Jukes's side, the pistol still in his hand.

'But they're not in uniform,' I said hesitantly. 'Can they be soldiers, Mr Pegg?'

'What else? Night manoeuvres. Don't want to be seen, do they?'

'There be a whole lot of them,' said Jukes, his voice

shaking. He added dourly, 'The law will have its way in this country, sure enough. What she did' – he jerked his head towards me – 'must have been wicked indeed that so many of them be eager to get her, Pegg.'

'I never meant this to happen,' I said. 'Please go – look to yourselves.'

'Too late,' growled Pegg. 'If we leave now, we'll be savaged by the dogs or shot by them soldiers most like. Accomplices, they'll call us. We're harbouring a criminal.'

'We'll be taken to the Capital, up before the Lord Protector himself,' Jukes said, his lanky frame quivering.

'And all for a kitchen maid,' said Pegg.

Below us they began to hammer on the outside door. My heart almost stopped.

The two men stared at each other. Pegg looked down at the pistol in his hand. 'I've a little notion that might work, Jukes.'

Jukes eyed the pistol apprehensively. 'You'll be in worse trouble if you use that on them.'

Pegg shook his head; his teeth bared in a ghastly smile. 'They want the girl, right? Well then, we shall give her to them nice and easy and not be seen ourselves.'

And his right hand swung to point the pistol direct at me.

9

The group of men who surrounded the tower began to thump their sticks on the ground in triumph. Earlier the dogs had sniffed a bodice taken from the missing girl's bedchamber, and minutes ago they had picked up the same scent in the grounds by the wall. Now they were going mad around the tower, panting and straining on their leashes: tough, rough-haired mongrels with sharp noses and even sharper teeth. She must be in there, the girl they were after.

Not long until the door was down. Even solid oak couldn't bear up against pickaxes.

In the dark and from a distance, it is easy to mistake a stick for a rifle. But soldiers do not carry sticks, and these men were not soldiers. They were rebels.

The leader of the group of rebels, a young man called Titus Molde, bent to feel for the dagger he always kept in his boot, and smiled to himself. He wasn't expecting any trouble, but it might be handy. He had spotted the two men with her and didn't know if they'd let her go easily. Number 102. At last they had found her. It would make all the difference to the morale of the cause, so badly damaged by the death of Robert Fane.

And he'd be glad to be out of this place. It made Titus Molde uneasy: the trees like ghosts in the moonlight, the whining of the wind. He was used to working in the night, of course, but he didn't like it. He wasn't devout any more, but at times he regretted he'd ever cast away his amulet.

Something flickered against the full moon. A large bird, neck outstretched. His hand went up automatically to his throat, to the place where his amulet had been. What could it be? What night bird had that wingspan – or was it a trick of the moonlight? And now another bird was following it, and another: a whole flock of great white long-necked birds, swooping low over the dark blowing trees of the copse and flying through the wind towards the men.

Then Titus Molde smiled again, at his own stupidity, as he realized what they were.

But the men in charge of breaking down the door looked up at the white birds flying against the stars, muttered together and put down their axes uneasily. Those holding torches shifted closer together, the ring of men around the tower beginning to break up. The dogs, sensing the tension, were barking, hackles up, and from far away in the Hall there came an answering howl from the imprisoned guard dogs of Murkmere.

'What are they?' said one of the men, looking up at the great heavy birds and rubbing moon-dazzled eyes.

'An omen,' said another.

The youth standing next to him gave a frightened moan. 'What do they mean in the *Table of Significance*?'

It was time to stop this, thought Titus Molde. He strode over. 'They're swans, can't you see that? Wild swans. They breed in the Wasteland.' These recruits from the city! Unfortunately, the local men were down at the gates.

The birds made no sound, no cry, as they circled beneath the moon. The wind buffeted the men's ears and hissed through the undergrowth around them.

Then there was a crash from far above their heads, from the top of the tower. Something fell through the air. Nerves on edge, the nearest men leapt back. One of them held the object up, turning it gingerly this way and that in moonlight. 'Broken glass,' he said. 'She's trying to break the window!'

'We'll be waiting for her if she jumps!' said another man.

'Be sure to catch her, then,' said Titus Molde. 'I want to take her back to the Capital in one piece.'

Another crash from above, and another, and then something invisible came hurtling through the air, followed by a lethal rain of smaller pieces. The men dodged back, but one brought his hand to his face with a cry of anguish and took it away, black with blood.

'We could try shouting up to her,' someone said to Titus Molde.

'She'd never hear, not with this wind,' Molde said. He hesitated, then yelled over to the men at the door, 'Hurry up with that, can't you?'

More shards of glass fell, the smaller ones blown in all directions by the wind. The men on the grass drew back hastily; those at the door of the tower pressed themselves against the wood for protection. They waited speechlessly to see what would happen next, mesmerized by the dark hole that had been the great window at the top.

Then they gave a low groan of amazement and fear. Something extraordinary was appearing out of the darkness up there, something inhuman – like a giant moth, with an eerie glow to the vast, furled wings. And even as they thought it a moth, the pale wings uncurled and they saw it was a bird.

It had not yet flown out. It perched, swaying, on the very edge of the hole.

And in its claws it held a girl.

Too frightened to care about losing their quarry, the men clutched at their amulets, letting the dogs loose.

Only Titus Molde knew what he was seeing. He'd heard about the flying machine that had been fashioned long ago by the late Master of Murkmere. It had never flown, so far as he knew. Was the girl so desperate she was trying to escape them in such a risky contraption? Something so fragile, so amateurishly built, could only crash. She'd fall through the wind to her death on the hard earth.

This went through his mind in a flash. A voice inside his

head screamed protest, then he was running towards the tower, shouting upwards into the mocking wind, 'Stop!'

Even before the word was torn from his mouth, the bird-machine had moved suddenly forward, had lurched over the edge.

The men below stood, transfixed. They held their breath. Alone among them their leader moved, gesticulating wildly, screaming something inaudible above the barking dogs.

The bird thing did not fall immediately. As if there was some impetus pushing it from behind, it went horizontally through the air for a short way, holding its height, the wind beneath its wings. Then it slowed. It seemed to judder in the air, hanging stationary but quivering, for a second.

Titus Molde shut his eyes. He felt air press on his forehead as something flew heavily over his head. He ducked involuntarily; the men behind him cried out.

When he looked around, black wings had blotted out the moon. The wind was full of birds. The swans were all about the men in a turbulence, beating the air so that the screams of the men were muffled by the *thump*, *thump* of wings. The men cowered down, shielding their eyes.

Titus Molde fell flat on the grass, protecting his face with his hands. His heart was banging in his chest: he knew that swans could kill a man. He heard the swans attack the contraption, beat it to the ground.

He lay motionless until he thought the vile birds had gone. He was full of fury and humiliation. He was the leader and he'd done nothing to prevent the girl's death.

He'd been too scared, without an amulet. Scared of birds that had no sinister significance in the *Table*, were no doom-laden omen.

The wind rattled the bare branches in the copse and lifted his hair. The dogs had fallen silent. His men would not get up from the ground until he did. He'd best stand up and go over to the debris left by the shattered machine, the dead body in the midst of it all.

But when he raised his head and looked up, there was nothing to see. Beneath the empty stars his men lay huddled on the ground: pathetic bundles of rags and spent swagger, sticks at all angles, useless. A couple of dogs nosed at them and whimpered.

The swans must have flown away into the night. But neither, on the stretch of moonlit scrub before him, was there any sign of the flying machine.

THE WASTELAND

I

Someone was lifting my head. I didn't want them to do that, it hurt too much.

I drew my brows together with the faintest flicker. I was too hot. I heard murmuring. Then I slept.

Later there was the rim of something hard against my lips. I opened my mouth. A bitter liquid. The air smelled of something faintly familiar.

I groaned. Again, the murmur came, then the soothing touch of cool fingers on my forehead. I recognized the scent in the air now, but I was too tired to make sense of it. Hay, new-mown. And something that stank of animal covering me.

Another time when the touch came, I opened my eyes. Eyes looked down into mine. I shut my eyes again, and slept.

Later, I was given water.

One day I said, 'Who are you?'

My lips were cracked: it was painful to move them. My voice sounded old and rusty. But when I looked over from the straw pallet on which I lay, I could see a man sitting on

68

a stool by the fire and I knew him. He had watched over me during the days and nights that had passed, had lain healing hands on my head, covered me with sheepskins. Sometimes I had watched him move about this dark, smoky place, as he tended me. There had been someone else, too – a young man – but he was not here now.

The older man had been gazing into the fire, but when I spoke, he looked round, startled. Then he rose stiffly to his feet. He was a giant, broad and strong. As I shrank back, pressing myself down into the bedding, he went across to an opening in the wall, and in a voice to match his size shouted out into the beam of white daylight, 'Erland!'

Then he came over and spoke softly to me, pulling up a stool and sitting on it with a grunt a little way away, as if he sensed I might be frightened if he came too close – though I knew he had looked after me most gently.

'My name is Gadd, Miss,' he said. 'You've been very poorly. I think you hit your head.' He spoke with the round vowels of the Eastern Edge. 'I gave you feverfew to cool you.'

'Thank you,' I whispered. I bit my lip at the thought of the intimate tasks he must have done for me, but his face showed only respect and concern.

'My son will be here shortly,' he said. 'He'll be pleased you've woken proper.'

I nodded, and raised my hand weakly to feel my head. I couldn't feel any bump, but my hair was filthy, matted with dirt.

'Your hands were in a state,' said Gadd. 'I couldn't get the blood from beneath your fingernails without distressing you.'

My hands – my wrists and forearms! Surely, he must have seen the number branded on my skin? His face showed nothing.

'I can wash myself now,' I said, anxious.

'Slowly does it. You must rest as much as possible. My son found you, Erland. He carried you here.' He spoke of him with shy pride.

'Where am I?'

'Why, in the Wasteland.'

I started. 'The Wasteland?' I was sure I must still be on the Murkmere estate.

I looked wildly about me, at the odd, circular walls of plaited reeds. I was lying in a dwelling made entirely from grass: even the floor covering was woven from rushes. There was no roof: the walls curved up to a central hole that let out smoke from the fire.

'I didn't know anyone lived in the Wasteland,' I said.

'There was a village here on the river road once,' said Gadd. 'I still make use of its well and grazing ground. No man could live here otherways.'

'So the river road is close by?' I whispered.

'You're lying right on it, Miss, though you'd scarce call it a road these days. But if you've the eyes to see it, it be there.'

Gadd's eyes were narrow slits of light, permanently half

closed, as if against the sun, and surrounded by waves of brown wrinkles. They were so disconcertingly direct I thought he must know my destination. 'Erland found your wings.'

'I was escaping...' A wave of terror caught me. 'Soldiers...'

He clucked his teeth. 'Easy, lass. There be no soldiers here.'

I relaxed back into the sheepskin coverings and fell silent, breathing in the fragrant green scent of the place, a mingling of the burning rush lights above me, the sheaves of cut grasses and the young sappy wood on the fire. In the shadows I saw the glint of scythes propped against a wall, the dull sheen of cooking utensils hanging from hooks in the roof. There was little furniture, save for a rough-hewn table, a stool and a ribbed wooden chair.

As I listened to the fire sparking, I must have closed my eyes, for when I opened them Gadd had gone and there was a youth crouched on the matting not far from me. He was staring at me, but as soon as he saw me look over he bent his head. His straight fair hair fell forward into his eyes.

I said painfully, 'Thank you – for bringing me here.'

He looked at me again. Under the fall of fair hair his eyes were deep-set and grave above a jutting nose, but now a smile lit his face. He was lanky and long-limbed in his rough breeches and patched jacket; he'd not yet filled out to his full strength like his father, but he was tall and broad-shouldered, and moved with a quick litheness, unlike his father's stiff gait.

'What is your name?' he asked. His accent was not as strong as his father's.

'I have no given name,' I said, in a low voice. 'I've been called Scuff – for part of my life.'

He considered the name solemnly, then shook his head. 'You must find your true name.'

'How long have I been here?'

He shrugged. 'Time passes differently in the Wasteland.'

'How did you find me?'

'Your wings are still out there, in a reed bed that cushioned your fall.' He jerked his head towards the opening in the wall. 'You weren't moving, so I lifted you up and brought you here.'

'Your father nursed me,' I whispered.

'He's a healer.'

I thought of Gadd's cool touch on my forehead, all he'd done for me. 'I wish I'd the means to pay him.'

'Money would mean nothing to him,' said Erland gruffly. 'He cared for you because you were hurt.'

I didn't know what to say, faced with such unquestioning kindness. Tears filled my eyes. Though I couldn't say such a thing to this grave, unworldly youth and his gentle father, who together had saved my life, I wished I had died when I fell from the air. There was nothing to live for.

* * *

I had no way of telling how much time was passing, nor did it matter to me.

I lay listlessly on the pallet, listening to the fire crackle or to Gadd and Erland talking to each other as they moved about, preparing food, bringing in clanking buckets of well water or cow's milk, sharpening blades. Their thoughtfulness was endless. They rigged up a reed screen to preserve my modesty, and brought me bowls of water to wash myself in.

When it grew dark outside, they pulled my pallet closer to the fire and I would watch Gadd plaiting reeds into baskets and mats to sell, for although the rheum had stiffened his legs, his fingers were nimble and clever. I would scarce touch the fish they cooked for supper, and it seemed too great an effort to talk. But I'd notice how easy they were together in conversation, how they'd joke and tease each other in their soft voices. As Erland passed Gadd's stool, he'd ruffle his father's greying locks in mocking impudence; in return, Gadd would pretend to box Erland's ears or clap him on the rump to chivvy him to his duties.

And in their eyes there was such affection that deep inside me something woke and twisted with emotion.

During the day I was often on my own, for Erland went out whatever the weather, and Gadd only stayed behind if the rheum was bothering him badly, for he needed to tend the animals. But I did not have the desire or strength to go out with them. I scarce had the energy to do more than empty the bowl they'd given me for a chamber pot: the few dragging steps to the latrine ditch they'd dug in a clump of silver birch. Not far away I could hear the lowing of a cow, a goat bleating, but my eyes didn't leave the ground. It was too dangerous.

I'd often finger the amber stone that Aggie had given me, dangling it like a solid drop of sunlight on its leather thread, touching the smoothness that had saved me from the sky.

Or had it?

Sometimes at night I would dream. The dreams would be a blur of images: Pegg's hand on the pistol; the upturned faces of the soldiers; the brands burning below in the darkness; the dogs howling and straining on their leashes. I'd feel Pegg's pistol in my ribs, the leather flying harness cutting into my body.

And then I'd drop into space.

I would cry out in terror and wake to find Gadd by my pallet, hushing me, smoothing my hair back from my face. Then I'd whisper over and over again, 'How did I survive such a fall?'

Gadd said nothing. He sat there quietly, a dark soothing presence, until at last my trembling ceased.

But there was a curious thing. Sometimes on waking I had the sensation of wings beneath me. A sea of feathers held me up so that I floated on the night wind. It seemed that I skimmed the air, rose into the glittering, dark blue firmament and sailed beneath the stars. I flew on, light as a bird, and all the time there was a force beneath me, supporting me, guiding my way. Whether it was dream or memory, I had no notion.

All day long, the seagulls mewled over the rush dome above my head. I stared into space for hours, hearing their plaintive cries above the spitting of the fire, and my mind felt dull and empty. I wondered if I were going mad. When Gadd and Erland came back they often found me sitting on my pallet, huddled in the sheepskin coverlet and gazing fixedly at nothing.

One afternoon Gadd came over to light the rush lights on the shelf above my pallet, and surprised me. I'd pulled my screen across to give them the impression I was asleep, but I was lying on my back staring blank-eyed at the patterns the plaited rushes made as they met over my head in the darkening shadows.

He sat down on a stool close by me in the pool of green light and sucked on his pipe in silence for a while, not looking at me.

I sat up and pushed back my matted hair. 'It's the dratted seagulls,' I said fretfully. 'They are sending me mad.'

He said nothing.

'I'm sorry,' I muttered at last. 'I don't know what can be wrong with me.'

'Your soul yearns for what it's lost,' he said calmly, 'and for what it's not yet found.'

It was the truth, I realized, and my eyes pricked.

'I'm thinking that soon it will be time to set about your new life,' said Gadd.

Panic gripped me at once; I clutched the sheepskin. 'Please, I beg you – could I stay here? I could cook for you both, keep house?'

He looked about him, smiling. 'A housekeeper, here? But it would not be seemly, the three of us living together in one room. Besides, Erland be away most times. It would not do – the two of us together.'

'Please, Mr Gadd!'

'During the winter it be bitter cold in here. In the summer I be out all day and sometimes nights, given good weather.'

'I wouldn't mind,' I said, but he shook his head.

'It be no life for a young girl,' he said gently. 'Be there nowhere else you can go?'

I thought of the letter in the pocket of my cloak, and said with reluctance, 'I have an address where I may find employment, a house in Poorgrass Kayes.'

'Aye, it be where I sell my work. Erland will take you there in the dory.'

My heart sank. 'But not yet, Mr Gadd?'

He considered me a long moment. 'Not yet.'

2

After that day, things changed for me.

The following morning, after the animals had been tended and we had eaten our breakfast of oatmeal and dried herring, Gadd set off with his fishing rod. I expected Erland to follow. By now I knew he hated being inside during daylight. Even in the evening he was never still. He moved restlessly around the cramped space by the fire and never settled to his weaving as his father did.

Now he beckoned me to the opening in the rush wall. 'Close your eyes,' he said.

Puzzled, I obeyed. I felt him guiding me, then gentle fingers on my face. He turned my head to the light. 'There! Don't you feel it? The change in the sunlight?'

Radiance lit the insides of my lids; I could feel warmth on my upturned face. It stole through me from the tip of my head to my feet. It bathed my cold skin, warmed my thin blood. When I breathed I could smell it in the air: a green warmth, as if everything in nature was breathing.

In pleasure I opened my eyes and saw Erland's smile. 'Summer's on her way.' He held out his hand, as if to pull me outside.

At once I was frightened. 'What are you doing?'

'Going to check the boats. Come with me.'

'But I . . .' I couldn't think of what to say.

Somehow I found myself outside the shelter, clutching the amber at my neck. The light was strong after so many days in darkness. It was as if I'd emerged from the cellar. I rubbed my dazzled eyes and the light softened into a green-brown water-world.

I saw the grass and wattle dome of the shelter where I spent my days. I saw shingle and tall grass and pools, glistening like tears, all the way to the rim of the sky. There were islands of silver birch and gorse, with bright yellow flowers like tiny drops of egg yolk, and high in the sky, seagulls wailing over a strange, flat land.

It was the first time I had raised my head to look at it. I took my hand away from the amber. 'It's beautiful!' *But there's too much space*, I thought.

'It's a wild, magic place, with its own rules,' said Erland. 'You have to respect it.'

He began to pick his way along a finger of shingle between water and reeds. His leather bag swung against his side. He wore no jacket over his rough calico shirt, as if it was already summer; his hair shone in the sun. I knew he was smiling again, a secret smile, at the fairness of the day.

My legs were weak from lying around so long, and it was difficult to keep up. Erland was disappearing into a sea of reeds; at my feet, silver water oozed over the shingle. 'Wait!' I wailed.

He halted at once. His contrite face looked back at me. 'For a moment I forgot,' he said, and held out his hand to guide me.

I should talk to him in an interesting way, I thought, *then he won't forget me*. But I didn't know what to say. I knew he wasn't one for idle conversation; he would be more used to birds and fish, than girls. The silence grew heavy between us, but Erland seemed content with it, looking ahead, his face lifted to the sun. After we had been walking on firmer shingle for some time, I could bear it no longer.

'Where do you fish?'

'By the river or in the creeks,' he said, still gazing ahead. 'Sometimes I cast from the bank, sometimes take the punt out.'

'What's a punt?'

'A long boat, flat-bottomed. You pole it through the water. My father uses it when he cuts reeds for thatch.'

I stared about, seeing nothing but tall grasses and splinters of still water. 'Where are the creeks?'

'You come on them suddenly. The river's not far off, running near parallel with the sea. There's more water than land in the Wasteland.'

'Gadd cuts the reeds in summer?'

Erland nodded. 'He's only two months at most to cut and spread. If I'm here, I help him.'

'Spread?'

'You spread the reeds out to dry them,' he said patiently. 'You have to dry them in the open air. He'll harvest by moonlight too, if the night's clear.'

'What does he do all winter?' I said, nonplussed.

He gave a sudden laugh. 'Struggles to keep himself and the animals alive. It's hard, here on the Wasteland. If he's time to spare, he weaves baskets and matting.'

'And you? What do you do?'

'It's hard enough making a living for one, let alone two. My work takes me elsewhere. But if I'm here, I'll sail the dory down to Poorgrass Kayes for him – sell his work in the market.'

I did not want to think about Poorgrass Kayes. My legs ached; there was no sign of the river. 'Let me sit a minute,' I begged.

Erland nodded, and I sank down on the bright turf, between cushions of pale pink thrift. The water around us mirrored the reeds: I could see the sky reflected, a gull winging overhead. I leant forward, parting the reeds, and suddenly saw a face gazing back: large eyes; pallid cheeks; long, matted hair. *I'm ugly now*, I thought.

Erland sat down beside me and unfastened his leather bag. He took out a long mahogany box. 'This was my grandmother's toiletry box.'

With great reverence he showed me what was lying on

the faded silk lining inside: two yellowing lace collars; some faded hair ribbons, neatly rolled; a little waxy square of what looked like soap sitting in a glass bowl; a tortoiseshell comb. He held the box out to me. 'Borrow it, if you like.'

'Are you sure?' I said, touched.

'She'd like to think of it being used.'

I took out the glass bowl and sniffed at the soap: it still contained the faint, pleasurable fragrance of lavender. When I tried to fit the bowl back in, something was stuck in the lining, something that pricked me: a sharp point sticking out. When I pulled it, more and more came out. It was a single feather, long and white, the barbs crushed.

A shiver went through me. I laid the feather quickly down on the grass and touched the amber stone at my neck.

Erland picked the feather up, holding it to the sun. 'A swan's feather.'

'You dare touch it?' I saw he wore no amulet himself.

He smiled. 'My grandmother always watched the swans at Murkmere.'

'Murkmere? But that's where I came from!' It slipped out carelessly. I hadn't meant to tell him where I'd lived – Erland or his father.

'I know,' said Erland. He was still looking at the feather, smoothing the barbs with his careful fingers.

'How do you know?' I demanded, bewildered and suddenly apprehensive.

'I know because that's where we met, you and I.'

I shook my head. 'We've never met before.'

He laid the feather down and turned to me, his eyes on mine: sombre eyes, deep-set. For the first time I noticed their colour: dark grey, almost black. 'Don't you recognize me, Scuff?'

I shook my head again, fiercely; I was frightened now.

'I lived at Murkmere too,' he said softly, 'when I was a little boy. One day by the mere you rescued me. You took me home. Don't you remember?'

I did remember.

'The little lost boy was you?' I said in disbelief. I stared at the youth beside me: long limbs and fair, stubbled beard, the little child long gone. And yet there was an ageless quality about his face.

He nodded and gave a small smile. 'The other girl wanted me to live with the swans, I believe!'

'That was Leah. She was a strange girl.' I hesitated; I stared at him still. 'But you are older than I am. The child I rescued then was young, younger than I was by a good deal.'

'Haven't we told you that time passes differently in the Wasteland?'

'How can it?' I said. 'It must obey the same laws, surely?'

'This is not a place for formal measurements, for mechanical clocks or even sand timers,' he said curtly. I thought I'd irritated him. 'I feel I've spent many different lifetimes here.'

'But that can't be so,' I said, half smiling.

'You know nothing,' he said, suddenly angry. 'You think I'd lie to you?'

'No, no,' I stammered, taken aback. 'Of course not.'

'Well, then. Believe it.'

After a while, I said timidly, for I could see he was brooding on it, 'But if you lived at Murkmere, why did you leave?'

There was a long silence. I thought he was still angry but then saw he was mulling over his words. 'My father has told me that after my grandmother died, I wandered off – perhaps to look for her, he thinks. I don't remember. He searched the estate, begged Silas the steward to order the keepers to drag the mere, but Silas refused. I don't know what brought my father here to search for me in the Wasteland.'

'You were here?'

He nodded.

'And you never went back?'

'We never went back. My father wouldn't work for Silas any more. He's always been good with his hands. Somehow he managed to make a life for both of us here.'

'But – weren't you ever lonely?' I couldn't imagine it. I thought of the bustle and chatter of Murkmere in the days of the Master, all the servants rushing in and out of the steamy kitchen quarters.

He grimaced. 'I never missed the company of other children, but my father made me go to the village school.

Each day I'd have to leave the reeds and water to go and study books.'

'Then we must have had the same teacher, for I know Miss Jennet, who taught in the village. She now lives at Murkmere and has taught me!' It gave me pain to think of Miss Jennet.

'She was a fine teacher,' said Erland, 'though I was no scholar. She would box my ears.'

'Mine too!' I said, forgetting my bitter thoughts. We smiled at each other.

'You look nice when you smile,' he said. 'Not frightened any more.'

'I'm always frightened,' I said in a low voice. 'The world is too big.'

'Is it the birds that frighten you? You wear an amulet.'

'Most people wear amulets,' I retorted. 'Are you so brave you'd defy the birds, or aren't you a believer? Did you never attend Devotion and listen to the scriptures in the Divine Book, never learn the *Table of Significance*?'

He is heathen! I thought.

'How can any bird mean wickedness?' he said. 'They are all the Almighty's creatures. They behave as their natures guide them, and He has given them those.'

'Oh,' I said. I thought a minute. 'Do you believe He has given us our natures as well?'

'Indeed He has.'

But mine is a bad nature, I thought. *He can't have given that to me.*

84

'You look frightened again,' said Erland. 'Is it because you think they will catch you?'

He gently touched the brand mark on the inside of my bare forearm; it was showing where I had rolled up the sleeve of my blouse in the warmth of the sun. I snatched my arm away at once and bent my head so that my hair hid my face.

'I've noted it before, I couldn't help it,' he said. There was such compassion in his voice I pushed my hair away and looked at him.

'I came to Murkmere from one of the Orphans' Homes in the Capital,' I said at last. 'In the Homes they brand the children when they first arrive.'

He looked grim. 'They should not do such a thing to any child.'

He was so innocent, I thought. 'It's to identify us. They can reclaim us to work for them without wages if we run away later and are found by the Capital's Enforcers. It's called – Recompense.' I stumbled over the word. 'They see it as a return for our keep when we were small. You can never escape if you've been in a Home.'

In silence we looked at my scar, a raised whiter mark on my white skin – the number 102, and a square to show I was from the Gravengate Home – then I covered it up again. But I had not minded showing it to him.

'You escaped,' said Erland.

'I was sold to Silas, the steward at Murkmere. Sometimes they'll sell off the children as servants. I was small and weak. They thought I wouldn't be any use to them.'

'So that's why they're looking for you? For their Recompense?'

His eyes were gazing into mine, clear, concerned. I would have to tell him the truth, or some of it; it would not be right to keep silent. 'I'm putting you and Gadd at risk,' I burst out. 'I'm a wanted criminal, Erland! Soldiers of the Lord Protector are looking for me. They've traced me after all this time. If I'm found they'll take me back to the Capital and try me in the Courts. I'll get the death penalty, most like!'

He was silent; I couldn't tell what he was thinking.

'You'll be sorry now that you took me in,' I said in a small voice. 'Shall you tell Gadd?'

He shook his head. 'He may know already – he knows most things. We looked after you because you needed us, not merely because you rescued me long ago.' He paused. 'I think my grandmother took a fancy to you. She often talked about you afterwards – the girl with no name.'

'You must wonder at my wickedness,' I said nervously. 'You must want to know about my crime.'

Erland looked away from me, at the soft feathery tops of the reeds. 'Let the Almighty judge what's wicked and what's not,' he said. 'It's not for men.'

The Almighty has allowed me to survive in spite of my crime, I thought. A tiny flicker of hope stirred inside me. Then I said, 'But it's men who make laws. And I've broken the law and so I must be punished. That's why the soldiers came for me.'

'There are no soldiers here,' said Erland.

'Does anyone ever come?'

'Sometimes we find the drowned bodies of vagrants in the marshes. Bands of them sometimes group near the river in summer. But the Lawman keeps the only chart of the Wasteland and the ground is always changing. You are safe.'

Later, when Erland took me back to the shelter and left me there to rest, I heated water and washed my hair with the soap, its lather still richly creamy and soft. Then I combed my clean hair free of tangles.

It took a long while, but when it was done I sat in the afternoon sun until my hair was dry. The evening clouds were darkening overhead when I went back inside to stoke up the fire for supper. Canvas sail bags were lying against the wall. One had rolled too close to the fire for safety, so I picked it up to put with the others.

It was strangely soft. Curious, I looked inside the neck of the bag. At once I flung it away from me and clutched my amber. I had to sit in Gadd's chair until I grew calm.

Feathers.

But they were beautiful, not threatening, those silver-white feathers, like the single feather in Erland's grandmother's box. I knew the sail bag contained the swanskin I remembered seeing in their cottage long ago.

Erland cared nothing for blasphemy; he had kept the swanskin in memory of her. All he'd said to me was true.

Erland returned before Gadd, as I was setting bowls on the table. I had recovered, was in control of myself, the bag safely with the others.

He stared at me. 'You look different.'

I'd forgotten my new-washed hair. I felt awkward under his gaze and bent my head so my hair swung around my face. 'Do I?'

He came across to me and gently, tentatively, took a strand from my face. 'It shines in the firelight,' he said, as if he held a treasure between his fingers.

I looked up at him, at his solemn, old-young face, the slight frown between his brows that I was beginning to know so well. I looked into his eyes and saw the surprise and wonder in them as he looked back at me.

Something altered in the air between us.

'I shan't call you Scuff any more, but Silky,' he whispered.

A footfall made us turn. Gadd was standing silently in the doorway, watching us.

3

From then on I went with Erland into the Wasteland each day.

He taught me to fish in the creeks, to cast and ply the line. He took me deep into the spring reed beds, a shifting, secretive sea of tawny-green, broken by willow and alder. The seed heads were higher than my head; I could hear nothing but the wind soughing through them.

Sometimes we saw swans drifting on the hidden pools. *Such mystical creatures belong here*, I thought, as I watched their lazy, almost sensuous motion through the water. 'Don't they mind us coming?' I asked Erland.

'They'll be building their nests soon,' he whispered. 'They might attack a stranger then if one went too near. But they're used to me.' He gazed at them under his heavy brows, his face softening. 'The cob and pen court again each spring, you know.'

'Then it's right that swans should signify True Love,' I whispered back, standing close to him.

Something curled into my mind, a dream or memory,

faint as smoke. A flash of white, then a feeling, nothing more, of wings beneath me, lifting . . . For a second it was with me, then it had blown away.

When the strength had come back into my legs, Erland took me to the river, along the causeway road that was only a line of flat stones, so overgrown it was almost hidden. The river stretched all the way to the sky. Low yellow-green banks, nibbled by narrow inlets, bordered a muddy shore. Drifts of birds flew low over my head, startling me; the air was full of their eerie wailing and piping. There was a smell of salt on the breeze, of mud, of unknown things.

Erland taught me the names of the birds: redshank, red-legged as its name; black and white oyster-catcher; avocet, with its upturned beak. I remembered the *Table of Significance* and knew these birds carried no omens, yet still my unease lingered. The Wasteland remained an alien, mysterious space to me, though I tried to like it for Erland's sake. I longed to please him, to make him love me.

He must love me already, I thought, for on good days he seemed so entranced by my presence: smiling, full of light, his moodiness banished. Sometimes, when we were walking, he would take my hand and swing it loosely in his, cheerful as the morning. He would call me Silky, then. *He is mine*, I thought, *he truly loves me*. Once I pressed his warm hand, hoping he would press mine back. I gazed at his cheek, his eyes, his hair, his strong profile, as we strode along. I'd never seen a youth so handsome.

Yet other times he would turn from me and stare over the shimmering marsh water to the far horizon, and his face would be shut against me.

'What's in your mind, Erland?' I said, at last. 'You are thinking sad thoughts again.'

He turned to me at once; he stroked my hair as if he gentled a pet. 'How can I be sad when you're here, Silky?'

But I was disturbed by a trickle of unease. *Lovers should tell each other their thoughts, shouldn't they? But if I love him, then he must love me.*

'Your coming here has made me think many things,' he said. 'What I shall do when my father dies. Shall I be an ordinary man and live out my days like any other? I only wish I could.'

I looked at his unhappy face and longed to say, 'Then come away with me, Erland, come now,' but I was too tentative.

He shrugged his shoulders abruptly as if to shrug his thoughts away. 'And what of you, Silky? You have great things ahead of you, I know it.'

I had to laugh. 'How can you know it? You say it to please me, but I know nothing about the working of the world, Erland.'

'That is now. You will learn it. It will take time.'

'Your time or mine?' I said it in jest, but at once his face closed against me.

And so some days he would be withdrawn and morose,

and I would try to cheer him until he became again the attentive companion I knew.

In the shelter I avoided his eyes as if mine might say too much and show Gadd my secret love. If secret it was. In the evenings, I would sometimes look up to see Gadd watching me warily, a troubled look on his face in the firelight. But I was careful to show nothing, to go about cleaning pots after supper in an unconcerned way. It gave me a thrill to pretend that nothing had changed between Erland and me, that everything was as it had been in those drear, dark days before we went outside together.

'I am glad to see you better,' Gadd said.

'Yes,' I said cheerily. 'The Wasteland air's so very bracing.'

'Be careful. Too much can make one light-headed.'

I was feeling so happy inside that night, I wanted to share it. I looked at his long face, poor old man. 'What say you to a song, Mr Gadd? We should entertain ourselves. A roundelay, perhaps, with the three of us.'

Because I was so careful not to look at Erland, I couldn't see what he thought.

'I rasp like the corncrake when I sing,' said Gadd. He sucked his pipe. 'You sing us a verse or two, Miss Scuff. It be a long while since I heard a maid sing.'

All at once I was shy; my happy confidence disappeared. I hid behind my hair, but I could see that they were both looking at me expectantly. I couldn't let Erland down. He might love me all the more if I sang: I would make him fall in love with my voice.

First I gave them that rousing old song of the haymakers, 'Lift Your Pitchforks High and Holla: "Harvest's Home Tonight!"'. They both appeared to enjoy it and gave me a little clap when I'd finished.

Then I cast around in my mind for a song to bring a change of mood. I fixed on a haunting ballad I'd heard as a child: 'I Left My Love by the Amber Gate'. It is said that somewhere in the Capital there is a fabulous, ancient gate made from amber and gold. Perhaps the woman in the cellar had sung the old song – or someone in the streets of the Capital – I don't know. I was surprised at myself for I'd forgotten I knew it, but every word came out perfectly. It is a sad song, for the girl's lover dies in the magical place at the Gate, where the sky rains with 'stars and crowns'.

I sang sweetly that night. I knew it, as you know when you do something your heart is in. I thought of Erland's precious love and sang for it; and as he and his father sat and listened by the fire, I captured both of them in the spell of my singing.

Afterwards there was silence. I looked from one to another, my heart beating quick. They stared into the flames, each lost.

Gadd roused himself. He said huskily, 'That was well done. Thank you for it. You sing like the nightingale.'

I knew it was a compliment but I touched my amber quickly, for the nightingale can sometimes signify Death to those who hear it.

Erland raised his head and looked at me. 'Beautiful,' he murmured. Our eyes met.

'You sing now, Erland,' I said hastily, for I did not want Gadd to think anything of his comment.

'I don't sing,' said Erland. His face was shadowed.

'Please, Erland.' He shook his fair head.

I shouldn't have pressed him further, but I felt bold after the success of my singing, and so I did. 'You're a coward,' I said, laughing. 'I have sung. Now it's your turn.'

'I never sing,' he muttered.

'But your voice can't be like the corncrake's too! Let me hear it.'

'No!' He leapt to his feet, knocking his stool over with a thud on to the matting. His shadow flickered over the walls as he went in two strides to the doorway. Without looking back, without further word to either of us, he ripped the sheepskin hanging aside and disappeared into the night.

It was suddenly very quiet in the shelter, except for the hissing of the wood on the fire, as the cold night air found its way inside. Blown smoke billowed around us. I felt my eyes smart and a great gulp rise in my throat.

Gadd shook his head and rose stiffly to straighten the hanging.

'What have I done?' I whispered, when he came back to the fire.

He settled himself again with an effort and gave his pipe a steady suck before he answered. 'Erland does not sing.'

'But he was so angry. I don't understand.' My voice trembled.

'And he would not want you to try,' said Gadd. 'Don't concern yourself over it.'

'But he may come to harm,' I wailed, 'out in the dark – alone.' I thought of the Birds of Night, and shuddered.

Gadd grunted in amusement. 'Erland? He be a wild creature himself in the dark. Sometimes we fish at night . . .' He looked over at me and it was too dark to see his expression. 'You should leave soon, before the season starts, before things go further.'

I knew what he was saying to me. He had known all along about our love and disapproved of it. I was dismayed; but Gadd seemed deep in his thoughts and I could say nothing. I wanted reassurance and comfort, and only Erland could give me that. If he loved me he would come back soon, apologize for his temper and smile at me, and on the morrow he'd take me out again.

When Erland did finally return, I was asleep. But the next day he took me out fishing and never mentioned the previous evening. Nor did Gadd say anything more to me about leaving. I thought, *Perhaps he has accepted that we love each other*.

And so time passed, a green time of fine rain and pale sun and troubled happiness, until the morning there were two moons in the sky. And that was my last day on the Wasteland, though I didn't know it.

4

That morning when we went out, I could still see the moon, fat and full in the sky as if it were too lazy to leave. A second moon peered milkily from behind the clouds. I knew it was the sun in hiding, though it gave no warmth today. The Wasteland looked a desolate and gloomy place without the sunlight, the stunted trees and bushes tinged grey.

Erland frowned up at the sky. 'There's a spring storm coming.'

'How can you tell?'

He shrugged. 'It's in the air. The birds sense it.'

He began to stride away and I ran to catch up with him. I didn't know where we were going.

'I must secure the boats.'

'When will the storm come?' I panted, perturbed by his sudden urgency. Erland didn't slacken his pace. 'Maybe tonight, maybe not for another day or so.'

Down by the river everything seemed the same to me. There was no sunlight on the water today; wind ruffled its dull surface. The tide was on the early ebb and had not yet drained the muddy inlets that wandered over the marsh between the old grassy dyke wall and the river.

I watched Erland manoeuvre the punt close to where the dory, the small flat-bottomed sailing boat, was already moored in a wide creek. He weighed the rope's end – the painter, he called it – down with heavy stones on the bank. Then he checked the dory's mooring. 'Should be safe enough.'

Good, I thought. *Now the day can be peaceful, as it always is*.

There was a distant explosion of noise, so sudden, so violent in the stillness, we did not have time to move. We stood, rigid with shock, blasted by sound. The birds rose in a tumult of cries and beating wings.

Erland came to life before I did and pulled me down on the springy turf.

'What was that?' I cried.

He held me close. 'A gun.'

I'd never heard gunshot before; I was trembling.

He raised his head. 'They must be on the river somewhere. Soldiers from Windrush – fooling about, most like.' Only soldiers and the Lawmen in the main towns had a licence to carry guns.

'You said no soldiers ever came,' I hissed.

'They don't. They must have a chart.'

'Did they see us?'

'Don't know.'

'They'll see the boats!'

'Plenty of boats on the river.'

I lay, scarce breathing, his arm still around me. Mud seeped up through the turf; I tasted the grit of sand in my mouth. The birds settled back; the air closed around us. For a moment everything was still. Then, unmistakeably, we heard the creak and squeak of wood, and slow but regular, the dip and splash and surge of water being pushed away. Not far from us a craft was being rowed over the river and coming closer all the time.

'I'll go to the bend and look,' whispered Erland.

'No, don't! Stay with me!'

But he was already wriggling away like an eel beyond the dory, along the bottom of the dyke wall where it followed the bulge of the shore.

I lay where I was, my heart thumping. There was laughter not far away: high-pitched, excited. Two male voices, with the slight hoarseness of youth: one, more educated than the other, sounded tipsy. I held the amber stone and prayed to the Eagle, a wordless prayer for protection. Two young soldiers, relishing a day's freedom on the river. Let that be all it was.

The voices were closer.

'There he is again, damn him – thought I'd got the ruffian!'

'You'll waste your shot, Sir. And be had up for murder.' The accent of the Capital.

'Not for killing a vagrant. Doing the law a favour. It's a

game, Chance, cheer up. Plenty of shot left. Where's he got to?' A whoop. 'There he is!' Another blast of sound as the gun was fired. Birds flew squawking and piping in all directions amid insane laughter from the youth. There was a sharp, burning smell on the clean air.

Had Erland been hit? There was no cover here. I pressed myself harder into the tufty grass. My heart thudded, for I remembered the name, Chance. It was the soldier who had come into the kitchen at Murkmere, the young Corporal. The soldier with him must be the Lord Protector's son, Caleb Grouted.

The boat scraped over shingle. They must have found somewhere to land without having to wade through mud. I heard the distant crunch of boots as they climbed out, a flurry of startled birds, high-pitched giggling from the youth with the gun, a tipsy snatch of song, *A-hunting, a-hunting, a-hunting we will go!*

Where is Erland? Very cautiously I lifted my head.

The two young soldiers stood on the grass at the bend in the river. They were looking straight towards me, staring over the desolate marshland. Chance had the painter of the rowing boat in his hand; Caleb Grouted held his musket cocked, the leather holster dangling loosely. They were looking for Erland; they couldn't see him, but I could, and my heart lurched.

He lay, almost submerged in water, in one of the shallow inlets between the dyke wall and the river. He was closer to the soldiers than he was to me, hidden only by the height of turf and low sedge above him. But he was trapped. If he moved, they would see him.

'This place gives me the creeps, Sir. Let's go.'

'He can't hide from us, Chance, not here. He's somewhere about and we'll get him.' Caleb Grouted swung his musket slowly across the landscape.

'He could be dangerous.'

A sudden wild giggle. 'Not when he's shot at, he won't be. We'll make him dance, Chance!'

I stood up.

I think I had a notion that they would see me and realize I was the girl they'd been hunting, would be distracted and Erland could escape. I can't remember. At the time it seemed the only thing to do.

I don't think Caleb Grouted noticed me immediately. But in that minute a great many things happened.

Erland turned his head, perhaps to check where I was. He saw me stand up and an expression of horror crossed his face. At the same time Caleb Grouted spotted him, and with a shout of triumph, raised his musket to take aim.

5

Even from the boat, Chance had recognized the girl, as soon as he saw her with the vagrant. They were standing not far from the grassy wall that ran along the reach of the river. She'd been half hidden behind the man, but Chance had known at once the shy, sideways tilt of her head, her long sweep of hair.

When their search for the girl – Number 102 – at Murkmere had proved futile, Caleb Grouted had produced the Wasteland chart he'd ripped from the wall of the Lawman's hut. Chance heard Mather say, 'Excellent foresight, Lieutenant Grouted', and he had ground his teeth with envy.

Then Mather had ordered Caleb to carry out a preliminary survey of the river, with a view to searching the Wasteland for Number 102. Chance was told to accompany the Lord Protector's son and guard him.

Chance had never actually believed the girl could have reached this fearful place alive, but all along the Gods had been on his side. They had granted him this stroke of luck.

He said nothing to Caleb about seeing the girl; he was going to arrest her himself. If he said anything to Caleb, then Caleb would take all the glory. Chance's plan was to go ashore while Caleb was distracted by the vagrant, seize her at gunpoint and shackle her to him for the journey back in the boat. She would be his prisoner by rights and Caleb could do nothing.

But Chance didn't like stepping on to the shifting shingle; when he took his first step, stones, mud and sand moved under his feet and his musket banged against his back. He looked with distrust at the short coarse grass that stretched before them in the grey light. Caleb, impatient, headed off in front. He spotted the vagrant again and, with a shout of triumph, raised his musket.

And the girl stood up.

The birds came from nowhere, it seemed – the swans.

As Caleb raised his musket, they rose from the inlet beyond him in a fury of white feathers. They hissed ferociously, outstretched necks like snakes. Their wings created a slamming and booming of air that seemed to vibrate to where Chance stood transfixed. In the churning storm of wings and necks and beaks, Chance couldn't tell how many there were; he'd never seen so many swans together.

They circled Caleb. Caleb, whimpering beneath them, tried to aim his musket. Then they flew lower so that they were just above his head. Chance saw him dodge and duck, his musket wave wildly. He was too frightened to move, to go to Caleb's rescue.

Suddenly there was an explosion of gunfire. Chance had the impression of something heavy falling from the sky through a cloud of white smoke.

At once the swans ceased their attack and veered off. He heard the thrum of their wings as the great birds cleaved the air laboriously.

In the distance Caleb crouched down. He began to sob: loud, noisy sobs of relief.

Chance came to himself at last. He trembled with shock. *The swans are the guardian spirits of this place*, he thought. *He'll be damned.*

Caleb stumbled back towards him, red in the face and wild-eyed, clutching his smoking musket. An acrid smell clung to him. 'I shot one, didn't I?' he said, with triumphant bravado. 'I shot a swan, filthy creature. I frightened them all off. I killed a Bird of Significance and survived. What does that mean, eh, Chance?'

'Not good, I reckon,' muttered Chance, still trembling.

Caleb seized him by the collar of his jacket. 'You fool. It means I'm more powerful than they are. You saw, didn't you? They're only weak creatures, after all. It died, shot with one of my musket balls! Only wish I could have killed that vagrant. Those blasted birds got in my way!'

Chance, half throttled, automatically balled his fists, but before he could throw a punch, Caleb hastily released him. Chance glowered and readjusted his collar.

'Not a word about this back at camp, understood?' growled Caleb. 'Say nothing to Mather. I've the power to make things very unpleasant for you, don't forget. Could get you discharged – like that.' He snapped his fingers.

Chance nodded resentfully. 'Goin' to leave it behind then, are you, Sir – your trophy?' he managed to say, with heavy sarcasm.

Caleb stared. 'What?'

'The bird you shot.'

Caleb opened his mouth, thought better of answering and brushed past Chance to the boat. Chance followed sullenly. There was no way he could search for the girl now, yet she had been so close to him – still was, no doubt. On the other hand, this place gave him the creeps. He wanted to leave smartish in case those swans came back.

Behind them the Wasteland was silent.

POORGRASS KAYES

1

Gadd took me to Poorgrass in the dory that self-same day, as soon as he had made Erland as comfortable as he could.

He washed Erland's wounded leg with a vinegar mixture to quell the bleeding, then dressed it with a sour-smelling poultice of yarrow. When that was done, he said we should set forth immediately while the tide was on the ebb and in our favour. There would still be light enough to get us to Poorgrass, and him safely returned on the flood tide before nightfall.

I was shocked. 'Must I leave while Erland is in this state, Mr Gadd?'

Outwardly, Gadd seemed his calm self, but his face was grim. 'You say one of the soldiers saw you?'

I nodded miserably. At the time I had scarce cared whether they did or no. I thought Erland dead, that the Lord Protector's son had shot him as the swans flew about his head. It had been impossible to see what happened in that frenzy of feathers, the fog of white smoke.

But it was a flesh wound: the musket ball had ripped

past Erland's thigh. There was so much blood, though, that I had to tear up his shirt and my petticoat to staunch and bandage his leg before I could help him limp back to the shelter. He couldn't tell me what had happened: he was speechless with pain.

'It be wisest to leave now,' said Gadd quietly. 'The soldiers may return and search the Wasteland any time. You'll be safest in Poorgrass, with your new employers.'

'Shall the soldiers come here to question you, do you think?' I asked fearfully. 'Shall you tell them the truth, Mr Gadd?'

'What truth be that?' said Gadd, shrugging. 'Nay, you've told me neither your given name nor birth place. And Erland be too ill to speak, so I shall do his talking. Nobody knows nothing, I shall say. All we did was take in a sick young maid and tend her till she be well again, as we would any of God's creatures.'

I looked at Erland lying helpless on his pallet beside the fire, as I had done myself until only recently. His eyes were closed: he slept; and how dearly I wanted him to wake, to protest that I must stay to look after him, that I was his love. In the song about the Amber Gate the maiden tends her true love, who is sick unto death, and words from the refrain kept running in lunatic fashion through my head: *And shall he wake no more? And shall he wake no more?*

'You will give Erland my address, won't you, Mr Gadd?' I begged. 'I'll be allowed time off, I'm sure, to see him next time he comes selling in Poorgrass Kayes. Get word to me, I beg you, of how you're both faring. You'll remember where I am, with the Bundishes of Gull House?'

I prayed Gadd's memory still worked: he was an old man, I thought dismally.

'Erland will find you, wherever you be.' Gadd moved jerkily about the shelter, sucking in his breath as he bent to pick up sail bags and ropes.

'I'm sorry for the trouble I've caused,' I said in a low voice. 'All this is my fault – and now you have to put yourself at risk as well as Erland.'

'Bless the maid,' he said, his smile strained. 'Erland would have been shot whether you was there or no. They be like that – soldiers.'

My old clothes had become too ragged and filthy to wear. I was dressed in a skirt that Gadd, in the kindness of his heart, had roughly stitched for me from a piece of supple leather, and a warm sheepskin jacket that had once belonged to Erland when small, as had my laced leather boots. I took a brush of boar's hair and brushed myself clean of Wasteland mud. At least my old frayed bodice had had a wash in hot water only two days before. As for my face, I rubbed it with a wet cloth until my cheeks stung, and then I combed my hair, tying it up with string for lack of ribbons or bonnet.

But in truth I little cared if my employers thought me some outlandish country clod. My heart was heavy.

I looked my last on Erland's peaceful face. 'I will see you soon,' I thought, but immediately into my head came the maddening refrain: *And shall he wake no more?*

I shut the mahogany box that he'd given me and tucked it under my arm. Then we left.

'Oh, Mr Gadd!' I gulped, crouching down uncomfortably as the dory rocked in the current, the sail billowed wildly and the waters fought beneath the hull, 'I'm not sure I like this!'

'You'll not need endure it long,' said Gadd shortly. He pulled on a rope somewhere and the sail became taut. Suddenly wind and water were moving us along in a surge of speed. But I could not understand how it was we remained afloat, given the fearful straining sounds of rope and sail and wood. And over our heads was the incessant mockery of the herring gulls, and all around, the cold grey surface of the river waiting to gulp us down.

I shut my eyes; it seemed the safest thing to do. 'I can't swim,' I whispered to myself.

Holding the tiller steady above me, Gadd said, 'I cannot swim neither, and have never had need to yet.' I took comfort and opened my eyes a crack to see where we were.

'Look,' said Gadd. 'See Poorgrass Kayes? There be her watchtower.' Indeed, there the tower was, rising against the overcast sky and easy to mark, since the land was flat all the way.

'It is no distance at all!' I exclaimed. I felt considerably cheered.

'Little by land, further by water,' Gadd said.

And so it proved. Though my eyes watered with looking, the tower never seemed to draw any closer. The river widened and narrowed and widened again, as we sailed past mudflats, salt marshes and low mounds of samphire and seaweed.

But at last the mudflats gave way to dykes, the long shingle banks protecting the farming land that sheltered behind them: fields still mostly bare and brown, divided by draining ditches. Sheep clustered down by the river and sheltered around the few stunted, windblown trees; they skittered off when we passed close.

Far beyond our little boat, the grey river flooded into the horizon and become part of the vast grey sky. 'Is that the sea?' I asked.

'The town sits before the bar,' said Gadd. 'It be the sea, right enough.'

'It's too big,' I murmured, in dismay. This place was to be my home. Could you live in a port and turn your back on the sea?

Gadd found a mooring for the dory on the nearest quay. Above us warehouses of dark brick rose from the long causeway, which was thronged with merchants and seamen, bartering and arguing over piled barrels and bales of wool. Around us sailors threw their ballast over sails hung between boat and quay and shouted to each other in words I didn't understand.

My head rang after the peace of the Wasteland; my heart sank to my boots.

Two young men from a fishing smack helped me on to the quay, and Gadd after me. They doffed their woollen caps to us, then said something to each other, laughing. An old fisherman, chewing a lump of mastigris as he sat on a bollard, stared at me expressionless and spat out a stream of orange-stained spittle.

There was a trawling net by my feet full of dead fish: the reek was overwhelming. For a moment I thought I'd be sick.

Gadd and I looked at each other. Gadd twisted his old leather hat between his hands. 'Now then, Miss Scuff, tide's turning. I must get myself home.'

'Of course you must, Mr Gadd,' I said. My feet rocked beneath me with the remembered motion of the river. I felt oyster shells splinter beneath my borrowed boots. I swallowed hard. 'I don't think I realized Poorgrass was so very far . . .'

'You have the address safe?' said Gadd.

I felt for the parchment tucked into the pocket of Erland's old jacket, and nodded.

'Then fare you well, maid.'

That was all he said. He turned and scrambled awkwardly back down into the dory. The young fishermen watching didn't help. When Gadd glanced up, they moved back to their black-hulled smack, shoving at each other and making a lot of noise.

I couldn't watch Gadd sail away and leave me. I shifted the mahogany box more securely under my arm, then bent my head, crunched over scattered fish bones to the causeway and slipped quickly into the crowd.

I was tempted to go up one of the alleys between the warehouses. It would bring me out into the town where someone might well know the Bundishes and where they lived. The house couldn't be far.

I could see a marketplace down the end of one alleyway. I hesitated at the opening. It was dank and narrow; filthy urchins played in the puddles. A man came out from a hidden doorway and spoke roughly to them. He looked over at me. My scalp prickled; I walked on hurriedly.

Gull House is in Kaye Street, I thought. *It must be here on the causeway somewhere.*

I began to search along the warehouses, weaving my way in between the groups of haggling merchants before the open doors. Most were too engrossed in their business to pay me any attention, but when I wandered out on to one of the quays, a sailor looked up from coiling rope to stare at me, eyes gleaming in his weather-beaten face. He smiled; he seemed friendly.

A small boy crouched nearby, feeding a plump cat a dish of milk. I looked at the milk thirstily. I'd had nothing to eat or drink since breakfast at first light.

'All alone, Miss? You somethin' to sell?' The sailor's eyes went to the mahogany box under my arm.

I tightened my grip on it. 'No, indeed, Sir,' I said quickly, and turned back to the causeway. I'd heard the sound of the Capital in his voice.

'Wait. That's a nice piece. That wood comes from faraway places. I seen such trees growin'. Could fetch you a good price.'

'It's not for sale,' I said. 'I have the offer of employment here. I've no need of money.'

'Lucky girl,' the sailor said, smiling a broad, white smile. 'I don't like to think of you goin' hungry.' He looked at my clothes and smiled again. 'Remember me if you change your mind – Butley by name. I could bring you a good price back from the Capital. Gravengate Docks is my regular run, takin' brick or salt along the coast.'

'Gravengate?' I breathed.

'Gravengate. This is my girl here – the *Redwing*.' He gestured at a broad, three-masted barge lying against the quay, its rust-coloured sails furled. 'And if I'm not mistaken, you're from the Capital yourself.' He came closer. 'Regular number of us here, there be, not just the summer plague-runners but soldiers too.'

I was suddenly frightened. For all his face was so friendly, I wondered if he could be being paid by the Militia to interrogate strangers. 'Do soldiers come here to Poorgrass?' I asked, my heart beating hard.

'To Poorgrass? 'Course they come, for a bit of off-duty relaxation, if you understand my meanin'.' He winked. 'It's wild fenland where they are, the military camp at Windrush Creek. Only sheep. No ladies.'

I relaxed. 'You know Poorgrass well, then, Sir?'

'Well? Me and Shadow . . .' he gestured at the small boy '. . . are back here all the time, ain't that the truth, Shadow?'

The boy looked up and nodded, and the cat weaved round him, purring. The tip of its tail was white, otherwise it was coal black. 'And Plushey,' the boy said.

'And Mister Plush, can't forget him.'

I made a decision. 'Would you know the whereabouts of Gull House in Kaye Street, Sir?'

His bright eyes measured me. 'Is that where you'll be workin'?'

'It might be,' I said carefully.

'It's by the stream, what they call a gull local.' He jerked his head. 'Follow the causeway till you can't get no further, then the street roundwise. Can't miss it.' He was chuckling to himself now.

I felt uneasy; I didn't like the way he was looking at me. Now his eyes were on the amber at my neck. I pulled my jacket collar together and turned away. 'Thank you, Sir.'

'Wait. Shadow will go with you. He knows Kaye Street like the back of his hand, don't you, Shadow? You don't want to be hangin' round Kaye Street in the dark tryin' to find your way, a young lady like you.'

Chuckling again, he bent to his ropes, the cat rubbing against his legs. The small boy sprang ahead of me back along the quay, as nimble and delicate in his movements as the barge cat. 'I've nothing to give you for this, I'm afraid, Shadow,' I said. 'I've no money till I'm paid.'

He grinned at me, his dirty face mischievous. 'I'll come and collect it later, then, Miss!'

'Is that your father?' I nodded behind us at the sailor's back.

'Lawks, no. That's the bargemaster. 'Is brother is mate and I'm barge boy. There's more crew to help with the loadin' and unloadin', but I do the important stuff like climbin' the riggin' and lookin' after Plush.' He puffed out his scrawny chest and then laughed mockingly at himself. ' 'E's important too, is Plush, 'cos 'e eats the rats.'

I wondered if he was an orphan, if he'd ever been in a Home. A shapeless woollen tunic hid his thin forearms and any branding mark. 'Why are you called Shadow?'

His lively little face lit up. 'It's a nickname, see?'

'I've a nickname, too,' I said. 'It's Scuff. Maybe I had a proper name, a given name, once, but I don't remember it. I was nicknamed Scuff because I wore shoes that had belonged to someone with bigger feet.'

He looked down at my borrowed boots and grinned again. 'I'm called Shadow for a reason, too.' He pulled me closer. He smelled of warm grass and salt. 'I'm like a shadow, see?' he whispered. 'That's 'cos I'm a spy for 'imself, for the bargemaster, Mr Butley.'

'Why does he want you to spy, Shadow?' I asked warily.

He looked at me sideways, put his finger to the side of his nose. 'Others could be jealous of our cargo, know what I mean? I keep a watch on 'em, report back. They don't know I'm listenin'. I'm just a shadow on the wall and ever so small.'

I was relieved. 'You sound useful, Shadow.'

'Oh, I am.' His eyes glinted. ' 'Ey, Miss Scuff! Could do the same for you, report back. If there's anything – anyone – you want watchin'.'

I shook my head quickly.

'You could pay me – later,' he offered chirpily.

'What makes you think I need someone to watch for me?' I said, my heart beating faster.

He laughed carelessly. 'Why, everyone's watchin' some person else, ain't they?'

On the causeway I was afraid of losing him, but he stuck by my side like a limpet, grabbing hold of my jacket to guide me. They were beginning to light braziers and lamps outside the warehouses. Once I stopped to warm my cold hands, but Shadow pulled me on. 'You shouldn't stop, Miss.'

It was true I could see no other females about in the fading light. I was doubly glad Shadow was with me. I might have missed the continuation of Kaye Street altogether, for the causeway ended abruptly in the brick wall of a dockyard and there was only a dark alleyway between the wall and the last warehouse. Shadow darted into the gap, but I hesitated.

'Can this be right?' I said in a low voice, for some seamen were looking at us curiously.

He nodded. 'Yes, Miss, you'll see the gull in a minute.'

And he was right, for the narrow gap between wall and

warehouse widened at the end into a puddled street with a wide, open drain down one side, full of rushing water. In some places it had risen to pour over the cobbles. The wind funnelled down between the buildings on either side of us and rippled the shiny surface of the water into tiny sharp waves, but it could not blow away the stench of sewage.

I looked at the water in horror in the dusk. Shadow pulled me on to a line of raised stepping stones. 'This way.'

There was no one about. The buildings that lined the street appeared to be warehouses, shuttered and dark. Then we passed an ironworks. The main part of town lay to our left. I was filled with doubt. Was this where Miss Jennet's relatives would live?

Then I heard creaking in the wind. 'See,' said Shadow, and pointed.

There was a house on the slope above us, a town house once fine and imposing, with a brick exterior, four storeys and wide stone steps leading up to a pair of elegant, painted pillars that supported a porch over the front door. Over the years the paint had peeled away, and salt and rain had eaten at the exposed brick. A faded sign swung in the rising wind.

I looked at it, scarce believing my eyes: a sheep by a wriggling blue stream, crudely painted. Miss Jennet had never said I'd be working in a tavern.

'Shadow, this can't be the house!'

He shrugged. 'Long Gull, you said.'

He was fidgeting, looking up at the windows of the house. I could see candlelight on the first floor, where the shutters had not yet been closed.

'No, no – Gull House – it was your master who said . . .'

'Plenty of ladies come 'ere, Miss. I've brought 'em. You'll be right enough. They'll give you a bed for the night, least.'

My heart sank. I remembered such places – houses of ill-repute – from my time in the Capital. 'It's the wrong house,' I said firmly.

'Is it Gull 'ouse you want, then?' He looked up at the house again, then back at me.

'Do you know Gull House, Shadow?' I said suspiciously.

He looked shifty. 'Could do. Plenty of grand 'ouses in the centre of town.' He began to cough, a barking cough that echoed down the empty cobbles. He wiped his mouth, his thin chest heaving, his large eyes fixed on mine.

I thought of trailing after him in the growing darkness of a strange town, a boy whom I didn't even know I could trust to find it. While I was hesitating, the door opened as if on cue.

A woman stood on the step. In the dusk I couldn't make out her face, young or old, but her clothes were tight around her shapely figure, her hair down and loose over her shoulders.

'Mistress Bundish?' I said uncertainly, and even as I said it I knew my misgivings were justified. 'Mistress Elizabeth Bundish?'

There was a pause. She turned to Shadow – I couldn't see her expression – and then back to me. 'And who's asking for her?' Her accent was genteel, yet she was no lady, I thought. All I wanted now was to leave this place as fast as possible.

'I'm sorry,' I said politely, climbing the steps so she could see me. 'I believe I have mistaken the address. I'm a stranger here . . .'

'A mistake? Then why don't you come in, my dear, and let us sort it out? It will be dark soon and at the least we may lend you a lantern.'

Her voice was gentle and kind; I should not judge her so quickly.

'Go on, Miss,' urged Shadow. 'We could do wiv the light.' He was jittering about on the step below me, as if he were cold.

Some instinct rose to protect me. I stepped back, almost at the same moment as Shadow must have pushed me forward. Encumbered by the box, I almost fell at the lady's feet, and might have done so, if she hadn't gripped my arm herself to raise me up. Her hand beneath my arm was like a claw.

I saw her other hand go out to Shadow, press something into his outstretched palm. Suddenly I was inside the wide, candlelit hall, and Shadow, with a gleeful jingle of coins, had disappeared into the darkness outside, as the door shut.

2

Immediately, I struggled free of her powerful clutch on my arm, but already she had whisked a key from a pocket at her waist and locked the front door.

We gazed at each other, breathing fast: she with exertion, me with fear. She was a tall, wiry woman, richly dressed in stiff violet taffeta. 'You are a pretty one,' she murmured, her rouged lips smiling. 'I could see it even in the half-light.'

'What is this?' I faltered. 'You are not Elizabeth Bundish, are you? Why are you imprisoning me here? I've nothing valuable in my box, if that's what you're after.'

'Your box?' She looked down and saw it clutched to me. 'My dear, it's not your box I want.' She gave a gurgle of laughter.

I looked around wildly, at the graceful staircase curving upwards at the end of the hall and the silken chairs standing either side of an open doorway. Of course she would not want my box. 'What then?' I demanded.

She did not answer. Instead, she took out the key again,

slow and deliberate. She held it aloft so I should mark it, then she unlocked the front door. 'Leave, if you wish,' she said softly, 'you are free to go,' and she held the door open so I could see the dusk pressing down on the black cobbles and the greasy, oozing water. 'I must warn you that a pretty girl – so young too – should not be alone at night in Poorgrass Kayes.' She clicked her tongue. 'As a mother once, I find it beholden on me to offer you a bed for the night. Indeed, I cannot bear to let you out again. It would be very irresponsible of me.'

I hesitated, looking out at the darkness. When I turned she was watching me expectantly, even humorously, thin brows arched. Her angular face and crooked smile did not seem evil. There was a warmth about her, a charm. A fire crackled from the room along the hall; and there was a rich smell of cooking meat in the air, and of sweet-scented flowers.

She gestured again at the open door. Cold night air seeped damply against my face. 'There, leave if you wish.' She parted her hands to indicate it was my choice, not hers, and the candlelight gleamed on her silver bracelets.

I looked at her direct in her black-ringed eyes. 'I would be free to leave in the morning?' I said, to make certain.

'You need to find your Mistress – Bundish, you said? I can help you find her, I'm sure. I know the town well. Let us discuss it properly tomorrow when you've rested.'

'I can't pay you for a bed,' I said stiffly.

She shook her head, put her arm around my shoulders.

She was wearing a musky perfume; face powder had creased around her eyes. I hung back from her closeness, but she wouldn't allow me; and somehow she was leading me down the hall and into a parlour, golden with candlelight and hung with wallpaper of yellow silk. A china bowl filled with hyacinths sat on a polished chest. She pressed me down on a couch amongst velvet cushions and perched herself opposite on an embroidered chair, leaning forward to tinkle a little brass bell on the chest.

It was delightfully warm and cosy; the fire blazed merrily in the wrought-iron grate. It was so long since I had been in a house, sat comfortably – so long since I had been truly warm! I put my box down carefully on the parquet floor, and looked around, avoiding the lady's appraising gaze.

This house did not seem like a tavern, unless they had no visitors. Where were the drinkers? The noise of ribald conversation? The clash of pewter and chink of glass?

Shortly after the bell had rung, a girl poked her head around the door, saw me and stared. She looked a few years older than I was, her fair hair in ringlets. 'Connie, fetch the decanter and two glasses,' said the woman.

I shook my head when the drink – an amber liquid in a small, stemmed glass – was offered. The girl, Connie, having brought the glasses on a tray, had now disappeared after further inspection of me, and we were alone again. I felt almost too tired to speak.

'Drink,' urged the woman kindly. 'A sip or two. It will do you good. You are much fatigued, I can see that.'

It was true, the drink did me good; a glow suffused me from my head to my feet. I had meant to take one sip only, but found I had swallowed the lot, and that my glass had been refilled. My head began to swim. The woman took an enamelled tin from a corner cupboard and offered me a savoury biscuit, then another. They were delicious: salty and sharp with cheese. I wolfed down several, though I tried to eat them slowly; I licked my fingers for the last of the taste when I thought she wasn't looking.

'Now, let us exchange names.'

This was the hard part. 'I am called by a nickname, Scuff,' I said in a small voice. In this beautiful room it seemed a silly, inelegant name.

She smiled again. 'Nothing more glamorous than "Scuff"? Perhaps we shall find something else that suits you better.'

'I am only a kitchen maid, Madam,' I muttered. 'I am used to it.'

'Mine is Anora Drazel, though you may call me Anora, as my girls do.'

'Anora?' It was hard to get my tongue around it. 'Your daughters call you that?' It seemed disrespectful, though it was a pretty name, the prettiest I'd ever heard.

She had an unexpectedly deep laugh. 'They are not my daughters. They are girls like you whom I've not had the heart to turn away. They end up in Poorgrass for all kinds of reasons, and then they stay – they stay here with me.' She smoothed the violet taffeta of her skirts. 'In return for a bed and food, they help me. I don't ask for money.'

'I've been a kitchen maid a good while,' I said. 'I'm willing to do any housework you want in return for a bed tonight, and perhaps' – I looked at the tin – 'a few more biscuits.'

She gave her deep laugh again. 'Indeed, you shall have more than a few biscuits! But I won't ask you to work tonight. Tomorrow, when you are rested, will be time enough. Besides,' she leant forward again, her eyes on my face, 'although a little housework would be helpful, there is something else I require of you, if you are willing.'

'What is it?' I said, suspicious again.

'You may have seen the sign outside. This house was once an inn, but sadly run down when I bought it. I have brought it up in the world, thanks to the generosity of my dear departed husband. I now hold salons every week, Scuff. We have plenty of rich merchants and seamen passing through, willing to spend money on entertainment.'

'Salons, Ma'am?' I said doubtfully.

'Anora, please. Salons are parties, with music and singing.'

'Your guests dare break the Curfew?' I said, wide-eyed, for all towns had a Curfew and it could mean arrest if the Lawman found you out after dark.

She gave an elegant shrug. 'The Lawman usually turns a blind eye to what goes on here. He knows my salons are much sought after. My girls are a great attraction, you know.'

'Why, what do they do, Ma'am – Anora?'

She smiled. 'Each has a special talent. I train them well.'

'I can sing a little,' I said. 'I've never been trained, though.'

'You can sing? Excellent!' She clapped her hands together, more like a little girl than a grown woman; she had large hands, with pointed nails that shone with a rusty glaze. 'I knew as soon as I saw you that you would more than do.'

'Do for what?'

'Do as a replacement for poor little Sukey. She is unable to sing tomorrow. But you shall sing for us instead. You shall sing for your supper!'

'I'm only singing one night, if you please, Ma'am. I must find my new employers.'

'Ah! Tomorrow is our most popular night in the week. Our guests will love you, I know it. Will you give me a verse now, so I can hear your voice?'

I hesitated, but she smiled at me so encouragingly, I could not refuse to sing, although I had never felt less like doing so. I gave her the first verse and chorus of 'So Sing Success to the Weaver'. My voice shook a little.

'Charming,' she said at the end, and smiled her crooked smile. 'You will do very well.'

She rose with a stiff rustle, and held out her hand.

'Come, we shall find some supper for you. You shall meet the girls!'

I did not take her hand, but I picked up the box and, holding it fast to me, stood up unsteadily and followed her.

3

There were three girls in the panelled dining room: Connie, with her fair ringlets, and two dark-haired girls, one of them around my age.

Madam Anora introduced me and told me their names, but what she said floated through my head. I merely noticed that the three of them were beautifully dressed, had perfect table manners – 'pleases' and 'thank yous' forever on their lips – and that throughout supper they did not stop staring at me, at my strange garb and ravenous eating.

A much older woman brought the food to us. She had a tired, sallow face, and was a housekeeper of sorts, I supposed, since she wore a cap and apron. She carved our servings of roast beef on to plates of painted china; each place setting was laid with silver cutlery, and she brought cut glass jugs of wine that she set down on the gleaming mahogany table.

Madam Anora's late husband must have been wealthy indeed, I thought, but I was too tired and hungry to dwell on it. I was now cautious enough, however, to drink only water.

I scarce listened to the conversation: gossip about gentlemen they knew. Everything Anora said was greeted by tiny shrieks of laughter from the girls, who talked in high, affected little voices and giggled a good deal too much.

In the pointed golden flames of the candelabra Madam Anora looked radiant, and not at all as if she were missing her late husband. 'I always insist the girls dress in their best for dinner, even if it is only the family present,' she said to me, during a lull.

'The family?' I said, bleary.

'I look on us as a little family, my dear – my girls and myself. Sometimes we entertain gentlemen, of course, especially before one of our salons. But during the week we tend to be just the five of us together at supper, don't we, girls?'

'Yes, Anora,' they chorused.

She put her hand to her mouth. 'I was forgetting . . .' Her black eyes glittered with sudden tears. 'Poor, dear Sukey – she is no longer with us. But we have you instead, Scuff, a gift from the night.' She looked around at the girls, who had fallen silent without her to lead them in conversation. They never talked amongst themselves, I noticed. 'Scuff is to sing tomorrow evening in place of Sukey.'

The three girls nodded at me, seemingly polite and interested now. I thought I saw a shadow pass over the face of the younger dark-haired girl, but perhaps I had imagined it.

We had finished our apple pie. I laid my spoon down on the exquisite plate, which I had scraped clean. *In return for all this food*, I thought uneasily, *I must excel at singing tomorrow.*

When the nero leaf and liqueurs were brought round, Madam Anora frowned at the housekeeper. She spoke so harshly I felt sorry for the poor woman. 'Do you never remember that we must not indulge before a salon? Such ruination to our voices – our complexions . . .'

The housekeeper retreated with the silver tray, her face impassive. The girls barely glanced at each other, but I felt something pass between them. We gazed silently at the table, laden with our empty plates.

'Forgive me, girls,' Madam Anora said, with a tiny yawn, patting her hand to her mouth. 'I shall have an early night. Don't linger yourselves, for tomorrow is an important evening.' She dropped a kiss lightly on each girl's head and swept to the door. For a moment I thought she had forgotten me, but she glanced briefly at the younger dark-haired girl before she closed the door behind her. 'Becca, look after Scuff. She can have Sukey's bed.'

The girls sat still and silent for a moment, and so did I, for I did not know what else to do. I thought they might be waiting for the downtrodden housekeeper's return. But then Connie nodded at Becca, and Becca jumped to her feet and darted to the door and listened. 'She has gone,' she whispered.

'Are you sure she doesn't listen the other side?' said Connie, stretching languorously.

'She is too eager for her nero leaf,' said the other dark-haired girl, Rose, in a low voice. A subdued giggle went between the two.

Becca looked frightened. 'Oh, hush! She might come back.'

'Then we must do our duties,' said Connie, and the three of them began to drift around the table, passing cutlery to each other with little smiles.

'Does the housekeeper come back for the dishes or do we take them through to the kitchen?' I asked.

Connie looked nonplussed. 'The housekeeper? Oh, you mean Anora's mother, old Ma Drazel.' She gave a giggle behind her hand at my surprise. 'She'll be looking after Anora now – she'll put her to bed.' She looked sideways at the other girls, but they did not meet her eyes.

I stood, uncertain, while they floated about, loading trays with the used china, wiping the table, snuffing out the candelabra. It took a long while.

'Can I help?' I said.

'Oh, no,' said Connie. 'Anora likes it just so, in case we have gentlemen staying for a late dinner tomorrow night. You would not know what to do.' She lifted the bowl of fruit to the sideboard and dreamily checked its position between two silver candlesticks.

'She should learn, though,' said the older dark-haired girl, Rose. She had long black eyes and a face like pale, carved wood. 'She will need to help in the future.'

'I am not staying long,' I explained. 'I will be leaving the morning after the salon.'

All three girls looked at me in astonishment. 'No one leaves here once they have come, unless Anora wants them to do so,' said Connie primly.

'Is that what happened to Sukey?' I asked.

There was a pause. They seemed taken aback, then Becca and Rose looked at Connie, who appeared to be the leader of the three. 'Anora wanted Sukey to leave – yes,' said Connie. 'Once she was ill, she was not so popular at our salons any more, you see – she didn't bring in so many gentlemen.'

'We bring lots,' said Becca, nodding her head like a jack-in-the-box.

'Our singing is most excellent, is it not?' said Rose, with her faint exotic accent, and the three of them smiled reassuringly at each other.

I looked from one complacent face to another, the three of them determinedly happy. 'But you could leave if you wanted to?' I asked uneasily.

Connie looked blank. 'Why should we want to? The salons bring in money and we have our share.' She nudged Rose and giggled. 'And then in return for a little kiss or two the gentlemen give us tips. And where else would we be clothed and fed so well?'

'We'd be out wandering the dark streets homeless, like Sukey is now,' said Becca, shuddering. 'Like we all were once, before Anora rescued us.'

'Dear Anora,' said Connie fondly.

'Dear Anora,' echoed the other two.

Then they turned their attention to me. 'Scuff – that's an odd name,' said Connie, wrinkling her little nose.

'I wonder what name it is that Anora will give you,' mused Rose. 'She has given us all new names, you know. Miss Constance, Miss Rebecca and Miss Rosamunda.' The three of them curtseyed in turn and simpered at an imaginary audience. There was something grotesque about the way they did it: they reminded me of three overdressed, overlarge puppets.

Connie straightened and shook out her skirts languidly. 'I scarcely remember my real name,' she murmured.

'I would not know where to go if Anora sent me away,' said Rose.

'But she will not do that, will she?' said Becca, anxious again. 'Turn us out?'

Connie and Rose turned to her at once and draped their arms about her. 'No, no, of course not, little one – not if we don't give her any reason to do such a thing,' and then they all smiled and murmured sweetly at each other again.

It seemed that our duties were done in the dining room, and that Ma Drazel would return to take the dishes down to the kitchen to wash them.

'We should go to bed now,' said Connie, yawning. 'You know what Anora said.'

They nodded at each other, and in what appeared to be a nightly ritual, each took a candle from the candelabra on the table. There was one left, I noticed. 'You may take Sukey's candle, Scuff,' said Connie and she presented it to me with a little flourish, as if it were a gift. Then they kissed each other most affectionately, as if they were indeed sisters, and filed out.

In the hall Becca noticed I had picked up my box. 'Leave it,' she whispered. 'You must leave it for Anora. She takes all our things when we first arrive.'

I gripped it more firmly. 'She'll not take this,' I said, and refused to be swayed by her pleading face.

She led me up the curving staircase, a finger pressed to her lips lest I should talk on the way up and disturb Anora, whose bedchamber was on the first floor. On my journey through the silent house I saw dark bedchambers beyond open doorways, but our chamber was on the top floor, a room within the attics. It was furnished adequately enough and without the damp chill of Murkmere, but after the luxury of the downstairs rooms I was surprised.

I looked at the two narrow little beds either side of the empty fireplace, each neatly made and spread with a counterpane of bleached wool on which lay a folded nightgown and a woollen wrap. There were two empty china candlesticks on the mantel, waiting for our lighted candles, two chairs with rush seats, a jug and two washing bowls, two prayer mats side by side on the floorboards.

I stowed my box beneath the bed that Becca indicated, and she handed me the nightgown, shaking it out for me as if expecting me to wear it. The fine cambric was crumpled and had a faint odour, a sweet-sour girl smell.

The cupboard was crammed with dresses, all as fine as the one Becca was wearing. 'Did Sukey not take her clothes?' I asked, climbing reluctantly out of my skirt, but keeping my chemise and drawers on so I did not have to wear Sukey's nightgown next to my skin.

'They didn't belong to her by rights,' said Becca, pulling her nightgown over her head. 'You'll wear them now. Anora will get rid of your old clothes.'

'I don't want that,' I said, removing a hairbrush so that I could pile my clothes together on one of the chairs; the hairbrush had long curly brown hairs caught in the bristles. 'I don't mind wearing one of those gowns for the salon, but I want to keep my own clothes.'

'Oh!' she said, and sat down on her bed, chewing her lip and staring at me. Her eyes brimmed with tears that shone in the candlelight.

'What is it?' I said gently, for everything seemed to upset the poor creature. 'I didn't mean to offend you.'

'I was thinking about Sukey,' she whispered. 'She didn't remember her real name – Miss Suzanna she was called during salons. We find it so hard to remember things about our past lives once we're here, and we don't want to, anyway.' She sniffed and wiped her nose on her lace sleeve in a way that Anora would not have approved. 'But I keep thinking about her wandering about the streets without knowing who she is now, and she's so ill, you know – she has the spitting sickness.'

'You mean,' I said, 'that Anora cast her out when she was dying?'

Becca blinked the tears from her eyes and looked at me earnestly. 'It wasn't Anora's fault. Anora wanted to protect us from catching it. She had to send Sukey away. Any employer would have done the same. She explained that to us.'

The spitting sickness was greatly feared, it was true: though it did not affect so many, it lingered longer and was as lethal as the Miasma – the plague – itself.

'Anora hates disease,' said Becca, sniffing. 'In the summer we get plague-runners from the Capital docking in Poorgrass Kayes. Anora's always fearful that one of their passengers will attend a salon and bring the infection with them. She makes us scrub ourselves with vinegar and lemon after each salon and inhale the vapour from a special brew she boils up herself.' She shuddered, and looked at me, red-eyed. 'I came here with my parents on a plague-runner, you know. We came to escape the Miasma – it was bad in the Capital that summer – then when we arrived in Poorgrass, my parents couldn't find work, try as they might. They went back to the Capital eventually, but I – I'd met Anora by then, so I stayed.'

'So you do remember who you are,' I said. 'Why don't

you leave this house, and try to find your parents again?'

She shook her head violently. 'Oh, I couldn't, not now. I'd be too frightened to leave Anora.'

'If I had parents, I'd risk anything to find them,' I said, but she shook her head again.

'Anora says they are most likely dead. She is my mother now.'

There was a sudden rap on the door, then Connie's soft voice in reproof. 'Becca, my dear, so much talking! Do you want Anora to come up?'

'Sorry, Connie, dear,' said Becca contritely.

'Don't forget your prayers. And wash first. We must be clean for God.'

'Yes, Connie,' and she scrambled off the bed obediently and went to the jug of water.

Side by side we stood at the bowls to wash ourselves. I was careful to hide my brand mark, for I thought that having lived in the Capital Becca would know what it was. 'I could pretend you are Sukey,' she said suddenly, as we stood there. 'You have much the same colour hair and build.'

'But I'm not Sukey,' I said.

She went on as if I hadn't spoken. 'Soon you'll lose your accent and talk like Sukey did – as we do, even Rose, who is from over the sea. Anora will teach you.'

A shiver went through me. 'I am not Sukey, and I don't want to talk like her – or any of you,' I said, surprising myself with my passion.

She looked bewildered, uncomprehending. 'Who are you, then?'

'I don't rightly know,' I said truthfully.

'That's what happens, you forget. Soon you won't care, you'll be Sukey if you stay here,' she said, and smiled in triumph. 'You will stay here, won't you?'

I bit my lip and did not answer.

She went to kneel on one of the mats. Pulling a red enamel locket, like a tiny seed on a chain, from the neck of her nightgown, she began to murmur to herself. She looked the very picture of a devout supplicant.

'You have such a lovely amulet, Scuff, much finer than mine,' she burst out after a while, sufficient prayers evidently having been said for the time being.

I put my hand over the amber at my neck protectively. Aggie's face came into my mind from a long while ago. 'It's not mine – it was lent to me,' I said in a low voice. 'I mean to return it to its owner one day.'

I was relieved she didn't ask more questions, in fact she scarce seemed curious about my past at all. Instead she gave me a reproving look. 'You should say your prayers. Sukey and I always said our prayers together.'

I knelt beside her on the other mat. I thought I should give thanks to the Almighty for letting me escape the soldiers once again, for giving me a safe lodging for the night. But instead of the Eagle's all-powerful gaze, I could only see Erland's white, stricken face as he lay on his pallet, wounded.

This was the price the Eagle demanded. In return for my safety, Erland had been hurt. I held the amber to me until it warmed in my clenched hand, and I prayed for his recovery most fervently.

I must find my employers, I thought. *For if I don't, Erland won't know where to come when he is recovered. I shall never see him again.*

4

I scarce slept that night, although in comparison with a grass pallet on the bare earth, my bed was wondrous comfortable. But the strong drink I'd been given made my heart pound. The sheets and woollen blankets felt strange and light after so many nights beneath sheepskins. They carried the same faint odour as my nightdress. I was lying in another girl's bed: a usurper. Outside, the wind rose to a shriek and threw rain, hard as hailstones, at the rattling window. This was the storm Erland had talked about; I prayed Gadd had returned safe before it.

All night, streams of water cascaded down the panes. Gradually, the room filled with the grey light of morning. Becca stirred and turned towards me sleepily, and her face broke into a beam of pleasure. 'Sukey! You've come back!'

'It's Scuff, not Sukey,' I said, hating to see the way her smile crumpled away.

'Of course it is. I'm sorry,' she said stiffly, and rose to pull on her wrap, shivering in the damp air. 'Come, we must arise, else Connie will bother us with her chivying. There's so little time.'

'What is it that must be done by the three of you until the salon?' I asked, curious. 'There's all day before it.'

'Anora always rests before a salon, and so must we, but not until after noon. During the morning we dust and polish and choose our dresses and wash our hair. We're all busy. Ma Drazel will be doing the cooking in preparation for tonight. The salon begins at six.'

'I must search out my new employers this morning,' I said.

Becca gave me a strange look then, but I didn't heed it. I went to the window to see if it had stopped raining. It was a sullen, overcast morning, but dry now. Below us was a huddle of mean cottages on a shingle bank, then half-drowned mudflats that stretched away until they met dark grey water.

'Hurry and dress yourself,' said Becca in an agitated way, and she thrust a dress at me from the cupboard. I shook my head and turned to the chair on which I'd piled my own clothes the night before. They had all gone, save my jacket with the precious letter in the pocket. I thought I'd not slept during the night, but I must have done so, for someone had secretly entered our room and stolen my skirt and shirt away.

'That will be old Ma Drazel, doing Anora's bidding,' said Becca, seeing me standing as if stunned. 'She creeps about so silently. That's why you must be careful what you say.' She flourished the dress at me again; it was made from charcoal wool. 'But see what you have instead. Is this not so much finer than your own? And tonight you shall wear silk!'

So in the end I took the dress, for I thought at least I would look respectable when I found Mistress Bundish later; and it had long sleeves that hid my scar.

We had our breakfast, the three girls and me, at a long table in the kitchen. It was in the basement of the house, a whitewashed room, airy but warm and of a good size, hung with copper pans that gleamed in the grey light from the windows. There was a long stove, well-blacked, and I could hear the furnace roaring in preparation for the day's cooking.

There was no sign of Ma Drazel. We had passed the larder on our way in, and I had seen the food laid out: bowls piled with fruits of all colours, pans of raw vegetables, carcasses of meat beneath stiff gauze covers. Ma Drazel seemed a methodical housekeeper, yet compared with Murkmere, how easy it would be to keep house here.

I could cook in this kitchen, I thought, and my eye lingered on the iron saucepans stacked on the scrubbed sideboard.

For breakfast we had fresh bread, with creamy butter and a jelly of plums to spread upon it, and frothy milk to drink. I had never eaten such a splendid breakfast before. Yet though the girls were fed so well, their pretty, rounded cheeks were pale as candle wax in the daylight.

'Do you go to the market in Poorgrass?' I asked, at some point.

'Oh, no,' said Connie, wide-eyed. 'Anora does not like us to walk in Poorgrass. It is not safe for us, she says. You were fortunate to arrive here unmolested last night. The fishermen are a rough lot, Anora says.'

'Do you never breathe the air outside?'

'Sometimes we do,' said Becca, leaning forward over the table. 'If the weather is fine, Anora takes us out in the pony and trap, out to the countryside. Then we walk a little, don't we, girls?'

'Yes, we do,' said Connie, nodding. She frowned at Becca. 'Becca, elbows. What would Anora say?'

Rose touched my shoulder and her long dark eyes crinkled. 'It is so good that you are with us. We are as we were before when Sukey was with us, four sisters together!'

'You shall be so happy with us – shan't she, Rose?' said Connie, and she squeezed Rose's arm fondly.

'So happy,' echoed Rose.

I did not protest immediately that I was not staying.

I looked thoughtfully back at her – at the three of them, smiling at me so warmly, so open-heartedly. I had always wondered what it would be like to have a sister, and, if I stayed, I would have three; I would be part of a family. This would be my home, and Anora – she would be my mother, as she was to them. I would be loved here, and safe. Was it really worth searching out Mistress Bundish, whom I did not know?

But what of Erland?

I could leave word for him somehow, so that he would know where I was. The stall keepers in the marketplace would surely know him and Gadd from the times they came to Poorgrass Kayes. Maybe I could leave a message with them.

It was easy – so easy – after all, to make the decision to stay.

'You are staying, aren't you, Scuff?' said Becca, and she leant across the table again, elbows forgotten, her round eyes fixed pleadingly on mine.

But when Becca asked me, I found myself saying as gently as possible, 'I can't be sure yet.'

I would seek out Mistress Bundish first, I thought, and talk to her. It might be that she would not want another servant, anyway, and then my decision would be even easier.

Becca looked crestfallen at my reply, but I noticed a meaningful glance pass between the older girls that made me wary, as if they knew something I did not.

'Come,' said Connie, rising languidly. 'We mustn't sit about chattering on a salon day. What would Anora say? Now, Scuff, we need flowers in the reception rooms. Can you arrange flowers in a pretty fashion?'

I was not sure what she meant, but she took me into the pantry and showed me a quantity of flowers standing in buckets, and some tall glass containers, cut with diamond patterns.

'Take the flowers out of the buckets and stand them in the vases, so they are not too crowded but show to their best advantage. Can you do that?'

'I think so,' I said. I took out one of the flowers and stared at it. It was most exotic to my eye, with long, pointed leaves and a neat oval head of closed, pale pink petals.

'These come from the Flatlands over the sea,' Connie informed me kindly. 'There are lots of foreign things here in Poorgrass Kayes that you will soon become familiar with.'

She left me to the flowers, and frowning a little, I set about putting them in the vases. I thought it seemed wrong and unnatural to uproot such beautiful flowers from the earth and bring them inside a house.

When I had finished, I picked up one of the vases and carried it carefully up the narrow stairs to the hall. There was no one about, but I remembered the room I had been in last night, the parlour where Anora had taken me, and so I took the vase in there.

The yellow silk wallpaper was too bright in the daylight; it did not seem as beautiful as it had by candlelight. The cushions, into which I had sunk so gratefully, were garish. In the bowl on the chest, the petals of the hyacinths were turning brown. I put the vase down hastily on a table, making sure the base was dry and would not mark the wood.

I put the other two vases into the front room, where the salon would be held. A thin daylight coming through the shutters showed the outline of an upright piano and overstuffed satin chairs and couches. Thick drapes were looped back with silky tasselled ropes; behind them were shadowy alcoves, with chairs placed together. My nose was sensitive after so many days in the open air: I could smell gentlemen's sweat and stale wine in the air, and it was not pleasant.

I put down the flowers on top of the piano. Silence hung heavily around me, so that I was startled when I heard a soft footstep. When I turned, Connie was watching me. 'I did not expect you to bring flowers into the drawing room.'

'Did I do wrong?' I said.

'Anora does not like us to come in here during the day.' She looked at me with a little gleam in her eye. 'But Anora is upstairs in bed.'

She went to the shutters and opened them. For a moment we were both dazzled. I could hear the outside world coming into the room: the trundle of waggon wheels over the cobbles, the shouts of children playing, the ring of iron on iron from the shipbuilders' yards.

Connie stared about her in surprise. 'It is not so very pretty, is it, in the light?' And she closed the shutters once more.

'What shall you sing tonight?' she said listlessly, leaning back against the piano in the sudden silence.

'I've not thought. What do you sing?'

'I play the piano,' she said airily. 'I had lessons, you know – in my old life. I came from a good family.'

I did not like to ask her more. 'And Rose and Becca?'

'Rose is a dancer. She has a special costume, like the one she used to wear. She came across the sea to marry a sailor here, but he did not want her. His vows were false. She was ruined, before Anora found her.'

'Ruined?'

'Ruined.' She nodded her head solemnly, so that her ringlets bobbed. 'It would have befallen Becca and me too, if Anora hadn't rescued us. Becca sings very passably, and the gentlemen like her because she is so young.'

'Madam Anora is lucky. What did she do before she found the three of you?'

Connie turned away from me. 'There have been other girls. We don't talk about them.' She moved to the door in the same sleepy way she did everything. 'I must go and see Anora now. We have to discuss the programme for tonight. Ask Becca to help you bathe. There is a hip bath in the basement and she will light the fire for you. You may have first turn as you are new.'

A bath – how luxurious that sounded. But I could not afford to linger; I must seek out Mistress Bundish before the morning wore on.

I put my eye to a slit in the shutters. It did not look so very frightening outside. I could see a stretch of cobbled street, the far gutter shining with water in the daylight. A cat trod delicately between the puddles, its tail held high: a black cat very like Mister Plush, the ship's cat.

I should like to meet with Shadow again while I am out, I

thought. *If I do, I will scrag him for tricking me in such a way last night.* Yet what would I have done if I had not found this place? Would I ever have found the right house before nightfall?

I hurried upstairs to fetch my jacket and the box. I had no hat, but perhaps I could borrow one from the cupboard. I found myself creeping up the staircase, as if I did not want to be heard, as if it was wrong to leave the house.

The hats were too grand, too embellished, for my taste. I shut the cupboard door on them and pulled my jacket over the grey wool dress. I felt for the parchment in the jacket pocket and pulled it out: *Mistress Elizabeth Bundish, Gull House, Kaye Street*.

Outside the window there was a swan on the mudflats, white against the brown-grey sludge. For a moment I could not move for emotion. I heard again the gunshot, the swans' commotion, saw Erland lying half-dead. Then I bent and picked up the box from beneath my bed.

What was I doing in this house? Its life of luxury and lassitude no longer tempted me. I would leave for ever – now.

I tiptoed down again in the same guilty way, and stole along the hall to the front door. The bolts had been pulled back, but the knob would not turn. I struggled with it for some minutes, my heart beating fast. I had to put the box down and use both hands.

'Miss! Miss! What are you doing?'

Instinctively, I picked up the box and held it against me. At the far end of the hall, standing in the parlour doorway, was the drab figure of old Ma Drazel. Her voice was unexpectedly sharp, not genteel like her daughter's.

'I must seek out my new employers,' I faltered. 'I will return shortly.'

'You cannot go without Anora's permission, and Anora is indisposed.'

'Madam Anora knows all about it,' I said quickly, thinking to make her understand. 'We discussed it last night. Please unlock the door for me.'

'I cannot do that, Miss. Only Anora unlocks the door. It is always kept locked for security, else we'd have every pecknose and prodstaff in here, pokin' about.'

I was quite at a loss to know what to do. She and I stood staring at each other. I saw I had underestimated Ma Drazel: her chin above the grey serge dress was as blunt as her voice, and as determined.

'What is it, Mother?' It was Madam Anora's voice, coming weakly from the landing above us.

'The new girl, Anora. Accepted your charity, but wants to leave already.'

There was a pause, a sigh, then Anora appeared herself in a long, quilted chamber robe, her hair awry. Connie hovered behind her.

Anora spoke softly and sweetly, a hand to her forehead; she was very pale. 'Oh, Scuff, dear – I had quite forgot. You wished to find your employer this morning, and I have such a headache I cannot help you today. Will tomorrow not do instead? Then I will come with you, and we'll find the right house together. After all, you have promised to sing for us tonight.'

I nodded miserably.

'Go downstairs, then, dear. Connie tells me Becca is in the basement preparing a bath. She will look after you.'

At least I would be clean when I left tomorrow.

I went down the stairs, the box still clenched under my arm, and found Becca in a cramped basement room at the front of the house. It had a fireplace in which Becca had lit a fire, a pair of dusty old armchairs and a three-legged stool; a narrow window looked on to the bottom of the area steps. The window had rusty bars across it, whether to keep thieves out or the girls in, I wasn't certain.

But it also had a door in the outside wall that would open into the area. It was, of course, closed. I told myself it would most like be locked as well, but it did not stop my heart lifting.

Becca was carrying in jugs of water to heat in a large pan over the burning coals; there was a hip bath set before the fire, and towels hung over a chair arm.

'I know what you have been doing,' she said, pink in the face and reproachful. 'I heard you in the hall with Ma Drazel. I thought you liked us.'

'I do,' I said, taken aback.

'I thought you wanted to stay.'

I hesitated. 'I'm sorry, Becca.'

She lowered her voice. 'You won't be able to leave, you know.'

'What do you mean?'

'Anora won't let you, that's all I'm saying. We all tried to leave at first.' She pursed her lips mysteriously, then she pointed at the water heating in the pan and said in her normal voice: 'Don't scald yourself. There's cold water left in the jug. Call me when you've finished, I'll use your water.'

'Thank you,' I said, trying not to stare at the outside door.

Once alone I rushed to the door and very quietly turned the handle. It would not budge. There was a keyhole beneath it, but no key. I went to the window and gazed out between the bars. All I could see was the line of steps disappearing upwards from the waterlogged area to the cobbled street.

I was about to turn away when movement caught my eye. The black cat was at the top of the steps, its white-tipped tail ramrod stiff. It was Mister Plush, I was sure. It began to trip lightly down, so close I could see its whiskers twitch at the smell of the turnip tops and other rubbish floating on the scummy water in the area. And then I heard whistling.

I put my hands through the bars and pushed up the bottom pane awkwardly. It was a sash window and so in two parts, like all the windows in the house. The pane grated up against the top pane; I could only lift it a little way. The cat paused on its way down the steps and gazed at me with cold, green eyes.

I called softly through the gap, 'Mister Plush?' Above, the whistling came closer.

'Mister Plush!' I called again, as enticing as I could. The cat ignored me, trod delicately down the remaining steps and, avoiding the water, sprang to the sill, where it arched its back and stretched.

I scarce breathed in case I startled it. A pair of small, scuffed boots came into view.

'Mister Plush! Where are you?'

'Shadow!' I hissed, fearful of Becca hearing in the next room. I struggled to open the window further, and the cat, alarmed, jumped back to the steps. Shadow would never see me now.

The boots were tantalizingly close. I put my hands through the gap and waved wildly. But Shadow did not see. In the end it was the cat he came for, murmuring as he came down the steps and looking all about him like a thief ready to run: 'What yer doin', Plushey?'

'Shadow! Help me!'

He straightened with the cat in his arms, the shock on his face replaced by wariness. 'Well, if it ain't Miss Scuff! How you doin' in this fine establishment?'

I glared at him, quite unlike the meek girl he had met before. The cat jumped down from his arms and began to pat gingerly at a floating fish head. 'It isn't fine at all, as well you know.'

'Why's that then, Miss Scuff?' he said, all innocent.

'These girls are kept here to make money for Anora Drazel. They're prisoners and so am I. It's your fault I'm here. You got me in and you've got to get me out!'

He looked most discomforted at that, and began to scratch his head. 'Don't rightly know 'ow I can do that, Miss Scuff.'

'Once I'm with my new employers, I'll pay you for it,' I said urgently. 'But I need your help to escape.'

'I dunno,' he said, shaking his head. 'If I gets on the wrong side of Madam Anora through 'elpin' you, then that's me income gone.'

'I've no money to give you now,' I said, angry and frustrated.

He waded through the vegetable peelings and squinted through the window, heedless of the water soaking his boots. 'You got that box, ain't you?' he said slyly.

I was dismayed. 'You want my box?'

'Mr Butley will pay me good for it, I reckon. I'll help you if you passes it to me under the winder.'

'Give it to you now?' I stammered. 'But can I trust you after last night?'

He had the grace to look ashamed. 'I don't like to think I let you down. I see now yer not that sort of girl at all, Miss Scuff. But 'ow are we to work yer escape, eh?'

'I don't care,' I said desperately. 'I want to be away by tonight. There's to be a salon here and I must sing for my supper, as I said I would. But afterwards can you create some commotion so I can slip out through the front door?'

He looked blank. I said as patient as I was able, 'Anora won't expect you to help the girl you've only just brought here escape. She'll not suspect you.'

He shrugged, very doubtful. 'Maybe.'

'You must think of something!' I said, exasperated. 'Come back at nightfall. That's when the salon begins.'

He appeared aghast at such a demand. 'You will come back?' I insisted, still doubtful of trusting him; but after much frowning consideration he gave a nod.

'Cross me 'eart, Miss Scuff. I'll think of somethin' easy enough once that box is in me 'ands.'

I hesitated, biting my lip; I knew it was exceeding foolish to put any faith in him. But I was desperate. In the end, most reluctant, I lifted the box on to the sill and saw his face brighten at once. We had to raise the window still further. Something tore inside me when the box left my hands and I saw it clutched to Shadow's filthy, ragged chest. It was my last connection with Erland, and it had gone.

He raised his hand and gave me a cheeky salute. Then he turned tail and nipped up the steps, whistling to his cat.

I didn't think I'd ever see him again. I pulled the window down and turned away.

5

As the evening drew closer, there was great bustle and anticipation in Madam Anora's household; I watched it all and bided my escape.

Anora went from room to room in a rustle of silk and a cloud of heady fragrance. She lit candles, closed shutters and drew curtains, though there was still weak daylight outside, clasping her hands together with pleasure as she surveyed each effect. No longer the suffering invalid, she gave me a warm smile as I approached.

'Ah, Scuff, our new girl!' Her eyes were bright beneath darkly glossy lids. There was rouge along her cheekbones and powder in her hair; she was dressed in deep purple satin. I thought she looked very handsome for an older woman.

I said, 'What should I sing, please, Ma'am?'

Her eyes swept over me and she gave her crooked smile. 'It will not matter what you sing, my dear. The gentlemen will be charmed by you – charmed. Now you must go and change before the light fades.'

Becca was in a fluster when I arrived upstairs. 'I shall be in trouble if you are not ready in time.'

I looked at her: her curled hair, blue silk gown and rouged lips. 'I am not used to such finery.'

She shook her head. 'Oh, fiddlededee! Listen to you.' She looked along the row of dresses in the cupboard with an expert eye, and pulled out one of raspberry silk, with lace around the bodice and elbows. I looked at it in sudden joy: I'd worn only black and grey before. Then she found buckled shoes and cream satin ribbons. She pulled the gown over my head and fastened all the little covered buttons at the back. She giggled when I did not know how the skirts should be arranged upon each other, so that each showed a hint of the one beneath, and how to fold the sash to show the smallness of the waist.

When Becca was finally satisfied, I looked down at myself a little perturbed. I could not see how my hair looked after all her artful arranging, though she had left my face unrouged. But I did not feel myself any longer: I too had become a passive, overdressed puppet.

'I shall call you Sukey now,' said Becca, with a mischievous grin, and she bent to do up the buttons at my elbows. I heard her give a gasp, then she looked at me, her eyes wide.

In dismay I realized I had forgotten to hide my scar. Without protesting, I let her take my wrist and examine it. Her face was hidden, but I knew she would realize what it meant.

'Your scar . . .' She faltered, and seemed to search for what to say. 'It's an old brand mark, isn't it?'

'I was in a Home once, yes,' I said quickly, 'but there is no shame in it. No one needs to know – we can keep it a secret, you and me.'

'You must never return to the Capital,' she said, breathing fast, 'lest you are reclaimed. You must stay here safe with Anora.' When she looked at me, her face was childish and lost. 'It must have been dreadful – in the Home.'

I shrugged to make light of it, my heart beating fast. 'I left the place when I was small.' I tried to keep the urgency out of my voice. 'So will you help me, Becca? Will you forget you ever saw my scar? Say nothing to Anora – to anyone.'

'I won't, I swear,' she said, seemingly determined. I was touched; I did have a friend in the world, after all.

'We must hide the mark,' she said, chewing her lip. 'The sleeves of these evening gowns are too short. If only we had a bracelet!' Then she fetched a lace handkerchief and a velvet ribbon. She folded the handkerchief into a neat square, put it over my scar and tied it on to my wrist with the ribbon. 'There! Plenty of girls wear their kerchiefs that way. It does not look strange at all.'

I prayed not. Tonight I would be gone, I thought. Once I had delivered my letter into Mistress Bundish's hands and was in her employ, I would be safe, I was sure. I took the letter from my jacket pocket in case Ma Drazel should come snooping again, and slipped it into my bodice.

Feeling a little easier, I followed Becca down the stairs to the bright candlelit hall, and into the parlour. Connie and Rose, curled and perfumed, were giggling nervously together on the couch: Rose in her dancing costume, which was bright yellow and flounced almost to the knee.

Anora whisked in, the wine glass in her hand already half drained. 'Merely to steady the nerves,' she said gaily. 'But none for you, my dears, before you perform. Now – we will do as we always do, you understand. I shall greet the gentlemen and once they are somewhat merry and relaxed in the drawing room . . .' she winked roguishly '. . . I shall announce you one by one.'

She inspected me, then nodded approval. 'Scuff – you shall be Miss Susanna tonight. You look enough like our dear Sukey for our usual patrons to be quite taken in once they are in their cups.'

She looked from me to the others; the wine glass quivered in her hand. 'Tonight you must all be especially charming, for a little bird has told me we may have a special visitor coming.' She lowered her voice and her eyes gleamed. 'Word from my young spy is that the Lord Protector's son staying out at the Windrush military camp has heard about us!'

The girls burst into a babble of questions while she nodded and smiled. 'He will come incognito, of course, so that no one recognizes him.'

I sat, stunned and silent.

Becca touched my hand as soon as Connie and Rose, still talking excitedly, had followed Anora out. 'You are gone so pale. What is it?'

'It is very bad, Becca,' I said, 'or it may be, I don't know. He may bring soldiers with him.'

'You think they will send you back to the Capital as Recompense?'

I nodded mutely and she took my hand, and we sat close, my fingers trembling in hers. She did not shriek or twitter or ask more questions; she was no mere puppet after all.

'But you look so different now,' said Becca at last, very earnest and solemn, 'so different in your finery. And you have a name – Miss Susanna. No one will know that you have not always owned it.'

'I hope it will be enough,' I said.

6

Dusk fell outside. For a long while we heard loud raps of the knocker as the guests arrived and were greeted by Ma Drazel, who showed them into the drawing room. The fire leapt in the grate each time the front door opened, for we had the parlour door wide to listen.

The men brought with them the damp night air and their deep voices. Next door the conversation and laughter swelled: Anora's low gurgle echoed by guffaws from the gentlemen. Connie and Rose were called in, and the piano began to tinkle beneath the merriment; there were sudden bursts of clapping. It grew very warm once they had stopped arriving: I could smell the wine and food, and the hot eagerness of the guests.

Then Becca was called in and I was alone.

Then Rose came for me.

They were sitting – lolling – about, and were already some way drunk, I think, for their eyes had that bulbous, glassy gleam. I do not know how many guests were in there, perhaps upwards of thirty; it seemed to me there were red shining faces everywhere, and stout legs in satin breeches that might trip me up. Some had even brought their floozies: overpainted women in tight bodices.

I bent my head and made my way between the chairs to the piano, where Connie had stopped playing and was engaged in polite talk with a seedy-looking fellow in an embroidered waistcoat. I could see Anora waiting for me, half-impatient, but with her crooked smile placed on her face. 'Ah, Sukey, dear,' she whispered to me, putting her glass carefully down on the piano.

I did not correct her.

'Miss Susanna will sing for us,' she announced to the assembly, and hiccuped discreetly.

There was a tipsy roar as I stepped out, and some began to clap. I could still hear talking, but thought I should begin. I fixed my eyes on a far alcove where there was a plaster statue of a girl with a tiny linnet on her shoulder; she was almost naked. *The Eagle preserve me*, I thought, and I began to sing.

I gave them 'Come, Let Us Frolic While We May', for I hoped it might sober them up with its mournful message of mortality. My mouth was very dry; I could scarce get the words out. All the same, my weak little rendering was greeted with leery applause.

As the clapping died away, I heard the knocker go again, the front door open. A cold draught blew into the room, and more guests – two young men, youths. Darting around them like a puppy was Shadow.

I felt a rush of heat to my face and my heart began to beat quickly. I dared not look more closely, for with one quick glance I had recognized the Lord Protector's son, Caleb Grouted, and with him, Corporal Chance.

I lowered my head and melted back behind the piano and Connie's seated figure. I stood against the curtains where I hoped the candlelight would not reach me, and looked around for Becca. She was seated at a table in an alcove nearby, with an old gentleman, who was almost asleep – or drunk – his lolling head propped on his hand and his powdered wig off and sitting on the tabletop like a large iced cake.

I could see Anora at the end of the room, seating the two young men with many a curtsey and coquettish flutter of her fan. She knew who they were, although they wore no uniforms. The other guests paid them little attention, continuing their carousing and making an immodest amount of noise.

Somewhere Shadow hovered beyond the candlelight; I could no longer see him. I prayed he was still there and making some plan for my escape. I wondered how I could ever leave the room without being seen.

I slipped over to Becca. 'Sing in place of me,' I pleaded.

She looked up in surprise. The old man gave a gentle snore. 'But what will Anora say?'

'Please. It's important.' She understood it was by my face, and stood up immediately. She went to the piano and whispered to Connie, who began the first bars of the song that begins 'Sweet Sir, I Must Say No', while I drew back, away from the candles.

Becca sang with gusto and a great deal louder than I had; but it seemed that some of the guests were discontent. To my dismay and alarm, I heard mutterings of 'Can we not have the other one again – Miss Susanna?'

I could hide no longer.

'There she is,' someone cried, and the next moment Anora had glided over to me and had pulled me into the candlelight in front of the piano.

'My voice has gone,' I muttered to her, trying to shrink into the polished floorboards. I dared not raise my head.

'Nonsense, girl,' she hissed, endeavouring to keep the smile attached to her face. Her eyes had a hard glitter. 'Sing them something – anything! You know who is here!'

She moved back so that I stood alone before them all. I looked up at last.

Caleb Grouted would have no idea that I was the girl he had been looking for, since he had never seen me face to face. I could not see if Corporal Chance recognized me, for he sat in shadow. I began hesitantly to sing 'I Left My Love by the Amber Gate', for I could not think of another; it was the song that came into my head, with all the words complete.

Gradually, the murmuring ceased and, apart from the crackling of the fire and the occasional snore from the gentleman in the alcove, there was silence in the room. The strange dreaminess of the song seemed to hold them all, like a magical binding of beasts. For the length of the first verse, their glassy eyes grew focussed, their befuddled faces sober.

Then the spell was broken. I hesitated a little too long before starting on the second verse. In that moment the Lord Protector's son leapt to his feet and shouted thickly, 'And what do you know of the Amber Gate, Miss Susanna?'

I stared at him in bewilderment. Was this some trick question to trap me?

'It is merely a song, Sir,' purred Anora, but her hands clenched together in agitation at her bosom. 'It has naught of fact to do with the old story of the lost gate. Does she not sing it to your liking?'

'Aye, let the wench proceed,' shouted another guest. 'What nonsense is this?'

'Get on with it!' hissed Anora, glaring at me.

But the words had gone.

I stared in consternation from one face to another, trying to remember the words of the song, while the murmuring grew to a grumble of impatience. Caleb Grouted had subsided into his seat, muttering. Chance had shifted into the candlelight and was staring at me too hard, his mouth compressed.

I lurched sideways, as if faint. It was a desperate ploy, but as if I had rehearsed her, Becca rushed towards me, crying out, 'She needs fresh air!' She bent over me, and whispered in my ear, 'I'll get you out!'

I leant on her heavily, my eyes half closed. 'Whatever

happens, you'll always be my friend, Becca.' Did I think it or say it? I hope I managed to say it, for it was in my heart and still is now.

Connie rose as soon as she saw us and made as if to help support me from the room, but suddenly Anora was there, brushing both of them aside in fury. She whipped a tiny bottle under my nose. I knew I was lost, then.

'You will recover and sing on!' she said grimly, and held me fast.

7

The smelling-salts were vile; I flailed in her grip, choking. Becca and Connie, on either side of us, gave little cries of distress; one or two of the guests began to protest.

And then, cutting through the confusion by the piano, a boy's high voice yelled out from the doorway: 'Look to yer backs, Sirs! The Lawman comes!'

I don't know what happened then, there was such uproar in the room: shrieks and swearing and commotion. Caleb Grouted and Chance were somewhere in the midst of the throng pressing forward to the door and out into the hall. Connie had blown out the candles. Anora had left my side immediately and was nowhere to be seen.

'She's gone to open the back door,' whispered Becca, in my ear. She pulled at my arm. 'Come upstairs with us now, out of the way.'

The other girls had already disappeared. The Lawman was the last person I wanted to see, but I hesitated a moment in the confusion and darkness, and lost Becca. Then I felt a tug on my skirt. It was Shadow. 'Wot yer doin', 'angin' about?' he hissed fiercely. 'Look slippy!'

In bewilderment, I let him drag me from the room, which had now almost emptied. The front door was wide open on to the dark street. I could hear running water outside, and quick footsteps – people leaving the house, or coming towards it?

The steps died away into the distance, and then suddenly it was just Shadow and me outside on the cobbles and the house was behind us; and we were dashing down Kaye Street, towards the riverfront.

The moon was out over our heads like a great silver ball, bouncing off the rooftops. A touch of frost nipped the air and cut through my thin silk gown. 'Shadow!' I gasped, struggling to keep my skirts from dragging in the rivulets of filthy water. 'Shadow! The Lawman!'

His eyes glinted in the moonlight. 'Nifty wheeze, eh?'

'You mean, it wasn't true?'

'Nah!' He looked scornful. 'That lot gets taken in easy. Terrified of losin' their tradin' licences. The Lawman round 'ere, 'e's dozy, always tucked up snorin' instead of doin' 'is duty.'

I was overcome with gratitude. 'Thank you, Shadow. I could never have escaped without you.'

He put his hand out to slow me. 'Careful,' he whispered. 'There's people about.'

We could hear footsteps clipping the cobbles along a side street a little way behind us. It sounded like two different pairs of feet, but their owners were trying to tread softly, warily. The hairs on the back of my neck stirred.

Shadow put a finger to his lips, then pulled me into a narrow doorway out of the moonlight. He kept a grip on my skirt as if he suspected I might flee in fear, and we waited, my heart hammering.

After a minute they came swiftly past us, two male guests from the salon, still breathing heavily, too intent on their flight to notice us. They must have left through the back door, gone past the cottages and cut through. We stayed where we were, scarce breathing, straining our ears.

More footsteps, not so quiet this time. As they came closer I heard a voice: young, careless, arrogant, the words slurred with drink. A voice I knew.

'Wasn't worth staying for, anyway. Glad to be out of it, eh, Chance?' Feet scuffled as Caleb Grouted nudged Chance. 'Still, if we'd been caught there, Mather would not have been pleased, nor my pa for that matter.' A snigger, then, peevishly, 'Where are those damned horses? Hope you know your way in this squalid little place.' The Lord Protector's son kicked out and a fish head flew past my skirts.

I couldn't hear what Chance replied, but I saw him, clear in the moonlight. He seemed sober, looking to left and right as he strode along, as if watching for any sign of the Lawman. I felt Shadow's clutch tighten on me as he reached us; Chance looked away across the street and then straight at us in the doorway.

His eyes rested on us for a second, swept on and he passed by.

'Close shave, eh?' whispered Shadow, after their footsteps had died away into the night.

I took in a breath of cold, salty air. My teeth were chattering. 'Thank the Almighty!' I said, and I put my hand up to the amber on its thong. 'But where can I hide till it's light?'

'Easy. You can rest safe on *Redwing*.'

'On the barge?'

He nodded, and I caught the flash of his teeth. 'You stay 'ere a mo.'

'Don't leave me!' I said, frightened.

'I'm only gonna nip down the end of the street, see it's all clear.'

I waited, shivering, in the rank hole of the doorway, my shoes grating on fish-bones, my arms wrapped round me for warmth. Shadow's small soft boots made no sound on the cobbles beyond, so I could not guess where he was. It seemed very quiet, and the tall bulk of the warehouses on the other side was gloomy and oppressive, throwing the street between into darkness. I was beginning to worry about what could have happened to him, when a dark arm reached in at last and grasped me.

'Got you!' hissed the voice of Corporal Chance. 'I knew it was you.'

I couldn't say a word. I was too busy kicking, squirming. I knew everything was over, but some instinct for survival drove me to struggle as he wrenched me out of the doorway. I could hear him grunt as he tried to keep hold of me. He was behind me now, gasping with the effort of holding me; he had pinioned me to him, his arms around my chest so that I could scarce move.

'I heard you sing,' he whispered hoarsely into my ear. 'A girl from a Home shouldn't sing like that. Not as if she still had a heart.'

I looked down and saw the muscles bulging beneath the worsted of his jacket sleeves as he held me. The backs of his hands were bare and smooth. I lowered my head, and sank my teeth into the hand closest to my mouth.

Then out of the darkness came Shadow, flying like a little raggedy crow. As Chance straightened with a yell, Shadow came running straight at him from nowhere and butted him plum in the middle. It was a hearty *thwack* and maybe got him where it was most painful, for next minute he was lying groaning on the cobbles.

'Scarper!' shouted Shadow, and hand in hand we belted down the street like mad things, me with my skirts held up round my waist.

There were braziers burning along the causeway and wharf-keepers and watchmen about, but Shadow avoided them, dodging into the dark nooks and crannies between warehouses.

We arrived out of breath at the quay where the *Redwing* was moored. I was trembling and Shadow had to help me along now, for I could scarce move my limbs any more.

'On with you, then,' said Shadow, and he helped me

across on to the deck. A tiny light gleamed at the top of the tallest mast.

'This way,' said Shadow, and he led the way down a ladder into darkness. I hung back, but he tugged me down after him so that I almost fell, and pushed me into a narrow passage lit by a hanging lantern, and on through a door.

Once he had lit a stump of candle I saw I was in a tiny cabin. 'This is mine,' he said with pitiful pride, looking around at its only furnishings: a bunk, a sea chest. There was scarce room in there to twirl a turn.

'You can 'ave it,' he said. 'I'll sleep in the galley.' He looked at me, his head cocked. 'Are you in trouble, Miss Scuff?'

'Why should you think so?' I said, trying to unscramble my wits.

'I've a nose for it.'

'I am, indeed,' I burst out, too weary to dissemble. 'Those were soldiers after me!'

'And one of 'em a very important personage. My, what 'ave you bin and done, Miss Scuff?'

I shook my head weakly.

'Never mind,' he said, with a wink. 'Yer safe wiv me. Now, rest a sec, and I'll bring you a toddy.'

I didn't know what that was, but I sank against the edge of the bunk in the dim light and waited. I could hear voices somewhere – outside, or in the boat? Had Shadow told the bargemaster, Mr Butley? Could I trust either of them?

Shadow returned, after an eternity it seemed, but he

was alone and holding a pewter mug in triumph. 'Swill it down,' he ordered, pressing the mug into my cold hands, where it burned them.

I put it to my lips tentatively: hot, sugary water – sweet, very sweet – with a powerful kick to it. I could feel the heat of it trickle through me as I sipped.

He grinned at me. 'Just what the quack ordered, eh? Guarantees a good night's kip.' He nodded grandly at the chest. 'And you can 'elp yerself to what's in there.'

He seemed about to leave me again.

'Wait,' I begged; I had all sorts of questions.

'I must go,' he said. 'Mr Butley will be wonderin' where I am. Sleep tight.'

And then I was alone.

I perched on the end of the bunk and tried to calm myself. After a while I stirred and opened the chest to see if I could find something warm to put round my shoulders. There was a pair of boy's dirty breeches that looked as if they could stand on their own legs, and a tatty cloth jacket lying on top of a couple of folded blankets. I poked round the cabin in the candlelight to see if I could find the mahogany box, but it wasn't there; there was nothing else in there at all.

I didn't blow out the candle before I climbed into the bunk; I left it burning, careless of safety, and lay down in my underskirt and the jacket, pulling the blankets over me. They scratched and smelled damp and sour. The bunk was a wooden board with a thin straw mattress that prickled through my skirt. But I was exhausted, and glad of the warmth glowing in my limbs from the drink. I must have fallen fast asleep, in spite of the strangeness of lying above an unknown deepness of water.

An unfamiliar motion finally woke me. I was aware of having to brace myself very slightly where I lay. I heard a sucking, slapping sound beneath me, the creak and complaint of wooden timbers.

I opened my eyes and saw daylight filter through a tiny porthole, moving and flickering over the wooden walls of the cabin. Even then I think I was too bemused, too dazed with sleep, to understand. Then at last I roused myself and knelt up to look out.

Land moved past outside. There were no houses or cottages, only shingle banks tufted with coarse grass. We were approaching the rivermouth, would soon be over the bar. The noise of rushing water increased, though the flat-bottomed barge remained steady. I heard feet on the deck over my head, and realized I had heard them through my dreams.

Sometime while I was asleep – perhaps only recently – the *Redwing* had set sail.

I threw myself off the bunk and at the door, twisting the handle, frantic to get out, to alert someone so they could let me off. What had happened? Why hadn't Shadow woken me?

The door was locked.

I flung myself back at the porthole. I could see a grey

expanse of choppy water, little waves, white-topped, pointed like arrowheads. They looked sharp enough to pierce the timbers of the boat. I could even see – close enough to swim to if I'd been able – a muddy shore where waders pecked. A fan of swans bobbed serenely with the waves, as if the violence of the current was nothing to them.

I began to batter at the door with my hands again, shouting out, 'Shadow! Shadow!'

I heard his light quick steps outside; a key turned in the lock and he was there, looking as innocent as you please. ' 'Ow did you sleep, Miss Scuff?'

I dodged past him, but he caught me at once; his small wiry arms were surprisingly strong. ' 'Ang on.'

'I want to get off!' I cried, struggling.

He pushed me down on the bunk none too gently. I glared up at him.

'Too late, can't turn about now,' he said earnestly. 'Listen. I locked you in for safety last night. They was prowlin' all around, two of 'em, after you. They raised up the Lawman to help search. Lucky you was sleepin' fast, for they made some racket.'

'Why didn't you wake me this morning before you set sail?' I demanded suspiciously. I glared at his cheeky little face, his beguiling grin. Was he telling the truth?

He looked injured at my ingratitude. 'Wot, and leave you all alone in Poorgrass with them fellers around? This is 'uman kindness, this is, to take you on wiv us. Mr Butley says it's all right wiv 'im. You can 'ave free passage in return for a bit of cookin' and bottle washin'.'

I put my head in my hands. There was a bitter taste in my mouth – from the toddy last night or my own feelings of dread, I wasn't sure. 'I needed to stay in Poorgrass!' I said at last. 'That was where I was to find employment.'

He beamed at me encouragingly. 'Plenty employment where we're goin'. If you'd stayed in Poorgrass, you'd 'ave bin caught.'

Perhaps he was right.

I looked at the porthole, at the cloud-filled sky moving up and down: it was all I could see without kneeling on the bunk. I thought of Erland left behind. How would we ever meet again?

My throat seemed to close up, so that I could only whisper the question.

'*Where are we going?*'

But I knew.

Part Two

The Capital

GRAVENGATE

1

I'm back in the place where stone arches cast shadows on the ground and lead away to darkness. I'm still small enough to wriggle through between the stones, the old secret way. I remember the bitter smell of dead stone, the ripple of secret water. I've been here before, long ago.

I go to the gate, but slow, because I'm so weak, and run my fingers over it. I feel again the curls and whorls of gold, the smooth pieces of amber they hold, like chips from the sun. If I held a candle to it, it would glow: my amber gate. I see the faintest sheen of light on the surface of the water beyond. When I was here before, warm fingers held mine.

I go back to the steps and climb them. I crawl through the hole again. The Eagle has His back to me. His wings are spread, but He can't fly. The ravens can fly, but they are silent.

Hunger gnaws at my belly. They give us so little food in the Home. I think of food all the time. There are baskets of meat for Him, laid out on the purple cloth. How can He eat meat when He is made of stone?

It's silent in the Cathedral, but He hasn't heard me. He doesn't turn. So I help myself to the smallest basket. And still He doesn't turn. He'll never see me, with His stone eyes.

My mouth's wet. Raw flesh. I spit it out, but still something oozes down my chin. Dark gobs spatter my white pinafore. When I look down, my hands are crimson with the blood of the sacrifice. I shall never wash them clean. And then the ravens start shrieking so I know I am found out. I have committed the greatest crime of all: I have stolen from Him.

And as I run, I drop my Number.

I opened my eyes. Erland was sitting on the sea chest close to me, with the moon in his hair.

'Hush,' he said. 'You were moaning in your sleep.'

'I must have had a nightmare,' I murmured. I could not remember it. Then I roused myself, startled. 'Erland! You've found me!'

'I've been with you all the while,' he said, with his old smile, half-rueful.

'How is your leg?' I whispered.

He stretched it out; there was no bandage around it. 'I told you Gadd was a healer.'

I was bewildered. 'Have you stowed away?' We'd had several stops since Poorgrass to take on more cargo, but I'd hidden in the cabin. 'You must be careful.'

'You didn't see me. Nor shall anyone.' He leant towards me and dropped his voice low. 'Listen. I shall try to stay with you, if I can.'

'The *Redwing* is headed for the Capital,' I said in distress. 'It's so far from the Wasteland!'

His soft voice soothed me. 'Hush now, and go back to sleep.' I could feel his hand, rough-palmed but gentle, stroking the hair back from my forehead. 'Silky,' he whispered.

'Dirty,' I muttered, and heard him laugh before I slept.

2

Some weeks earlier, on a damp spring night in the Capital while Mather was still away on his abortive mission to the Eastern Edge, agents working secretly for the Lord Protector made an extraordinary and fateful discovery. The Protector's personal finances were low, so on his orders they were methodically looting every church in the city. That night they stole into the ancient Cathedral through the ruined entrance. A verger was asleep in a pew, his candle guttering. They looked around. Little of value here: the Cathedral's gold had been ransacked long ago. In the end it was a tiny, wizened beggar, sleeping in the apse, who unwittingly led them to a treasure beyond imagination. He had fled from them in fright – to vanish, seemingly, into a pile of fallen masonry.

On their return to the Capital, Mather and his bodyguard, Chance, were summoned to see the Lord Protector.

They had the honour of being taken to the Palace of the Protectorate in the Protector's own coach. Chance was suitably awed: he had never sat before on a padded velvet seat, in a vehicle decorated with gold leaf.

He stared out through the window as four black horses pulled them at a smart trot over the smooth paving of the Central Parade. It was difficult not to feel unnerved by the fierce gaze of the black Eagles on plinths either side, all the way up to the Palace at the end. Their eyes, made of marble that gleamed in the sun, could almost be alive.

Instead, he looked between the statues, at the green lawns of the pleasure parks beyond the Parade, where daffodils were in flower. He imagined himself taking off his boots and stockings, feeling the grass between his toes. His eye followed the paths that ran into the shrubberies; he pictured himself wandering between the weeping willows on the edges of the ornamental lakes, where swans glided on the glittering water and white pavilions rose from little man-made islands.

It was a peaceful scene in the spring sunshine. But that wasn't surprising. Except for a knot of gardeners in the far distance, the parks were completely deserted.

The Protector's people were hard at work, and those that had no employment – the countless homeless, the sick or elderly, the criminal underbelly – lay low in daylight hours. And away from here, there were plenty of places to hide in the reeking slums and narrow waterways of the old city. Once, Chance thought, he might have had to do that, too – if he had ever managed to escape from the Gallowbrook Home.

Mather was regarding him coldly from the opposite seat. 'You will leave all the talking to me, Chance. Understand?'

Chance nodded.

'I have reported exactly what you said to me: that you saw the kitchen maid from Murkmere in Poorgrass four days ago, being manhandled on to a barge named *Redwing*, bound for Gravengate. That is correct? You are absolutely sure you saw the brand mark on the girl's forearm?'

'Yes, Sir,' stammered Chance. 'It was full moonlight and her arms were bare and all.'

Mather gave him an odd look. 'A good deal to observe from afar, Corporal.'

'I saw the brand real close, Sir,' said Chance earnestly. He had had time to perfect his story. 'I went to rescue her, 'cos I thought she were a damsel in distress, but these ruffians kept pullin' her one way and I pulled the other way, and then I thought they'd turn on me. They had knives, Sir, and I was unarmed, bein' off-duty and all. Then one of 'em pushed me violent, and I fell on the quay and they had her on the barge. By the time I'd fetched the Lawman, the barge had sailed. A spritsail barge, it was, Sir, with a square topsail.'

'So you said. They are two a scathing on the Eastern Edge.'

'Lucky I'd made particular note of its name and destination, Sir.'

'Indeed.' Mather frowned. 'And all the time Lieutenant

Grouted was too incapacitated by drink to help.'

'Or maybe frightened, Sir,' said Chance, making the most of his story.

'The Protector won't countenance any defamation of his dear son,' Mather said sharply. 'I've reported merely that you saw the girl and recognized her from Murkmere.' He sighed in exasperation. 'How that barge gave the Ports Lawmen the slip, I can't imagine. Still, it should arrive at Gravengate tomorrow.'

He looked out of the coach window and cracked his bony fingers. 'Nearly there.' He glanced back. 'And – well spotted, Corporal Chance.'

'Thanks a lot, Sir,' said Chance modestly. He felt a glow of pleasure flush his cheeks.

At the end of the Parade there was a turning circle, with a vast black statue of the Protector himself standing triumphant before the gilded wrought-iron gates of his Palace. His eyes – made from the same marble as that set in the Eagle heads – watched their coach slow and turn. It entered between the gates and came to a stop before one of the many pillared entrances.

Chance followed Mather in, trying to look nonchalant. Mather seemed to know where he was going. As he made his way through each antechamber, footmen bowed low to him and Chance noticed the quick flicker of fear in their eyes. The Chief of the Interrogation branch of the Militia was well known in the Palace.

The mechanical clocks in the Palace were chiming

the eleventh hour in mellifluous harmony as Mather and Chance were ushered into the presence of the most powerful man in the country.

The Lord Protector, Porter Grouted, was seated at a desk in his elegant morning room, wearing a silk dressing gown over his breeches and sipping a small glass of fortified wine. He was surrounded by papers. Next to him on a marble pedestal, a gold bust of the Eagle gleamed dazzlingly in the sunlight from the long windows. Two rows of bewigged courtiers sat bolt upright on ornate chairs placed a discreet distance away and watched the Protector warily. There was a tense atmosphere in the long room, but there was nothing unusual in that.

The Protector rose as a footman announced Mather's arrival. He waved his courtiers away with an irritable, blunt-fingered hand.

Mather did his obeisance to the Eagle as was proper, then saluted the Protector; Chance copied him clumsily. There was the sound of hasty shuffling behind them as the courtiers retreated in relief, but Mather did not turn; he kept his eyes on Porter Grouted.

Though Chance did not dare stare directly at the Lord Protector, he had the impression of a short, bull-like man emanating a terrible power and energy. The Protector's bald head gleamed like a round polished stone; his body was stocky, but well-muscled. The silk dressing gown did nothing to soften him.

'Ah, Mather. You've taken your time gettin' back, haven't you?' It was a harsh voice, and the displeasure in it sent a chill through Chance.

'It's always four days by road, My Lord,' said Mather coolly. It took a brave man to stand up to Porter Grouted, but Mather had had long experience of dealing with him; he recognized and respected someone who liked control as much as he did. 'We must do something to improve our roads from the Eastern Edge.'

Grouted snorted. 'What, and make things even easier for the rebels? We'll have 'em bangin' on the gates of the Palace before we know it.'

'I think not, Sir,' said Mather. 'They seem in disarray since the death of Robert Fane. My spies tell me they cannot decide on a new leader. We found little organized resistance against us in the Eastern Edge, and where we did, we dealt with it.'

The Protector gave an unpleasant smile. 'I'm sure you did, Mather. I wish I could say the same thing about the rebel movement here in the Capital. I need you here, man – I shall grant you new powers. That firebrand, Titus Molde, has been stirrin' things up since Fane's death. He could become the next leader. That would be bad, very bad.' He strode to one of the long windows and inspected his perfectly manicured lawns. 'Rumblin's of rebellion – I sense 'em all the time, in the secret places of the city. I'd like to trap Molde like the sewer-rat he is.' He sucked at his lower lip.

Mather shifted position. 'You have read my report, My Lord?'

'Ah, yes. The girl, Number 102, the real purpose of your trip to that benighted part of the country.' Porter Grouted returned to his desk and pulled a parchment from the heap. 'We certainly don't want the rebels gettin' hold of her, since, accordin' to what you say here' – he tapped the parchment with a thick forefinger and jerked his head round to stare at Mather – 'she didn't die after all!'

A pulse flickered in Mather's hard grey cheek. 'When we returned to Murkmere the day after our initial search, we discovered the girl had endeavoured to escape in the old flying machine.' He cleared his throat. 'A group of men had frightened her, according to two footmen.'

Grouted frowned. 'A group of men? Your soldiers?'

'No, Sir. We believe they may have been rebels, mustered both from the Capital and the Eastern Edge. I fear Titus Molde was behind it.'

The Protector's eyes bulged. 'Molde! You mean he was in the area?'

Mather nodded grimly. 'For Robert Fane's funeral, I assume. We were unable to discover anything about the funeral – or, indeed, Molde's whereabouts – from the villagers, though we used all the usual methods of interrogation. The footmen themselves were unable to furnish us with any descriptions of the men. It had been too dark, they said. The fools mistook the rebels for the Militia!'

'And the girl?'

'At first we believed the flying machine had crashed in the Wasteland and that the girl had died. That is, until she was sighted in Poorgrass by my Corporal.'

Grouted gave a furious laugh. 'All in all, not a lucky trip for you, Mather.'

Mather did not flinch. 'I had the Wasteland searched, of course, but it is not an easy area, as you know yourself.'

'Too much damned bog,' muttered Grouted. He pursed his lips and stared at the report; his lips were fat and sensual, and made a slight sucking sound in the silence.

'Well, at least we now know the girl's bound for the Capital. You'll give the necessary orders, Mather? Post men at the city docks? We could even close the Gravengate itself if the barge, *Redwing*, is seen on approach.' He hit his fist against the parchment and it crumpled to the floor.

'You need have no worries, My Lord,' said Mather calmly. 'We will be waiting for the girl, and this time at least we shall know she is dead.'

'It was my bodyguard here – Corporal Chance – that identified the girl,' said Mather, leaning back in his chair and stretching out his legs. He had been granted permission to sit down, and the footman had given him a glass of the sweet wine. It had clearly made him feel in generous mood.

Chance stood behind Mather's chair and felt his knees quiver as the Protector looked him over with a flick of his almost lidless eyes. 'You're younger than my son, but you know him, do you?'

'Yes, My Lord.' *All too well.*

'Fine boy, my Caleb,' the Protector said fondly. 'Better-looking than his old pa, too. He can get a little overexcited from time to time, but that's his age. He'll settle down.' He chuckled to himself, then gave Mather a sharp glance. 'He's doin' all right, ain't he – Caleb? Provin' himself a natural soldier, no doubt?'

'He is – a natural, certainly, My Lord. And he has attended interrogation sessions and shows potential in that area.'

'Good!' The Protector slapped his knee. 'Give him a few years and he'll be Commander in Chief of the Militia. I'll appoint him myself if necessary.'

'He may have to quell his fondness for the bottle, Sir,' Mather said drily.

The little eyes went gimlet hard. 'What are you sayin', Mather?'

There was a sudden silence; Chance hardly breathed.

'My boy likes a drink – like his pa,' growled the Protector. 'No harm in that. He can hold it, too. Understood?'

'Of course, Sir. I was certainly not implying—'

Porter Grouted brushed his words aside impatiently. 'Enough. Something important has come up. I need to talk to you alone, Mather.' He looked at Chance. 'You can scarper until you're needed.'

'Yes, Sir.' Chance stepped back from Mather's chair.

'Wait a minute, sonny,' said Grouted unexpectedly. 'I

think we'll let you have a special treat, since you're a friend of my lad's. Shall we let him see the skin, Mather? I like to show it off – my prize possession.' He grinned to himself. 'I take a look at it each day to remind myself I've got it. Now, where's the key to the room?' He began to thump among the papers on the desk. 'Blasted thing, where is it?'

There was the sound of a scuffle at the double doors. The Lord Protector raised his head and bellowed down the room, 'Is that you, Boy Musician? Eavesdroppin' again? Get those useless pins of yours down here!'

3

The guards by the door stepped back in shock, as a youth dodged through them and came skidding over the floor to stop just short of the group by the desk. His wild, curly hair was long, as was the artistic fashion, and he had a stringed ratha tucked under his arm, like a small, glossy pet.

He looked terrified. Chance couldn't blame him but he felt some contempt: he was adept at hiding his own fear.

'You wanted me to play, My Lord?'

'You think this is a time for music, sonny?' Grouted gave a snort of derision. 'I have a secret matter of state to discuss with Officer Mather in complete privacy. Take this young soldier off and show him the swanskin. Entertain him for the next half-hour. Here's the key to the door. Don't lose it. If you do . . .' he paused '. . . I will kill you personally.'

'What's your name?' whispered the boy once they had left the morning room. He was still trembling, Chance noticed. He himself had stopped shaking as soon as they were out of the Protector's presence.

'Chance,' he said tersely. 'That's all I've got.'

'Nathan Kester – Nate,' said the boy. He had an open, eager face. He stuck out his hand in a friendly way and Chance, nonplussed, found himself shaking it.

He followed Nate Kester through a panelled antechamber and up some steps into a passage lit by burning lamps. Two guards stood watching them suspiciously from the far end. 'What's this skin thing, then?' Chance asked Nate.

Nate shifted the ratha under his arm and slowed. He kept his voice low, looking warily at the guards, and moved into the shadows between the lamps. 'It's a swanskin. Haven't you heard? We've the daughter of the late Master of Murkmere here in the Palace. It belongs to her.'

'I was there – at Murkmere – myself a few days ago,' Chance said loftily.

'Really?' said Nate. He looked impressed. 'On business?'

Chance nodded. 'Secret mission.' He paused for the importance of that to register and then said, 'Miss Leah says she's one of the avia, doesn't she? That she's a swan girl? Did she go crazy while she was wanderin' the streets?'

'She might not have been wandering the streets,' whispered Nate. 'She was found, soaking wet, on the banks of one of the ornamental lakes. And the swanskin was in her arms.'

Chance shivered in spite of the heat of the oil lamps. 'Don't believe in 'em, the avia. No one can be half bird, half human. It's just an old story. What's goin' to happen to her, then?'

'The Protector's waiting for a medical report.'

Chance nodded. 'Sick in the head, that's what she is.'

Nate frowned. 'The medical specialists know what they must say if they value their lives. The Protector wants her passed as sane so he can take her round the country to show what happens to those who think themselves on the same level as the Gods. He says he's keeping the swanskin so she won't fly away. I think he's joking, but I'm not sure.'

'Sounds as if you believe it yourself,' jeered Chance.

Nate shrugged, non-committal. 'He'll put Miss Leah on trial for blasphemy. She's condemned herself out of her own mouth, poor thing.'

'Poor thing?' You are soft, Chance thought.

'She looks so desperate, so unhappy. The Protector keeps her prisoner, you know – his own niece!'

Chance wasn't interested. 'Let's see this swanskin, then.'

They approached the guards, who recognized Nate and let him pass. They stared at Chance as he followed; he felt uneasy in spite of his uniform.

'This is the room,' said Nate. He stopped outside an iron-studded door and briefly explained about the key to the guard on duty.

'Be quick about it, then,' the man said reluctantly. 'You'd better not be having me on, young Kester, or it'll be more than your life's worth.' He moved a little way off. Chance looked at the door in astonishment: the Protector certainly had the skin well guarded.

'It's got a room all to itself,' whispered Nate, as he turned the key.

All there was in the room was a glass case, shining in the light that came from a single high window. They moved across to it and stared down at the swanskin, lying inside the case on a backing of black velvet.

Chance drew in his breath. The skin was a dazzling white against the black; each perfect feather lay snugly upon the next. At that moment he longed more than anything in the world to touch the swanskin, to force his hand through the glass and sink his fingers deep into its softness. He'd break the case, smash it to smithereens if Nate wasn't there, then he'd grasp up all the beauty of the skin and press it against his face. But at the same time, the sight of it filled him with revulsion and fear. He remembered the swans on the Eastern Edge, the attack on Caleb Grouted.

He shuddered. What was he thinking of? He hated swans. He turned away, and found himself shaking. 'Let's go.'

Nate was still staring down. 'You know the Significance of swans?'

'Don't believe that stuff no more. Had enough of it rammed down my throat once.'

He didn't elaborate, and Nate didn't question him. He murmured to himself, 'True Love . . . Messengers . . .'

'Messengers from where?' scoffed Chance.

'From the spirit world, perhaps.'

To Chance's relief Nate led the way out of the room

then, locking the door behind them. The guard nodded at them grudgingly as they left.

The double doors to the morning room were still firmly shut, so they had to wait in the antechamber outside. It was impossible to talk privately here: a swarm of guards eyed their every move. They perched on hard gilt chairs; Chance bit his nails, Nate strummed a few idle notes on his ratha.

Heavy footsteps sounded in the adjoining antechamber and a stout man came in, red in the face and mopping his brow in an agitated way with a large silk handkerchief. One of the guards brought in a sturdier chair and he sank on to it, breathing fast. He glared at Nate, who said politely, 'Good morning, Doctor.'

'Nothing good about it in my view. That girl threw her slippers at me just now. She really is exceedingly vexatious. Wouldn't let me examine her. Foul-mouthed, too. Called me . . .' He thought better of it and shut his mouth primly.

'Are you talking about Miss Leah?' said Nate, looking interested.

'Who else?' said the doctor wearily.

'Is she mad in your opinion, Doctor?' said Nate innocently. He nudged Chance.

'It is certainly difficult to establish her sanity while she behaves like this. Any more of it and we shall have to use a straitjacket.'

'Isn't that – a little extreme, Doctor?'

'Are you questioning my methods?' The doctor glared harder.

'No, no, of course not.'

'It's for her own good. She's dangerous.' The doctor felt his nose tenderly. 'A straitjacket is the answer. I've used them in the madhouses to great effect. I'm here to suggest such a measure to the Protector.'

Nate was silent; he stared down sombrely at his long musician's fingers.

A moment later they were called in to the morning room, leaving the doctor fuming impatiently outside. The Lord Protector and Mather were standing by the windows deep in conversation that cut off abruptly as the boys came in. The Protector held out his square hand for the key and locked it away in his desk. He didn't ask Chance what he thought of his precious exhibit; indeed, he seemed distracted, in a mood of suppressed excitement. His eyes gleamed; he chortled to himself. Evidently the private discussion had gone well.

'So that is all for now, Mather,' he said, beaming at his Chief Interrogation Officer. His teeth were even and yellow. 'But we will have much to plan in the next few weeks, eh?'

'Yes, indeed, Sir,' said Mather thoughtfully. 'It's certainly an unexpected and interesting development.'

'A very interesting development, Mather, and we shall use it to our greatest advantage,' said the Lord Protector, and he gave another of his unpleasant smiles.

4

I didn't dream of Erland again.

As I lay in my bunk, I'd picture us leaving the Capital, setting off together for the long walk back to the Eastern Edge. In my imagination the sun shone, blackbirds sang among the white may blossom and the candle flowers of the chestnut trees shimmered above our heads. Yet though I thought of Erland every night, he never came again to me.

All the way down to the Gravendyke estuary, the *Redwing* had hugged the coast, passing sandbanks that stuck out like drowned fingers where the water was shallow. The bargemaster had ordered a fine supper when we reached the Capital in a few hours; I wouldn't be able to cook it until we arrived, but thought I'd busy myself with preparing the vegetables meantime.

I'd scarce picked up the knife when the bargemaster, Mr Butley himself, came down the ladder into the tiny galley unexpectedly. I had the sleeves of the boy's jacket that I'd worn all voyage rolled up over my wrists, and wasn't fast enough to cover my scar.

He had sharp eyes, Mr Butley. I didn't like the way he was always staring at me; I didn't like being alone with him. Usually Shadow was there, thieving food from under my nose, but today he was busy on deck.

'You have your sea legs now, little maid,' Mr Butley said, giving me his glint-eyed look. 'You've settled well to the life of a ship's cook.'

'I'm grateful for my safe passage, Sir,' I said, politely. 'It's the least I could have done.'

He straddled his sturdy legs to the shifting of the boat. 'How old are you, Miss?'

'Fifteen, I believe, Sir.'

'No parents?'

I turned back to the carrots on the wooden board. 'No, Sir.'

I could sense him looking me up and down. 'A comely girl, slender but strong, straight-legged and in good health,' he murmured to himself, as if listing my assets. 'An excellent cook, a willing worker. In addition, one amulet – amber, very fine.' Then, louder: 'What will you do in the Capital?'

'Find employment, Sir.'

Suddenly he was behind me, breathing into my ear. 'What other talents do you have, little maid?'

I twisted round, holding the knife casual in my hand; I let him see I had it there. 'I can sing a bit, Sir.'

He pretended to look downcast. 'Nothing more than a song to reward your generous skipper? Not a kiss or two?'

'I will come on deck and sing for you now, if you will let me pass, Mr Butley,' I said firmly. 'You won't be disappointed. It's all I can offer, but I know by your kindness to me that you are a gentleman.'

He stared at me a moment, then his eyes dropped. 'Very well, but you must sing loud to drown the gulls.'

And so I put down the knife and climbed up after him, and found myself on deck for almost the first time.

At first I was dazzled by the sea light, the brightness of the water flowing on every side until it merged with the sky. It was alive, I was sure of that, because it never stopped moving; but I couldn't work out where such a vast watery body would keep its soul.

Shadow came up with a grin as I emerged, a coil of rope in his hand. 'Good afternoon, Miss Scuff!'

The bargemaster put his hard hand on my shoulder. 'Miss Scuff is going to sing for us. Give those damned birds some competition, girl!'

He lifted me on to the cabin roof before I could protest. Mister Plush was up there already, curled into a tight knot, drawing any warmth from the wood. I felt alarmingly high up, with all that space around me. My hair blew in the damp breeze, the great rust-coloured sails creaked above my head and there were only the mizzen shrouds to hang on to until Shadow came to perch beside me.

After I had sung and the bargees applauded, it began to drizzle. Mister Plush stalked away to slink under a tarpaulin. Shadow's face was pinched with cold, but his eyes were bright. 'I'm lookin' forward to me supper,' he whispered. 'What shall I do when yer gone, Miss Scuff?'

'Shall you miss me then, Shadow?' I said, teasingly. 'Me, or my suppers?'

'Put yer arm around me, Miss Scuff, pretend yer me big sister this once.'

It gave me a strange, tender feeling – to put my arm around his bony little back and have him nestle against me. We sat there in the damp, sharing our warmth between us.

'But where's the river?' I said.

'Why, we're at it. See the markers?'

On the port side I heard doomy clanging, like a call to judgement; it was the bell-buoy swinging with the surge, and now I could see it clear, as we rode the waves and passed between it and a tall stone rising from the water on the starboard side.

The skipper bellowed, 'Look to the depth, boy!'

Shadow scurried to the bows and threw out a lead line; he chanted the depth back until we were safe through the sandbanks and had a channel of withy sticks to guide us. The estuary of the Gravendyke lay all around: mudflats and marshes; a grey landscape blurred by mist.

Mr Butley's brother, the mate, peered behind the mizzen mast. 'That spirit bird again,' he muttered. 'Appears out of nowhere. I swear the same swan has followed us from Poorgrass!'

Mr Butley was checking off each withy on the chart. He

didn't turn. 'Look to your sails, not to swans, for omens, brother. We'll never reach the Capital unless we harden up!'

From the galley porthole I could see ramshackle cottages, huddled together behind little quays. A child with a bucket waved to us. Cows wandered along the bank or stood foolishly, hock-high in water, as if transfixed by our ghostly appearance from the mist.

I didn't look for a while after that, for I wanted to leave the galley tidy. It was a surprise when Shadow put his head through the open hatch. 'We're on the outer reaches of the Capital, Miss Scuff!'

We were passing houses that teetered tight together to the very edge of the mud, some half drowned by water already, the river lapping up their walls. Between them were crumbling landing-stages and jetties, stone quays and docks. Beyond the mud, the banks were crowded with vast brick warehouses and wharves, and almost hidden by the forest of masts that stuck up from the moored boats.

Above my head came shouts of warning and command, the flapping of sails as boats changed course. When I scrambled halfway up the ladder to look out through the hatch, boats surrounded us. They covered the scummy surface of the river like a million water beetles. There were other barges like the *Redwing*, then all the smaller boats winding their way between us. Chalk boats trailed a film of white dust through the black wash of coal boats, which were laden with filthy sacks and black-faced men in aprons. Scavengers slid by, piled with stinking rubbish; corpsers, with their grisly cargo. They were all tossed about and half sinking in the turbulence from the larger schooners and sloops. And the smell came to me, the smell I remembered all too well: the river stink of mud and rot that hung over the whole city.

As the first of the prison islands loomed out of the murk, I was filled with dread.

'How far upriver will we go, Shadow?'

'Through the Gravengate to the trading basin, most like,' Shadow said, coming down into the galley after me and pinching a piece of raw carrot from under my nose. He peered out of the porthole and shook his head. 'Nay, seems we're holing up in Sowerditch tonight. The skipper must be thinking there's too much traffic round the Gate and he'll not get a berth to unload. He'll leave it to the next high tide.'

The Sowerditch wharf was full of dirty water, bordered by leaning houses with windows on the same level as the *Redwing*. We could see straight into the squalid rooms, and the people inside could stare back at us. Shadow amused himself by pulling faces at an inquisitive red-faced trollop until she snapped her shutters together. There were shouts and thumps as mooring ropes passed between us and the next boat, the long rattle of the anchor chain being let out.

We ate our meal as the afternoon wore on. Shadow sat

tight by me on the bench; Mister Plush was on his lap, green eyes fixed on the herring roes I'd put on a platter. The bargees ate heartily, their faces shiny with grease in the light of the oil lamp. Mr Butley kept plying me with toddy, which I tried to refuse.

'It's only a couple of hours until Curfew,' I said, nervous. 'I must leave soon.'

'No one keeps Curfew in this part of the Capital,' said Mr Butley, chewing on a lamb chop. 'They're a lawless lot. Shadow and I will deliver you safe to a respectable boarding house for the night, where they'll lodge you in return for kitchen work.'

I did not trust the bargemaster. I shook my head. 'I'll manage, thank you.'

When the meal was finished and I had cleaned up as best I could – for we had no water left in the bilges – I felt a shy tug at my skirt. I knew it was Shadow and I must say goodbye to him.

I turned from the sink and he presented me with a canvas bag on a long strap. When I looked inside I saw the mahogany box. 'Take it back,' he whispered. 'It's yours,' and he put his finger to his lips to show that Mr Butley mustn't hear.

'Won't you get beaten?' I said anxiously.

He shrugged, nonchalant.

I hugged him. 'You are a friend, Shadow, a true friend.'

Something came into his eyes then. 'I do want to be a friend to you, Miss Scuff,' he said, looking up at me earnestly; his dirty face had the tracks of tears. 'Believe it, I do.'

Then he slipped from the galley before I had a chance to say goodbye.

Though I'd had so little of the toddy, my head was starting to swim. I tried to pull myself together; I combed my hair with the tortoiseshell comb and wiped my face with an edge of cloth. My clothes were dirty, but at least I'd not stand out in this part of the city.

Then I put the box back in the bag and put the strap over my neck. Lifting my skirts, I climbed the ladder for the last time. I was clumsy, especially with the box banging against my legs. When I looked back down into the galley, it seemed to blur before my eyes.

I stood on deck, swaying a little and blinking in the grey afternoon light, the box under my arm.

Two bargees stepped forward. 'Come, we'll help you disembark, Miss Scuff.'

I didn't refuse their help; I knew I needed it to struggle to the wharf-side across the boats that lay along us. When I'd placed my feet safely on the muddy stones, I wondered if I could walk steady, all alone.

'We'll guide you,' said one, and he took a firmer hold of my arm. Neither man listened to my protests. With a boatman gripping each arm, I was almost carried from the wharf.

The toddy was drugged! I thought hazily.

I looked back as I was borne between the houses and I saw Shadow on deck. I heard his thin cry: 'I'm sorry, Miss Scuff!'

Has Shadow betrayed me all along?

'What are you doing?' I mumbled to the men, the self-same men that had listened to my songs that morning. 'Where are you taking me? You've no right!' Panicked, I began to twist in their grip, forcing them to stop.

'Mr Butley's orders, Miss,' panted one of them, as he pinioned my arm. 'You are a cheat, Miss, Mr Butley says so.'

'What?' I cried.

The other one chimed in, shaking his head. 'You took back the box that was to pay for your passage.'

'Our skipper don't like to be the loser on a deal,' said his friend.

Outrage seized me, clearing my head. 'It was given me . . .' I began. Then, 'Take the box back! It's in the bag.'

For a moment the bargees looked disconcerted. 'Mr Butley said we was to take you to the slave market.'

At his words I began to struggle in real terror. 'Take it yourselves then, keep it! Only let me go. Don't sell me, I beg you!'

'We'll get a share of the proceeds if we sell you. What would we do with a box?'

'And you'll 'ave a roof over your head tonight,' said the other. 'Now, come along like a good girl.'

Now they gave me no opportunity of stopping, but

swung me along so that my feet scarce touched the ground. I might have been a bale of merchandise; I suppose I was, to them. I could feel my heart beat thickly; I remembered hearing about the slave markets and what happened to those who were sold. If they were sold as servants, they were lucky, though they'd always carry a stigma.

But sometimes girls and women were bought for prostitution, or taken north to the coal mines and never saw daylight again. Others were bought to work in the chalk pits and lime kilns, where their lungs drowned in dust; or in the blubber factories, where I'd heard they made soap from human fat.

All this ran frantic through my mind as I was pulled along. The courtyards and alleyways reeked of urine and rotting vegetables. Packs of wild dogs nosed the rubbish, snarling at each other, fighting over old bones. Ravens, pecking at the cobbles, shuffled out of our way with raucous croaks, so that I longed to touch the amber beneath my bodice.

I was desperate for help, but the streets were deserted. The hour of Curfew was coming; even in the open places the light was beginning to fade. Only a beggar huddled in a doorway, peered at me dully as I was dragged along.

Then suddenly I saw my salvation: a lamplighter, coming down his ladder from the lighted oil lamp.

'Help!' I cried out. His grease-smeared face turned towards me. 'Please – help me!'

But in the pool of yellow light he saw the two muscular

bargemen. He grabbed up his trimming scissors and pitchy rope and vanished into the dusk, without even waiting to collect his ladder.

'You shut your mouth, you hear?' growled one of my captors, his face brutish. He shoved his fist under my nose and I was dragged on.

The slave market was being held on a scurfy patch of open ground surrounded by ruined buildings, their staircases open to the wind. The auction was almost over and the crowd beginning to leave. As we arrived, two rough-voiced assistants came up and took details from the boatmen. Then they led us towards the centre of the ground. The bargees held me fast; there was no chance of escape.

On the makeshift platform three tiny children were roped together, their faces gaunt in the light from the flaming brands. They looked scarce old enough to work, but their parents had brought them here to sell. I could see a ragged couple hovering below, waiting for the auctioneer's speech. The mother was wringing her hands and weeping; the father didn't look at his children but at a sprouting weed by his feet.

'We have here a girl and two boys, in good health, meek, easy to train. One lot, or separate. What am I bid?'

The two boys were sold immediately to a prosperous-looking businessman, accompanied by a bodyguard and a link-boy bearing a lamp – a factory owner, perhaps – but the little girl was rejected.

She ran in joy back to her mother, but the father prised her away and forced her back to the platform. Her sobs were terrible. Eventually she was sold to a hard-faced madam in a stiff black hat for a single scathing. The mother wept as the father took the paltry coin, his face bitter.

'And now we have a pretty young maiden, ripe for work, an experienced housekeeper and cook, sound of limb. Also, one amber amulet, of very fine quality. Items to be sold together or separate.'

The two bargemen and the auctioneer's assistants thrust me up on to the platform; the bag with the box was flung after me. Almost blinded by the flaring brands I could see nothing, only hear a ripple of interest from the people that had remained in the ground. The assistants kept firm hold of me.

'Turn around, Miss, lift your skirts – show us your shapely ankles – now roll back your sleeves,' ordered the auctioneer, breathing roast onions in my face, and to my horror, his own repulsive, podgy hand came at my breast to pull out my amber.

I closed my eyes and did as he told me; I had no alternative.

I felt I could not sink any lower than to be sold as if I were an object, and had no soul. How could I face Aggie again, if her mother's amulet were separated from me and sold to a stranger?

In my shame, I tried to cast myself far away in my mind – to Murkmere. And immediately I thought of Miss Jennet:

of what she would say in such a situation. *It does not matter what these people think of you, but what you think of yourself.*

So I held my head proudly and looked, clear-eyed, into the dusk beyond the flames and the ring of gawking, orange-lit faces below me.

And suddenly I saw out of the corner of my eye against a ruined wall the pale glimmer of a shirt – surely the calico shirt I had mended for Erland and that I'd seen him wear so often? But when I looked back I saw it was a trick of the light. The moon was rising above the broken buildings, a full moon that shone in the puddles of the open ground.

At that moment the Curfew bells began to toll warningly through the Capital, a tuneless clamour of many different pitches. The auctioneer was in a hurry to have the business of the evening over and be safe inside his walls. He prodded me further forward, to the very edge of the platform.

'So, ladies and gentlemen,' he shouted. 'What am I bid for this willing young creature? See her straight limbs, her strong back? She is an excellent hand in the kitchen, I have the strongest recommendation from her former employer. It would be a veritable crime, ladies and gentlemen, to start with a bid less than a double revere. Come and have a closer inspection if you wish.'

To my horror dark figures stirred in the crowd. Several people were moving forward to climb on to the platform: to poke me all over, inspect my teeth, finger the amber. I tried to struggle, but the auctioneer's assistants held me more tightly still, and down below the bargees, eager for their money, were ready to help.

Two women were the first to climb the steps: one, panting with the exertion, and bulky – I could make out her shape but little more in the torchlight; the other, younger, agile, reached the platform first. She stepped out of the darkness, seized up my bare forearm and peered at it.

'I thought so!' the girl exclaimed, in tones of triumph. 'She is an orphan.' She held my arm out to the auctioneer. 'Look at that brand mark, Sir. See the square after the number? She was one of ours at the Gravengate Home. We've the right to claim her for Recompense. She's our property!'

I stared at the girl. I saw the flames gleam in her little currant eyes. I knew that smirk. It was the same expression she'd had on her face when she used to taunt me at Murkmere.

I'd never expected to see Doggett in the Capital.

5

The same evening, Mather and Chance were back at the Palace of the Protectorate. For what would be the final time Mather was to interrogate the Protector's special prisoner: his niece, Miss Leah Tunstall, formerly of Murkmere. Chance himself had never before seen the girl whom everyone in the Palace whispered about, the girl who might be one of the despised and blasphemous avia.

Full of curiosity he followed Mather into a courtyard, past the armed guards that stood to attention at the entrance to one of its corner towers. He noted that the prisoner had been confined as far away as possible from the main Palace building with the Protector's reception rooms. He could hear her yells blasting down the shadowy stone stairwell as they climbed.

'Get out, you doltheads, out of my sight!'

There was a crash above them.

A man came hurrying down, almost falling over his feet. It was the doctor from the day before, redder in the face than ever. He glared at Chance, then at Mather. 'I don't advise seeing her just now. Ill-tempered little . . .' He floundered as he registered Mather's uniform, spat out 'Pah!' and blundered past them.

'There will be no more medical checks on Miss Leah from today, Doctor,' Mather called down after him. 'They will not be necessary.'

The doctor stopped short and looked up. Hope suddenly lightened his heavy jowls. 'Really, Officer? On whose authority?'

'There is only one who could give such a command,' said Mather, with a touch of reproof. 'The Lord Protector himself will inform the medical team shortly.'

It seemed to Chance that the doctor went on his way with a positive spring in his step.

Two more physicians in long black tailcoats came out through a chamber door as they reached the top. They were shielding their heads, wisely it seemed, since a shoe came flying out after them and almost hit Mather in the face. The guards either side of the door stepped aside with the alacrity of long practice.

Chance bent and picked the shoe up. It was a blue silk shoe, elegant but uncommonly large for a female. He followed Mather in and as the door was locked behind them, presented it to the girl crouching on the floor. 'Your shoe, Miss.'

'Who on earth are you?' She glared up at him from the middle of a ring of assorted objects – more shoes, books, belts, bottles – her ammunition, he thought. The room was bordered with broken plates, though he noticed she'd sensibly eaten her luncheon off them before she began throwing. 'Are they sending boys to interrogate me now?'

Mather looked with disapproval at the disorder on the floor and sidestepped it fastidiously. 'This is my bodyguard, Corporal Chance, Miss Leah. I've not brought him before.'

Leah gave a hollow laugh. 'An excellent precaution to bring him today, then, Mather. I've a feeling you're going to need him.'

Mather did not look in the least disconcerted. 'I think not. I have some good news for you, Miss Leah. Your doctors are being dismissed. You'll suffer daily examinations no longer.'

Leah listened, then gave a suspicious frown. The frown, daunting though it was, made no difference to her beauty, Chance thought. She was, in fact, the most beautiful girl he'd ever seen, with pearly translucent skin and long fair hair that gleamed silver in the candlelight. Her bare feet were large, it was true, but delicate-boned and somehow of a piece with the rest of her, for when she stood up she was exceedingly tall in her blue silk dress, as tall, almost, as Mather.

'Sit by the fire, Mather, and tell me more about this change of heart,' she said drily, pulling a fringed shawl around her shoulders.

'If you will sit also, Miss.'

They both sat down, Leah curling herself gracefully into an armchair of quilted silk, Mather stiff-backed and stiff-faced in another.

The chamber was sparely but luxuriously furnished, as was fitting for the Protector's niece. It did not resemble a prison cell, but that was what it was. Chance, hovering awkwardly around the perimeter of their conversation, noticed bars on the window between the heavy velvet drapes. Outside the locked door of the chamber he could hear the guards stamp and shuffle in the cold.

'So, what's brought this about?' said Leah. 'Dismissing the medical team! What's my uncle scheming now?'

'Really, Miss Leah. I thought you'd be pleased.'

'Oh, I am.' She shot out her words like bullets. 'I'm fed to the teeth with those fools, forever pestering me with their idiot questions.' She put on a high, pernickety voice: ' "If I put the swanskin round my shoulders now, what did I think would happen?" ". . . What had I eaten during my time as a swan – weed or insects or little fish?" ". . . Had I made a nest somewhere in the pleasure parks?" ' She glared at Mather, but he didn't flinch.

'They needed a lesson in the art of interrogation from you, those fine physicians. First they'd asked their damn fool questions, then they'd examine me each day to see if I was sprouting wings yet. It would take three of them – two to hold me down, one to look.' She shuddered, then laughed again: a hysterical sound that echoed round the stone walls. Her dark eyes, ringed by the delicate mauve shadows of recent illness, were desperate. 'Wings! If I'd grown wings I'd fly away! I long for wings!'

'That is all over, Miss Leah. The Protector will be sending the physicians away tomorrow, after their final report. The reason for their dismissal is . . .' Mather paused. His expressionless eyes were on hers. 'The reason is that the Lord Protector believes you.'

Leah let out a shriek. 'What?' She threw herself back in the chair, hands clasped together. Chance could see that this was an act; that she was not amazed at all, but wary and suspicious. He wondered if Mather could see it, too.

'The Lord Protector believes you are indeed one of the avia,' said Mather gravely.

A look of genuine fear crossed her face before she could hide it. 'What's he going to do about it, then? Kill me?'

'Why should he kill you?' said Mather carefully.

'People kill things they don't understand, they feel threatened.' She looked sideways at Mather. 'You should know that, you of all people, Mather. People are frightened of the avia – superstitious. The avia is a cursed race, so they believe.'

'The Protector will not kill you. Indeed, he wants you to put it in writing.' Mather leant forward, his eyes on hers.

She licked her lips as if her mouth was dry. 'What do you mean?'

He pulled a small roll of new cream vellum from his pocket and unrolled it. 'Write a short statement to say you are one of the avia, and sign it. Swear it on your life.'

She looked taken **aback** for a moment, then she laughed scornfully. 'You really must think I'm mad. This statement will be an excuse to murder me. If the Protector says he believes me now, it's because it suits his purpose. What I want you to tell me, Mather, is what that purpose is.'

'The Protector, your uncle, will tell you himself once you have written your declaration and signed it. He needs to know you have not changed your story.'

'It's no story!' she said furiously.

'Write it down, then.' He held the vellum out, and added with a chilly smile, 'He has no plans to kill you, I can assure you of that. How do you think it would look to the people if he had his own niece murdered?'

'Come, Mather. You know as well as I that he could arrange to get rid of me quietly, without anyone knowing.'

'Write this statement,' said Mather softly, still holding out the vellum. 'It will open the way to your freedom.'

'Then I have no alternative, do I?' she spat out. 'If I'm imprisoned up here much longer I think I'll die!'

She snatched the roll of vellum and stalked over to a little desk in the corner, making the candles flicker. She paused, as if in thought, then Chance heard the scratching of a quill, the patter of the sand-sifter on the paper to blot the ink. She shook the sand off into a silver bowl. Then she came back and waved the vellum under Mather's nose.

'There! I've written your declaration.'

Mather took it. In his dry, clipped voice he read out: '"I, Leah Tunstall, do swear on my life that during my

215

wanderings in the Capital I was not myself, but inhabited two bodies, half girl half bird."'

'Satisfied?'

'It will do.'

'Now, give me back the swanskin!'

'The swanskin?' said Mather in feigned surprise. 'I have no authority for that, Miss Leah. You must ask your uncle yourself.'

She went paler still, if that were possible. 'But if I am to be freed?'

He rose to his feet, the vellum in his hand. 'Be patient. Your uncle will come to you shortly. He has something to tell you that will change everything.'

6

Following his visit to Leah, Mather went straight to the Lord Protector's private apartment in the Palace. Chance, following close behind Mather as always, marvelled at the number of guards it took to protect one man: they were standing outside the main anteroom of the apartment, their hands hovering about the leather holsters of their pistols, and looked simultaneously bored and nervous.

Grouted was having an informal supper with his son, Caleb, who, by his father's order, had been given special leave from his military duties. They were seated at a small table in the panelled library, surrounded by shelves of gold-tooled, leather-bound books that reached to the ceiling. Apart from some tomes on taxation and foreign investment, the books were beautiful fakes: from the early years of the Protectorate, books had been banned for containing heretical ideas. From the alcoves set into the shelves, a set of bronze statuettes of the Eagle glared a warning.

Grouted had called for entertainment from the Boy

Musician while they ate, and the room was filled with the sweet, haunting music of the ratha, played very softly. This wasn't an occasion for family chat: the Protector had just presented Caleb with a new and highly significant proposition, and Caleb was having some difficulty in taking it in at the same time as his roast pork.

He swallowed a large mouthful and frowned. 'Say again, Pa. What's the link between this cousin of mine and your discovery of the Amber Gate?'

'Coincidence, my son – the Gods have sent us Grouteds a divine coincidence.' The Protector leant forward over the snowy tablecloth. 'It so happens that on top-secret orders from me my agents have been – let's call it – "takin' an inventory" of one or two minor churches in the Capital, with a view to appropriatin' their treasure – to finance some recent buildin' work here in the Palace, you understand, let alone all my other expenses. The priests don't need it, I do.' He mopped his fleshy lips with a napkin. 'Well, what happens next is I suggest my men take a look at the old Cathedral. And what do you know? They find that a recent fall of masonry has opened up an old stairwell no one ever knew existed. And guess where it goes?'

'The crypt, Pa, you said,' Caleb said, bored.

'The crypt! And down there they find the fabled Amber Gate in all its glory. Gold, Caleb, gold like you've never seen. My men have searched for the Gate for years, all over the Capital. Never guessed it would turn up underground, along with a lot of corpses. Anyway, once that gold's melted down . . .'

'And the coincidence?' said Caleb.

The Protector smacked the palm of his hand down on the table. 'Why, that we'd captured Leah Tunstall at the same time. It ain't so much the Amber Gate that's significant, my boy – though that's a nice little extra, you might say – as the ceiling of the crypt. It seems to be some kind of prophecy.' His bald head glistened in the candlelight as he nodded emphatically. 'If you marry your cousin Leah our line will be secure – that's what those paintings down there are tellin' me, and the Palace seer confirms my interpretation.'

His time in the Militia had not improved Caleb's table manners. He shovelled in his roast pork, his handsome face sulky. 'But marriage, Pa! It's a bit sudden. Takes a chap time to get used to the idea.'

'My son, my son . . .' began Porter Grouted. He gazed at Caleb with sentimental pride. 'I know it's a big step,' he went on more slowly, choosing his words carefully. 'But it's a step towards securin' your future and the survival of our lineage. A father can do nothing less for his son, especially in my position. The rebels are almost at our gates, Caleb. The people may swing to them, and if they join forces in revolution, then we shall lose everything, includin' our lives – you and me.'

Caleb scowled. 'And this marriage will stop that?'

His father brandished a fork. 'It's all foretold, Caleb.

I tell you, I've seen the prophecy with my own eyes.'

Caleb pouted. 'What about the girl, Leah? I've met her once, you say?'

'You came with your mother and me to Murkmere many years ago. She was about five, your cousin.' He chuckled. 'Spent your time pinchin' and bitin' her, I seem to remember.'

Caleb smiled, the same unpleasant smile as his father's. 'Did I make her cry?'

'It was you that cried. She bit you right back, spiteful little thing. She was a skinny, wan shrimp of a child, all arms and legs.'

Caleb spat out a piece of gristle. 'Don't like the sound of her, Pa. She sounds ugly. Ugly things make me want to wipe 'em from my sight.'

Grouted chuckled again as the ratha paused at the end of a melody, and began another. 'Oh, you won't want to wipe her, son. I can guarantee that. Wait till you see her!'

There was a knock and Mather entered without announcement, followed by Chance. Caleb looked at Mather and from where he was sitting clumsily half saluted, thought better of it and started in on his pudding; Chance, he didn't give a second glance.

It was known that the Lord Protector disliked being interrupted during the process of eating, and today it was his favourite sponge pudding and syrup. He laid down his spoon with a show of resignation and frowned.

'Mather. Like a bent scathin', always turnin' up. Well, spit it out, man. What did she say, my niece?'

'She has written the declaration, My Lord.'

'Give it here, then.' He seized the roll of vellum. There was a pause. The ratha played even slower and softer. Chance glanced over at Nate. He plucked the strings with a look of intense concentration on his face. It took concentration to play and listen at the same time, thought Chance.

Grouted slapped his thigh. His little eyes were jubilant. 'What would I do without you, Mather? We have her confirmation – in her own handwritin', we have it!'

Mather twitched his upper lip into the semblance of a smile. 'I believe so, My Lord.'

'Believe so? What is this, then, if not a confirmation?'

'She has not admitted in so many words that she is one of the avia,' said Mather carefully.

'Stuff, man! When we picked her up, that's what she was sayin', wasn't it? She's avian, no doubt about it, and probably the last of 'em. And she was clutchin' the swanskin that belonged to her mother! It was always said that Blanche Tunstall was one of the avia, and we know the avian trait is inherited through the maternal line.'

Mather sucked in his thin cheeks. 'Miss Leah was delirious when she was discovered, My Lord. She was out of her mind, running a high fever.'

Grouted snorted. 'She was found on the bank of one of the park lakes. She was soakin' wet, wasn't she? So was the swanskin. And the fuss when it was taken from her! It had to be prised from her fingers. Nearly broke 'em myself to get at it, but it would have looked bad for an uncle to do that. What further proof are we lookin' for? She's a swan girl.'

'She was wet through, it's true, My Lord, but the parks are not lit at night. In her delirium she might have fallen into the lake by accident.'

Grouted spoke through gritted teeth. 'You're bein' too precise, Mather. An excellent quality when extractin' information, but at the moment no use to me at all. This document tells me that she says she is avian and it bears her signature. If I read it like that, then it is so, man. Understood?'

Colour tinged Mather's grey cheekbones. 'Yes, Sir.'

Caleb had been absorbed in stuffing himself with pudding throughout their conversation and giving the occasional snide glance at Chance. As if it had just dawned on him that it was Leah they were talking about, he said uneasily, 'What happens if she doesn't like me, Pa?'

'Doesn't like you?' snarled his father. 'What the hell do you mean?'

Caleb stiffened in his chair, an apprehensive look on his face. He was clearly used to his father's tempers. 'No need to fly off, Pa,' he muttered. 'Only wondering, that's all.'

'It don't matter whether the chit likes you or not, son. Get that into your head.' The Lord Protector spoke louder, looking furiously over at the Boy Musician. 'And as for you, you can stop your confounded pluckin'! If we had a singer, it might be a darned sight more cheerful than these dolours of yours!'

He glared back at Caleb as silence fell. 'Leah's future is tied up with yours, that's all there is to it. And she's damned lucky to have a future. I could have had her arrested and tried by the Supreme Court for her role in what happened at Murkmere three years ago, but what have I done? As a dutiful uncle I've taken her in, let my best physicians tend her and nurse her back to health, and now I'm offerin' her wealth and security. She'll accept it, all right.' His tone softened; he leant across and patted Caleb's hand. 'She's only got to set eyes on you, my handsome boy, and she'll accept, ain't that so, Mather?'

Caleb smirked, and helped himself to more pudding.

Mather coughed. 'With reference to all this, Sir, it really is imperative that we find the girl, Number 102, and deal with her as fast as we can. Members of my team have spent all day at the Gravengate.'

'But no sighting of the barge yet?' said the Protector. He took a generous spoonful of syrup and sucked it, narrow eyes sharp on his Chief Interrogator.

'Not at the Gate itself, no,' said Mather uncomfortably. 'I've taken the liberty of dispatching men further afield. They are searching the wharves on the way up to the Gate. They should report to me at first light tomorrow. The *Redwing* will be found, never fear, My Lord.'

The Protector pushed his pudding bowl away and blotted

his lips again. 'Oh, I don't fear, Mather. Nothing frightens me. You should know that by now.'

'I do know it, Sir,' said Mather quietly.

They looked at each other with cold eyes. It seemed to Chance that the temperature in the room fell by several degrees. 'It is you who frighten others, Mather,' said the Lord Protector with a grim smile. 'That is why I employ you, ain't it? That is why you are my right-hand man. You do so excellent well at it.'

Mather bowed his head and the Protector rose to his feet.

'And now, Mather, let us go tell my niece the good news. Come, Caleb, it's time you set eyes on her. What a day for the dynasty, eh?' He strode to the door, a jaunty swing in his step, then turned. 'You don't need your bodyguard, Mather. He can stay here until we return. Let's not overwhelm my niece in her chamber – give her a chance to have an intimate chat with my son.' He gave a guffaw. 'They can get to know each other, eh?'

As Chance stood and saluted, Caleb pushed by and his heavy military boots ground into his feet. He grinned. 'Sorry, did I step on your poor little toes, bodyguard?'

Then the three of them had left the library, the guards outside had swung the heavy double doors together and Chance and Nate were alone.

Overwhelmed by the fierce bronze glitter of the Eagle statuettes, the grandeur of so many books and the sudden hush, Chance felt he should whisper.

'What in the name of the Eagle was all that about?' he asked Nate.

'Haven't you heard?' said Nate. 'I thought that superior of yours might have told you.' He, too, had lowered his voice. 'The Lord Protector has decided that his son's going to marry Miss Leah.'

'I guessed a bit from what they were sayin',' said Chance defensively. 'How do you know, then?'

'I was in here earlier when the Protector told his son. I've been prescribed for the Protector, you see – by his physicians. He was complaining of gout and they thought music would balance his humours. Any time now I could get thrown out, of course, but I make sure he scarcely notices I'm here. He likes showing me off to visitors – makes him look a man of culture.'

'You mean he's really goin' to marry his precious son off to an avian?' said Chance. 'Thought he hated them like everyone else.'

Nate fiddled with a string on his ratha. The candlelight cast shadows on his open face, making it look suddenly secretive. 'He's changed his mind. Something to do with a prophecy, I think.' He twanged a few melancholy notes. 'Can you imagine a wild, beautiful creature like Leah married to that brute Caleb?' he said softly.

Chance shrugged. 'If she's avian, she's cursed anyway, cursed by the Eagle. Marriage to Caleb is what she deserves.' It was worth saying it to see the shock on Nate's face.

'What do you know about the orphan girl, Number 102?' said Nate, changing the subject abruptly. 'Your Mather and the Protector seem very keen to hunt her down and deal with her – whatever that means – before the marriage. What's her connection with all this?'

'I don't know,' said Chance truthfully. He was about to tell Nate of his own ambitions for capturing Number 102 when it struck him that the Boy Musician was a mite too inquisitive. He gave him a wary glance and shut his mouth again.

But tomorrow he'd put his plan into action. Number 102 – he knew exactly where to start looking for her, after all. He knew the brand on her arm meant she had come from the Gravengate Home. There was a good chance that if she'd left the barge, she would have been reclaimed by now.

He'd go armed, of course. This time he meant to trap her.

7

'You could have knocked me down with a feather when I saw it was you up there on the platform,' Doggett said to me, as she hurried me along through the pools of lamplight. 'Little Scuff that we all thought was dead!'

Mistress Crumplin let out a small scream. 'Pray, Doggett, don't talk of feathers! Blasphemy, girl!' She looked nervously into the shadows and clutched the amulet around her neck. 'It will be the last Curfew bell soon. Hurry!'

I found myself almost glad to see two familiar faces from Murkmere, even though one was my old rival whom I'd never trusted, and the other – housekeeper there until three years ago – my single source of terror and pain in that place. But Mistress Crumplin no longer seemed so fearful now I had grown: indeed, she looked almost ridiculous in her bulky grosgrain skirts and her oversized bonnet. Her face, peering out between the black ribbons, seemed to have shrunk and lost its colour: it had the same peaky, frightened look as all the city's dwellers.

I'd been rescued from a worse fate perhaps, but I was

still returning to the Home where I'd spent two bitter, hungry years.

'You don't say much, girl,' panted Mistress Crumplin, as we hurried along. She pressed a none too clean handkerchief to her nose as we passed a dog's rotting corpse.

'Give her a chance, Dorcas,' said Doggett. 'She's recoverin' from the shock of that slave market. Bein' sold – the shame of it! However did you come to that, Scuff? Good thing we was there lookin' for a servant, weren't it, Dorcas?'

'We'll give you good honest work at the Home,' said Mistress Crumplin. 'Work you're used to – scouring and scrubbing and such. Cleaning up after them little varmints – always vomiting, or wetting theyselves.'

I saw Doggett smile in the lamplight. 'Oh, there's plenty to do. We've not had no spare time before, have we, Dorcas?'

'You're working in the Gravengate Home – both of you?' I faltered.

'Mistress Crumplin – she worked at the Palace for a while when she left Murkmere – didn't you, Dorcas? – for all that it was only six weeks before you got yourself throwed out!' Dog giggled.

Mistress Crumplin straightened her bonnet. 'Mistress Slyde – she's Matron of the Home these past few years – took me on immediate as Housekeeper. There's no disgrace in that. It's an excellent position.'

Doggett nudged me. 'As for me, I told you I was comin' to the Capital, didn't I? I've not been here long, mind – not had time to find meself a husband yet. Dorcas was kind enough to employ me as Assistant Housekeeper, so here I am.'

'What about Aggie?' I said in a low voice. 'How are they faring at Murkmere?'

'Aggie was for ever talkin' about you and all. She was sure you wasn't dead, though she were cold to her aunt a good while after. And Miss Jennet – well, she said she'd not forgive herself if you had gone and died.' Doggett's voice soured. 'I doubt no one misses me.'

'Aggie relied on you, Dog,' I said. 'She must miss you.'

I drew my jacket closer round me. Mistress Crumplin saw the amber stone and her eyes gleamed. 'Why, ain't that Miss Aggie's?'

'She gave it to me.' I did not want to be thought a thief.

'You don't want to be showing off such a jewel in Gravengate, young lady. Attracts all manner of vagrants. Best give it to me for safe-keeping.' She held out her hand eagerly.

I shook my head and pushed the amber down my bodice, out of sight. 'I'll keep it hidden, Mistress Crumplin. I must give it back to Aggie.'

'If we all had amulets like that one,' she said, with a sniff, 'we'd not fear the Night Birds of the Capital, would we, Dog?'

We all jumped as the last Curfew began to toll over the

city; the grimy church we were passing joined in, with a sudden loud clanging from its crooked bell tower. A dark cloud of pigeons flew up around the belfry, disturbed from their roost. Before I could touch the amber, Mistress Crumplin gave me a spiteful prod; her fingers were no less painful than they had been.

'Oh, my, we're late! Come along, girl, do!'

Before us a giant bird rose out of the night sky, its wings outstretched; I saw the shine of its eyes. But it could not fly from its plinth. It was one of the Eagle statues of the Capital that I had so feared as a small child, with their sinister marble eyes that seemed to watch every movement of the people toiling beneath them.

We hurried by, out on the riverfront, where houses of dark, cracked stone leant over the black water. I knew I was near the Home now, for we were walking towards the holding column of the Gravengate and on the far side of the river I could see the great square wheelhouse, its metallic facing engraved with silhouettes of the Birds of Night. From it, the chains that formed the Gravengate would shortly be wound up above the water level to block the further passage of shipping upriver after dark and keep the city secure.

As a child, at first I had watched from the windows of the Home whenever I heard the grinding of the Gravengate's wheel. I saw the chains rise, to lie over the surface of the black water like serpents; weed, rubbish, even grey, bloated corpses caught amongst their rusty coils.

Sometimes the huge links trapped the living, for as the chains were raised, the smaller and flimsier boats tossed in the turbulence, throwing out their human cargo, and the last cries of drowning sailors mingled with the seagulls' wails.

They meant nothing to me: those deaths. I had lived with a dead body in the cellar for three days. But after a time I stopped watching the Gravengate rise from its dark secret bed: there was no novelty in it any longer.

Mistress Slyde was a tall woman in middle-age, with a hard mouth and straight, greying hair drawn back so tightly into a bun that it looked as if it had tugged all kindness from her face. Even in the tallow light I could see her dark clothes were immaculately starched and pressed.

'Is the girl healthy?' she asked Mistress Crumplin, stalking in a wide circle around me. She shot out a hand and pinched my upper arm so painfully I flinched. Her mouth tightened. 'There's some muscle on her, I grant, but is she used to hard work?'

'Oh, yes, Ma'am. I can guarantee it. We all worked hard at Murkmere.' Mistress Crumplin twisted her hands together earnestly, her voice shaking. She was frightened of this woman, I thought, frightened of losing her livelihood in the dark, dangerous city.

'Then find her some clothes,' Mistress Slyde said, as if I wasn't there with the two of them in the dim basement kitchen. Her nostrils twitched as she spoke. 'Discard what she's wearing, burn the lot. And her hair is far too long, and lice-ridden, no doubt. Tomorrow I shall cut it all off.'

Mistress Crumplin bobbed a nervous curtsey. 'I trained this girl at Murkmere myself, Ma'am. You know how hard it is to find staff these days. I can assure you she is a good kitchen maid . . .'

'You may use her in the kitchen, Crumplin. But I wish to use her, too.' Mistress Slyde came closer and, holding a candle to my face, examined me from all angles as if I was a cow at market. 'She hasn't a pleasant expression, I fear – not an amenable girl, for one of her lowly degree. Never mind, hard work should cure her rebellion. If it persists, we'll take her back to market and sell her off. Meanwhile, there's plenty for her to do here. Send her up at eight to help me with the girls' dormitory.'

Mistress Crumplin gave me a stiff black shift to put on over my bodice and drawers, and a pair of yellow stockings. 'You'll wear 'em if you're wise,' she said, as she saw my face. 'They frightens the rats away. We all wear 'em,' and she pulled up her skirts to show me her own lumpy yellow ankles. Then in spite of my protests she carried away my raspberry silk skirt and Shadow's jacket. I managed to rescue Miss Jennet's letter and store it in my box, but I never saw my clothes again.

For the next hour maybe I worked alone in the kitchen, moving awkwardly in my unfamiliar clothes as I scoured pans and washed dishes. As the darkness came down outside, cockroaches ran from beneath the skirting boards, scuttling over the floor and work surfaces. Wherever I trod, I could feel bodies squash beneath my boots. The whole room moved.

Mistress Crumplin was snoring by the fire. She had poured herself a large glass of neat slowfire and drunk three-quarters of it.

'I knows I can rely on you, Scuff, my dear,' she said as she settled herself. 'Like the old days, ain't it? Now, if you're a good girl all will be well for you, but if you ain't – well, Mistress Slyde ain't one to be reckoned with, I'm warnin' you.'

I didn't hear a squeak or sigh from the children. They would have returned from the neighbouring building, where I remembered spinning flax all day. It was as if ghosts inhabited the house above me. But I knew they must be there, for there were so many dishes to clean, and they were so shining I'm sure they had been licked clean by the children, as we used to do. The pans, on the other hand, were encrusted with ancient food, even rust and mould. But I was not surprised; I knew Mistress Crumplin's slovenliness of old.

I must bear this for tonight, I thought. *Tomorrow I'll escape . . .*

Dog was winding the standing clock in the hall. She came back with the key after a while and made a great display of helping me, though I think she was more eager to talk. 'I've not said nothin' to Mistress Crumplin about harbourin' a criminal here, Scuff.'

'You don't believe I'm truly a criminal, Dog, do you?'

'Whether I dos or don't, that don't matter. You help me in the house and that, do my work for me, and I'll help you. I'll not say nothin' if you work hard. But if I find myself gettin' weary, then I shall complain. And I might complain to you, then again I might complain to Mistress Slyde.'

'You know I am a hard worker, Dog.'

'You've escaped them so far, Scuff, you must be lucky, eh? But what if the Militia come knockin' on our door?'

'Why should they think I'm in the Capital?' I asked, but my mouth was dry.

'If they see your arm – Number 102 – that's a giveaway.' She snatched my wrist and I drew it away at once.

'They can't check everyone,' I said. 'There are too many in the Capital. I believe they think I'm dead.' I looked at her. Could I trust her? What if they offered a reward for information?

She gave a hollow laugh. 'You might as well be dead workin' here! I tell you, Scuff . . .' she gave a quick glance at the snoring housekeeper and lowered her voice '. . . that Slyde, she's a right bossy cow, and the pay's nothin' neither. As for you, poor little orphan girl . . .' she looked mock-sad at me '. . . bein' reclaimed, you won't get nothin' to pay your way.'

A bell rang impatiently somewhere above us. Dog gave me a shove towards the door. 'That'll be Slyde wantin' help with the girls, third floor. Her husband sees to the boys at night, top floor.'

'Husband?'

She pulled a face. 'Twin of her, he is. You wouldn't want to meet either of 'em in your worst nightmare.'

The narrow stairs were in darkness, but I needed no candle to feel my way up. Time moved backwards. It was as if I'd never left that smell of mildewed walls, old food and unwashed bodies. Beneath my feet, the bare boards creaked in the same mournful way. I could hear the solemn *tick-tock* of the tall hall clock below me, the slow echoing *tick* of deathwatch beetle in the narrow walls around me, the scratching of mice behind the skirting.

A terrible weight of oppression and helplessness descended on me. I was back and there was no escape.

It was a tall house, and the girls' dormitory on the third floor was the first lighted room I came to. In the yellow glow of the oil lamps Mistress Slyde was walking around the two long rows of low iron bedsteads, her shadow, an elongated stick figure, jerking along the walls. In the beds lay two dozen or more little girls; in some, two or three shared together. Though the shutterless windows were open to the night, there was a smell of sickness and stale urine in the cold room.

As I came in their heads turned towards me, and a thin murmur arose, abruptly cut off when Mistress Slyde beat her long ruler on the floor. The children's hands fluttered on the sparse coverlets like so many trapped birds; their faces were wan and full of fear.

I stepped past the filthy prayer mats and quickly bowed my head to the wooden Eagle head that was fixed to the near wall. 'You wanted me, Mistress Slyde?'

She pointed with her ruler to an empty bed by the door. 'You will sleep there, 102. You can get the children up in the morning, six of the clock. Make sure they say their prayers, lest any should die before evening. They must strip their beds and fasten their clothes properly before breakfast.' She came closer and frowned down at me. 'You will keep good order, 102. Report to me any misdemeanours and the child responsible will be punished. So will you, if I hear too much noise. Understood?'

I nodded dumbly. The children gazed at me, their eyes dull. Someone was whimpering very quietly.

'From seven in the morning until six in the evening they work in the factory close by, spinning flax. You will remember the place, no doubt.'

I bit my lip and again I nodded.

'You will clear the breakfast dishes when they have left, and do their laundry. I will give you further instructions then. Any questions?'

The order of the day hadn't changed since I'd been there. Without thinking I blurted out, 'Do they still get no time to play?'

'One day a year is for play, that is plenty,' snapped Mistress Slyde. She gave me an angry, measuring look. 'There is no time for such trifles. Play only encourages bad behaviour.' She looked round at the rows of beds.

236

'Speaking of bad behaviour, where is the child who was silent at Devotion tonight?'

No one made a sound. Even the coughing and snuffling stopped.

'Where is she?' Mistress Slyde began to go slowly from bed to bed, tapping the ruler against her lanky flank as she stared down at each child. She watched their eyes.

'I thought so! You again!' In triumph she wrenched the coverlet off a cowering child in a threadbare nightgown, and nodded at me brusquely. 'Ring for Crumplin and Doggett. I need more help with this.'

The little girl clasped her arms about her thin chest in a feeble attempt to protect herself; her eyes were terrified, enormous in her starving face. I could see the red bites of bedbugs on her forearms and bare feet. She began to wheeze: there was a sound like the crackle of parchment in her chest.

I went to the door and picked up the bell with a heavy heart. Mistress Crumplin and Dog arrived after some long moments during which no one moved or breathed, and the child's crackling went on and on.

I was sure Mistress Slyde would hit the little girl with the ruler. I felt sick.

'This ungodly child must be pressed,' said Mistress Slyde. 'We must press the wickedness out of her.'

Mistress Crumplin and Doggett went forward eagerly enough. They knew what she meant; it had happened before.

Mistress Crumplin's face was red, her lace cap awry, but Mistress Slyde did not notice; she was too intent on the child's punishment. She had begun to breathe heavily. A hand clasped her amulet. She bowed to the Eagle and muttered something.

The three of them moved very swiftly.

They went to the spare iron bedstead by the door and tugged off the filthy bedding, all but the horsehair mattress. They lifted the bedstead and carried it over to the little girl's bed, where they set it down over her like a prison. The base, with the mattress sagging through, almost touched her frightened face. Then they fetched the bedding – the dirty sheets and coverlets – and draped it so that it all hung down over the sides.

I could see her no more, but I heard the *crump, crump* in her chest.

I thought of the bedbugs running in the darkness around her, crawling on her face, her hair. 'Oh, please,' I cried, and started forward. 'She'll suffocate!'

They ignored me. Instead, they heaved themselves up and sat on the top of the bedstead. They began to drum the heels of their boots against the iron bars. Their combined weight made the bed sink right down on the one beneath.

Its mattress must be pressing against the little girl's face and body, I thought. *She won't be able to move in the darkness and din.*

Mistress Slyde's mouth was a hard line; her eyes had the

gleam of madness in the oil-light. I could not bear to look at Mistress Crumplin and Doggett, so complicit in her cruelty.

I could do nothing, and I hated myself for it. I stood, twisting my hands together, and watched helplessly, while the terrible rhythm of their beating heels went on and on and on.

At last it was over. The two women and Dog had extinguished the oil lamps and left, leaving me with the candle stub.

'Help me!' I whispered to the children. 'We must lift the bed off.'

No one moved. Frightened eyes gazed at me. I could hear no sound from the lower bed.

'Quickly!'

The panic in my voice roused them at last.

It took several of the strongest and biggest girls to help me lift that iron monster off the little child below. Her lips and closed eyelids were tinged blue, but she was breathing, for I could hear the crumple in her chest.

We wrapped her in a blanket and carried her to the window, where the night air was blowing in, damp but mild. I began to rock her in my arms; I held my warm cheek against hers. 'Wake up,' I breathed. 'You're safe now.'

And then I began to sing softly to her, an old nursery rhyme I think it was, about the 'lily-white boys' who are the sweeps' climbing-boys. She opened her eyes, and suddenly smiled, as if she'd gone to heaven.

And so I continued singing, and when I looked around they were all creeping closer to crouch in a circle round me – all the little girls. The smallest one laid her head on my arm.

'Will you sing to us every night?' she asked, at the end of the song.

What could I say? I was too choked to answer; I tried to smile.

'Tell us a story,' whispered the little child in my arms. 'Make it about me.'

I thought a while. Then a story came into my head that the woman in the cellar would tell to me, and this was the bareness of it, without any of the whys and wherefores I put in.

'Once there was a great city, where the people were very unhappy because they worked so hard and didn't have enough to eat. They'd heard of a gate that stood at the entrance to a land of plenty, where everyone had all the food they wanted and were happy for ever. The gate was like a tree, with beautiful golden branches from which amber stones hung like fruit.

'One day they found it, as you do if you look hard enough for something. They began to pass through – all the mothers and fathers and little children – and then they shut the amber gate carefully behind them.

'But one little orphan girl hadn't passed through. She was the last, too small to keep up. She could hear the footsteps of the people fading away beyond the gate, and she wept bitterly. Then she saw that she was small enough to squeeze between the golden branches.'

'So she reached the land of plenty, too?' said the child I held.

'She did, indeed,' I said.

'And that little girl is me,' she said, smiling.

I sang them another song, then I tucked them all into bed. The little girl touched my hand when I came to her. 'There was once an amber gate in the Capital, you know – like the one in your story – but it's lost.'

'Perhaps one day it will be found again too,' I whispered. I stroked the hair from her face. 'What is your name?'

'I don't have one.'

'No more do I.'

She clutched my fingers. 'Will the Eagle forgive me for not saying my prayers? He frightens me. The words stop in my mouth.'

I looked over at the dark head jutting from the wall. 'He's the Almighty,' I said, at a loss. I kept my voice low in case He should hear. 'He's made by man to look frightening to make sure we're good.'

I had to bend my head to hear what she said.

'When I look in His face, there is no love there.'

8

Next morning, after a breakfast of thin oatmeal, Mistress Slyde marched the children out in a sickly troop to the clothing factory. I collected the wet sheets from the beds and took them in a basket down to the kitchen, where Doggett eyed the soaking, stinking pile with satisfaction.

'That was my job before you came,' she remarked.

I had nothing to say to her.

I mixed boiling water with vinegar in a vast pan and put the lot in to soak, pushing them well down beneath the surface with a wooden prod. The kitchen was full of steam. Doggett lounged on the table, swinging her heels while she watched me.

'Where is Mistress Crumplin?' I asked at last, irritated by her idleness.

'Gone to market,' said Doggett. She winked at me through the steam. 'Had a hard time of it, gettin' her up this mornin'.'

I stared at her. 'You're not frightened of her any more, are you, Dog? You were once.'

'Tell you what, Scuff, I despise her now. Why, Miss Jennet was a far finer housekeeper and kept me to the mark. I respected her.'

'You should go back to Murkmere, Dog,' I said. 'Aggie was fond of you, I do believe it.' I added, 'Maybe you will find your heart again there.'

She didn't meet my eyes. 'Mebbe I will,' she muttered, then, 'What about you? Will you stay here a while?'

I stirred the sheets. 'I think so. The children . . .'

She shook her head. 'If you makes 'em love you, you won't be doin' 'em no favours.'

'I can at least protect them!'

She climbed off the table and came over to me, fiddling with the ties of her apron. 'I know what you must think of me. We do things here we'd not do in better places. If I don't do what that cow wants, I'll be out on my ear with not a scathin' to my name.'

'But if we don't stand up to her, nothing will ever get better,' I said. 'We could do it together.'

'And both be thrown out into the streets? I'm not riskin' my position, I'm tellin' you. As for the children, you stop thinkin' of them as human after a while. The drudgery makes you hate 'em in the end. They're such pathetic scraps and there's always more where they come from, like insects.'

'I was like them once,' I said quietly.

Doggett stared at me and had opened her mouth to speak when a knocking sounded above us. She frowned.

'Tradesman. Always comin' to the front door instead of goin' round the back. I'll go up.'

I caught her arm. 'It may be soldiers, Dog!'

'Nah, why should they think you're here – you said it yourself.'

She had gone. I stood in the middle of the kitchen, chewing my lip.

But it was Shadow she brought back down with her, Shadow with Mister Plush in his arms, like a baleful velvet cushion.

'This rapscallion says he wants you.' She glared at him suspiciously.

Shadow was unabashed, but I could see he was in a state of agitation that was nothing to do with her. He was jittering about from foot to foot, brimful of something, ready to burst with it.

I looked at him bitterly. 'I know him, Dog. He must have followed me here last night. I thought of him as a friend, till he helped in the selling of me.'

'Mr Butley made me, Miss!' said Shadow earnestly, his most innocent expression on his face. 'He threatened me with the ship's lash if I didn't. If he finds out I'm here, I'll get it, sure enough. That's why I must be quick.'

Doggett brought her face down to his. 'Spit it out then, you little varmint. Stop clutterin' up our kitchen.'

'There are two men lookin' for you, Miss Scuff!'

Immediately a cold hand seized hold of my heart.

'Men?'

'I've come to warn you. They came at first light this morning and asked to see the skipper, Mr Butley. He told 'em he'd seen the number on your arm. It's you they're lookin' for, certain sure. They said immediate about searchin' the Orphans' Homes – I was there, listenin' in. I knew you were here, 'cos I'd followed you, but I said nothing. My lips was stuck fast together. I said I knew nothin', that you was a good woman and a good cook. That whatever you'd done couldn't 'ave been so very wicked.' He looked at me expectantly.

'Thank you, Shadow,' I said faintly.

'I wanted to protect you, see? You must leave now, hide someplace.' He looked up at me wide-eyed through his matted hair. The cat in his arms stared at me, too, unblinking. 'You are my friend, Miss. I said so, didn't I?'

'And you're mine, Shadow.' He stuck out his hand and I did the same, and we clapped our palms together in our old salute, much to the cat's displeasure. Then Dog bustled them both away before I had a chance to say goodbye.

She rushed back down again, seconds later, to find me staring abstractedly at nothing. 'What are you doin' dreamin'?' she shouted at me. 'Move yourself! Get out of here!'

I started, and stared at her. 'But it was you who told the soldiers at Murkmere about me. Why are you protecting me now?'

She had the grace to look ashamed. 'I didn't do nothin' the second time, and I said nothin' when the first lot came back after you'd gone. Anyhow, now I'm givin' you the chance to go, and I won't tell, honest. This time I'm not thinkin' of me own advantage. You're a good girl, Scuff, and always have been, so go. You've more wit in you than you had – you'll survive.'

And then the knocking came again.

They didn't bother with waiting to see Mistress Slyde. They allowed Dog upstairs to fetch my bag, but made her give it to them. They took me straight out then, leaving Dog gabbling by the front door. 'She's innocent of everythin', a good girl!'

The clock behind us chimed a doleful midday as the two men marched me out of the dark hall into the drizzle. I didn't look at their faces, but I did notice they were not armed. Why should they be? They were big, strong. They didn't hurt me; they had no cause, for I walked docile between them and didn't protest. There was no use.

We didn't go far: through the crowded back street behind the warehouses on the river – the long one that is called the Cut – past the stalls of fishmongers and butchers. The men, dressed in the dark jerkins and breeches that many soldiers wear when not on ceremonial duty, stuck either side of me and I made no move to escape. There were no thoughts in my head, only a dreadful feeling that my doom had finally caught me up and there was nothing I could do about it.

We were still in Gravengate because every now and then

I saw the great wheelhouse across the water as we passed an opening on to the riverfront. The tide was out and there was mud under the jetties; seagulls wheeled over our heads.

'In here,' said one of the soldiers. They guided me towards the back door of a tavern that stood on the edge of a black canal.

'Here?' I said, confused.

For answer they pushed me inside, urgently but not ungently. Then they crowded in behind me and shut the door.

We were in some sort of lobby at the back of the building. From behind a door facing us came the deep roughness of male voices and the clash of pewter; the air was thick with the stale smell of stingoe, the peppered beer. A dilapidated flight of stairs led upwards.

One of the soldiers nudged my back. 'Up you go.'

There was only one flight. At the top was a landing with two closed doors. The man behind me pushed me forward and opened one of them, keeping hold of my arm as he led me inside. Then suddenly, bewilderingly, he let me go; the door was slammed behind me and I heard the key turn in the lock on the other side. They were still somewhere near – perhaps in the next room; there was the sound of voices raised in argument, but I couldn't make out what was being said.

The room was small, furnished only with a pallet on the floor and a couple of shabby chairs. The floorboards were littered with old stubs of nero leaf rolls and stained orange with the dried spittle of mastigris. A cracked window looked out on to the canal below. A single swan had appeared, sailing along on the black water. It looked so pure, in the filth of the city.

But what Significance could it have for me now? I thought; and if I'd not been so frightened I would have cried for my lost hopes. I had no chance of True Love now, or use for any Messenger. I could only wait to hear my fate.

My heart beat faster. Footsteps were approaching the door. The key turned in the lock and the two men came in, filling the tiny room. I was still at the window and I pressed against it, my heart in my throat.

'My name is Titus Molde.' The first man spoke abruptly. He was in his early thirties perhaps, well-built, meaty; his jerkin strained across his chest. Beneath it he carried a slight paunch, surprising in a soldier. He looked me all over. 'We'll not hurt you. Sit down.'

I had to sit down anyway, for my legs were trembling.

He sat down too, although the chair protested. Closer, he had a blunt face and frown marks engraved on his forehead. Like all soldiers, his bright gold hair was cut almost to his scalp: a prickly crown. He did not look pleasant.

The other man stood with his arms folded across his chest. He was youngish also, lantern-jawed, with dust-coloured hair.

'You have led us a merry dance,' said Titus Molde. 'All

the way from Murkmere. It seems we have succeeded in finding you at last. But I need to check a few details. Show me your arm.'

It was a brusque command, not to be disobeyed. I held out my arm, the one with the brand, for I knew that was what he wanted to see. He leant closer; he smelled of sweat, like raw onions. He gripped my forearm in his calloused fingers and turned it over to study the scar.

'Number 102 and the Gravengate symbol.' He drew in a breath of satisfaction. 'See, Flint?'

The other man peered closer and nodded. 'You were right. She's the one.' He looked at me in a sort of awe, as if one so young could yet do something so wicked.

'Better make double sure,' said Titus Molde. He nodded at the bag on the floor. 'Have a look in there, Flint. See if there's anything to identify her.'

My precious mahogany box was brought out and opened. Flint squinted inside. 'Toiletries. A comb, soap. Ah, this looks more like it.' He brought Miss Jennet's letter out and passed it across.

Titus Molde broke the seal and scanned it swiftly. 'We already know this girl was at Murkmere. So – she can cook, she can clean, she can sing too. No relevant information.' He turned to me and his eyes raked my face. 'Tell me, do you remember your name?'

'Scuff, Sir,' I faltered. 'That's what they called me at Murkmere.'

'You were purchased at the Gravengate Orphans' Home

by the late steward of Murkmere, Silas Seed. Is that correct?'

I nodded.

'Do you remember being called by any other name before that?'

I shook my head.

'Do you remember where you were before you were in the Home?' He was impatient and having difficulty keeping his voice hushed; it was by nature loud and domineering.

'I was still in the Capital,' I said. 'We lived in a cellar below the streets, Sir.'

'We? Who was with you?'

'A woman. She looked after me. She told me . . .' my voice trembled ' . . to call her Mother.'

The two men exchanged glances.

'What happened to her?' said Titus Molde.

'She died. I was hungry. I went above, and that was the day they caught me for the Orphans' Home.'

His face was grim. 'But before the cellar?'

I shook my head again. I was puzzled that he didn't ask about my crime. 'I don't remember,' I whispered.

'Is the number enough to convince them, Flint?' Titus Molde stood up and began to stride around restlessly in the cramped space, going from window to door and back again, and all the while staring at me. The reek of onions grew stronger.

The other man stood back, staring at me also. 'They'll take your word for it, Titus.'

'I don't think so. There's too much to prove, too much riding on it.'

Titus Molde came back and sat down.

'I want you to tell me everything, anything you can remember.' He sounded as if he would not stand for any waste of words.

My mouth was very dry. 'I committed a crime, Sir, as you know. I do admit it. It was a long time ago.'

A quick look passed between the two men.

'Recount it, then,' said Titus Molde impatiently. 'It may help.'

I wrung my hands together. 'I know I committed a terrible blasphemy. I was young, Sir, and very hungry, that's all I can say in my defence.'

'Stop havering, and tell us.'

And so I confessed everything.

9

That evening Titus Molde ordered some food and candles from the tavern below, and he and Flint took them in to the girl, Number 102. She was crouched on the pallet in the fading light, and started as they came in.

Flint lit a candle and stuck it on a platter. The girl took no notice of the bread and meat, but snatched up the cup of watered wine and gulped it down.

Titus Molde examined her critically, kneeling beside her and bringing the candle so close she flinched, though she did not move away. He wasn't aware of how he must appear to her by the same flickering light: a burly young man in the sweat-stained jerkin he'd stolen from a soldier, no pity in his face and the light of madness in his eyes.

She was a pretty girl beneath the dirt, he thought, though too small and scrawny for his own taste. She had her mother's striking dark blue eyes, her father's nut-brown hair. She would inspire awe in his group when he chose to show her. She had the blood of the legendary leader Robert Fane in her veins: she might be a brave girl. She was what he, Titus Molde, needed to become the next leader of the rebels, the man who would one day take command of the country. He would use her to advance his own ambitions. Hadn't his voices told him to do so?

Titus Molde had been listening to the voices in his head for a while now.

Even before Robert Fane's death they would whisper to him how he, Titus Molde, would make an even greater leader. When Robert Fane died, the voices rose in such a buzz of excitement that Molde had to shake his head to clear it. They had chosen him, they were saying; they would help him. Now was his chance.

Titus Molde told no one about his voices, not even Jed Flint. If he did, they might go away and help someone else.

Since the girl had confessed her 'crime' to him earlier that afternoon, the voices had suggested an extraordinary idea to him – an idea which, if it worked, would open the way to his taking over the rebel leadership without opposition.

'Listen to me carefully,' he said to her, trying to keep his voice calm though excitement filled him. 'You have confessed to me and you know your punishment is most like to be the death penalty. Stealing from the Almighty Himself is the most heinous crime of all, punishable by death.'

She gazed at him with eyes that were filled with despair and said nothing. It helped that she seemed to assume he and Jed Flint were soldiers.

'If I said to you I had the power to grant you life and freedom on one condition and would do so if you fulfilled it, what would you say?'

She looked at him in astonishment and frowned, as if she did not believe him. Jed Flint stirred, raising his eyebrows in question at Molde, who ignored him.

He repeated, 'What would you say to that condition?'

She croaked out, 'Why, yes. I'd say yes.'

He paused to shake his head, then took a deep breath. 'You would have to stay here for a few days until I'd made arrangements. You'd have all you needed – food and warm clothing – and I would ensure you were safe in the meantime.'

She looked around her. 'Here?' she faltered.

'It is the safest place for you. It would be a secret agreement between us. Only my trusted colleague Jed Flint here will know.' He watched her carefully. Excitement burned like a fever in his blood. He had to speak loudly above the voices. 'Do you still say yes?'

She nodded again, large-eyed.

He did not want to frighten her immediately, so he smiled; he did not know he had a brutal mouth. 'You do not know what the condition is yet.'

She shook her head, fervently, as if she did not care – as if it did not matter to her and she would do whatever was asked of her. She appeared increasingly amazed – confused – and that was good. Lucky for him again that she had spent so much time in a cellar and was easily duped.

'You will swear on the Divine Book?' he said.

For a moment she seemed anxious. He waited, regarding her face without compassion. *So young and smooth, so innocent*. Then, as he knew she would, she nodded, as if swearing on the sacred scriptures was reassuring to her and could not involve her in anything wrong.

Flint, looking bemused, brought in a leather-bound book from the other room, where it was often used for the swearing-in of new members to the cause. The girl put her hand on it and said in a tiny voice, 'I swear.'

'Good,' said Titus Molde. 'And now I shall tell you what you must do.'

'Holy Wings, Titus, what have you made her agree to?' said Flint, in admiration and horror.

It was a short time later, and he and Titus Molde had left the tavern and were returning to their lodgings in the meanest and cheapest part of the city – among the summer plague pits. They kept to the shadows along the riverfront, in the direction of the Gravengate. It would be dark soon, and dangerous for Titus Molde of all men to be out after Curfew in case he was discovered by the Capital's Lawmen, commonly known as the Enforcers.

The two men moved quietly past the deserted warehouses, their heads together, talking low, while they smoked their nero leaf rolls. The entwining wreaths of smoke behind them dissolved almost immediately into the damp air.

Molde's boot sank into a deep pool of mud and he pulled it free with a curse. But inside he was jubilant, still simmering with excitement. He wondered how far he could trust his old ally, Jed Flint, or whether he would have to kill him in the end to ensure his secrecy. The voices would advise him.

'That girl's the figurehead that could draw the splits amongst us together, Jed,' he said. 'She could unite the rebel factions all over the country – with my help, of course. She needs to prove to our own men that she possesses the legendary courage of her father. Then they'll accept her. The other group in the Capital, the old guard in Seacoal Lane, won't have any choice. We'll ride roughshod over them. It will be her and me together, and they'll have to agree to it. They won't get her unless they accept me – for leader.'

'I'll back you in anything, Titus, as you know, but this is profoundly risky,' said Flint carefully. He looked at his leader's face in the dusk, but through the nero leaf smoke could only see his eyes glittering with dreams of the future. Sometimes he wondered if Titus Molde was going mad. 'We've found her, yes, but to deliver her straight into the wolves' lair . . .?'

'The only risky part is getting her into the Palace,' said Molde. He inhaled deeply and blew smoke out through his nose. He needed to relax. He could feel his whole body tensing itself for action that would not come for a while yet.

'We've never had anyone in the Palace before,' said Jed Flint.

'The Messenger – he gets in all the time, doesn't he?' Molde said dismissively.

Flint stared at Molde with incredulity. 'But murder – assassination! Using Robert Fane's daughter to kill the Lord Protector's son! The Messenger will be appalled by the plan.'

Molde rounded on Flint in the shadows and caught him by the collar of his jerkin. 'He won't know! You won't say anything to him when he returns to the Capital, you understand?'

'Right! I understand right enough, Titus,' spluttered Flint. Molde released him and he found he was trembling. 'You know you can trust me. Haven't I given you my support all these years?' He straightened his collar reproachfully. 'When do you propose to tell our men we have her? Before the Seacoal Lane lot get to hear, I take it?'

'I'm not telling them,' said Molde shortly.

'What? You mean you'll keep her secret?'

'No one else must know any of this,' said Molde heavily. 'Not yet, not until she's killed the boy. If she fails, they may not accept her. Besides, it's too dangerous. If it gets out, the three of us could die: the girl, you and me.'

'The girl's likely to die anyway, isn't she?'

Molde gave a short laugh. 'If she succeeds once she's in the Palace, then it won't much matter. Good for me if she doesn't die, good for our cause either way – that's how I see it. The assassination will put an end to the Protector's dynastic ambitions and throw the whole of the Ministration into a frenzy of horror and confusion.' He rubbed his hands together. 'Then while the Protector is in deep mourning for his dear son, the rebels will strike and I will lead them!'

'You think the girl will pull it off?' said Flint. 'Succeed in killing Caleb, I mean? She's scarcely more than a child and seems so innocent of worldly ways, so gullible. Hardly surprising, I suppose, given those years she spent protected by the woman in the cellar.'

Titus Molde blew out a ring of nero leaf smoke and watched it curl up towards the holding column of the Gate. They were now almost opposite the wheelhouse on the far side, close enough to the opening to see between the dripping chains into the wheelroom itself, where the slumped, resting figures of the turning-men were silhouetted against the burning lamplight. On the facing around the outside walls the engravings of the Birds of Night were silvered by the rising moon, wings raised, bills stretched forth to strike.

Molde was not afraid of the Night Birds: he admired their cunning and ruthlessness. He knew his voices did, too.

'She'll kill Caleb,' he said. 'Unless the Palace guards kill her first.'

10

I was so terrified, I would have said yes to anything.

A simple little word that would make me a murderess, but save my life. But which of us was worth saving for the other – Caleb Grouted or me? Was one life ever worth more than another?

Shut up in that tiny room I had time to regret what I'd said a million times. But I had sworn to kill Caleb on the sacred texts. If I broke my oath I would be damned.

I was trapped.

I didn't have the courage to ask why Titus Molde wanted Caleb – a fellow soldier and son of the Lord Protector – dead. Some kind of military rivalry, I thought. I must have sensed Molde was ambitious; I knew he was dangerous.

As the days went by, marked by the tolling of the Curfew bells morning and night, I tried to pray. My knees grew red from kneeling. Sometimes tears would run down my face and I couldn't stop them. I knew there was no escape, either from that room or from what lay ahead of me. My task, Titus Molde called it.

The tavern keeper's wife brought me food and drink and emptied my chamber pot, but she never spoke to me, merely looked frightened when I tried to speak to her. I thought that she must have been forbidden to do so by the soldiers, Molde and Flint.

Molde came to visit, while Flint lurked by the door. The visits were brief, as if he merely wanted to check I was still alive; and he was brusque. If I asked a question he would brush it aside as a problem of little consequence.

'How will I get near Caleb?'

'I'll tell you when the time comes.'

'How will I get into the Militia's headquarters? Will you take me in, Sir?' I had a picture in my mind of him marching me in as a prisoner and then releasing me secretly in order for me to carry out my task. By now I had imagined it many times.

He stared at me irritably and then shook his head as if a gnat whined round it. 'Caleb isn't at the headquarters any longer. He's on long leave, in his father's Palace.'

'The Palace of the Protectorate?' The picture jolted.

'We'll plan to get you in there. Caleb's about to get married, to Leah Tunstall of Murkmere – as soon as she agrees.' He glanced at Flint by the door. 'The Protector's working on her.'

'Won't be long, then,' said Flint, with a grin that stretched his lips.

I'd taken in but one thing. 'Miss Leah is in the Palace?' I stammered, staring at them both. 'But she'll remember me from Murkmere most surely.'

'The girl has a point, Titus,' said Flint.

Molde shrugged impatiently. 'We'll disguise her, if necessary. It's not a problem.'

Early on the morning of the second day, Molde came alone, when I was walking around the little room, stiff after lying on the pallet. The bells for the raising of the night's Curfew had rung only recently.

He pressed something cold into my hand.

'Get used to the feel of this,' he said. 'It's what you'll use. I want it to become part of you.'

I looked down. It was a dagger.

I would stand at the window for hours, fingering the handle of the dagger, hoping to see the single swan gliding below me. If I saw it, it would be a symbol of hope to me, of redemption. But it did not appear again.

On the morning of the third day both men came together. Flint was awkwardly carrying a bundle of clothes, which he flung down on the pallet.

'You're to have a bath this morning,' said Molde. 'The woman downstairs will take you into the kitchen and stay with you. Flint will be outside the door so don't try anything. Then you must dress yourself in these garments.'

He held up a dress between his finger and thumb. It

was made from coarse dark red wool and had long tight sleeves. On the pallet were other garments: a bodice, petticoats, white stockings, a black shawl. A pair of wide kid boots. And a black felt hat with a half veil.

Molde saw my eyes widen at the veil. 'You'll wear the hat as well this afternoon,' he said. 'And thereafter. You caught the plague last summer but recovered. The pustules left bad marks on your forehead so you veil yourself.' He came closer and looked down at me. 'That is your story. Repeat it to me.'

I did so, my voice trembling.

'And you must never lift the veil, you understand? On no account must they see your eyes.'

I nodded, bewildered.

'The dress should fit you well enough.'

'Whose is it, Sir?' I faltered.

His face hardened. 'That doesn't concern you. She is dead now. She was of a similar height and build. You must never, ever, roll up the sleeves, of course – never show your scar – in case someone sees it and realizes you are from a Home. That would jeopardize your task. You'll find the boots wide enough to hold the dagger.' He looked at me meaningfully.

'I'm making arrangements to get you into the Palace. Never forget that I'll be waiting for you to carry out your task.'

I shook my head.

'This will be your last morning here. When I return this

afternoon I'll be bringing a visitor with me. Be dressed and ready. Do you understand?'

I nodded. 'I am to go, then?' I stammered, unable to believe that freedom lay ahead at last.

Titus Molde glanced back at me as he left, and nodded. 'The little songbird shall fly her cage.'

He was a blasphemous man.

II

I had to have a bath under the curious eyes of the tavern keeper's wife. I knew Flint was outside and would come into the steam-filled kitchen on the slightest provocation, so I dared not complain. I washed with the dried-out chip of soap she had handed me and tried to pretend she wasn't there. Afterwards, I dried myself as best I could on a rough woollen cloth that was already none too clean, and dressed in the clothes of the dead woman.

The skirts of the dress were a little long, and the boots a little big, but I was used to that. I had worn second-hand shoes all my life: my toes were bent and curled from them. In any case, I was glad to be rid of the black shift and yellow stockings at last.

In the stuffiness of my room my hair soon dried. The last two days had been warmer; the heat in the little room would grow unbearable with the coming of summer.

I combed my hair with the tortoiseshell comb and tied it back with one of the faded ribbons. I put on the hat and veil and pulled them well down, then I looked at myself in the mirror from the box. Many women in the Capital wore veils to hide their wrinkles, so I would not look too out of place. It felt odd to have the scratchy net against my forehead and beneath it my face looked strange to me, too: peaky and apprehensive, my eyes robbed of colour.

I put the comb and mirror back in the box, on top of the reference from Miss Jennet. Last of all, I slipped the dagger in its sheath down the inside of my right-hand boot. It was a short, straight dagger; I could feel it there, like a splint. I waited, and my heart seemed to beat out each second heavily in my ears.

I heard the key turn in the lock on the other side of the door. Flint opened it and stood aside so that his visitor could enter.

He was a boy, a little older than me, and well dressed in a jacket and waistcoat of fine green wool, his ruffled shirt open at the neck to show an amulet of green jasper stone, his curly hair shiny and clean. He looked exceeding wary, but he had an honest face. He was certainly not a soldier; I couldn't tell who he was. He was carrying a ratha, cradling it, I should say, as if it was the most precious thing on this earth to him; and the wood had a glow to it as if it was loved.

He stared at me, and then at the room in all its shabbiness and squalor. 'Why is she locked up?'

'For her own protection, Master Kester,' said Titus Molde. He'd put on a solicitous deference quite unlike his usual dominant manner. 'We don't trust the landlord here. The Saggy Bottle tavern is frequented by a rough sort. We thought it safest to lock her in and keep the key. She's not been in the Capital more than a few days. I knew her father and like to take care of her, don't I, Mr Flint?'

By the door Flint nodded. 'He's a good guardian, Master Kester, the best.'

Such lies! I almost choked. I looked imploringly at the boy, but he couldn't see my eyes. *Take me away.*

He stared at me again, uneasily. 'She can sing, you say? I'd like to judge her voice for myself.'

Molde jerked his head at me. 'Go on then, girl, show the young gentleman you can sing.'

'Now?' I had no desire to sing in this dreadful place, which had been my prison.

Molde frowned at me warningly; my heart sank.

'Please, Miss,' said the boy. I thought I saw sympathy in his expressive face, some understanding. He gave a half smile of encouragement. Titus Molde sat down on a chair and folded his arms; Flint stood in the doorway, watchful.

And so I did my best for the boy, though my voice was thick and trembled. There was not enough air in the room. I sang 'I Left My Love by the Amber Gate'. After I had sung a verse or two I faltered to a stop. 'I remember no more, Sir.'

The boy was looking exceeding interested. 'That's an old song, is it not, Miss? What do you know of the Amber Gate?'

Caleb Grouted had asked the self-same question at Madam Anora's. 'Nothing much, Sir,' I said hesitantly. 'No man knows whether there is such a thing or no. I heard the song as a child.'

'Don't we all wish we could find the Amber Gate?' said Titus Molde, winking at the boy. 'Wealth beyond dreams, eh, Master Kester?'

'But it has some sacred importance, hasn't it, Sir?' said the boy, and frowned. 'If there is indeed such a thing, it shouldn't be desecrated.' He turned and regarded me gravely. 'I'll take you on, Miss. I can tell you have a sweet, soprano voice, which will improve with practice and good food.'

'Your master will approve, you think?' said Titus Molde.

The boy laughed then, and covered it with his hand. 'My master's not musical, Sir. It is his guests who will appreciate her singing. But her songs may soothe his temper and therefore be good for his health.'

The two soldiers glanced at each other. 'He's unwell, Master Kester?' said Titus Molde solicitously.

'His physicians fear for his choler from time to time. They prescribe the playing of music to calm him. That's why I'm there.' The boy smiled ruefully. 'But though I play music, I sing like a saw on wood. That's why I was so fortunate to meet you and hear about . . .' He gestured at me. 'What is your name?'

I hesitated. 'In my last employment they called me Scuff,' I whispered. 'It's a kind of silly nickname, Sir.'

The boy held out his hand. 'Nate, please, not Sir.' He shook my hand in a warm, friendly way. 'You know your master is to be the Lord Protector?' I nodded. 'Come, bring your things and we'll go.'

He gestured down at the bag that contained my box. I picked it up, but he took it from me courteously and slung it over his shoulder, all the while moving to the door as if he could not wait to get away; as, indeed, no less could I.

'Thank you for your introduction,' he said to Molde and blushed. 'I'm afraid I've nothing to reward you with – no money in my pockets.' He gestured at his clothes. 'It's all show, I'm afraid. My master provides these fine garments so I don't disgrace him.'

Titus Molde smiled, and clapped him on the back so that he almost fell. 'Master Kester, I need no reward for helping my dearest friend's daughter! Good luck to you.' Then he patted my hand in an affectionate-seeming gesture. 'And I'll look forward to hearing of your progress in the Palace, child.'

He stared at me with narrowed eyes as he said those last words, as if to make sure I understood that I'd never be truly free until I'd done what he asked of me. Both men watched silently as I followed Nate Kester down the stairs, almost tripping over my long skirts in my hurry.

All the time, deep in my boot, I could feel the dagger unyielding against my ankle.

The Palace

I

There is a dark shadow that hangs over every child in the Capital. It is the shadow of wings.

In the streets, ravens and kites peck and scatter the heaps of stinking refuse, filling the air with their harsh tumult. By the river, the gulls cry forlornly, swooping low over the masts of ships at dock. On every street corner, there are the soot-blackened statues of the Great Eagle on their plinths.

That afternoon when I emerged at last from the Saggy Bottle tavern with Master Nate Kester, the chains of the Gravengate had been wound up across the river. Above the lethal net of links the sun flickered on the metal facing of the wheelhouse so that the engravings of the Night Birds seemed to move. I could almost hear their foul screeching and cawing.

Panicked, I pushed at my veil, forgetting why I wore it. I was in a stranger's clothes. *Who was I?*

Nate Kester looked at me in concern. 'Are you faint? We've a long walk ahead.'

I shook my head. 'It's nothing.'

'Perhaps you are anxious about working at the Palace,' he said kindly. 'My father was Keeper of the Keys to the Capital and worked in the Palace all his life, so I suppose I'm used to it.' He made a wry face. 'I've been Boy Musician several years now. In return I get my keep, as will you.'

We were walking along the riverfront, passing large houses, each with its own gilded water gate. Gulls flashed and wheeled above the oily shingle and squabbled among the muck and weed. The sun was hot on my back, holding the threat of summer, the return of the Miasma.

'I've only a reference, no identification papers,' I faltered.

'So your guardian said. Stolen from you your first night.' Nate shook his head, watching me. The ratha under his arm gleamed in the yellow sunlight. 'The pick-pockets are appalling in the Capital.'

I was sure he didn't believe the story. 'How will I get through without them?' I said, nervous. 'Will they search me?'

'I've briefed one of the guards, a friend of mine. He's on duty in the security office today.' Nate smiled; he had an open, engaging smile. He'd have many friends.

He stared at me. 'If you removed your hat and veil, it would give you more air.'

I pressed my hat down more firmly, worried he might take it from me himself, he looked so concerned. 'I have terrible scars – on my forehead, you know – from the Miasma. Last summer, it was.'

Now he looked at me in astonishment and respect. 'You survived the Miasma? You must have a strong constitution.'

'Like an ox,' I assured him.

'Strange. You look so fragile. There's no telling, is there?' He peered closer. 'You were lucky not to be scarred on your cheeks and chest. They are still – perfectly smooth.'

'Tell me how you heard about my singing,' I said quickly.

'I was in a tavern not far from the Palace.' He blushed again. 'It's a respectable place, I do assure you – the Dancing Bear. I go there from time to time and I suppose people know I play a bit. Someone asked for a tune, so I obliged.' He stroked his ratha. 'Then one of those men with you asked for a song. I explained I'd no voice for singing, and we fell into conversation. It ended with him offering me the opportunity to hear his own little "songbird". I was curious, I suppose.' He hesitated. 'When I saw you, I knew I had to rescue you, however ill you sang.'

'Rescue me?'

'You looked so distressed. Something wasn't right. That room – locking you in like a prisoner . . . They kidnapped you, didn't they?'

I shook my head.

He sighed. 'You look frightened again. At least they didn't try to sell you. Did they harm you in any way?'

I tried to keep my voice steady. 'They did nothing to hurt me.'

We walked on in silence. We had left the river and the

tall brick houses that we passed now had once been elegant, but had fallen into disrepair and ruin long ago. Their marble front steps were chipped and broken; the wrought-iron railings and imposing porches broken or hidden by thick fronds of ivy. On one balcony a woman in a tattered silk dress, grubby wig perched askew on her head, tried to hang sacking over a broken window.

It was difficult to breathe beneath my veil. I felt dizzy with heat.

Nate looked at me. 'Why don't we break our journey at the Cathedral? It's close by. We can rest there.'

We walked across a square of cherry trees towards the great West entrance.

I have been here before – once, long ago.

Wings of stone grew out from the walls of the Cathedral and threw shadows at our feet. Above us rose a magnificence of gables and pinnacles and long columns. The windows were decorated with stone tracery as delicate as lace; the spire dazzled like silver in the sun, and in the ribbing live ravens perched as motionless as the stone birds around them. I looked up and clutched my amber, then I saw that Nate was not afraid.

On all sides of us people streamed over the grass.

'This Protector has little time for churchgoing,' said Nate. 'But my father told me that in the old days the Protectors used the Cathedral on great religious occasions. They always had the Ceremony of Anointment there, and state weddings and funerals. It's falling into ruin now, but there's still some kind of folk memory that brings the people here from all over the city.'

Prayer mats were spread out beneath the pale pink cherry trees. I lingered longingly by the religious icons displayed for sale, for they were such pretty things: the five Birds of Light, each intricately carved in wood, and stone eggs painted to represent the World Egg.

'Come,' said Nate, looking warily around. 'There are thieves about here.'

I'd noticed a tiny wrinkled man staring at us from beneath a tree where a stack of Legend sheets were displayed. When I looked back next he was nowhere, had vanished into one of the shadowy alleyways off the square, perhaps. There'd been something strange about him: he'd not been dressed in rags, but feathers.

Nate steered me beneath an arched gable; the stone was crumbling, the doors long rotted. I touched the stone as I went through, feeling the cold strike my fingertips. I remembered the feeling of the carved grooves in the stone, the feeling that the place was entering me through my flesh and bones.

We stood in the nave. All around us in the central aisle men and women with careworn faces murmured their prayers, their desires and fears rising up into the high vaulted roof with the ravens that flew in through the open entrance. The sun glowed through the colours of the stained-glass windows, so that it seemed the kneeling figures had been sprinkled with rose petals. They looked in supplication towards the stone statue of the Great Eagle on the altar while their small round-eyed children perched on the edges of pews like rows of starlings.

We sat down in an empty pew. I was glad when Nate moved a little way from me. I closed my eyes and felt the Cathedral breathing its chill breath all around me.

This is where I committed my crime.

That morning long ago I'd managed to escape from the Home before we left for the weaving factory. Finally, I must have wandered into the square. It was early, the Cathedral almost empty.

But someone saw me as I ran away afterwards, my mouth covered with blood, the lump of undigested sacrifice heavy in my belly – the Bird-Scarer, who is employed by the vergers to wave the ravens away from the sacrificial meat. He pointed at me; he had a loud, accusing voice and I was frightened. The ravens flew up in a black, croaking cloud.

I ran and ran, all the way back to the Home. It was the only place I knew. They whipped me. They didn't know what I had done, only that I had given them the slip that morning. Then I was sick over their boots.

I had nightmares for weeks afterwards. *Krak-krak-krak.*

I'd dropped my handkerchief in the Cathedral. It had my number sewn into it. Number 102.

* * *

When I opened my eyes I saw there was a different Bird-Scarer now up in the chancel by the altar, a gangling youth with a pockmarked face. He looked scared to death himself as he flapped the big black birds away from the meat.

A voice in my ear said, 'Little one,' so suddenly, I thought it was in my head. 'Little one!'

Bright eyes crinkled at me from a wrinkled, walnut face.

'Who are you?' I stammered, drawing back in alarm. To my horror, a little claw-like hand tried to lift my veil.

Nate slid along. 'Don't bother the young lady, Gobchick,' he hissed sternly.

'Aye – Gobchick,' said the tiny man sadly. His eyes were ageless, but his face was old and pitifully thin: the grooved skin clung to the bones of his cheeks.

'Go away,' repeated Nate. 'Leave us alone.'

'I don't believe he intends any harm,' I said.

'Gentle,' nodded the old man. 'Gentle Gobchick, my Master's Fool.' A single tear rolled from his eye. 'Cast out,' he mourned. 'Cast out! Time for laughter gone.' His feathered costume was worn and tattered, the colours faded by sun and run together by rain.

'We've no money,' I said softly. 'We can't help you.'

'Don't need money. You're my little one.'

'You're mistaken,' I whispered. 'I don't know you.'

He clutched my sleeve again. 'Come with me, little one! Come, see Gobchick's place.' He clasped his brown palms together then put them to his gaunt cheek to mime sleep. 'Master should have asked me, his Gobchick. Gobchick knows about the Amber Gate.' He put his head on one side like a bird, and his eyes slid away.

'The Amber Gate?'

He nodded fervently. A smile lit his face. He stroked my hand, although I tried to draw it away. 'Gobchick show. You come with me, little one.'

'He used to be the Protector's Fool,' whispered Nate. 'He's cracked in the head these days. He must have taken a fancy to you. Come on, we'll leave.'

'He says he knows about the Amber Gate.' The name seemed suddenly strangely enticing to me. But now I could not even remember the words of the song I'd sung.

The man had curled his small, hard hand around mine and was pulling at me with surprising strength, so that I found myself rising. I heard Nate grumble as he slid out of the pew after us. Gobchick capered and chattered like a small child, giving little beckoning gestures to draw me on down a side aisle, past candlelit chapels to the Birds of Light. Behind, Nate kept his head bent, as if embarrassed to be seen in such company.

But no one saw us, no one looked up from praying or moved their gaze from the Great Eagle; no one saw when Gobchick slipped behind the altar screen.

But then he chittered in alarm. There were men working beyond us in the gloom of the apse: stonemasons, with mallets and pickaxes. I could see a huge pile of broken stone under an arch that was supported by wooden props. Closer, two were sitting around an oil lantern in a pool of yellow light, eating bread and passing a flagon between them. As we hesitated, they saw us, stood up and suddenly a soldier stepped out from the shadows between two stone piers. I shrank back against Nate. He was armed with a rifle.

'Apologies, young Sir,' he said, with grudging respect as he took in Nate's fine clothes. 'Can't go no further. Lord Protector's orders.'

'Our mistake,' Nate muttered.

'Exit through West door only, meantime. I'll accompany you, if you don't mind.'

There was no sign of Gobchick's darting shadow; the sight of the soldier had frightened him away. Nate and I were hurried through the Cathedral. When we looked back we could see the soldier standing under the arched entrance, looking after us.

I could see Nate was flustered and cross; my own heart was thudding with dismay. 'You shouldn't have followed Gobchick,' he said. 'He only wanted to show you his den.'

'Den?' I said breathlessly.

'He sleeps somewhere in the Cathedral.'

'I'm sorry, Nate,' I said, and added hesitantly, 'It's only that – I've always had a curiosity about the Amber Gate.'

'He's cracked, I tell you,' Nate said. 'He can know nothing.' In the sunlight his face was full of fear. 'Things have a way of getting back to the Protector. I don't want to be reported for spying. If he thinks you're the enemy, he doesn't wait for you to prove it.' He drew his hand across his throat, meaningfully.

I felt a sudden pain in my boot. The sheath of the dagger had slipped and jammed against my ankle bone. And I'd never finished praying for forgiveness.

2

Nate felt an overwhelming sense of relief when the girl had been cleared by Palace Security and they could both leave the building that housed the administration offices of the Protectorate.

Bathed in the afternoon sun and covered with the golden-pink buds of honeysuckle, it did not look in the least sinister. But cunningly hidden behind the high, dark green firs at the end of the Palace gardens was another building: the recently built Interrogation Centre.

It was well known that the Lord Protector had become paranoid about security. Last autumn, the rebels in the south had managed to join up with those in the Capital, and lead a mob down the Central Parade almost to the gates of the Palace, before they were routed and most of them slain. Since then, even the recent death of the great rebel leader, Robert Fane, on the Eastern Edge, had not allayed the Protector's fears of secret attack.

Bernard the guard had waived the need for any identification papers; he merely made a quick show of examining the girl's reference and then stamped a pass with the Protector's initials beneath an Eagle's head. He handed the pass over, with a grin and a wink for Nate, and gestured that she was free to go through.

He thinks we're courting, thought Nate, blushing with embarrassment.

He led the girl across courtyard after courtyard: past the great Council Chambers, where an ornate stone fountain shot streams of shining water high into the air; past the Offices of the Ministration, bordered with neat, freshly tilled flowerbeds; past the orangeries and ice houses. Next, the formidable domestic quarters that housed the entire force of Palace staff, down to the under-scullery maid, the gardener in charge of weeding, and the boy who fed special titbits to the swans on the Palace lake.

All the time Nate watched the girl covertly.

She had the most beautiful singing voice he had ever heard, even though it came out from under the dreadfully unflattering veil. He thought of what they could achieve together when members of the Ministration or foreign dignitaries were entertained at the Palace; how they would be celebrated for their concerts, her pure, high voice complementing to perfection the haunting notes of his ratha.

'What is *that*?' The girl's voice was trembling.

Nate was jolted from a delightful reverie of acclaim. The clapping died abruptly in his ears as he realized where they were.

The courtyard through which they were passing was overlooked by a tower at each corner, and from the top of one of these towers a large gilded cage hung from a pulley. A bedraggled girl crouched inside the cage, glaring defiantly through the bars at a small group of spectators below: Palace staff who had come to goggle and jeer. The girl's fair hair stuck to her scalp; her clothes were limp and crumpled, as if they and their owner had been out in all weathers.

Nate's heart twisted. 'She is Miss Leah Tunstall, the Protector's niece. The cage is – a punishment.'

The girl looked appalled, as well she might. 'Miss Leah,' she whispered oddly. 'Why is she being punished?'

'She refuses to marry the Protector's son, Caleb Grouted,' said Nate, and added, under his breath, 'So would I, if I were in her position.'

'But those people – don't they know who she is?'

'No doubt, but they also know it's rumoured she's one of the avia. They insult her because they are frightened. There's always a crowd staring up at her, as if they expect her to turn into a bird any moment.' Nate gave a small smile. 'But she gives as good as she gets. Sometimes she's emptied her piss-pot out on them.'

'But the Protector can't keep her outside for ever! She'll die!' Her veil shifted as she turned to him. Her eyes were huge and accusing – as if he were responsible – and they were an unusual dark blue.

'He cages her in it as long as he dares,' he said. 'A couple of days and nights at a time, then he brings her in. He's trying to wear her down, so she'll agree in the end.'

Even as Nate spoke, there was a flurry the other side of the courtyard and the Protector himself strode across, followed swiftly by several members of the Ministration in their dour black Council robes. They had emerged from a meeting in the Chambers and looked grim and purposeful as they glided behind him, their long robes swishing over the cobbles. The goggling group of Palace staff turned and fled as soon as they saw them, their faces apprehensive. They knew they would be in trouble for leaving their work.

Among the gloomy, black-garbed throng, two figures in dark grey uniform stood out. Nate recognized them: the Protector's Chief Interrogation Officer and advisor, Mather, and Mather's personal bodyguard, Corporal Chance.

Chance carried a black leather case. He looked down at it every now and then as if to check it was still safely closed, his narrow face intent and nervous above the stiff grey collar.

Mather stepped in front of the members of the Ministration and went to the Protector's side. He said something to him in a low voice and beckoned to Chance. The three of them came to a halt under the cage, not far from Nate and the girl.

She hid behind him. *She's terrified*, Nate thought, *and no wonder, poor thing!*

It was a bad time to introduce her, yet he knew he would have to do so. Nothing ever escaped the Lord Protector's lizard-like eyes: they flicked all about him, watching for any lapses in security. There was no way he and the girl, Scuff, could go back the way they had come without being seen. It was best to stay where they were.

But the Protector had not yet noticed them: he was intent on Leah. The two men muttered together; the members of the Ministration stood in a black huddle.

Leah watched the debate beneath her ironically, her pale face pressed to the bars of the cage. Suddenly, as if bored by the lot of them, she yelled down, 'Leave me alone! Go away!'

A hail of stale bread rolls began hitting the ground around the group, some finding their targets and smacking the black hats off the heads of the Ministration, bouncing off their shoulders and paunches.

The members of the Ministration began to retreat in an unseemly muddle, clutching noses and heads. The Lord Protector did not move.

'Leah, my dear!' he called up mildly. 'I wish to end this as much as you. You've only to say the word, one little word – "yes" – then you'll be free.'

'Free!' Leah retorted. 'Bloody Wings! I'll tell you what I think of your "freedom"! I think it pukes, it craps, it . . .' and she shouted out a string of swear-words so horrible that even Mather looked a little startled. The Ministration moved even further away, raising eyebrows as they murmured 'Blasphemy?' at each other, then nodded solemnly in agreement.

'Leah,' called the Protector again, his tone reasonable. 'I see you've not lost your spirit, girl, but this has gone on too long. I've a little proposition that will ensure your own release. What do you say to a bargain bein' struck between us, eh?'

Leah paused in the act of tilting a bowl of cold soup. 'What bargain?' she yelled down suspiciously.

'I've somethin' you want. Your precious swanskin.'

Leah put the bowl down.

The Lord Protector beckoned to Chance. Chance opened the leather case and the Protector took out what was inside and held it up for Leah to see.

There was utter silence, as if a spell had been cast: in the courtyard of the four towers no one moved or spoke. In the sunlight the swanskin was a pure creamy-white, the tips of the feathers gleaming as if dipped in pearl dust.

'Your swanskin,' called the Lord Protector. His voice echoed through the silent courtyard. 'Thought you'd like a glimpse of it. You can have more. You can have it back again, yours for the keepin'.'

Leah reached her thin white arms through the bars. Her shout throbbed with passion. 'How? When?'

'Marry my son, my handsome Caleb. You can have it back on your weddin' day.'

There was a long pause.

'Before, or after the wedding?' Leah said at last.

The Protector gave a little chuckle. 'Well, after, of course, once you've taken the vows of marriage. You might go flyin' off if you had it before!'

'You swear?'

The Protector nodded.

'I'll choose the oath, then,' said Leah slowly. 'You agree?'

'Whatever you wish, my girl.' The Protector shot a look of triumph at Mather. Nate thought: *Oaths mean nothing to the Lord Protector. He believes in nothing but himself.*

'You are to swear on your Anointment Rite that you'll give it to me,' shouted Leah. 'If you break the oath, you lose the authority to be Lord Protector of this land.' It sounded like a curse.

'I swear,' said the Protector easily. He held up his right hand. 'I swear on my Anointment Rite.' He touched the swanskin. 'If I don't give this back to you, Niece, I forfeit my Protectorship. Now you – you swear, girl.'

Leah's voice was unsteady. 'On my mother's swanskin I agree to marry Caleb Grouted, son of the Lord Protector.'

'Good.' The Protector clapped his hands together, smiling around. His eye caught Nate's, and then registered the girl beyond him. Nate saw him note her, pass on.

'Ministers!' the Protector shouted. 'I have great good news! An engagement is announced between Miss Leah Tunstall, my beloved niece, and my own dear son, Caleb. I shall hold a Council Meeting immediately after luncheon to discuss the weddin' plans.' He gestured at the guards standing to attention on either side of the entrance to the tower. 'You! See that Miss Leah is freed and that her maids attend her.'

The guards disappeared, in a rush to do his bidding. A low, shocked hubbub arose among the Ministration on the far side of the courtyard. They clustered together in a tight knot of horror, some shaking their heads surreptitiously. The Lord Protector ignored their reaction. Not waiting to see the cage that imprisoned his niece hauled in safely, he swept triumphantly away, with Mather at his side. His path led him directly past Nate.

'So, Boy Musician, are you going to tell me who your companion is?' he growled, staring at the girl, who quickly bobbed a terrified curtsey.

'A singer, My Lord,' stuttered Nate. 'She has the most exquisite voice, I do assure you, Sir. She will sing for you, Sir – accompany me when I play.'

'Did I ask for a singer?'

'Er, not exactly, Sir. But you've often complained that *I* don't sing. You've said you prefer singing to the sound of the ratha.'

'If she drowns you out, that will be something.' The Protector peered closer at the girl, trying to look beneath the veil. 'She can give me something rousin', can she? None of your plaints and moans?'

To Nate's surprise, the girl suddenly spoke in a nervous but clear voice. 'I can sing japes, chorus songs, ditties and frolics, Sir, if those are what please you.'

'Excellent.' The Protector was evidently in a good

humour and willing to allow for Nate's audacity in employing the girl without permission. 'Security's cleared her?' He glanced at Mather, who stiffened like a wolf scenting prey.

'Yes, Sir.' Nate produced the pass hastily.

'Excellent,' repeated the Lord Protector. 'Who knows, we may even have her singin' at the weddin'.' He strode off, smiling to himself, with Mather following.

Tagging behind his commanding officer, Chance looked over at Nate and then at the girl. Nate saw his eyes narrow. For a second he hesitated, then he hurried on.

The Lord Protector enjoyed a cigar filled with finest-ground nero before going to the Chambers for the start of the Council meeting. The early afternoon was too warm for a fire, and he lounged in the leather armchair before the empty grate, his muscular legs in satin breeches splayed comfortably apart, squinting at the smoke as it drifted in curls through the sunbeams.

Opposite him sat Mather, who had refused both cigar and after-luncheon brandy, and had a pile of Council papers on his knees. Chance hovered behind him, not listening to the conversation. His legs ached, he was sweating in the heat of the room and sick with frustration and fury.

Over the past few days he had been mulling over and over in his mind how he'd been too late arriving at the Orphans' Home in Gravengate, how that stupid hussy who'd opened the door to him had said, 'My, another soldier!'

What soldier or soldiers had got there before him and arrested her? Had they been sent on Mather's orders? He had heard nothing. Yet if he asked Mather, it would show up his own incompetence.

Mather's dry voice broke through his churning thoughts.

'Have you thought where the marriage service will take place, My Lord?'

The Protector's eyes glinted. 'We shall have it in the Cathedral, Mather, where else? The Amber Gate crypt must be on show – that's the whole point. The guests must see the ceiling.'

'Clearing the remains of the blockage and work on the steps may well take another couple of months, My Lord.'

'I scarcely think we'll be prepared for such a great occasion in *under* two months, man!' The Protector sipped his brandy and licked his lips. 'The Cathedral façade must be cleaned, new doors fitted at the West entrance. No one must be able to get in – or out – until the service is over.'

'You refer to Miss Leah?'

'Particularly Leah. I don't want her doin' a last-minute flit. But it's also the rebels I'm thinkin' about – keepin' 'em out, providin' proper security for our guests.'

Mather cleared his throat. 'Speaking of guests, Sir, how do you think the Ministration will take this betrothal?'

'No need to be delicate, Mather. You saw their faces. But they'll accept it, they'll have no choice. I shall quash any quibbles personally. Besides, once they hear about the prophecy, they'll see which side their bread is buttered. They'll be imprisoned for treachery if they don't.'

Mather plucked at his papers. 'The weather is growing warmer, Sir. If we have a heat wave again this summer, the Miasma will rise over the Gravendyke and the canals of the Capital and we'll have plague stalking our streets.'

Porter Grouted shrugged. 'So? We'll be in covered carriages, we'll not catch it ourselves.'

'The foreign dignitaries will keep away.'

'Let 'em. Makes your job easier, don't it?' Chance saw the Protector smile evilly at his right-hand man; his pate glowed in the sunlight like smooth, tanned hide.

Mather pursed his lips. 'It will cost, Sir – shall we be able to raise yet more credit? You need ready money, I fear.'

'Taxes will have to be raised, that's all,' said the Protector impatiently. 'I'll tell the Treasury fellows at the Council meetin' this afternoon. We can't touch the Amber Gate yet.'

Mather was expert at interrogating tax-dodgers. Chance could not see his face but he knew that his expression would be one of cold calculation mixed with secret pleasure.

'I believe there is no tax yet on property, Sir. You could investigate that possibility with the Ministration treasury. There are many dwellings in the Capital, slums or no . . .'

'An excellent idea, Mather.' The Protector drained the

balloon glass and put it down. 'To Council, then. And first of the celebrations, Mather, will be an official pre-nuptial reception to introduce my son and his young wife-to-be to the members of the Ministration – a small supper dance, I think.'

He popped a freshening lozenge into his mouth and leapt to his feet, thoroughly invigorated by his discussion. 'The Boy Musician can play his wretched instrument, and that pretty young chit he's brought in can sing. I'll get him to compose somethin' special for the occasion – what do you say, Mather?'

Chance hurried behind his master and the Lord Protector. *Always hurrying*, he thought to himself resentfully. *Always at someone else's beck and call – no chance of glory*.

The sunlit courtyard outside the building that housed the Council Chambers was full of activity. Members of the Ministration in the long black Council robes and white wigs, their hats under their arms, were scurrying across or stood talking in small groups outside the pillared entrance of the building. When they saw the Lord Protector, they stood aside respectfully for him to enter.

The Protector paused, and spoke in an undertone to a tall young man standing in the shadow of a pillar. Chance knew who he was. He was the mysterious, secretive person they called the Messenger; he had spotted him a few times himself, slipping through the Palace buildings and courtyards.

Grouted's voice carried easily to Chance's sharp ears. 'You're givin' us your latest report, ain't you, my boy? You've already heard the news, I take it? You wouldn't be any good at your job if you hadn't.'

'The engagement between Miss Leah Tunstall and your son?' The Messenger stepped from the shadows and his fair hair caught the light. 'Congratulations, My Lord. You must be very pleased.'

'Oh, I am, my boy, I am.' The Protector winked at Mather. 'It will secure the longevity of my line.'

'Indeed, My Lord?' the Messenger said politely.

In great good humour, the Protector tucked his brawny arm in its silken sleeve into the young man's. 'I'll shortly be makin' a special announcement to the Ministration, but I don't see why I shouldn't tell you first – eh, Mather?'

Heads bent in conversation, the three of them entered the Council Chambers together.

Chance knew he must remain outside with the guards. Sulkily, he kicked at a loose pebble. That was what he wanted – to have that sort of recognition and esteem. To be like the Messenger, whoever he was. Now that would bring power all right.

3

'We must rehearse,' Nate said to me. 'Let's amaze them at the supper dance with our music-making!'

He shook his head over my untrained voice. He made me do breathing exercises every day and sing scales before we began rehearsing the song cycle that he had written himself with much labour and head-scratching. He tried to teach me to read the squiggles on his sheets of music, but I was a poor scholar. He had to lead me through it himself in his gruff, growling voice and play the notes for me to copy.

I could understand why he'd never sung in company.

Once, at the end of a long day in the music room, he put his head in his hands. 'What's the matter?' I said anxiously. 'Is it my singing?'

'It's not you, Scuff,' he muttered. 'Never you. I can only strive to write music that is halfway worthy of your voice.'

'What is it then?' I said, concerned, for it wasn't like him to be low.

He lifted his head and his face was bitter, quite unlike

the cheerful, enthusiastic boy I thought I knew. 'It's him! He owns my soul and doesn't value it!'

I was shocked by his talk of souls. 'You mean – the Protector?' I said in a low voice, for I didn't think our elderly chaperone, drowsing over her tapestry stitching in the corner of the room, should hear. 'But he's the Lord's Anointed, isn't he? The Lord Protector, Nate – doesn't he have a right to our souls if anyone does?'

'No one does,' whispered Nate, quick and fierce. 'Not any man, least of all him. Haven't you seen the poverty and misery in our streets? And that's surely echoed in the country. I hate him, Scuff, not merely because he has no music in his heart, but because of what he is. He sent my father, who was Keeper of the Keys, to his death. He ordered him – an elderly man – into the plague-ridden streets to lock up all the public buildings. He was forced to drive out the homeless sick sheltering inside and it broke his heart. Soon afterwards, he died of the Miasma himself.'

'I am so sorry, Nate,' I whispered back, appalled. 'But why do you work here if you feel this way?'

He dropped his head back into his hands. 'The truth is, I'm the most contemptible coward, Scuff!'

'How so?' I was taken aback by his misery.

'If I were brave, I'd leave – escape. Or I'd have confronted the Protector when he ill-treated Miss Leah, his own niece. And now he's arranged this marriage for her – to his son who is a deranged animal – and I can do nothing, only compose music in its honour! There's terrible irony in that, don't you think?'

I had a sudden understanding. *He loves her, and he knows it is hopeless.* I touched his hand gently.

'Listen, Nate. If you are a coward, then so am I. You are braver than you think: that is what someone said to me once, and I say it to you. The time may come when you have to make a brave choice.'

He ran his hand through his curls so that they stuck out wildly. 'I'm trapped here, Scuff. There will be no choice. It's a livelihood, and, God knows, it's hard enough to survive in the Capital. I could never find another position where I was allowed to play music all day.'

And play he did, sometimes like someone possessed. Day after day, as the weather grew warmer, we rehearsed in his rooms in the Palace. Outside, blossom drifted from the trees and tender green shoots curled open. Grass sprouted in the square in the courtyard, was cut and grew again. Flowers pricked through the neatly hoed beds and opened out in frills of pink, white and yellow. Sometimes ravens would fly down and strut through them, crushing their petals into the earth.

Nate would be cross when I wandered over to the window. 'We'll never succeed unless you concentrate, Scuff.'

'I'm sorry,' I said meekly. 'It's only that summer's coming and I long to be outside.'

'You won't soon,' he said gloomily, 'not when the Miasma comes. This place becomes a fortress then.'

Indeed, the Palace already felt like a fortress to me – reassuringly so. I felt secure, for although I could not get out, nor could Titus Molde reach me.

I'd been given a stuffy bedchamber, with a tiny wig closet. It was outside Nate's apartment, a maid's chamber, but Nate had no maid. I'd been presented with a set of garments more appropriate for my new position than the old red dress I'd arrived in; but though I wore the fine dresses and undergarments, I didn't wear the slippers. I kept on my veiled hat and my wide, too-large boots, and most horribly hot they were.

At night I took the dagger from my boot and slid it under my pillow. Sometimes I'd creep with it into the wig closet and curl up in the darkness among the mouldering wigs on their stands. It made me feel safer – as if I were back in the cellar long ago – but I still couldn't sleep for worrying how I'd ever arrange to be alone with Caleb and fulfil my task. I'd not come across him yet, for he had his own grand set of rooms next to the Protector's.

One day when sweat was prickling under my hat and I was trying not to yawn through my singing, there was a knock on the door of the music room. A guard stuck his head in.

'Miss Leah wishes to attend your rehearsal, Master Nate.'

Nate went white with shock. He nodded curtly.

My heart sank. I tugged the veil down and bent my head as I stood at the music stand; my hands clenched themselves into anxious balls. But why should Leah recognize me after three years? She would never expect to find the little kitchen maid from Murkmere here at the Palace. Most important of all, she didn't know I could sing.

Miss Leah swept in and the chaperone drew out a velvet chair for her to sit on, in the corner of the room.

I looked across at Leah from under my veil. Although her silver-fair hair was dressed with ribbons and shone like glass, her yellow dress did not suit her pale complexion. She was shockingly thin and looked unhappy; her eyes had dark rings beneath them as if she could not sleep for weeping. She clenched and unclenched her hands in her lap. Yet I remembered that fierce gaze, those dark grey eyes that could destroy a strong man in seconds, or so it had seemed to me once. Surely her spirit hadn't died?

'Sing something to cheer me,' ordered Miss Leah. She arranged herself in the chair, large feet sticking out from beneath the taffeta skirts, her back very straight. 'That's what I long for. I am bored, so bored. Give me something merry. Remind me of happiness. It is possible it still exists, somewhere?'

Nate went pink to the roots of his hair. 'Er, the song cycle we're rehearsing is reasonably merry, Miss Leah.'

'Is it religious?' she demanded.

'Why, yes, it is,' he said eagerly. 'It tells of the first great wedding in the celestial skies, between the Robin and the Wren. "All's Right in the Heavens", it's called.'

She made an impatient movement of her hand. 'If it's the tosh you've been asked to compose for the supper dance, then think again. Give me something that speaks of . . .' she thought a moment '. . . of sap rising, earth warming, waters beckoning. You must have something in your repertoire?'

Nate shook his head, crestfallen. He appealed to me. 'Do you know anything that might please Miss Leah?'

I saw her tight face, her desperation. I sensed his wounded pride, his desire to please her above everything. I found myself nodding.

I began to sing, 'When the Sweet Curlew Calls O'er the Marshland'.

She relaxed. A tiny smile plucked at her lips. She began to tap one of her large feet.

'I remember that song,' she said, when it was over. 'I thought it was only sung on the Eastern Edge. I'd never expected to hear it in the Capital.' She looked keenly at me. 'You have a pretty voice, girl. I might come again.' She smiled graciously at Nate. 'With your permission, Boy Musician? I should like to hear more of your ratha playing too, of course.'

Nate blushed again, and gave a funny little bow.

'Incidentally,' she said to him, as if she had only then remembered it, 'I believe my uncle, my dear father-in-law-to-be, wishes to see you at once to discuss your composition for the supper dance.'

Then she went out, with the chaperone fluttering beside her and the guards leaping to attention. Nate left too, almost running, in her wake. I breathed a huge sigh of relief; I was alone in the room. I stretched my arms; flexed my fingers; twirled, carefree.

And she was there right beside me at the music stand, noiseless in her slippers, looking down on me, for she was a tall girl.

'Show me your music,' she said sweetly.

I bent my head and passed the music over. My hand holding the sheet of parchment was quivering.

But she had not recognized me. She took the music without another glance at me. 'I see I've left my wrap on the chair over there,' she said vaguely. 'I should take it back with me. Fetch it for me, would you?' She looked down at the music.

I was glad to leave her. I went across to the chair, picked the wrap up and brought it back. I made to move away, but she grasped my wrist.

I gasped and looked at her. With a shock, I saw her eyes were full of tears.

'Scuff? It is you, isn't it?'

I nodded; there was no point in doing anything else.

'Scuff!' For a moment it seemed she could not say anything. She shook her head, as if bemused.

'I thought it might be you,' she said at last, 'and when you fetched my wrap, I knew so at once. The way you walked – your boots are still too large!' Her laugh turned into a sob. She pulled out a lace handkerchief and blew her nose. 'I want to know how you got here – everything – and there is no time!'

'Will you give me away now?' I said, in a low voice.

She stared at me in amazement. To my own wonder I saw that tears still stood in her eyes. 'Give you away?'

'Don't tell anyone I'm from Murkmere, I beg you.'

'I see – you've come to rescue me!' She looked about her wildly in sudden hope, as if expecting a hidden band of heroes to leap out from nowhere and carry us both to freedom.

I shook my head and her face fell. 'I am here quite by accident, Miss Leah,' I said gently. 'Or not exactly accident, but . . .'

'You are here to take news of me back to Aggie? I long to see her, Scuff, I even long to see Murkmere.' She flung her hands out hopelessly. 'Marry Caleb! That's my fate now.'

'It may not be,' I said quietly. 'Don't despair, Miss Leah. Don't give in.'

She looked at me with tragic eyes, and a sudden hysterical laugh came from her. 'You've changed, little Scuff, you know that? And I never knew you could sing!'

'If you don't give away that you know me,' I whispered, 'I may be able to help you.'

She was startled; she opened her mouth to speak. And then we could say nothing more, for the guards came running in with disgruntled faces, having searched various apartments for her. Then Nate returned, too, unnerved by his curt ejection from the Lord Protector's chambers and wondering if Miss Leah might possibly have been mistaken . . .

* * *

Leah came again to our rehearsals.

Nate was flattered but flustered by her visits, and didn't play his best. He tried to look at her at the same time and his fingers fumbled over the ratha strings. His face went very pink; I could see sweat beading his forehead.

Leah sat listening silently, and although we could never talk, our eyes would meet across the polished floor. She looked feverish sometimes, with a glitter in her dark grey eyes as she tried not to fidget on the velvet chair. I knew she was waiting – hoping – for some sort of sign from me. She'd no notion of what it was I was planning.

Sometimes I would see the Lord Protector's son, Caleb, walking through the courtyard, deliberately making the ravens fly up around his head. Once he brought his musket and fired it at them, laughing like a maniac through the white smoke. He must have forgotten that ravens signify Death.

Soon you will be my victim, I thought, as the sound echoed round and round outside, striking off the walls and vibrating against our windows, *and I will be a murderess*. But I would have my life, my freedom, back.

I thought of Erland then, and an ache went through me; there was a hopeless longing in my heart as spring turned into summer.

Sometimes I'd see the Chief Interrogation Officer, Mather, and the young bodyguard, Corporal Chance, hurry through on their way to see the Lord Protector, and

I'd have to dodge back so they couldn't see me. *I am living on borrowed time*, I thought, as each morning I slipped the dagger down between my ankle and the soft kid of my boot.

It grew warmer still. Outside, the fresh green leaves turned dusty, the grass yellowed. I opened the windows wide and the air that came in was tepid. I often gazed out of the windows when I sang, for by now I knew the words and notes of Nate's composition by heart.

And that was how I saw him.

I knew him immediately. He was walking quickly across the paving of the courtyard, the fair, flopping hair on his forehead lifting as he moved. He wore a black silk cloak that flowed from his shoulders. I must have stopped singing, or gasped perhaps, for Nate looked up frowning.

'What ails you, Scuff?'

I felt dizzy. My heart seemed to stop, then start again with a great rush of heat.

I clutched the music stand. 'Who is that?' I asked weakly, my voice coming from a long way off.

Nate looked over at the window. 'He's called the Messenger. I've seen him about in the Palace.'

Erland had almost gone from my sight, round the corner of the building opposite. I found it difficult to breathe. I wanted to run out after him, but my limbs would not move. 'Why is he here?'

Nate shrugged. 'I've no notion. What's your interest in him?' He looked at me curiously.

I pulled myself together. 'Nothing,' I faltered. 'For a moment he reminded me of someone I knew once.' I put a hand to my forehead. 'It's very hot in here. Shall we stop for a little while?'

'Of course.' Nate pulled out Leah's chair at once, and I sat down gratefully. He fussed around me, contrite. 'I'm to blame. I've been obsessed with this wretched piece – I've worked you too hard.'

I shook my head speechlessly.

'Rest there, I'll fetch you water.' He went off in a rush, looking worried. He would be thinking of the supper dance so soon – tomorrow – and of the calamity if his singer were ill.

I wasn't ill; I was filled with such joy I wanted to dwell on it without distraction.

Erland, here in the Palace! It could only mean that he had been following me all this time, had managed to trace me here without being discovered himself, would rescue me before I was forced to fulfil my murderous task.

I only had to wait and he would find a way to reach me, I was sure of that.

Erland, my faithful love.

4

Late in the afternoon before the supper dance, the chaperone brought in the new clothes I was to wear: a simple silk gown in soft sage-green, high-necked and long-sleeved, as I had requested; a small matching hat covered with tiny rosebuds, swathed with a veil; cream silk slippers.

She tried to take my old black felt hat from me and sucked her teeth when I would not let her have it. 'I'm ashamed to show my scars,' I said.

She gave me a sharp look. 'In my time I've seen everything, Miss. I've even seen those suffering from the Miasma. The pustules usually appear in the armpit and groin.'

'I was lucky. Perhaps that's why I survived.' I sent a quick apology heavenwards for my lie.

Later, I dressed alone in my chamber, trembling with anticipation as I pinned my hair up beneath the little hat and pulled the veil down so it hid my eyes. The dress had been made to my measurements. It was the first to fit me properly; the first that had not been passed on to me, though I could not call it truly mine. I dropped the amber stone down safe beneath the bodice.

I gazed at my reflection in the little mirror from my box: my face scarcely visible, mysterious, unfamiliar. Who would guess that my heart was bursting with hope?

All day I had been waiting for Erland to seek me out. I did not understand by what miracle he was there in the Palace, and yet I knew it had been him I'd seen. He must have planned my rescue – he must!

'Why aren't you wearing your new slippers?' asked Nate, when he came to fetch me and saw them beneath a chair. He was very fine himself, in a silk jacket that matched my green dress and with his curls subdued by water.

'They are uncomfortable.' I sent up another prayer. 'My boots don't show, do they?'

'They are quite hidden. Indeed . . .' he added with a gallant effort '. . . the whole of you looks uncommon pretty.'

'And you look quite the gentleman.'

'You think so?' I could see he meant: *Will Leah think so?* He was in a fidget, his mind elsewhere: on Miss Leah or his music or, possibly, his stomach. His cheeks had a green tinge, as if he were about to be sick.

'I hate performances,' he hissed to me, as we left the apartment and set off down the passage. 'What if they don't like 'All's Right in the Heavens'? It will not please Miss Leah – I'm sure of that – for it is not merry. The Protector won't like it, for it's neither a frippery nor a chorus piece.'

'It has a good melody running through it,' I said, for his face was so glum. 'And you are a wonderful musician.'

'You think so?' he said, a little brighter. 'I wish Miss Leah thought so.'

'I do, and so will others.'

He looked gloomy again. 'We're only the prelude before the quartet takes over and the dancing begins. They'll be too busy drinking and talking to listen to us.'

I prayed they would be, for I wanted to draw as little attention to myself as possible.

The supper dance was to be held in the gardens behind the Protector's chambers. We had been ordered to be there before the guests arrived, for Nate was to play his ratha as they progressed along the path beneath rose-covered arches and on to the main lawn. Later we would perform the song cycle.

My heart was thumping; I forgot all about my task, even about Erland.

'What if my voice dries?' I whispered.

'It won't.' Nate took my hand. Our palms stuck together: we were each as nervous as the other.

It was a windless evening, warm, with a low sun slanting hazily across the lawns and shimmering through the white linen of the pavilions erected on the grass; the light caught the gold emblems of the Eagle that decorated the draped entrances and turned them to fire. Somewhere birds sang, hidden by the thick leaves of summer. The guards with their grim, intent faces and dark uniforms blurred into the shadows between the trees.

Those who were performing the Illustratives were already arranging themselves around the edge of the lawn, and would not move for several hours. They were to represent significant events from the Divine Book: the Laying of the Great Egg, the Battle of the Birds, the Great Betrayal, the Anguish, the First Wedding. There was no Illustrative of the avia story, since it is not included in the accepted scriptures and would have shown little tact on this occasion.

I stared at them, those strange human statues, their bird costumes vivid against the darkening grass, and I saw their eyes blink. A shiver went through me; I touched the amber stone at my breast and looked around for Nate.

I found him in the supper pavilion, absently wandering between the embroidered screens and the couches plumped with silk cushions. Around him fountains sent sprays of shining drops into the scented air; honeysuckle and pale pink clematis twined up the tent poles.

'We shouldn't be here,' I whispered. 'This is for the guests!'

'We're better than any of them, Scuff. Anyway, no one's here yet.' He grabbed a crystal glass, bubbling with a pale yellow liquid, from under the outraged eye of a footman and took an enormous gulp. 'It's the best seccer,' he whispered wickedly, like a naughty child at a grown-ups' feast. 'Try it!'

'I daren't,' I said, and dragged him away.

There was a murmur of voices along the path behind us and we separated quickly, Nate to his ratha playing. I had a last glimpse of his face, greener than ever, as he disappeared beneath the roses. The seccer had been a mistake.

We were to perform on a raised circular stage on the lawn, beneath a delicate, trellised roof covered with white flowers. A footman had begun to light the tiny lamps that hung from it; already moths flickered around the points of light.

I knew where I was to wait: behind an ivory screen that stood on the grass to one side of the stage. Someone had thoughtfully arranged some gilt chairs and music stands here, perhaps for the quartet that was to perform after us. I sank down and tried to breathe calmly.

At first, I could still hear birds singing their evening songs and, very faintly, the plaintive notes of the ratha. I grew calmer.

Soon after, the voices grew louder; there was laughter, some of it very close to where I sat hidden. After a while I risked a look through the fretwork border of the screen. The shadows were longer. Twilight had fallen and the colours glowed against the dark grass: the long shimmering gowns of the ladies, the rich velvet of the gentlemen's jackets. I was looking for Erland, but I didn't expect to see him in this company, for why should he expect to find me here?

And yet he was the first person my eye lit on, walking alone beneath the last rose arch, between the lanterns on the path.

My heart leapt like a fish. He was coming towards the guests on the lawn – towards me.

But then he lingered; he stopped. I saw him bow several times in a most accomplished fashion; he conversed with several people. His hair was unpowdered, but he wore a blue silk frock-coat that looked very elegant. He walked over to the Lord Protector and his son Caleb and Miss Leah, who were standing together to receive the guests. I could not see their faces for their backs were to me, but I saw Erland bow to Miss Leah – they did not speak – but then he bowed to the Lord Protector, and the Lord Protector shook his hand most heartily.

What could it mean? My Erland from the Wasteland on such easy terms with these people?

I sank down on the chair again. I think I put my hands to my face. I was trembling all over.

Shortly after that Nate came around the screen. 'No more time to be nervous, we're on!' He pulled me to my feet, and gave my hands a squeeze. 'Courage, Scuff!'

'I cannot sing,' I whispered.

'The show must always go on. Come, the Protector's about to announce us.'

Somehow he pushed me up on to the stage, up some little steps at the side. Although the lamps had been lit, no one had yet noticed us. I was scarce aware of the crowd of guests drinking and talking as if we didn't exist; their faces were blurred.

Then the Lord Protector stepped up and went to Nate's side. I stood by a marble pedestal that held an urn of pale pink lilies; in the dusk, their fragrance was sickly sweet.

The Lord Protector clapped his hands. Instantly, there was silence. Faces turned, eyes fixed on him. Everyone was looking, now.

I heard the Protector say '. . . great cause to celebrate . . .' '. . . especially composed for this historic occasion . . .' '. . . the Protectorate's very own Composer and Musician . . .' The words in between were lost to me.

And then the slab of his hand landed on my silken shoulder: '. . . and introducin' a new young singer to you all, a little maid who has a big future here in the Palace.'

There was muted applause. The Protector stepped down. Nate sat gingerly on the fragile gilt chair set there for him, and tuned his ratha.

Time seemed to slow. Faces came into focus through the twilight. Leah's white and miserable above her dark grey silk, her hair severely pulled back so that her nose seemed more prominent, her beauty destroyed. I knew she'd done so deliberately. Caleb Grouted, next to her, drinking too heavily, his handsome face flushed beneath his wig. He threw an arm around her shoulders, but she flinched away.

And Erland? I did not look for him.

Halfway through the song cycle the guests began talking. Quietly at first, then louder. I saw Nate's face, and sang my best for him. The cycle ended; there was some desultory applause, people moved into groups and the talking began again, louder than ever. Nate slumped over his music stand and I moved to comfort him.

And then I saw Erland come out of a pavilion, hover on the edge of the lawn, talk to a man whose white wig caught the last of the dying light.

I will make him notice me, I thought.

I opened my mouth and the sound came out by itself. I began to sing 'I Left My Love by the Amber Gate'.

Nate looked up at me startled, and then he began to play softly behind my singing, for he had a gift for picking up melodies when he'd heard them but once. I heard my voice soar, true and sweet, as if it did not belong to me at all, but was a bird, flying through the air, delighting in its freedom. I did not think about the words, but I know they came out right.

The guests were silenced, utterly silenced. And I saw Erland stop talking to his courtier friend and look over at me.

5

I waited, but he did not seek me out.

A footman brought us food and drink behind the screen, while we heard the orchestra tune up for the dancing, which was to take place in the largest pavilion. I tried to cheer Nate, but my own heart was heavy, my thoughts churned.

'Be careful what you sing in public, Scuff,' he said unexpectedly, 'particularly when you sing for the Lord Protector. The ballad you sang about the Amber Gate . . . He might think you know more.'

'But the song's mere fancy, Nate! I was sung it when I was small.'

'The Protector has searched for the Gate in secret for years – to fill his coffers.' Nate spoke bitterly. 'If he thinks you have been sent to spy on him . . .' He stared at me, a question in his eyes.

'What are you saying?' I cried. 'I am no spy!' *I am an assassin.*

'Hush – hush.' He shook his head, his hair no longer neat but springing back into its curls. 'I'm sorry. It is only

that you are so – secretive. You have told me so little.'
Seeing me still disturbed, he added with a wry smile, 'At
least the ballad made them listen, which was more than
my music did.'

'Miss Leah listened to you, I'm sure of that.'

'You think so?'

Silence fell between us, for I could think of nothing more
to say. Beyond us, we could hear muffled farewells as
guests began to leave. We looked through the screen and
saw the Lord Protector leave, with his guards, Mather and
Chance, slipping behind, almost invisible in the night in
their dark grey uniforms. It was still warm; the temperature
had scarce fallen.

Nate said, 'I'm returning to the apartment. Will you
come, Scuff?'

'I'll stay a little,' I said.

He looked anxious, even put out. 'You'll stay without me?'

I felt a spark of anger. 'I'll be safe enough on my own,
Nate. Don't concern yourself. Go.'

He went, but I had no time to feel contrite. *I must find
Erland*, I thought, *since he has not found me.*

I stood up and peered again through the fretwork of the
screen. The lawn was deserted, even the Illustratives
long gone. There was still music coming from the largest
pavilion, where the dancing was taking place; there must
be a few guests remaining in there.

I had no care for my safety; I was determined. I took off
my hat and loosened my hair so that it fell down around

my shoulders. Though younger than most, I might be any guest in my elegant green dress.

I set off across the lawn, the sheathed dagger in my boot pressing into my ankle. My silk skirts swished about my legs, hiding my inappropriate footwear. A cool dampness rose up and touched my skin and there was the smell of cut grass in my nostrils.

The guard at the entrance to the pavilion inclined his head slightly as I walked in past him.

Then as if by magic I was standing in an enchanted forest where the air was filled with sweet music. Above my head, birds perched among the blossom; the night sky was lit by a thousand stars. In a clearing amongst the trees, dancers swayed together.

My heart pounded with shock; I clutched my amber. I put my free hand out to a tree trunk for support. And then, slowly, I realized.

The trees were cunningly made from painted paper and wood; the blossom, from scraps of silk. The starry night sky – so beautiful, so romantic – was painted canvas, covered with netting that held tiny lanterns. Even the clearing with the dancers had a wooden floor; beyond it musicians played, hidden in the trees. The birds perched on the branches would never fly; the eyes looking down on me were sightless.

It made me marvel that one could be so utterly deceived.

There were few guests remaining on the dance floor, and the candles were burning down. In the dimness I could see Caleb slumped upon a rustic bench beneath a cherry tree, his eyes closed, his wig tipping. I couldn't tell if he was asleep but he looked the worse for wear. I looked all about for Erland, but couldn't see him.

Someone moved close to me. At once I turned, but it wasn't Erland. It was Mather's bodyguard, Chance, the boy who had confronted me in Poorgrass. I'd thought him gone with Mather and the Lord Protector. I gazed at him in alarm, unable to move for terror.

But in that place and in the soft darkness between the trees he couldn't know who I was. He hadn't recognized me in my finery. He stared at my dress, my hair. He looked stupid – or crazed – standing before me without speaking; his features thick, his mouth half open. He was breathing fast; he smelled of sweat and seccer. He was standing too close; I thought he'd accost me.

I slid away from his wine-drenched breath, wrinkling my nose; I couldn't help it.

'Wait,' he said, urgently. 'Wait. Will you – would you – dance with me?'

I shook my head for answer, for I dared not speak. I turned my back on him and moved quickly away into the darkest spot I could find. When I looked round he was disappearing through the opening in the pavilion and out into the night.

I didn't move. I waited apprehensively, but he didn't return.

I would wait a moment longer, then leave myself. Erland wasn't here.

And then my gaze was drawn to the couple dancing alone on the floor.

They moved with such perfect grace, I drew in my breath.

They were both tall, slender. Their silks shimmered in the candlelight – cloudy pewter and sky-blue – as they curved and leant into one another, their fair heads close together, their beautiful faces rapt and intent and strangely similar. They gazed into each other's eyes as if no outside force could break their gaze; as if they did not know the outside world existed.

The musicians stopped playing to watch them. Voices trailed away, the few guests remaining stood silent. The only sounds were the soft click of the dancers' shoes, the rustle and sweep of the girl's dress over the floor.

What are you doing, Erland? I cried, in my heart. *You love me, not Leah!*

I was forced to watch; I could not drag my eyes away. I felt such pain I thought I would die there and then.

For I saw now that all along fate had intended them for each other, Erland and Leah. It had always been so. They had been created from the same mould; I had never stood a chance. I would kill Caleb now and then turn the dagger on myself, for my own life was no longer worth living. Everything I'd hoped for – love itself – was lost.

I turned away from the dance floor. I believe I may have begun to move towards Caleb, still asleep on the bench. Behind me I was dimly aware that the music had begun again. Someone passed me; people began to talk again.

I felt a touch on my arm. When I looked around it was to see Leah.

'Stay away from me!' I said, drawing back. A cauldron of emotions churned inside me. I looked at her with a hatred that it was too dark for her to see.

'Keep your voice down,' she whispered. 'Come with me, I beg you.'

Would she take me to Erland? Even then, I had some hope left.

I followed her to a darker corner of the pavilion. We were alone, hidden behind a clump of paper bushes.

'We can't speak long,' she whispered. 'The guards will notice.'

'What do you want?' I snarled, in my pain. 'Have you come to explain?'

'You mean to help me, don't you?' She seemed taken aback at the expression in my voice. 'I wanted to know . . .'

'Why don't you ask Erland to help you?' I hissed.

'Erland?'

There was no mistaking her amazement. 'I know your Erland too,' I whispered, savage.

'But how . . . ?'

'Has he not spoken of me?' I asked, a pathetic twist of hope inside me.

She shook her head; her hair had slipped down from its binding.

'He is a traitor, a two-timer . . .' I began.

She sounded alarmed. 'Don't speak of it . . .'

'I will speak of it!' I spat out. 'He was mine, and is now most surely yours. Look to him for rescue, not me.'

'I can't ask him. It would be impossible. It would endanger his position . . .'

'And what of mine? Why should I risk my own life for you?' A desire to hurt her engulfed me. 'You're avian – disgusting, despicable, *cursed*.' I spat all the words out with a huge, horrible satisfaction, and I saw her step backwards, a pale hand to her throat.

'Scuff? You don't know what you're saying. You don't understand.'

'You think because I am a little servant girl, I don't understand. You think Erland understands? Does he know what you are, Miss Leah?' It was surely not me, saying this with such ferocity?

She came towards me and laid a hand on my sleeve. Her eyes, shining in the dim light, were huge and dark. 'Please, Scuff, say nothing. Not for my sake – for Erland's. Don't betray him. Say nothing of his other life, whatever you do.'

'He will betray you in turn,' I whipped out. 'Why is he here amongst these grand folk? They are corrupt, and so is he. Watch him, Miss Leah.'

She drew herself up. 'You don't know what you're talking about. You understand nothing. Whatever Erland may have meant to you once, you must forget it, here of all places. Don't you see the danger you could put him in?' She stared at me, then added as a muttered afterthought, 'He is too old for you, anyway.'

'Then you are welcome to him,' I said furiously. 'You both deserve each other.' I flung away from her, but she came after me.

'Scuff, don't go, please understand. I've known Erland for such a short time and there's no future for us – everything is hopeless, for I must marry Caleb. I know you cannot help me now, you would not want to.' She paused; her voice shook. 'I give Erland back to you, Scuff, whatever I've taken. He is free for you.'

'But he does not want me now,' I flung at her. 'Not now he has set eyes on you! If I'd stayed longer in the Wasteland, it would have been me!'

It gave me a hollow satisfaction to see her start as I mentioned the Wasteland. She recovered, spread her hands. 'I didn't know you loved him, too.' She lowered her voice even further. 'I know so little of his past – it's scarcely ever safe to talk. Tell me – how did you meet? How does he live – in the Wasteland?'

He called me Silky.

I couldn't speak.

She hesitated, uncertain. 'There's nothing to cry for, Scuff, please stop.'

But then I stumbled away from her, from the pavilion; ran from the black lawns and the impassive guards; from Erland himself wherever he was, the coward and the cheat.

6

Some of the lanterns had burned themselves out. I blundered along the dark path; the white roses either side of me glimmered like ghost flowers. I had only shed one tear, one little tear for myself, and that had quickly dried. I burned with anger.

A guard with an oil lamp loomed in front of me. 'Where are you going, Miss?'

My anger died as if dowsed with cold water and was replaced by fear. I hesitated; for a moment I did not know. I was nothing – nobody – with nowhere to go. Then I stammered, 'My chamber, outside the Boy Musician's apartment.'

'Let me escort you, Miss. You'll be questioned if you walk alone in the Palace.'

I would not have known my way back through the silent courtyards with their darkened buildings. The yellow glow of another lamp approached us. It was a second guard, who said curtly to my companion, 'Who is she? Has she been verified?'

'I'm the girl who sang at the supper dance, Sir,' I managed to say. The second guard looked surprised.

'Have you not heard, Miss? The young master's asked for you. He's put word about that you're to be found and brought to him.'

My heart gave a sudden leap from its pit of despond. 'The young master?'

'Master Caleb, the Lord Protector's son, no less. We'll take you to him without delay. He's in his mother's room.'

The guard with me gave a muffled snigger. 'Ever his mummy's boy,' he whispered to the second, who gave a warning jerk of his head towards me.

I could not think why the Lord Protector's son should want to see me. And I was still bareheaded, without the disguise of my hat and veil that Titus Molde had told me to keep on at all times.

I was in such a state of anxiety by the time we reached Caleb Grouted's apartment that I could scarce walk. We passed his personal guards and entered a series of fine panelled reception rooms, where lamps still burned and gold-framed portraits of Protectors from another, gentler, age were hung upon the walls. The two guards with me led me to a door that stood slightly ajar, in a lighted passage.

'Someone will see you back afterwards. Knock first, Miss, and loudly – case he's saying his prayers,' said one of them, in a low voice. The other sniggered again.

'Will his mother be in there too?' I whispered.

The guard winked at his friend. 'Only in spirit, Miss. The Lady Sophia's been dead these long years. Passed away from the plague on Master Caleb's eighth birthday.' The other nodded his head in mock gravity, then they hurried away as if anxious to leave the apartment as swiftly as possible.

I stood, hesitating. This was my chance at last: I'd be alone with Caleb.

Or I could run – run straight into more guards, who might arrest me there and then.

I could hear Caleb talking within – muttering. The hairs rose on my neck. There was someone in there with him – the ghost of his mother! I peered through the opening.

I could see little: he had his back to me, had taken his wig off, and was kneeling beside what appeared to be a bed entirely covered with black silk, unless it was a coffin. I heard him clearly though, for he raised his voice to a wail: 'Mama! Mama! Tell me what to do.'

I took a deep breath and knocked firmly. I saw his face turned towards me in astonishment: a flushed, petulant, wet face, his handsome looks melted away by tears, his dark hair rumpled. But the red-rimmed eyes were wary and dangerous.

'Go away!'

'I'm sorry, Sir. I was mistaken . . .'

'No, wait. It's the chit who sang, isn't it? Come in. I asked for you.' His voice was thick with tears and drink.

He scrubbed his puffy face with a corner of the black silk as I entered, then held it against his lips, regarding me over the top of it like a small child as I took in the room. It was entirely black, except for the myriad of white candles burning on an ebony-topped chest and reflected in the mirror that hung over it. They seemed to devour all the air with their cold flames, for it was exceeding stuffy, but they brought no light for there was none to be had in that black, black room. Black drapes hung in folds over the great mahogany bed-head, thick black velvet curtains hid the windows, panels painted black covered the walls and ceiling.

It was a room of mourning, mourning that had grown into an obsession for the boy who had been eight years old when his mother died.

The portrait of a grave young girl hung over the bed; she gazed at me sadly and for a moment I looked back. The painting was of her head and shoulders, the only thing of colour in the room. She wore her dark hair coiled into the nape of her neck; her tragic eyes were remarkable and seemed alive.

'Look at her,' said Caleb. 'Go closer.' It was an order. I stepped a little closer. 'What do you think of her?'

'I know nothing about painting,' I stammered, 'but she is very beautiful, Sir.'

'That is my mama. You see – I look like her, don't I?'

'You have her eyes, Sir,' I said politely, and it was the truth. His eyes were a dark blue and still striking, though reddened by weeping.

'I ask Mama what to do and she tells me.' He looked at me expectantly, as if waiting for a reaction.

I hesitated. 'Was this her chamber, Sir?'

'Her bedchamber, yes. No one else shall have it, ever.'

He is mad, I thought, *and I am alone with him*. I licked my lips. 'Why did you want me, Sir?'

'I liked the look of you. Sing to Mama. She will like you too.'

My skin prickled. He made me face the portrait while he lay on the black bed and looked at me. I sang the shortest song I know, a lullaby about a sleepy thrush. Somehow the lady's calm, sad eyes, her dark-haired beauty, seemed to give me courage in that cold, dead room.

When I looked at him at the end of the song, he had tucked his thumb into his mouth and his black lashes were lying on his cheeks. I thought he might be asleep.

Now I could do it, I thought, *reach down to my boot, pull the dagger out, slide it from its sheath . . . He will never know what killed him. So easy, so quick, so quiet – so much blood.*

There would be too much blood on the black silk, a lake of blood. I could not let the lady see it. I turned away to tiptoe out.

'Not so fast!' His hand reached out and grabbed my dress; the delicate silk was crushed in his fist. He saw the shock on my face and his voice took on a whining note. 'I don't want you to leave us yet. Sing some more.'

'My voice is a little tired, Sir,' I whispered. 'Please let go.'

He flung himself back on the bed pettishly. 'No one loves me. Not you, not Leah Tunstall – whom I must marry, Papa says – not anyone but Mama.'

'Your father loves you, Sir.'

His face twisted. 'Papa?' He crouched up with his knees to his chest, pulled the black silk to his face again and began to rock himself backwards and forwards on the bed. 'I am frightened of Papa,' he moaned, shaking his head, 'frightened, frightened. Big bad man, so rough with little Caleb.'

He looked at me, rubbing his lips with the black silk; his eyes gleamed as he watched me. 'Don't leave me, sweet sparrow,' he crooned. 'Come here, little bird, come.' He stopped rocking. He murmured, 'If you will not come to me, then I must come to you – stop you flying away.'

He swung his legs off the bed in a sudden movement. Before I could draw away, he had grasped my hand. He was taller than his father. 'Now you can't fly, can you?' He looked down at me, smiling. I gasped as he dug his nails into the flesh at the base of my thumb. He shook his head again, smiling all the while; pressed harder. He seemed to enjoy my pain. 'No one can hear you, little sparrow.'

Beyond his arm I saw the portrait. With my free hand I pointed. 'Your mother can! She looks at you and weeps!'

His smile died. He swung round, letting go of me. With

a cry of anguish that echoed round and round that funereal room he threw himself face down on the great black bed.

And I escaped.

7

Chance felt the familiar shudder go through him as he looked down at the swanskin.

'What will you do?' Mather was saying to the Lord Protector. 'I presume you won't be giving it back to Miss Leah after the wedding.'

'Too right, Mather,' said the Lord Protector. He stared with satisfaction into the glass cabinet, where the swanskin lay in all its pure white perfection upon the black velvet. 'My dear niece must produce an heir first – my grandson. Don't want her flyin' off before that, do we?' He laughed loudly and took a turn around the cabinet, his hands behind his back. 'Besides, it's pretty, ain't it? Something to show off, meantime.'

To set such store by feathers! Chance thought briefly, then for the umpteenth time he began to churn over the night of the supper dance, a week ago now. He'd known the girl up on the stage, even before she started singing to the music of the ratha. How could he not? He knew everything about her: her small hands, her slight body, the way she dipped her head nervously. Even the grand dress, the hat and veil she wore at first, could not hide her from him.

So why had he not reported her immediately? He didn't know; nor why he'd been drawn back to the dance to see her after the Protector and Mather had retired. She had been standing so close to him! He could have told any of the guards. But instead, like a fool, he'd asked her to dance and she had scorned him.

So why hadn't he taken his revenge and informed Mather that he had discovered the girl, Number 102, within the Palace itself? Perhaps it was because the moment had never seemed right.

But now it was – now, while the Lord Protector was here, while the three of them were together privately in this small, hushed room.

Sweat broke out on his forehead: it was very hot, airless. There had been a heat wave the last few days. As he opened his mouth, the swanskin seemed to glitter in his eyes. He took a step back from the cabinet and Mather spoke.

'My Lord, more deaths have been reported today,' he said quietly, to the Protector. 'I fear the Miasma is beginning to seep through the Capital. Soon the members of the Ministration will become nervous of remaining in the city. Some have already left for their country estates.'

The Protector pursed his thick lips. He paced to the corner of the room and back again, his lidless eyes unreadable. Then at last he spoke. 'If I brought the weddin' forward, could you get the security arrangements organized in time?'

'When for, Sir?' said Mather calmly.

'The sooner the better. The day after tomorrow, say?'

Mather did not show any reaction. 'There would be no problem, Sir. There is excellent liaison between the Militia and the Enforcers. The men have rehearsed the event already. They all know their positions, they've been highly trained.'

'I'm sure they have,' said the Protector drily. 'So they don't fear the Miasma themselves, eh? Can't have 'em running from the scabby crowds.'

'They'll be issued with the new protection masks. They know the rules. Any deserters will be shot, you may take my word for it.'

'I'll make things easy for you, Mather,' said the Protector jovially. 'I'll bring Curfew forward a couple of hours that day. Say we time the weddin' for immediately after the bells have rung?'

Mather nodded. 'It will mean the crowds will have dispersed, certainly.'

'And their germs, Mather!' The Protector paused. 'Can't see any other problems.'

Mather sucked his cheeks. 'The scaffolding will still cover the West façade of the Cathedral.'

'The new doors will be in place – that's what matters, man. The steps to the crypt have been cleared and reinforced. The guests can be taken down after the service.'

'But the overseas guests – the heads of state, politicians, ambassadors and so on – we cannot inform them in time, Sir.'

'That won't matter.' The Protector slapped his thigh. He was full of energy, unaffected by the heat in the room. 'We'll make it a small, intimate affair, for the Members of the Ministration only. It will certainly lessen the security risk. We'll hold a big reception in the autumn instead for our foreign friends. We might even have some special news to give 'em by then – an heir on the way, eh?' He winked at his right-hand man. 'Meanwhile, we must let the Ministration know the change of plan immediately.'

'What about the Messenger?' Mather frowned. 'Sometimes I wonder if we are right to trust him.'

'Indeed, we must tell the Messenger. I don't believe you trust anyone, do you, Mather?' The Lord Protector smiled. 'I leave the prisin' out of traitors to you, my friend. I know you won't let me down. Any enemies in the Palace – or, indeed, at the weddin' itself – won't stand a chance.'

Nate held the tiny bird between his cupped palms. At first it had fluttered wildly; now it lay quiet. He could feel its heart, small as a thimble, jerking against his fingers. He went over to the open window. Beams of low orange sunlight slashed the floor.

'What are you doing?'

It was Scuff, coming through from her bedchamber. She looked pale, drained with the heat.

'A bird flew in.' He raised his hands and released it as he spoke. For a moment he thought that it was already dead, that it would fall, but then it flew off in a series of funny nervous little leaps before it soared into the air.

'A bird?' She swayed; for a moment he thought she would faint.

'A sparrow, poor little creature.'

'Nate, it signifies the Brevity of Life!'

He shook his head. 'You are mistaken,' he said gently. 'Sparrows signify Friendship.'

'But if a bird – any bird – flies into the house, it signifies Bad Luck, even Death!' She put a hand to the amber stone she always wore around her neck, and stared wildly out at the courtyard where the leaves had turned to crinkled ochre and ravens pecked in the dust beneath the trees.

'It depends which way you look at it,' he said, concerned by her reaction.

'For me, it must mean the second Significance. I have no friends.'

'You have me,' he said awkwardly. 'Anyway, some say the *Table of Significance* is nothing but a collection of old superstitions.'

'Hush, Nate! That's blasphemy!'

'I'm not sure I don't believe them.'

She stared at him. 'But you wear your jasper . . .'

'To keep me safe, yes. You need something like that in this place. It reassures me, I suppose.' He smiled lopsidedly, and fiddled with the pale green stone. 'You know – the cry in the night, the knife in the dark.'

Beneath her old black felt hat, she looked alarmed. Droplets of sweat pearled her upper lip. He wondered why she didn't take the veil off: it must be so hot and he couldn't care about her scars.

'Knife?' she said, in a high voice.

'Oh, nothing – it was a jest.' This was the first proper conversation they had had since the night of the supper dance – she had been so distant with him the past week he thought he must have offended her in some way – and now it was all going wrong.

'Look!' He thought he'd distract her. 'They've brought your basket. Certainly smells like raw meat.' He wrinkled his nose and grinned, pointing over to the far corner of the room, at a basket covered with a rough cloth. The first fly was already buzzing round it, but it was too hot to shut the window. 'Do you really have to go off on some mad venture the day before the wedding, Scuff?'

He thought, with a resentment he tried to push away, *We could use that time for a last rehearsal, now the wedding's so soon*. They were to perform a nuptial motet during the service, though there would be the Cathedral's choir to sing anthems and its musicians to play other traditional compositions, both groups employed again after a gap of years.

She was still standing by the window, dreaming, not answering.

'It's dangerous in the streets alone,' he added, more sharply. 'I wish I could go with you, wherever you're going.'

'I'll be careful. I'll wear my old clothes. I won't stand out.'

'But why won't you let me come too?'

She looked at him and a strange expression crossed her face. Yet she spoke gently: 'You can't, Nate. This is something I have to do alone.'

He was exasperated. 'But why, in the name of the Eagle? Why tomorrow? It's so hot – the Miasma's rising – the wedding's the day after . . .'

His voice trailed away. She wasn't going to tell him, he could see that. She hesitated before she spoke, and her words were odd.

'I have to go alone, Nate. I have to make – atonement.'

The evening of that same day, in the larger of the two upstairs rooms at the sign of the Saggy Bottle in Gravengate, the rebels Titus Molde and Jed Flint were in secret discussion, their chairs pulled close. Though he was sweating profusely, Molde's tankard of stingoe was untouched on the floorboards. He was passing on to Flint what the Messenger had told him mere minutes ago.

The room was in shadow; outside the sun was sinking over the great river in a fiery ball. Titus Molde rose and went to the window again to check that no one suspicious loitered outside the tavern. Below, the river glowed like molten copper; the boats on its surface looked as if they had been blackened by fire. There was less traffic than there had been two months ago: even those that earned their livelihood on the water were beginning to keep away now the Miasma was rising.

'So the wedding's to be held the day after tomorrow,' said Molde. 'That won't cause us any problems. Security will be tight, but I've planned for it for weeks.' He gazed out, unseeing. His stocky silhouette brooded on the far wall. 'I'll call a meeting first thing tomorrow, go over the details with the others one last time. Remind them of their positions and what they're to do.'

Flint looked unhappy. 'Have you been in touch with the Seacoal Lane lot?'

Molde's lip curled. 'They know our plans but they want no part in them. They feel the rebel movement has more "groundwork" to do before it acts. If we thought like them, we'd be sitting around until we were as grey-haired as they are.'

'What about the girl? Shouldn't we try to get her out of the Palace?'

Molde ignored the question. 'I know how I can speak to her tomorrow.' He grinned. 'Overheard two of the Palace kitchen staff complaining in the Dancing Bear at luncheon. Apparently she's asked for a basket of raw meat to be brought to her. I've put two and two together. There's only one place she can be going. I'll intercept her, force her hand.'

Flint's eyes widened. 'You're not still thinking of using her . . .?'

Molde looked across at his oldest ally with sudden contempt. He was weak, was Flint; weak men were dangerous. 'She's run out of time. If the wedding's to be held the day after tomorrow as the Messenger says, then that's when she must kill Caleb.'

Flint frowned and his long jaw stuck out, unexpectedly mulish. 'I don't like it, Titus. It was a mad scheme in the first place, but to force the girl to assassinate the Lord Protector's son in a public place that's to be guarded by armed Militia! She's the daughter of our late leader! What are you thinking of?'

Molde gave a short, furious laugh. The sun glowed redly on his face and corn-coloured hair so that for a moment he looked as if he had stepped from hell. The voices, nowadays a constant murmur in his head, increased in volume to a clamour. Even when he hit his forehead several times, they didn't quieten.

Flint stared at him. 'Are you all right?'

'Shut up,' growled Molde, shaking his head. His voice rose. 'Shut up! Shut up!'

Flint took a deep draught of stingoe from his tankard. 'Look,' he said steadily. 'You're not well, Titus. I don't think you've been well for some time. We should reconsider, seek others' views, too. Why, the men don't even know we've found her! We need to talk to the Messenger, maybe even the Seacoal Lane rebels. Why don't I go myself – now?'

'No! No!' The voices shouted in Molde's head. It took all his control to ignore them, to stop his own voice shaking with rage and say with a casual laugh as he advanced across the shadowy room, 'Why not, indeed?'

Flint set his tankard down on the floor. As he was about to rise, a sound made him turn in his chair. Titus Molde had come up behind him, was leaning over the chairback and slowly flexing his fingers as he looked down on him.

'Sacred flight!' said Jed Flint, in dawning horror. 'You really *are* mad!'

8

I had to have permission from the security office in order to leave the Palace.

They stared at me, dressed in the old red wool dress, the stinking, cloth-covered basket on my arm. I gazed back at them from under the veil of the black felt hat. 'Devotion,' I repeated. 'I wish to attend Devotion at the old Cathedral. They have a service at eleven of the clock.'

I must have convinced them, for they let me through, after giving the raw meat in the basket an exceeding hasty inspection.

It should not be so very difficult to find my way to the Cathedral. *I must remember it backwards*, I thought. The long avenue from the Palace led almost there, before it lost itself in a fan of streets that ended at the Cathedral square.

I set off, walking where Nate and I had walked weeks before; and as I left the Palace gates behind me, a huge weight seemed to lift from my shoulders.

But I had forgotten I must walk alone between the great statues of the Eagles on their plinths all the way down the

Parade. Their marble eyes caught the sun and shone directly at me. I kept my head down; I took care not to step on their shadows in case that made them angry. I put a hand to the amber stone at my neck.

Some of the way was shaded by the plane trees that bordered the parks. They were in heavy leaf, but their leaves were curling; beyond them the grass was dry and brown. The fountains no longer played. Only the lakes glittered in the sun, fed by the secret underground rivers of the Capital.

My feet grew sore and hot in the boots. Beneath the red wool my armpits were damp; sweat trickled down the small of my back. The smell of the raw meat made me feel sick. Between the trees there were patches of burning sunlight; I tried to keep to the shade, but the heavy leaves only seemed to trap the hot dry air beneath them.

The statues watched without mercy: this was my penance.

Now and then a carriage would rattle along the high paved road in a cloud of dust. From inside, faces, topped by wigs, gazed at me incuriously; the drivers, flicking their whips over the horses' backs, and the footmen, clinging to the carriage-backs, ignored me. I dragged myself along in the heat, a beggar girl with a basket.

Then all at once I had entered the streets I remembered, with the decaying houses that once had been so fine: the long windows with their broken shutters; the jagged ironwork; the weeds sprouting between cracked front steps where the sheen of marble had dulled.

A gaunt child, playing with a hoop, snivelled and sneezed as I hurried on. It was oddly quiet, as if everyone had already died.

I held my handkerchief close to my face: it was not good to breathe here. I could almost feel the Miasma, the invisible mist of death, rising from the sluggish water of the canal to my left, draining my healthy cheeks to corpse white. Passers-by pressed nosegays of wilting flowers to their nostrils. They did not speak; they avoided looking at each other – at me – as if that might somehow prevent them from catching the disease.

I could not have come at a safer time.

Even the market stalls were quiet, except for the stray dogs nosing around them. Beneath the tattered awnings the meat and fish were beginning to smell. I was giving them a wide berth, when I noticed a girl haggling with an oyster-seller. It was the girl's yellow stockings I noticed first, the rat-frighteners. I hesitated, but while I stood uncertain, she made her purchase and turned, and immediately she saw me.

'Scuff!' Her plain, pasty face, shining in the heat, split in a huge grin.

My heart warmed. 'Dog!'

'Well, now, fancy! How are you, girl?' She gave my old clothes a measuring look. 'Neither up nor down in the world, I'd say. Wot you been up to, then? I thought you was bein' took off to prison!'

'I was, in a fashion,' I said. 'There is so much to tell,

Dog! But I cannot tell it now – I should hurry.'

'We'll both tell our doin's to each other, then,' she said, 'at Murkmere!'

'You're going back?'

She nodded, beaming, her greasy plait swinging up and down under the battered hat. 'I thought over what you said, Scuff – about this place takin' my heart away – and I'm goin' back on tonight's plague-runner to Poorgrass Kayes.' She glanced at me slyly. 'And you're goin' back too, ain't you, Scuff, so we shall be there together again, us two and Aggie and all.'

'Oh, Dog, I wish it were so. I'd give anything to return there. But I've something to do, and I don't know I'll survive it.'

'You'd better, girl,' she said, 'for I'm wantin' to hear about those doin's of yours.'

'Goodbye, then, Dog.'

She shook her head. 'I'll not say goodbye.'

In the square the blossom had long gone from the trees and the grass was parched. The icon-sellers had gone. People lay huddled in the shade like bundles of rags. I thought they might well all be dead, but as I passed, an old man opened a rheumy eye, a baby began to wail at its mother's shrivelled breast.

A couple of feral dogs had followed me stealthily ever since I'd stopped in the marketplace. If I slackened my pace now, they'd attack me before I could throw them the basket of meat, before I even reached the Cathedral.

I hurried across the crisp grass and almost fell under the wooden scaffolding in my relief. One of the new oak doors stood open. The dogs skittered away, yowling, as I heaved it to, banging it shut almost in their jaws. The great arch of the entrance was over my head, cool air touched my face; I was inside at last.

The pews were crowded with people. I saw that first, as my eyes adjusted to the rainbow light from the great windows that streamed over the nave until it was lost in the darkly shadowed aisles on either side. Then I saw that even in the aisles they were sleeping, or sitting, or crouching – the refugees of the plague. The people of the Capital had come to their Cathedral, as they had always done in time of trouble. They were begging the Eagle for help, for shelter and sustenance, for life itself. The air vibrated with their pleas, their supplications: a murmur that rose and fell but never stopped.

It was heart-rending; I could scarce bear to listen. I edged forward, towards the chancel where the altar stood, so that I could pray, leave my sacrifice there and go.

I slipped between the arches at the side, between the stone plinths with their sculptures of the Birds of Light, past the individual chapels where candles glowed to the glory of the Lark, the Robin, the Wren, the Swallow, the House Martin. Ravens flapped around my feet and flew high into the vaulted roof. The same timid Bird-Scarer I'd noticed weeks before waved his arms pathetically, as if he mimicked them.

No one noticed me. I was only another supplicant, bearing a gift of meat to seek favour with the Almighty. I bowed my head in contrition and put down my basket with the others that were laid in the chancel, to one side of the altar. Tomorrow, before the wedding service, the offerings would all be removed. I hoped He'd have time to appreciate mine.

I went to sit in the nearest pew and raised my eyes to His chipped stone face. A battered stone bird, the sculpture was ancient; no one knew how old it was. According to official history – one of the state-approved texts Miss Jennet had so reluctantly given me – it had been discovered hundreds of years ago, when the Cathedral was first raised on the ruins of the one before. This Cathedral had been laid out in the same way as the old, and the bird had been put on the altar, for that was where He must surely belong. He was an Eagle.

I looked at Him now and saw He did not forgive me, would never do so; I had been mistaken. He condemned me for what I'd done and was about to do the very next day. He would never save me. The child in the Gravengate Orphans' Home had been right: there was no love in His eyes.

A terrible panic gripped me; I covered my face with my hands. The sweat had dried on my body and I was cold.

'Little one.' It was the fool, Gobchick, whom Nate called

mad. He was still here. His wrinkled fingers covered mine as I gripped the pew. 'Come, little one.'

I don't know why I went with him. I think it was the understanding in his eyes, shining at me out of the dimness: he had a fool's wisdom, and I trusted him.

He took me to the Chapel of the Wren, which was almost empty, the Wren being a small bird and not so powerful as the other Birds of Light. We kept our voices low before the burning candles on the altar; a bitter tang of incense drifted from the pierced burner hanging above our heads.

'You suffer,' he said, his old face creased in a reflection of my own misery.

'I've lost my love,' I whispered. It wasn't at all what I'd meant to say.

'You must give love as well as receive it. 'Tis a to-ing and a fro-ing.'

'But I did, Gobchick! I gave him all my love.'

'Is it your heart that hurts now, or your pride? Was it true love, little one?' he murmured, his head on one side.

I hung my head. 'All I've ever wanted is to be loved.'

'Old Gobchick loves you.' He patted my hand. 'You don't remember Gobchick.' When I looked at him, his soft eyes smiled sadly between folds of wrinkled skin.

'You came to Murkmere once, long ago.'

He shook his head. 'Why are you here? Not to see Gobchick.'

'I committed a sin,' I whispered, 'many years ago, when

I was a child. I ate His food. It belonged to Him and I stole it! I've come for forgiveness.'

'You needed the food. He has forgiven you.'

I shook my head; I couldn't believe him. 'He'll punish me for ever.'

' 'Tis you who punish yourself. You think the Gods eat? That they have need of food like us mortals?' He waved his hand towards the chancel. 'Those be bribes, child, all those meats. The Almighty has no regard for them. He sees each man as he is.' He leapt off into the shadows and beckoned to me, his eyes gleaming, the scruffy feathers scarce covering his scrawny limbs. 'Come with Gobchick, come.'

Without knowing why, I followed him, and found to my alarm that he had slipped sideways into the chancel, behind the altar. 'Gobchick coming here all his life,' he whispered. 'Knows this place. Nothing to fear. Knows two secrets.'

Gently, he took my hand and led me over to the statue of the Eagle; candles front-lit the rough-hewn head and breast, but we were hidden in the darkness beneath.

Gobchick pointed to the outstretched wings above us. 'See the words?'

I frowned, still fearful of being so close to Him. 'What do they say?'

'Gobchick cannot read.'

The lettering was faint, carved into the stone like secret writing, a line of letters along the curve of each wing. To read them I had to stand in the shadow cast by the great wingspan.

I strained my eyes. 'One says "Judgement Tempered by Mercy",' I whispered. 'The other, "Love Will Redeem Thee".' The words seemed meant for me alone.

I don't know how long I stood there, staring up at them, but at last I heard Gobchick whisper, 'See? No need to fear, little one.' His eyes slanted up at me. 'Now show you second wonder.'

He took a candle from the altar in the Chapel of the Wren, touching his forehead to the painting of the Wren that hung over it. 'She allows me this,' he muttered, waving the lighted candle in triumph. The few worshippers looked at him with blank faces, wrapped in their own sorrows.

'I should go.'

'No.' He gripped my hand. 'Important stuff. Come.'

'Where are we going?'

'Where you have been before.'

The workmen had finished, taking their tools with them. The apse was deserted, lit by a single lamp so that the arches were in darkness.

'Where are the soldiers?'

Gobchick shook his head. 'Gone, gone. Never come back.'

I wished I could believe him; I was sure they were somewhere about. My pulse quickened with apprehension. Outside, in the streets, time would be moving onwards to noon. It was a long walk back in the heat and dust to the Palace of the Protectorate, and I had only a morning's pass. I wanted to leave, now.

Gobchick capered about, the candle in his hand flickering. Behind him stone steps wound down into darkness. I felt a prick of fear: the crypt must be below, stone ledges filled with crumbling coffins. 'Down there? Is that where you sleep?'

'Follow me.' He peered up, his grin mischievous. 'You will see wonders.'

I let those little fingers close around mine again, a grip warm, yet surprising strong. I let him lead me down the first step, then the second. His eyes shone crazily in the candlelight. Where was I going with this ancient fool?

The walls pressed close. It was colder suddenly, and damp, yet not musty, as if fresh air came from somewhere. I thought I heard water. But there was something else.

For a moment I hung back, frightened. 'I've been here before.' My whisper echoed breathily around the stairwell . . . *If I held a candle to it, it would glow: my amber gate* . . .

I stepped out at the bottom and was in a great stone place, with stone underfoot and, beyond me, stone arches like trees that disappeared into the darkness: a stone clearing in a stone forest.

The candle flame wavered in the mysterious currents of air. 'Gobchick only carer now, Gobchick look after this place.' He shook his head so that the tattered feathers flew, his voice mournful. 'But Master comes now, so Gobchick hide. Days of laughter over.'

I turned about, staring. 'How did you know I'd been here before?'

I knew the place, but not well, as if I had once come across it in a dream, then dreamed the dream again.

By a pillar there was a dark tumble of rags, a pewter plate. Gobchick's den. This was where he must spend his nights – and many a day, too.

'Let me hold your candle,' I whispered. My heart thudded; I was certain of a sudden that there was a painted ceiling above our heads.

I held the candle high, and there was the gleam of gold leaf, the flash of white against vivid green and blue. There were twelve panels set into the vaulted stone, like the patches in a quilt. Each panel showed a swan – black-eyed, slender-necked, proud – swimming on a background of sunlit blue or turquoise, or the deep green of reed-shadowed water. Around its neck each swan wore a golden crown that glinted in the candlelight.

'Why ever did I come here? Why, Gobchick?'

Gobchick pursed his lips together, silent; his feathered costume made strange shadows on the stone.

There is a mystery in this place for me, I thought, *and I must discover it.*

I began to walk around, venturing further into the darkness with my single candle. I was frightened but determined. I tried not to think of the bodies stored in the corpse houses beyond the arches.

Then, where the dark was thickest, the candle picked out a gleam of gold.

It was a double gate, formed of curving golden branches that were studded with amber. As I took the candle closer, the amber stones caught the light. They were the colour of sunlight, from the pale straw of spring to richest autumn brown, and clasped in delicate frilled acorn cups of burnished gold. Exquisite golden birds with feathered tails were eating the fruit of the sun.

I looked between the branches where the two gates met, into the darkness beyond. My cheek pressed against a lock garlanded with golden ribbons. The amber glowed around me, tiny suns without heat. I could smell water.

'Gobchick!' I whispered, for he had appeared from nowhere beside me. 'You knew all the time the Gate was here – in the crypt!'

The Amber Gate was tall, higher than my head; beyond it was a curved brick ceiling – the beginning of a tunnel – and beneath the tunnel roof there was water. It was a river of cold, secret water, quiet, yet gently nudging at its narrow border of stone, as if moved by the power of the moon and tides far above it. I could make out a brick platform, a rusting iron mooring ring. A dark, damp breath came from the tunnel mouth.

'Where does the river go, Gobchick?'

'To Paradise.'

A little shiver ran over me. 'What do you mean?'

But he shook his head and grasped my dress urgently. 'You were little Clem then.'

What did you call me?

He looked up into my face. 'Are you the meaning of your name?'

He was mad, after all; he waved his head like a lunatic as I stared at him.

There was a sudden flare from the candle flame; in the stairwell, footsteps echoed, light moved. 'Someone's coming!' I hissed.

He danced about in front of me, gleeful. ' 'Tis safe. 'Tis friend.'

And Erland stepped out into the crypt.

9

I could not bear to look at him. Different emotions fought inside me, and I did not know what to say. *He must have followed me. He couldn't speak to me in the Palace, so he followed me today*. A tiny whisper of hope sounded in my head, but I knew it was false and I mustn't listen.

He came straight across. He was holding a lantern. 'Scuff? I've been so anxious for your safety . . .'

I tried to find words. I said stiffly, 'You forget. I have lived in the Capital before. Have you forgotten so much of our talk together on the Eastern Edge?' I looked at him in the eye, and thought he looked a trifle discomforted.

'There's so little time,' he began quickly. 'There are things I must tell you . . .'

'Oh, I know already,' I said, casual. 'I had word with Miss Leah myself, at the dance.'

He looked bewildered.

'I know you love her now,' I explained, very kind. This was too beautiful a place for what I was feeling. A little while ago I would not have been so bold, and I felt a faint satisfaction in myself.

'Scuff . . .' He seemed at a loss. Gobchick went to crouch by himself a little way away in the darkness. I looked bitterly at Erland and thought that in the light he looked older than the youth I remembered on the Wasteland: he was a man, not a boy.

'Scuff,' he began again. 'I'd bring you heartache. My life's a lonely one; it's always been so. Until I met Leah, I accepted that that was the way it was for me and I'd never meet another like myself.'

'And now you have?' I said, with pain.

'I'm not the right one for you,' he said gently, 'but let me tell you I love you now as I did in the Wasteland – no less.'

The turmoil inside me eased a little.

'Gadd did what he thought was best when he took you to Poorgrass Kayes. He knows my nature and was concerned for you. He was right, you know.' He sighed and followed one of the whorls of gold with his finger. 'I feared you'd be in danger, alone in a town like that. I'd let you down. I wanted to protect you, I tried . . .'

'I don't need protecting, not any longer. It's too late.'

'I was always with you in spirit, you know,' he said gently. 'I traced you down to the Capital, but had to leave you when I had the Protector's summons. There was too much at risk. Then I found you in the Palace. I knew you as soon as you began to sing.' He reached a hand out to me. 'Why are you in such a dangerous place, Scuff? Are there secrets you've never told me?'

I thought it outrageous that he should accuse me of keeping secrets, while hiding so much himself. 'They are not worth the telling,' I said angrily. I longed to tell him of my deadly bargain with the soldier Titus Molde, but I was sworn to secrecy. 'Why are *you* there? I thought you a boy from the Wasteland, unschooled in courtiership. You are so sophisticated, so mannerly – and so very friendly with the Protector! I thought you hated him and all he stood for.'

He looked around at the darkness surrounding us.

'Oh, there is no one down here but us,' I said. 'What are you so afraid of?' When he didn't reply, I made to move past him, though my heart yearned for him. 'I must return to the Palace.'

He gripped my arm. 'Don't go – don't sing tomorrow!'

I thrust his arm away and tried to sound cold and grand. 'Why not, pray?'

'I've heard the rebels plan to attack. The Cathedral will be a death-trap!'

'I am sure the Protector has security organized.' I looked at him, at his strong cheekbones, his secret shadowed eyes, and my heart broke. I pulled myself together. 'How is it you know of the attack?'

'I know many things, Scuff.' He spoke fast, urgent. 'In the time you were at Murkmere, did you ever hear tell of a packman named Matt Humble? He went to the house on many an occasion to meet with the steward.'

I was taken aback that he should talk of meaningless things while I felt such pain. 'I believe he took ale in the kitchens once or twice. What is he to do with anything?'

'Before he was murdered some three years ago, Matt Humble was a spy on the rebels' side. He would report to them what took place in the Palace of the Protectorate. He was able to move freely there because Porter Grouted thought he brought information from the rebels.

'After his death, another took his place, though young in scheming, then. But he also came from the Eastern Edge and he knew all Matt's secrets. How could he not? Matt had been the dearest friend of his father – whose name is Gadd.'

I stared up at him. 'You are a spy?'

He nodded. 'They call me the Messenger. I shouldn't tell you this. But I want you to know – to understand. I can't bear you to think I have betrayed the cause. But now you know the truth about me, let me tell you to escape the Capital now, before the wedding.'

I shook my head. 'I can't leave, Erland. There's something I must do and I'm bound to it.'

He stared at me. 'Tell me what it is.'

'I can't.' I shook my head and saw incomprehension in his eyes. I knew that if I stayed longer, I would not be able to stop myself from telling him everything, it weighed so heavily upon me. 'If all goes well tomorrow, I shall leave.'

'I'll do my utmost to help you.' He hesitated. 'I have to think of Miss Leah as well.'

Sudden furious jealousy knotted inside me. 'You think it is a spy's duty to rescue Miss Leah? What's she to do with any cause?'

He spread his hands, with the long fingers I remembered so well. 'She is a girl in despair at her fate.'

'And what of me? Leah has brought it on herself, while I never desired adventure. She should never have left Murkmere in the first place – leaving that huge house for Aggie to run and too few of us to help her. She thought only of herself!'

'That is not true,' said Erland quietly. 'There were many reasons why she had to leave. Her life was in danger.'

'Oh, to be sure,' I said, trying sarcasm. 'She merely had to put on the guise of a swan and she could fly away! Others, earthbound, had to do all the work at Murkmere, while she floated on the pleasure lakes and along the city's canals.'

He took a step back, as if buffeted by my anger.

'Leah is avian – cursed!' I cried. 'She has put herself in this pretty pickle with Caleb because she wants the swanskin back. She will not leave without it, even with you. She'd rather marry Caleb!'

There was a terrible silence between us. At last he said grimly, 'Then I shall get the swanskin for her.'

I lifted my chin. 'It does not matter to me what you do.'

'Tell me you will leave now, Scuff. I need to know you

are safe. It's important. You mustn't stay in the Capital.'

'You do not want me!' I turned my back on him and began to walk quickly away. 'You have chosen her now. Escape with her and go!'

I heard him take a step after me. 'Wait, you don't understand . . .'

'I understand well enough,' I said, over my shoulder. His figure was hidden in the darkness behind me. 'Don't bother about me. I'm not your true love. I'm only a kitchen maid, a girl with a number but no name.'

Gobchick gibbered frantically but I took no notice. I ran from them both, still clutching the candle.

I was at the stairwell and beginning to climb, when I heard Erland coming after me. I tried to hold the candle steady but the light jagged on the stone walls. There was a movement above me and at once I blew it out.

Too late. I stumbled out at the top, straight into the arms of a soldier.

10

He was alone, young, but armed; yet in the light from the lantern he carried he looked as alarmed by my sudden appearance as I was by his. 'Well, well,' he said. 'Spying in the crypt. Better skip out swift, Miss, and tell no one what you've seen.'

I mumbled thanks and fled from him, through to the main body of the Cathedral, and immediately found myself in the middle of a milling crowd.

At first I was relieved, for Erland would never find me now; but then I saw that something was horribly wrong. All around me bewildered men and women were being bullied from their pews, dragged into the aisles: the ragged, the infirm, new mothers with wailing infants, snivelling, frightened children, men with haggard faces. While I'd been below in the crypt, the soldiers had returned – many more of them.

They came in their dark grey uniforms, with their rifles and coarse, brutal faces, their mouths covered by plague masks. Stepping from the shadows, they chanted: 'Out, out, out!'

Near me a white-haired man was wrenched from his place. His weeping wife followed; behind them came a dark-haired girl, wringing her hands.

'Becca!' I said. It was Becca of Madam Anora's, in Poorgrass Kayes.

Her face lit up. 'To find you here, Scuff!'

'And you!'

We clung to each other; the crowd had jammed in the aisles, unable to move. The middle-aged man and woman on either side of her each clutched a handful of her shawl as if their lives depended on it. 'I came back to the Capital to find my parents, just as you said I should,' Becca said, trying to smile.

'And you did find them!' They looked kind and gentle and dreadfully frail.

'You said, "You are braver than you think," and so I was!' Becca said.

We hugged again and would have talked for ever, but around us the crowd had begun to move again, pushing and jostling. Our clinging hands broke apart and she and her parents were hidden from me at once.

Then the first shot was fired.

Around me there were screams, hysterical cries, as the crowd panicked. The strongest shoved the weakest aside. An old woman hobbled a step before someone's elbow caught her. Her hand went up as if she were drowning and she sank out of sight.

Another shot was fired, then another. In the shadows

soldiers were firing up into the vaulted roof, peppering the ancient stone with bullet holes. The ravens had long flown away. How long would it be before the soldiers were bored with that game, and started shooting the crowd?

I was swept along in the flood – too light, too small to resist the terrible onward movement, as everyone surged towards the doors. My hat was knocked off, my skirts dragged and torn. I had no breath to scream; I couldn't even breathe.

I was thrust out into a world of light and heat. Like water bursting through a dam, people on all sides of me were forced out by those behind them. Some lost their balance, stumbled over the others already outside, and fell heavily to the ground.

I staggered to a halt and collapsed on to the stones of the square. I was trembling violently.

The square was still filling up with those that had managed to escape from the Cathedral. The shots and screams were muffled now. The sun beat down. When I looked up at last it was to stare straight into the lost eyes of a woman with blood streaming down her face, before she was helped away by her sobbing children. Two soldiers carried out the crumpled body of a young girl, no older than myself, and laid it on the stone. Then another body – a child – its dead feet sticking out beneath the soldier's arm.

I dragged myself away, to a bench beneath a tree on the far side of the square. Vaguely I wondered what had happened to Erland, to Gobchick, to Becca and her parents.

I sat there with an empty head for a long time. Slowly, my trembling stopped.

The square was emptying at last. Waggons trundled through and removed the pile of bodies. Soldiers shouted in the distance. Men and women and children led each other away from the scene of desolation. There were splashes of dark blood on the stone.

I rose shakily to my feet and began to walk away. I took the nearest street in the fan that would bring me out on to the Central Parade. It was deserted. Word must have spread fast that there had been mayhem in the Cathedral: every surviving soul had shut himself inside.

The sun was directly over my head. Was it only noon?

I was so surprised, I did not see a man slip from the doorway in front of me until it was too late.

It was Titus Molde. I did not recognize him immediately, for he wore a black, wide-brimmed hat low over his brow and was unshaven, yellow bristles hiding his jaw.

I stopped in alarm, my hand to my mouth. At the same time his hand landed heavily on my sleeve as if to detain me. 'Oh, Sir, it is you,' I stammered, confused, my poor heart beating thickly. 'Why aren't you with the other soldiers?'

He paused, while still gripping my arm. He examined my face, too close, and I couldn't draw away. I had forgot the brilliance of his eyes. 'I am not on duty now,' he said.

'But I wish to speak to you, Miss. I need to know when you will do the deed. You remember our secret pact?'

I nodded, dumb.

'You have taken too long. It is the wedding tomorrow. Do it then, you understand? Do it then, or die yourself.'

I nodded again, and gave a little moan as he tightened his grip on my arm. With his other hand he swatted his head violently as if to dislodge a clinging insect. 'I shall be there, Miss, waiting, watching. And afterwards – afterwards we can be friends, accomplices. I'm expecting great things of you.'

Behind him there was the sudden grinding of wheels over the cobbles, the ring of horses' hooves.

With a curse Titus Molde dropped my arm and started round as a black coach came swaying down the street drawn by two horses, the driver behind them in the uniform of the Palace security guards.

The door with its gold emblem of the Eagle opened while the coach was still moving. As it pulled up beside us, Nate's curly head stuck out and his hand reached down to me.

'Scuff! Get in!' I'd never heard him sound so fierce.

I'd thought my limbs wouldn't obey after so many shocks, but somehow my hand clasped his and he pulled me in beside him. I was flung back against the black leather seat as the carriage careered off again, with a terrific jingle of harnesses and clattering of hooves.

I'd not even had time to see what had happened to Titus Molde.

'Thank the Eagle I found you!' said Nate, white-faced, as the coach steadied to a rumble. He still sounded furious. 'Do you realize I've been looking for you all morning? I heard about what happened in the Cathedral. You could have been killed! And all for a silly whim – insisting on going alone into the heart of the Capital on such a day!'

'It was not a silly whim, Nate,' I said, in a small voice. 'I had to go.'

'I bribed Bernard the guard to drive. I didn't think I'd ever find you otherwise!'

'I'll pay you back when I can, Nate.'

'Oh, stuff that! And the danger you were in when I spotted you – that ruffian – anything could have happened!'

'It was the man you took me from,' I said meekly. 'The soldier.'

'I didn't have time to see his face. Anyway that man is no soldier, that's nonsense.'

'He is, he is!' I stopped quickly for fear of further questions.

'What were you doing, anyway – seeing that vile creature again?' He sounded exasperated. 'You're nothing but a confounded nuisance, Scuff. I don't know why I ever rescued you in the first place!'

A lump of misery rose in my throat. Before I could help it tears began to spill from my eyes, plopping on to the black leather.

I turned my head so he wouldn't see. The tall houses

with their crumbling façades were blurred, and soon I couldn't see them at all. I gave a huge gulp that he must have heard, for suddenly a white silk handkerchief was placed on my lap.

'I didn't mean it, Scuff, you know,' said Nate's voice awkwardly.

'I'm sorry,' I hiccuped. I struggled not to cry, but more and more tears poured from my eyes as if of their own doing.

I felt his arm go around my shoulders and draw me close. 'Hush, my poor little Scuff, hush,' he murmured. He began to stroke my hair and wet cheeks with his gentle fingertips. 'It is the shock, my poor little girl, my little sparrow.'

That made me give a tiny smile in spite of myself.

After a while I whispered, 'It is the pity of it all I weep for, Nate – the terrible pity. Those poor people in the Cathedral – how could the soldiers be so cruel?' I shuddered against his arm. 'And it was on the orders of the Lord Protector!'

'You have been through such things today,' he said softly. 'What a brute I was to talk to you so!' He looked at me with kind, wondering eyes. 'You have even lost your hat! There, I knew you had no scars of any sort! You are quite perfect.'

'My hat!' I sat up in alarm.

He drew me back, with a sigh. 'We shall find you another one, if that is what you want. Is it your face you wish to hide? You have too many secrets, Scuff, too many from me and from others, perhaps. We must be honest with each other.'

I lay against Nate's arm and could not speak. I longed so much to unburden myself, but I'd risk losing his loyal friendship and endanger him most horribly. Then I thought of something certain to distract him. I whispered, 'You will not believe me, but I saw the Amber Gate this very morning. The stories are true!'

He sat up at that, detaching me gently from him. He gave a quick glance to check the windows were safe shut and looked at me gravely. 'I know. It is in the Cathedral crypt, which has been blocked over a hundred years.'

'You know?'

'Remember my father was Keeper of the Keys. So was his father before him. He knew many secrets of the Capital. He said that the city once took its name from the Gate, its sacred heart. *Ambergate.*'

'And he – you – told no one?' I was incredulous.

'I've lived with the secret since my father's death. He always said that on the day Porter Grouted found the Gate he would plan to destroy it – melt it down for his own coffers. And my father was right.' Nate's face was sombre. 'Grouted has read his own meaning into the mystical ceiling and that's why Miss Leah must marry his son. The Gate and the Ceiling – the two greatest treasures of the Capital, and Grouted plans to use them both for his own ends! One hears many things as a Boy Musician. Servants of the Protector are not expected to have ears.'

He paused and his eyes met mine with his clear, direct gaze. 'But you know all this, don't you, Scuff? You are like the Messenger, are you not?'

I shook my head earnestly. 'I told you the truth the other night at the supper dance. But you know about the Messenger?'

He nodded. 'My father knew. Father had turned against the Protector by then. He was upset by the way he treated the fool, Gobchick, throwing him out into the streets homeless when he grew too old to serve his purpose.' He hesitated and gazed at me sadly. 'If you are not like the Messenger, who are you, Scuff? Why are you in such fear of discovery that you must hide half your pretty face? You are not going to tell me, are you?'

'I can't, Nate.' We were moving smoothly along the Parade between the Eagles, towards the Palace of the Protectorate. I stared out at the pairs of marble eyes and they stared back at me pitilessly – the girl with no name. 'I don't even know who I am myself.'

And yet – and yet. I remembered suddenly that for a strange moment that day it had seemed Gobchick was about to tell me.

11

That night the temperature scarce dropped and the moon seemed to boil in the sky. It turned a deep copper red for nigh on three hours. I knew it to be the reflection cast up into the sky from the Capital – all the blood that had been shed that day. It was too hot to sleep, and I was too apprehensive. Yet I didn't crawl into the tiny wig closet for comfort; tomorrow I'd not be able to hide any longer and I must start by being brave now.

Late the next afternoon, I began to ready myself for the wedding ceremony. I'd washed in the blue-patterned bowl on the wash stand and dressed myself in the green silk I'd worn at the supper dance, when a knock sounded at my door and Nate poked his head around.

'Oh, Nate,' I said, for I'd not pinned my hair up yet, 'is it time to go already?'

He was still in his everyday jacket and breeches and seemed flustered. 'Miss Leah wishes to see you, apparently. She asked for you particularly. I hope she doesn't object to something in our music.'

'I know what it is, Nate,' I said, laying the tortoiseshell comb by the box. 'It isn't that, I assure you.' *She's going to beg for my help again!* I thought furiously.

'Be back here in plenty of time,' he said. 'We must get to the Cathedral before the Ministration arrives. Our coach is already waiting in the courtyard.'

'I don't intend to be long,' I said. I rolled my hair and coiled it at the nape of my neck, since there wasn't time to pin it up properly. I took up the new hat that Nate had ordered for me and was about to put it on when he stopped me. He was staring at me oddly.

'It's strange, Scuff, but of a sudden you look so familiar. Your hair done that way, your eyes – I've seen you before, I know it!'

'Why, you've known me all of several weeks now,' I said, half laughing, arranging the hat on my head and pulling the veil down over my eyes. 'Of course I look familiar!'

Then I had to push past him, for it seemed as if he'd never shift from staring stone-struck in the doorway.

'I could not leave for the Cathedral without seeing you,' said Miss Leah. She gestured impatiently at her personal maid. 'Go! I've no need of you now.' The young girl tiptoed nervously from the bedchamber, glancing at me from the corner of her eye as I stood in the doorway, waiting for Miss Leah to speak further.

She was sitting at the dressing-table in a crumpled chamber robe, staring listlessly at the creams and unguents cluttering the surface, as if wondering what they were to do with her: the shining glass bottles of milky face lotions, the fat pots of rouge, dishes of charcoal powder, bowls of white face powder, the flat tin boxes of waxed carmine crayons. The air was heavy with perfume from exquisite flagons, filligreed with gold. Hanging from the wardrobe door I saw the wedding dress she was to wear: slippery cream satin, its sleeves and hem embroidered with pearls.

Leah was bone-pale, unadorned, her hair hidden in a pearled snood. I could see her face in the triple mirrors, puckered with disgust and weariness, yet still so maddeningly beautiful. Her great eyes, that needed no blackening to rim them round, moved from the array before her and fixed on me in the mirror, as if she had thought at last of what it was she wanted to say to me.

'What is to become of me, Scuff?' she whispered.

'You will be a wife, Miss Leah,' I said, with some satisfaction.

'In order to get my mother's swanskin back, I must marry Caleb and give up Erland. That is my sacrifice.' She twisted her hands together.

I felt an unexpected twinge of pity for her. 'If the world were different, you and Erland would belong together – you are the same. I saw it at the dance.'

'What do you mean?'

'I believe you know, Miss Leah. I think you knew when the three of us were little children, long ago at Murkmere. You wanted to lead him into the water, to the swans' nest –

do you remember? I tried to take him from you, then – to save him from you – and I only wish I could do so again.'

'You must hate me to say such a thing!' She buried her face in her hands.

'But it would do no good if I could take him,' I said, more gently. 'I cannot change his nature. I understand that at last. It is like yours.'

When she lifted her head, her eyes were red. 'He is better than me, Scuff – much better. His nature is wholly good.' Her voice trembled. 'I fear he'll do something foolish today. He'll try to rescue me before I speak the vows. He'll forget that his duty as Messenger is to remain undetected by the Lord Protector. His first duty must be to the rebel cause.'

She turned on the stool with sudden energy. 'When I first saw you, you told me you might be able to help me. I needed to see you today to ask you – to beg you – not to change your mind now . . .' she spread her white fingers '. . . now you know about Erland and me.'

I swallowed painfully. 'My plan's not changed, Miss Leah.'

'I can't live without open water and sky,' she said, with a great sigh. 'I'd rather die than be without them.' She stared at me piteously. 'How can you help, though? What can you do?'

'I can't tell you, Miss Leah.'

She bit her lip. 'You must. I command it.'

I shook my head. 'I'm your servant no longer.'

I looked at her pale, tense face; she seemed to shrink into herself with despair. 'Will it help Erland, too?' she whispered. 'Only tell me that.'

Something about the bowed, tragic figure on the stool touched me and I relented. 'I have a dagger, Miss Leah,' I whispered back. 'I shall be close to Caleb at the wedding.'

She jerked upright. Her eyes widened, her hand went to her mouth. 'You can't!' she whispered. 'You'll die yourself!' She paused, then suddenly shook her head as if in contempt. 'You've no dagger. What a fool I am!'

I said nothing.

Her lips curled. 'You're only a child and you've always been a coward. You'd never use a dagger.'

Anger burned inside me. I bent and touched my boot, with its lethal secret. Her eyes followed my hand.

'In there?' she hissed, incredulous.

I nodded.

She shook her head again, this time sadly. 'Don't joke, I beg you.'

In exasperation I bent and pulled the dagger out, and in the same second she snatched it from me. I thought she was about to turn it on her own throat. 'No, Miss Leah!' I cried, reaching out, my hat falling off in my agitation. 'No, don't!'

After my cry the chamber was very quiet. We stared at each other without moving. She held the dagger behind her back.

'You must not risk your own life for us, Scuff. I know you're no coward. You would do so.'

'It's not for you,' I said miserably, 'but to save my own skin.'

She stared.

I nodded. 'I am a criminal,' I said in a low voice, 'wanted by the authorities. I have agreed to kill Caleb in return for my own life.'

'And you could do that – use this dagger in cold blood, even on such a monster?'

She gazed at me; I looked away. Suddenly she reached out with her free hand and turned my cheek towards her. 'I know who it is you look like! It has bothered me ever since I first saw you here, and now, with your hat off and your hair coiled, I see it.'

I was bewildered, unsure of the sudden change in conversation. Was this another trick to keep the dagger?

She said softly, 'It is the Lady Sophia, my father's sister, who was married to the Lord Protector. There is a portrait of her as a young girl hanging in the bedchamber she had before she died from the Miasma.'

'I'm a nameless orphan, Miss Leah, as well you know.'

She opened her mouth to speak and then we heard Caleb Grouted's raised voice outside. 'Out of the way, girl. I wish to see your mistress.' There was the sound of a scuffle and a squeal of protest from the maid.

Leah, white-faced with horror, thrust the dagger into my hand, as the latch lifted on the door and Caleb burst in. He was dressed in a frock-coat of pale yellow silk, his dark hair unpowdered, but oiled in ringlets. He lurched towards Leah, his lips parting wetly, and made a grab for her, as she stepped aside. 'Have you no kiss for your sweet boy on this special day? Can't a groom kiss his betrothed?'

'Not before the service, Master Caleb,' said Leah coolly. 'Go and ready yourself, else we shall be late.'

'Yes, Leah,' said Caleb, pretending meekness. He succeeded in catching her hand, which he squeezed and slobbered with a kiss before he released it. I saw her secret grimace as she hastily turned her face away, and he gave a whinny of laughter.

'Afterwards, then. I'll look forward to that. Eh, Leah?' He punched the air. 'They think me a real man for capturing you as my bride. That's what they all say in the officers' mess. Leah Tunstall of Murkmere, the most beautiful girl in the country!'

'Even though it was your father who arranged it? And held me here under duress until I agreed? Did you tell these lieutenants about the cage?'

He looked sulky at once. 'You shan't dare to speak to me so once we're married, Leah. You'll respect me then, if you know what's good for you.'

Leah was silent, and he turned and swaggered to the door. As he brushed past me he seemed to take me in properly for the first time. I clutched the dagger behind my back, praying that the trumpet sleeve of my dress covered it.

'Why, 'tis the little songbird.'

I curtseyed quickly, keeping my head down, then winced as I felt hard fingers under my chin, tilting my face towards him. He was frowning at me. 'You look different with your hair like that,' he said. He seemed at a loss. He dropped his fingers, still gazing at me stupidly.

I did not wait for him to dwell on it. *He is within seconds of remembering me from Madam Anora's*, I thought. *If he tells his father . . .*

I bobbed my head and fled from the room, past the astonished maid, past the idle guards chatting outside the main doors; out into the courtyard, where already the members of the Ministration were starting to assemble, their deep claret ceremonial robes dissolving into the shadow cast by the high walls. When no one was looking, I slid the dagger back into my boot and continued on my way swiftly, slipping through the busy passages. I only stopped at my bedchamber, to collect the mahogany box. I knew I would not be returning.

In his apartment Nate, dressed in his green silk jacket, was fitting his ratha into a new leather case, as tender as if it were a babe. He looked up in shock to see me without my hat, in such a state. 'Can we leave now?' I said urgently.

At once he took up his ratha and the sheets of music and we hurried out together, past the guard at the main door of the apartment and into the dull glare of the courtyard.

One of the distinctive black coaches of the Protectorate, washed and shining, stood in the shade, waiting for us.

The horses shook their heads as we approached, making the harness jingle. The driver doffed his leather cap. 'Tell him to hurry,' I begged.

We could do no more than a trot as he manoeuvred through the courtyards of the Palace. Around us people scattered from our path, glaring round in alarm and outrage.

I hid behind the velvet curtain at the window, but as we reached the main courtyard I peered out to see that the Ministration had increased in number: a claret-coloured parliament, silent in their ceremonial headdresses. As we swayed over the cobbles, the bird heads turned towards us – raven, rook, hawk, magpie, buzzard, jay – all turning as one to stare, eyes gleaming through the slits. The Ministration needed no plague masks: with the bird heads in place they had joined the Gods and were invulnerable.

Others were joining them, stepping out from the wide dark doorway of the Protector's apartment. There was the Lord Protector himself, in deep purple robes, holding his eagle head under his arm; Caleb Grouted, the sun shining on his oiled ringlets and the yellow silk coat; Mather and Chance, spruce and sinister in their dark grey military uniforms, ceremonial swords glittering at their hips. They all were waiting for Leah.

Our driver, nervous, must have flicked the horses with his whip, for we picked up speed as we rattled by and clouds of dust and grit and dried mud flew up under our wheels. We almost ran over Chance, who was standing closer than the others, and spattered his clean uniform with filth. I wasn't fast enough to pull the curtain across the window. As we passed, his furious eyes met mine and widened.

Then we were past the long line of waiting carriages, their eagle emblems gleaming in the hazy sun. I could see the drivers' faces shining with sweat as they waited patiently. It was suffocatingly hot in our own coach.

'Sacred wings, what's happened, Scuff?' said Nate, as we left the gates behind us and the horses began to canter. We clung to the arm-rests as the coach juddered from side to side. Warm, clammy air blew through as I jerked the window further open.

'I may be in danger, Nate,' I gasped, between the lurches. 'I don't know for sure.'

He looked more apprehensive still, and puzzled. 'I don't understand! You could escape. We've left the Palace.'

'I've sworn a sacred oath – I must keep it. I owe the Eagle that much, this time. I'll be safer in the Cathedral. They'll be busy with the nuptials.' But as I looked at Nate's nonplussed face, my heart was beating fast and my mouth dried, so that I had to keep swallowing.

A small crowd had gathered in the Cathedral square. A row of Enforcers and armed guards stood by the entrance ready to deal with any sign of disturbance, but after yesterday the people were subdued, their faces sullen and wary. It would not be long before the Curfew would drive them away, if the heat did not do so first. The late afternoon sun seemed to fill the whole sky, staining it a thick dark orange; the air was so dry it seemed to crackle.

Before we left the coach Nate passed me a plague mask. 'There have been more deaths in the last few days. Wear it until we're inside again.'

He wanted to carry the mahogany box for me, but I wouldn't let him take it and alighted with it under my arm. I felt most uncomfortable at the prospect of passing before those miserable, ragged people in my fine silk dress. And the first person I set eyes upon was Titus Molde, hat well pulled down, hunched over a stick like an old beggar, with a bulging sack on his back.

He looked up briefly, and gave me such a look it chilled my blood, even in such heat. I could not mistake the menace in that look, in the rolled white of his glinting eye. I thought he would confront me, but he turned away, his silent message of threat delivered.

I'd scarce had time to recover when a woman jumped out of the crowd and tried to snatch the mask from my face. Her face was greasy, her tattered dress marked with sweat. 'It's us needs protectin', not you grand folk from the Palace!' she shouted.

Around her others started muttering. The guards, alerted, moved forward; to my horror, one cracked his pistol butt against the woman's cheek. She staggered back, her hand to her bloody face.

Titus Molde had disappeared.

Nate took my arm and almost pushed me inside the

entrance of the Cathedral. It was dark inside today as if the light was too thick and heavy to penetrate the windows; the air was almost icy against my hot face when I pulled off the mask. The altar was brilliantly lit with candles, but the aisles and chapels were full of shadows, and in the shadows, the black lines of the empty pews and the lurking soldiers, ever watchful.

A small, chittering figure capered up to us from the darkness and touched my skirt. 'Gobchick!' A huge relief filled me that he was safe. For a moment, I hugged him; I could feel his heart thudding in its cage of bones. Then he peered up at me, his eyes mournful, frightened, as if he knew what I had to do, and ran off.

One of the soldiers saw him. 'Shall I go after him?' he said to his companion.

The other gave a contemptuous laugh. 'He'll not harm no one. He's naught but the Protector's lunatic fool, with a head full of fancies.'

The musicians passed us, on their way to set up their stands: elderly men and women, sombre-faced and shabby. Nate went to speak to the Master Musician about the programme. I sank down in a pew, the box at my feet, and tried to compose myself.

What can I do? I thought. Both inside the Cathedral and out I was beset by enemies.

Besides, it was too late to escape. From outside there came the muffled tolling of bells. The Curfew was beginning; soon the guests would arrive.

AMBERGATE

1

Chance sat with Mather in the stifling heat of their coach as it led the way down the Parade. He was still fuming, although he had managed to brush his uniform clean before they left. He'd seen the look of irritation Mather had given him, the smirks on the faces of the guards. Now he'd be a laughing stock, unless he managed to redeem himself first.

Behind them, watched impassively by the rows of Eagles on their plinths, a long slow-moving line of black coaches stretched all the way back to the Palace, surrounded by mounted Militia. The soldiers had pistols on the pummels of their saddles and were wearing the new black gauze plague masks; behind the masks their faces were grim, their eyes flicked over the dusty road ahead, across the brown parkland, checked the dying shrubbery. There was no flicker of life in the baked landscape; no breeze to lift the papery leaves. Overhead, the early evening sky had turned as livid as a weal.

Although they had the windows of the carriage open,

Chance was sure he could smell the swanskin, which was lying rolled up in a linen cloth on the opposite seat.

Earlier that morning, on the Protector's orders, he had gone with Mather to the room where it was kept. The Protector himself was there to oversee the opening of the cabinet and removal of the skin.

Mather had gestured to him impatiently. Chance had had to lift the swanskin from the case by himself and was forced to use both hands; he had been unable to touch the amulet at his neck, his iron locket. He cringed at the memory of the smooth slide of feathers against his fingers, the stiff yet springing shafts, a bony network dividing the softness.

'Gently, boy, gently,' growled Porter Grouted.

Why don't you do it yourself? thought Chance, screwing up his face in fear, as he gripped the feathers and started to lift the swanskin out. For an extraordinary moment he wanted to touch the feathers to his face, to stroke his cheeks with their softness and beauty. But then the fear and horror had come back.

There was so much of the swanskin, much more than he expected: the cloth was scarcely large enough to cover it. He had had to carry it out, and it was so much heavier than he could have imagined, as if it held the weight of water, like a memory.

And now it was filling the coach with its stink, he was sure of it. That stink of wild, weedy, watery places, of oily secretions and horrifying alien blood. He couldn't think why the Lord Protector didn't throw it straight back at Miss Leah, and good riddance. And today it was to be hoist on a golden pole in pride of place over the altar, like some sort of sacred trophy.

He noticed Mather was looking at it with equal dislike. 'When we reach the Cathedral,' Mather said, 'you will carry that thing in and give it to the two soldiers who are to bear it up the nave at the head of the procession. I won't be handling it myself, you understand? I have to check the security arrangements before the arrival of Miss Leah.'

'Do you want me to help with hanging the skin, Sir?' At least it would be a chance to walk in the procession, to be seen performing an official duty by all the men and women of the Ministration.

'I've men to hang it,' said Mather irritably. There was sweat on his upper lip. 'Just get it inside, will you?'

Never any thanks or recognition, thought Chance sullenly. To Mather he was merely a lowly servant. But soon things would be different.

That white face at the carriage window. There was someone who was frightened of him, over whom he had all the power in the world. The girl. Number 102. He had let her escape too many times. Her time was up and his was just beginning.

'Sir,' he said, careful to get the tone of his voice right: responsible, yet urgent. Sweat broke out over his body; he clenched his hands. 'Sir, I've not mentioned this to you before in case I was mistaken, but I've been doing some thinking and I reckon it's worth further investigation, Sir. I reckon the new girl singer at the Palace is Number 102, Sir.'

Mather frowned, sceptical. 'You must be absolutely sure, Corporal.'

'When her coach left for the Cathedral earlier, I knew I seen her before, certain sure. Remember I was that close to her in Poorgrass, held her wrist that time? I saw the brand mark! You remember, Sir?'

'Sacred flight!' Mather stared at him.

Chance nodded. A gleeful excitement was rising inside him. 'It's the same girl, Sir, I'm sure of it.'

'Certainly worth investigation, then, if nothing else.' Mather sucked his cheeks. 'We must lay our plans carefully, then, Chance. We don't want to frighten her.'

'Don't we, Sir?'

'If we do, she will escape yet again. Before we do anything else, we must make double sure all possible escape routes are closed to her. That will be easy enough, today of all days.' He leant back against the padded leather and cracked his knuckles. 'We shall trap our little songbird right there in the Cathedral. I shall speak to the Lord Protector as soon as we arrive.'

'And me, Sir? I'll be in this too, won't I, Sir?'

'You?' said Mather vaguely, deep in his own thoughts. 'Of course, Corporal. We'll need your earlier statement as proof.'

Chance stared out into the street, where small children

were cowering back from the rolling wheels of their coach: scummy children with starving faces, just as he had been once.

He was smiling to himself.

Porter Grouted and his son occupied the second carriage a little way behind; it was splendidly picked out in gold, as appropriate for the Lord Protector of the country himself.

Porter Grouted, resplendent in his rich purple robes, lounged at ease, his muscular body scarcely stirred by the jolts of the carriage as it went over the paving stones of the Parade. The sallow dome of his bald head glistened with sweat, but he hardly noticed the heat, as with satisfaction he surveyed his son on the opposite seat. He had not put on the ceremonial eagle mask yet and it sat next to him, glaring blankly ahead.

Caleb Grouted looked petulant. Every now and then he pulled at the yellow silk of his cravat as if it choked him. 'I wish I was marrying the little maid instead of Leah, Pa. Leah doesn't care for me and I don't care for her.'

'What's that?' A faint frown marred the Protector's complacent expression.

'That girl, that little maid who sings – I wish it was her I was marrying, Pa.'

Grouted sat forward, a menacing bulk. 'Damned nonsense. Most unsuitable. With Leah as your wife you'll fulfil the prophecy – establish our line for the future. That's your job now, son, and don't you forget it.'

Caleb subsided into sulky silence as the carriage swung into the streets near the Cathedral and began to lurch over the uneven cobbles. But his father had not finished with him. Unexpectedly, he gave a sudden chuckle.

'So you fancy that little hussy, do you? And on the eve of your weddin'! Grouteds have always had plenty of red blood in their veins.'

Caleb looked up. Keeping a wary eye on his father in case he should suddenly erupt into one of his unpredictable and powerful tempers, he said, 'That girl – she looks like Mama.'

There was a pause. From outside came the dull tolling of dozens of church bells; it was time for the earlier Curfew. The Lord Protector narrowed his eyes. 'What are you talkin' about?'

Caleb flinched from the lidless stare; he clenched the plague mask lying on his lap. 'I mean – she looks just like Mama does in the portrait.'

The Protector opened his mouth to speak. Before he could do so, his eyes rolled back and he gave a loud sneeze.

Father and son stared at each other in sudden fear.

'It's nothing,' said the Protector. 'A summer cold.'

But as he pulled a silk handkerchief from his pocket, his fingers shook very slightly. In an instant he had mastered himself.

'Tell me again – tell me about the girl, son,' he said softly.

* * *

Looking over the Master Musician's shoulder in the Cathedral, Nate saw the gleam of pale silk as the Messenger approached Scuff. He saw her stand up, give the Messenger a box; it was the box she'd brought with her in the coach.

Jealousy suddenly coiled in Nate's breast, surprising him. He knew Scuff loved the Messenger, had known it all along. What he hadn't realized until now was what he, Nate, felt about her.

Behind him the musicians were starting to tune up: he could hear the dolorous drone of the ecclesiastical woodwind. He winced; he'd always hated it. The mournful notes echoing through the Cathedral sounded like a dirge – as if someone was about to die.

The Lord Protector broke the news about the girl swiftly and bluntly to his Chief Interrogation Officer. They stood talking in hurried undertones in a patch of shadow by the great West entrance of the Cathedral.

'I want nothing to disrupt the wedding ceremony itself, understand, Mather?' the Protector said. Close by a soldier kicked away a sleeping beggar. 'Let's get my boy married first.'

'Right, My Lord.' Mather's hands twitched; he longed to get them on the girl. Another carriage rolled up and set down a member of the Ministration. When Curfew sounded the crowd had hurriedly dispersed, and now the square was dotted with figures in dark claret robes, the bird heads tilting to each other.

'But as soon as the service is over and the nuptial agreement signed by the couple, you can move in and arrest her.'

'Right, Sir.' Mather rubbed his twitching hands together.

'And, Mather, dispose of her without any undue bother, will you?'

Mather hesitated. 'Do I understand what you're saying, Sir?'

'You do, Mather.'

2

I bent to touch the dagger hidden in my boot, beneath my green skirts. From where I sat in the pew I looked around for Erland. At first I couldn't see him, then I saw he was sitting alone in the darkness of the Chapel of the Lark, across from the chancel. His head was bowed; he was waiting, too.

Already the minor officials were beginning to assemble before the Facilitator on either side of the altar: the clergy in their white vestments, slashed with scarlet; the scribes with their parchment and quills; the page-turners for the Divine Book, who went to stand beside the lectern. Vergers brought in a table for the Bird Cages and another for the signing of the nuptial agreement. Finally, a pair of padded, gold silk prayer mats were placed with reverence on the lowest step before the statue of the Eagle.

Then the choirmaster came in, chivvying his pinch-faced, meagre flock into the carved wooden choir stalls. In the shadows behind the arches, armed soldiers watched silently.

I felt Nate tug on my arm.

We were to wait in the darkness behind the Great Eagle on His altar, then move forward to stand either side of Leah and Caleb as they took their nuptial vows before the Facilitator. We would then perform a motet while they knelt before the Eagle for the Contemplation. That would be the moment I would act.

But I could not think about it.

We passed the musicians peering at their music in the half-light of the transept, then the choir stalls with their rows of ghostly faces. We ducked beneath the banners of the Birds of Light and the long golden pole that hung before the altar, and climbed the altar steps into the chancel. Nate held his ratha as if it were his salvation. My heart beat light and nervous as we stopped in the shadows cast by the altar screen.

They were beginning to come in.

The bodyguard Chance walked with another soldier, ahead of all the guests. Between them they carried a long rolled bundle, wrapped in a cloth. There was a swagger about Chance, a cocky air; his ceremonial sword swung jauntily at his hip.

Behind them filed the members of the Ministration in a long, silent procession, the candlelight gleaming on the feathers of the bird heads, outlining the sharpness of a beak, catching the glint of an eye. A moan arose from the choir stalls, quickly quelled by the choirmaster.

The Ministration filled the pews to almost halfway down

the nave. They sat motionless, the bird heads scarcely quivered.

Chance and the soldier came up to the chancel and climbed the altar steps. The soldier began to crank a handle hidden to one side. The gold pole came down in jerks, was lowered almost to the floor.

The Lord Protector entered wearing his ceremonial eagle head, to a roll of drums from outside. He was followed by various minions – bodyguards, footmen, soldiers – who melted away as he strode up the nave. I drew in my breath, for he seemed to have become the Eagle Himself in that moment, as his majestic purple robes swept along the stone to the front pew and the great head glared about. The musicians bowed their heads, touched their amulets; the choir murmured in fear. The bird heads of the Ministration bowed to him as he sat down.

Caleb Grouted came next, a sneer – or perhaps it was a smile – twisting his handsome face as he looked to left and right, acknowledging the bows of the Ministration. He made an obeisance and sat beside his father in the pew.

Chance and the soldier unrolled the bundle lying before the Eagle. I knew what it was immediately. It was a swanskin, like the one I had seen months ago in Gadd's shelter. But this was Leah's swanskin, and soon she, too, would see it. The two soldiers fastened the swanskin to a cord that ran the length of the pole, with an arrangement of gold clips. They began to hoist the pole over the first step of the altar, where Caleb and Leah would kneel for their vows.

There was an indrawing of breath from the pews as the swanskin was revealed. Surely it was sacrilege to display the skin of one of the avia in the Cathedral?

My own hand went to the amber beneath my dress.

From where I stood I had the back of the swanskin to me – the grey skin – but as it hung, it rippled and turned in the down-draughts from the vaulted roof, a banner of glistening white feathers, each tipped with gold as it caught the candlelight. This was the Protector's cruellest trick: to hang the swanskin so tantalizingly close, yet beyond reach until Leah had taken her vows. It would be the first thing she'd see on entering the Cathedral.

The musicians struck up the nuptial march.

It was difficult to see Leah at first: she was hidden by a grey mass of bodyguards. It was only when she reached the Lord Protector's pew and Caleb stepped out, that the bodyguards dispersed and I saw her white, clenched face beneath the pearled snood, her dark eyes staring up at the swanskin, her hands twisting and twisting together over her cream satin skirts.

The Facilitator came down the altar steps and she and Caleb stood before him, their heads bowed. The Facilitator's white gown had moth holes in the hem. My heart thumping, I stared at the back of his head, at the ruff of grey hair that ran around his pink scalp. It had become very dark in the Cathedral, as if a storm brooded above us.

The windows high above the glowing candles were dull and opaque.

Nate had shown me the words of the nuptial service, so they seemed almost familiar when I heard the Facilitator speak them in his deep, gentle voice.

'My Lord Protector, Members of the Ministration, we are here today to witness a marriage, as the birds of the heavens witnessed the first marriage of all, between the Robin and the Wren, who sit on either side of the Almighty . . .'

As his introduction went on, the Bird Keeper came in and placed the Cages on the table: the Robin in one and the Wren in the other. My eyes went to those poor little captive birds, half-dead lumps of feathers huddled on the floors of their cages, dazzled by candlelight into a state of shock. Even sacred birds, it seemed, suffered from fear. For indication of a good marriage it is said they burst into song after the vows, but a human singer is always provided should they not do so.

The words of that old song, 'Who Killed Cock Robin?' began to run around my head in the most macabre way. *'I,' said the sparrow, 'With my bow and arrow, I killed Cock Robin.'*

The musicians had stopped playing. Caleb, the Cock Robin, would be the first to take his vows.

Leah's eyes were contemptuous; she didn't look at Caleb. She didn't see the malice in his sidelong glance at her. In the darkness I bent and took the dagger from my boot and held it behind my back.

Then, unexpectedly, as the Facilitator was about to pronounce the vows for Caleb to repeat, the Lord Protector moved from his seat and strode forward towards the chancel. He left a surprised murmur from the Ministration seated behind him. My heart almost stopped beating. *He is coming for me! He knows what I'm holding!* The Facilitator stepped hastily to one side, startled from his gravity; the clerics eyed each other in shock. But even as I cowered back, the Protector stepped up to the lectern.

The great eagle's head lowered as he looked briefly, dismissively, at the Divine Book, then regarded his captive audience through the eye slits. There wasn't a sound throughout the Cathedral.

He took off the head. A cleric hurried forward to take it but he waved him away, and gripped it in one hand. He seemed equally imposing without it. His voice ground through the vast spaces of the ancient building, hitting the stone and coming back.

'Friends,' he began. 'We're gathered here for the weddin' of my son to my niece – a family occasion, you might call it. Yet you all know of the rumours concernin' Leah's late mother, and, indeed, of the mystery surroundin' Leah's time here in the Capital the past three years. When she was found half drowned she was clutching the very swanskin that hangs above us.' He paused, so that a hundred feathered heads could look up and regard the swanskin above the altar.

'We remember the legend of the avia, and some of you

may be concerned that the Ministration itself will be sullied by such a marriage, despite the new law allowin' it. As those of you who remained in the Capital for our recent Councils will know, Leah has declared in writin' that she is one of that mythical race. She is, indeed, avian.'

He paused as a muffled gasp of horror went up from some of the pews. Leah's face was expressionless, her eyes downcast. In the Chapel of the Lark Erland stirred restlessly, but I could not see his face. The back of the Protector's bald head turned swiftly from side to side: he was scanning the nave. I studied the bulge of flesh at the top of his neck as his voice grew harsher.

'Perhaps it is worth repeatin' my own personal views on this matter to you now, my friends, so that in future they will be your views as well.

'I believe we have misjudged and misinterpreted the avia through the ages. We have always thought them cursed by their double life – seen it as a punishment for challengin' the power of God Himself and wishin' to emulate Him.

'Yet what if through this double life the Almighty intended to bestow on them power and grace beyond the reach of ordinary man? My friends, I, your Protector, whose prime consideration is your well-bein' and that of my country, have come to understand only recently that all my life I've misinterpreted the legend of the avia. It is they that have the power, my friends, they who will grant us all salvation. If you marry earthly power with heavenly gifts then you can achieve no stronger union for the rulin' of a country. This is what the marriage between my niece Leah and my son Caleb will achieve.

'It was when I made a remarkable discovery below us in the crypt of the Cathedral that my views changed. As you know, the crypt had been blocked for many years. No one suspected it was there. Not only does it contain the legendary and priceless treasure of the Capital, the Amber Gate . . .' he paused, as a murmur of astonishment ran around the congregation '. . . but also an ancient painted ceiling, whose prophecy will be clear to you, as it was to me when I first saw it. Ladies and gentlemen, dear friends, after this service you will be led down to view these marvels . . .' he paused again for emphasis '. . . then you will understand.'

He moved away from the lectern and bowed to the Facilitator. 'Now get on with the nuptials, man,' he muttered. Then he went down the altar steps, the eagle head under his arm.

I thought it must have been a good speech, for throughout the Cathedral there was an enthralled and utter silence. The members of the Ministration did not speak or cheer or clap. They were eerily calm and unmoving. But as the Protector returned to the nave, they rose row upon row in their claret robes, and the bird heads lowered in submission. No one would dare question the Lord Protector's will.

Leah and Caleb knelt on the silk prayer mats, their heads bowed. Nate nodded to me and we went down to stand either side, so that we could perform our motet as soon as the couple had taken their vows.

The girl singer must stand by the man who is to be married. *The Cock Robin.* I looked at Caleb's black head, gleaming in the candlelight. Above us the swanskin moved softly, and for a moment Leah looked up and her eyes were desperate. I clutched the dagger tighter; my hand was slippery with sweat. *Now!* I thought, *do it now, while he mutters his vows after the Facilitator and his back is bowed*. Yet I was standing in full view of the entire Ministration and the Protector himself, the candles shining behind me. I would surely be stopped before the deed was done!

Unless I was quick.

I glanced behind me at the Eagle. I fancied I saw sadness in His damaged eyes.

The gilded cage was brought before Caleb as he knelt, and the Facilitator took his hand in his and placed it on the top. The robin inside did not stir. 'And I, Caleb Grouted, do swear . . .'

'. . . By the love I bear the Eagle and the first among His Heavenly Company, the Robin . . .' said the Facilitator, with a touch of reproof.

Caleb repeated the words in a mutter: '. . . to keep the words I have uttered pure unto my death-day.'

And then it was Leah's turn, and still I had not acted. The Facilitator waited, but she did not speak. 'I, Leah Tunstall, do take thee, Caleb Grouted . . .' He gave her the first line.

Her mouth opened; everyone in the Cathedral waited for her to speak. In the shadowy chapel I saw the pale gleam of the Messenger's silk coat.

Leah's gaze caught mine.

Behind my back I slipped the dagger from its sheath.

3

But now the moment had come I could not do it.

I blinked, perhaps I gave a tiny sound, for Leah looked at me again, her mouth still open to speak. But then my hand unclenched of its own doing.

With a dreadful clatter, I dropped the dagger on the stone.

But no one heard it. At that moment there was a commotion by the main door and two soldiers burst in, dragging a man between them who swore and bellowed like a maddened animal.

The bird heads of the Ministration craned around at the noise. The Facilitator stood frozen at the second interruption to his service. Whispering arose in the choir stalls and amongst the musicians. Quickly, I looked around for the dagger. It had slid beneath the nearest musician's chair.

The soldiers restrained the struggling man by the door, and an officer hurried forward to speak to Mather. I caught sight of the prisoner's furious face, the hacked gold hair, bright protruding eyes. It was Titus Molde, his hat knocked off and without the sack he'd been carrying.

'Sir, this man has been found loitering outside,' said the officer to Mather, his voice ringing in the silence.

'You know who he is?' said Mather. His voice carried back to the altar steps. 'One of the rebel leaders. You've done well. Take him away.'

Molde yelled something that was cut off abruptly as the soldiers half carried him out. A blast of heat hit us as the doors opened and closed.

In the front pew the Lord Protector was unruffled. 'Molde captured, eh? An excellent augury coming today, Mather.'

It was then I knew I was reprieved. My understanding of things turned a somersault in my poor mazed mind. Molde – a rebel leader? I could scarce grasp it after so long believing him a soldier. I was free of his impossible bargain at last. How long had I known I would never be able to kill another human being? Perhaps from the very first. Murder was surely the greatest wrong of all.

But if I was reprieved, Leah was not.

'On with the ceremony, then, Master Facilitator,' called the Protector, and he settled himself more comfortably. 'Let's hear my niece's vows.'

The officer said something to Mather in an undertone; they had a hasty conversation while the Facilitator waited for silence.

'What now? Why the delay?' growled the Lord Protector irritably. He'd not replaced the eagle head and I could see him glare about him.

Mather bent to whisper. The Protector shook his head. 'No! Let 'em deal with it!' He shouted across to the Facilitator. 'Hurry up, man!'

The officer hurried back down the aisle. The soldiers guarding the West doors murmured like a restless wind and the murmur was taken up by the others in the shadows behind the arches. As Mather slipped away to deal with them, the Protector ignored the whispering; he jerked his head impatiently at the Facilitator.

The Facilitator repeated the first of the marriage vows to Leah, his voice shaking a little. 'I, Leah Tunstall, do take thee, Caleb Grouted . . .'

Leah bowed her head. Caleb shot her a glance of pure venom. Then Leah spoke at last, her voice reedy and thin, like the wail of a drowning soul. 'I, Leah Tunstall, do take thee . . .'

She never finished. With a high sound like the ripping of silk, the swanskin began to split. Along the length of the golden pole the tear grew. Every person in the Cathedral saw it. They stared, motionless, as feathers flew loose and, caught in the down-draughts from the roof, eddied and swirled in all directions.

The swanskin was rent from end to end. It dropped heavily through the air.

I started back as it swept past my head, almost touching

my hair, narrowly missing the candle flames. A gasp went up. Someone screamed in the choir stalls.

A figure was struggling on the stone floor at the bottom of the altar steps, writhing beneath the skin, fighting through the feathers. One hand clawed at the floor, clawed at Leah, who drew back, ashen-faced; the other hand brushed frantically at mouth and nose.

Caleb was trapped. The Protector and the Ministration could not see him, for the musicians' stands hid him from their view, but the Facilitator, the clerics, all those in the chancel, stared down in horror. No one wanted to touch a skin that had belonged to a member of the avia.

I shook Nate's hand away; I moved quickly, with no thought. In one movement I threw the swanskin off Caleb, and was astonished. There was no weight to it at all.

He lay, sobbing for breath. He was scarce a man at all at that moment. I wasn't sure why I'd freed him.

Leah clutched the ruined swanskin to her breast. She looked around wildly. 'Erland?'

'Hush!' I whispered. But I could no longer see him in the Chapel of the Lark.

'Are you recovered, Sir?' called the Facilitator to Caleb, who was sitting up and swearing most vilely to himself – oaths that I alone could hear.

'No, I am not!' he shouted back. 'That thing . . .' pointing to the swanskin '. . . nearly killed me! What fools hung it? I shall have their guts!'

'Should we get back into our positions?' said Nate

nervously to the Facilitator. The Protector was standing up, would be coming to rally his son, bully the Facilitator into continuing the service. With a resigned expression, the Facilitator watched Porter Grouted – Lord Protector and Controller of the Church – step from his pew and march forward.

The muttering from the soldiers that had been silenced by the rending of the swanskin arose again, louder, more urgent. An officer ran up the nave towards the Lord Protector as he began to weave determinedly through the musicians' stands towards the chancel. A yell went up from the entrance: meaningless, filled with fear.

The Ministration stirred as they heard it, the bird heads turned towards each other. The Lord Protector stopped where he was, his face like thunder. He turned, sending vellum sheets of music flying. The officer said something, the Protector thrust him off.

But the members of the Ministration were rising, taking off their bird heads. Some were pushing others to get out of the pews, had even left the heads behind. I caught a glimpse of a woman's white face, streaked where sweat had run down through the powder. Mather was trying to get through them, to reach the Protector. I could see Chance running hither and thither to Mather with messages for him, orders for the officers.

'What on earth is happening?' said Nate, dazed.

And then I understood. We all did up by the altar. The smell had reached us by then: no longer the fragrance of the incense burners, but now the faint but unmistakeable smell of smoke drifted through the chill air of the Cathedral.

The Facilitator tried to keep his composure. 'I advise you not to move until we know what exactly is happening,' he said quietly to the Chief Cleric.

Nate gripped my arm. 'There must be a fire somewhere!' he whispered.

'Where?' I said bewildered, for how could a stone building catch fire?

'The scaffolding outside, I think.' He put out his hand to Leah, who still held the swanskin to her. 'Miss Leah, your safety must take first priority . . .'

'Oh, fiddlesticks! My life's not worth saving.'

Caleb scrambled to his feet. 'Well, mine is. My life's more valuable than hers, you numbskull. I'm the son of the Lord Protector. Where's Papa? Are they putting the fire out?'

'I'm sure it's being dealt with, Master Caleb,' said the Facilitator.

Through the agitation of the musicians there were glimpses of the Protector surrounded by bodyguards and anxious members of the Ministration. The noise came to us from a long way away, as if across a rough sea. Some of the musicians' stands swayed and toppled as the musicians rose to their feet in panic; sheets of music floated to the floor. Someone slipped, causing further commotion. The choristers were rising, leaving the stalls in a flood, jostling down the side aisles.

'What should we do, Nate?' I said.

The calm of the Facilitator was disappearing. 'My dear brothers in God, colleagues . . .' he protested, as the other officiating clergy broke from their line behind the altar table and began to cluster in small agitated groups. In their cages the birds began to flutter wildly. The Bird Keeper fussed around them, crooning in a high voice.

'We should put out the candles as a precaution,' said the Facilitator.

'Let me do it, Master,' said a young cleric. He fetched the long candle-snuffer from somewhere behind the altar table.

The Facilitator picked up a candle, stepped up to the lectern and raised his voice strongly.

'Fellow men and women, let us fall on our knees and pray forgiveness for our sins, lest our lives be cut short without the Last Words. Let us pray for courage in this moment of adversity. Let us remember the example of the tiny Wren, who flew through thunder and molten rocks to reach the Eagle's side and take her place in the peaceful heavens above the sky. Let us kneel at this moment and beg for her fearlessness.'

I could see some were kneeling, but most had not heard or were too panicked to pay attention. Leah remained on her feet, her face inscrutable. Nate and I sank to our knees, Nate, I think, to please the Facilitator, but I tried to pray and held my amber. I was not sure it would save me this time; I'd asked so much of it.

'This is punishment, Master,' shouted an elderly musician. He clutched his long samphrit to his chest as if it too were an amulet. 'We have committed sacrilege.'

A woman in Ministration robes close to the Protector moaned, 'We hung up the pelt of an avian, violating His holy place. We gathered to witness a marriage between our Protector's son and a member of the avia.'

People turned to glare at Leah; their hatred and fear were tangible. She went paler still, but she did not flinch nor drop the shreds of swanskin. Close to me, two clerics muttered together. 'The Protector spoke heresy.'

'This is retribution sent by the Eagle Himself!' shouted another musician, waving his sheet music.

The Lord Protector held up a hand. It was enough to stop the voices, at least near the chancel. His voice carried easily, a guttural boom with no trace of panic.

'My friends. I gather this is the work of the rebel, Titus Molde, who was arrested earlier. A sack of kindling has been found. He must have managed to fire the scaffolding outside the main entrance before he was arrested. However, there is another way out of the Cathedral, through the North door. If you allow the soldiers to guide you, you will find yourself escorted safe outside.'

There was a sudden blast of heat as one of the West doors began to char on the inside. Flickers of flame ran up the sides. A horrible shriek pierced through the Cathedral: someone had been standing too close.

Even on the altar steps I felt the heat touch us like the

searching of a blind finger. Then the last of the candles on the altar steps were snuffed out, and for a moment I could see nothing.

Caleb began to scream.

4

'I'm going to get my ratha case,' Nate whispered in Scuff's ear. 'Don't move!'

All around them there was a confusion of milling bodies. Someone must have extinguished the other candles in the Cathedral. In the darkness he could hear officers trying to control the panic, trying to usher people in the right direction, towards the North door. Caleb had stopped screaming and was shouting for his father.

The darkness seemed to lift a little; his eyes were adapting, but the air was filling with a fug of smoke. The back of his throat stung; his eyes smarted. As he fumbled for his ratha case on the floor of the chancel, he heard Scuff cry, 'Where's Miss Leah?'

His hands touched leather; thankfully, he fitted his ratha inside, and held the case to him. He looked around for Scuff. She had found Miss Leah; in the choking semi-darkness they were struggling down the altar steps to join the people crowding to the North door.

That was when the main doors blew in.

There was a huge explosion of flame and smoke, a roar. Sparks flew halfway up the nave, as if someone hurled burning stars. Heat blasted through the Cathedral, hotter than the sun. In a second the pews nearest the doors had caught fire. A snake of flame coiled through the pews in the Chapel of the Wren. A soldier beat at his head, where his hair was alight; a tongue of fire licked down the back of another man's jacket.

The bird heads of the Ministration fell to the ground and were crushed. People were shrieking, choking. They scrabbled their way to the North door, their hands to their throats, coughing, pulling up the necks of their ceremonial robes to cover their mouths, making strangulated cries for air. It was now almost impossible to breathe.

'Open the door, for God's sake!' shouted a voice somewhere in the smoke and others took up the cry.

'The rebels are outside! We're surrounded!' came another shout, despairing.

A tall figure was beside Nate, the lapels of his white frock-coat pulled up around his face. 'Get the girls! Get them down to the crypt!'

Nate stared up and made out the deep-set eyes of the Messenger. 'But – the guards!' he gasped.

'They've run, left their posts. The stairwell's clear. The air's clean down there.'

'Won't we be trapped?' protested Nate, but the Messenger had already vanished into the shimmering, spark-filled air.

With a crash the North door was opened, and as fresh air fed the flames, the fire inside the Cathedral intensified. The crowd pressed forward to escape, then swayed back in a panic-stricken body, as the sounds of a fierce battle outside echoed into the Cathedral over the crackling of the flames. Gunshot and a clashing of weapons, the shouts of men and from somewhere – outside or within the doorway – a horrible, muffled screaming.

'Quick, Nate!' Scuff had grasped his sleeve, was pulling him with her; beside her Miss Leah still gripped the ruined swanskin.

Nate came to himself, tucked the ratha case more securely under his arm. 'Not that way – to the crypt!'

He caught Scuff's hand, and she caught Miss Leah's and the three of them ran from the turmoil. In the apse the air was fresher, the area deserted. Nate blinked away tears: his eyes were streaming. Beneath the arches, oil lanterns burned in readiness for the showing of the crypt. He let go Scuff's hand, seized a lantern and made for the stairwell. 'Come on!'

The lantern light moved over the narrow stone walls and the steps leading down into darkness. Miss Leah hesitated and clutched the torn swanskin to her. 'What is this place?' she said wonderingly, her voice hoarse. 'I smell water.'

Nate could smell nothing but the smoke still in his nostrils and clinging to his garments.

'Is it far down?' said Miss Leah. Her voice trembled a little. 'I don't like enclosed spaces, Master Nate.'

'But Nate, there's no way out below!' Scuff said. 'The Amber Gate is locked, and you've no key.'

The two girls were hanging back from the dark hole, white-faced. In desperation Nate said, 'Do you want to be burned alive or slaughtered by the rebels? The air will be clean down there, the Messenger said so!'

'The Messenger?' said Miss Leah.

'He said to go down.' He felt a momentary pang at how the Messenger's name seemed to persuade them both to move at last.

He led the way down, holding the lantern high, and stepped out into the crypt. The three of them stood in the lamplight, looking silently around at the alcoves closest to them where candles had already been lit, and at the shadowed arches beyond. The air was cold and fresh, and as a tiny draught stirred against his hot cheek, he too could smell water.

Behind them footsteps slipped down the stairwell: not the ring of boots, but shoes, soled with soft leather. The Messenger emerged, holding a hemp bag in one hand and the wooden box Scuff had given him beneath his other arm. He'd found his way down without a light, Nate thought. He must see in the dark like a wild creature.

Miss Leah ran to him at once and put her hand to his cheek without speaking; she showed him the ruined swanskin. Nate could not see Miss Leah's face, but he saw the Messenger's expression as he set down the bag and box and took the swanskin from her. He was trying to hold the rents together as if he could somehow mend them with his fingers for her, and all the time she clutched his arm as if she'd never let go.

Nate saw that they loved each other. He wondered if Scuff had seen it too, and felt painfully for her.

The Messenger kept hold of the swanskin and clasped Miss Leah's hand with his free one. 'The Militia will overpower the rebels soon,' he said urgently, looking around at the three of them. 'There are few rebels and many soldiers. I couldn't see what had happened to the Lord Protector, but no doubt he has survived. We should wait down here until the fire burns itself out in the Cathedral.'

'You could have left with the Protector,' Nate blurted out, almost aggressively, and he saw the grave eyes focus on him. 'You could be safe outside in the open air by now. The Militia would have guarded you. Why come back to us?'

'Does it need explanation?' said the Messenger quietly. He turned to Leah, as Nate felt a flush rise to his cheeks. 'Take my bag, there's a water bottle in it. We could all do with wetting our throats, I think.'

They passed the stone water bottle around. Nate watched Scuff as she drank, her eyes on the Messenger. While he tried not to gulp more than his fair share, desperate to relieve his parched throat, he wondered if she would ever look at him in that way, or trust him enough to tell him what she'd been through. When this was all over, he'd compose a romance, play it to her on his ratha.

Slowly they all sank down and sat on the cold stone in the pool of lamplight. The Messenger opened the box and took out a feather, running his fingers idly over its softness, his eyes narrow as he looked into the darkness beyond the arches. Leah stuffed the bottle back into the hemp bag. She dragged off her pearl snood and flung it down, shaking her hair free. They stared around at each other, taking stock of their red-rimmed eyes and blackened faces, the drooping, bedraggled wedding finery, the once-beautiful silks and satins scorched from the smoke. *We look like a gang of street urchins*, thought Nate, as he settled his ratha case against him. He felt unutterably weary.

There wasn't a sound except the *drip*, *drip* of water and their quick breathing. The stones waited, stolid, unmoving. Time stretched. Nate's heart slowed. They were in another world from the tumultuous hell above.

'Look above you,' said the Messenger's voice softly. 'Do you see the swans, Leah?'

When Erland came into the crypt, his eyes went straight to Leah. I minded that, but I think I expected it. But then Erland looked at me, and there was something in his gaze that made me happy.

We sat down finally, for there was nothing else to do. We knew we would have to wait a long time before it would be safe to go back up into the Cathedral, and none of us could bear to think of what might follow then.

'Look above you. Do you see the swans, Leah?' Erland said. Above our heads the colours glowed; the gold leaf glinted in the candlelight.

'Do they have a meaning, I wonder?' she whispered, staring up. Nate beat a tiny tune on the leather of his ratha case. 'Can you tell me, Nate? Your father was Keeper of the Keys, I believe, and knew much about the city's history.'

He cleared his throat and began a little bashfully; even in the lamplight I could see him blush at being the centre of attention.

'My father always said this was a mystical ceiling, of great importance to the city, Miss Leah. Do you see that in each panel the swan wears the crown? The Protector chose to interpret that as a prophecy, to suit his own ends. He thought he could present himself as the begetter of a dynasty through your marriage to his son. He knew it would stop any members of the Ministration plotting to overthrow him and his son after him, if they thought Caleb was ruling by divine providence.'

I looked at the elegant circlets of gold. 'But the swans wear the crowns around their necks, Nate. What does that mean?'

'Power is a responsibility,' Erland murmured.

'It's a yoke,' said Leah. For a moment she looked frightened. I watched out of the corner of my eye as Erland laid his hand on hers.

'But perhaps the crowns and swans mean something

more than earthly power alone,' said Nate thoughtfully. 'That's what my father always said. Perhaps the Protector was nearer the truth in his speech this evening than he realized.'

I could not recall now what the Protector had said. At the time I had been too agitated to understand his meaning.

Leah was impatient, fretting. 'What now, though? Is there no way of escape from here? If we stay until the fire has burned out above, the Protector will have soldiers posted back around the Cathedral. He's determined on this marriage. We'll be caught as we leave! I'd rather starve to death down here than be captured again.'

'I'll stay with you,' I said quietly. I was still the girl whom Mather and Chance were after: Number 102.

'I'm going to look at the Amber Gate,' she said restlessly. We were all recovering in our own ways, but Erland still looked weary. So Nate took a candle and went with Leah, for he was always courteous and I sensed he was eager to see it for himself – this marvel of which his father had spoken so often – but I wanted to stay with Erland, to have him to myself for a moment.

We saw the candle flicker as Leah peered into nooks and crannies on the way, searching for any means of escape. Their voices echoed back to us, their exclamations of wonder as they found the Gate.

Erland leant towards me. 'There is something I must tell you.'

But even as he spoke we heard Leah call in sudden excitement, 'I see a boat!'

I could see her trying to push against the gold branches. 'There's no boat, Miss Leah, and there's no key to the lock either,' I heard Nate say despondently.

'There is a boat. Look, there!'

Erland and I glanced at each other and he picked up the lantern. In spite of our weariness we almost ran.

With more light we could see what Leah said was true. As I looked between the golden branches, there was a boat stirring softly with the dark water, touching the brick platform beyond the Gate. It was a long, flimsy craft, with oars stowed in the hull. 'Perhaps the tide has drawn it through the tunnel,' said Nate, puzzled. It seemed magical – miraculous – to see such a thing, as if it had floated to us in answer to our desperate need.

'If we could reach it – unlock the Gate . . .' said Leah. I saw her face was lit with longing now she saw the possibility of a new life so close. 'Can't we think of something?'

Nate shook his head. 'There may have been a key once, an age ago . . .'

'Amber Gate . . .' I whispered to myself. I looked up at the curving branches, the birds surrounded by luxuriant fruit: the gate of plenty, the gate to Paradise. Amber and gold . . .

A memory flicked into my mind. Long ago I had played with treasures – his treasures – and he had let me. 'Gobchick!' I said. 'Where is he?'

We called his name, to no avail. His den was empty, his blankets in a heap. We took candles into the darkest alcoves behind the arches, where the shelves of coffins were, the jars of skulls, the stone boxes of bones. I was nervous at being so close to dead men, but I knew I had to find him.

'You are brave these days, Scuff,' said Erland, in a low voice, when I had come out into the open from another alcove.

'Only on the outside.'

'That is all anyone ever is.'

'What was it you wanted to say to me?'

'Later – when this is over.'

There was a tiny sound of movement, so near it chilled my blood. But it was not one of the skeletons come for us, but Gobchick, curled up in an empty coffin that was only half pushed into a bottom shelf and stuck out over the stone floor. He was whimpering quietly, and when I held my candle close he put his little hands over his eyes like a child.

'Why, Gobchick,' Erland said gently. 'Why are you in here? Were you hiding from us?'

He shook his head. I saw with pity that he was trembling.

'There are no soldiers down here, don't be frightened.' Erland held his hand out and Gobchick took it and climbed out stiffly, as if his joints pained him. This was too damp a place for an old man.

'Gobchick,' I whispered. 'Will you show me your treasures, as you used to do?'

He looked at me with eyes that were as sorrowful as a dog's, yet he did his little shuffling walk hand in hand with me back to the den that we had searched already. 'Are they here?' I looked doubtfully at the tumble of bedding on the bare stone floor.

For answer he let go my hand and disappeared in the blink of an eye. I had no notion where he had gone. But he wriggled out of the bottom shelf between two coffins with a little sacking bag, the kind that usually contains church money. 'May I look?' I said.

He nodded.

I knelt down with him beside me and I poured the contents of the bag out on to the stone. The others kept back and did not press us, so it was we two crouching on the floor with the candlelight glinting on Gobchick's hoard of treasures, as I ran my fingers over them, turning them over, separating them. I knew what it was I looked for.

I could hear him crooning over them: gilt buttons of all shapes and sizes, a foreign coin of tarnished silver, a baby's pewter teether much bitten, coloured beads, a broken ivory comb, part of a gold locket, three pearls. Sharp-eyed as a jay, he had picked them up from the floor of the Cathedral and lovingly stored them away.

How long had he had some of them? Did I remember playing with any of them? I didn't know. I was bitterly disappointed. My head drooped. 'I thought there might be a key. Did you ever have a key, Gobchick?'

A curious sound came from him. When I looked at him I saw he was weeping: tears coursed down his wrinkled cheeks. I could not bear to see him cry. 'Why, what is it? You've lost the key, is that it?'

He ducked his head. I knew suddenly that he still had it.

'Please, Gobchick. If we stay here, we shall all die, most like.'

'You, little one?' he said, with a wistful look.

'That is certain sure.'

At once he put his hand into his feathers. When he brought it out again he held a key. When I took it from him it was solid gold and heavy, and it held the warmth of him.

'This is the key to the Amber Gate,' I said with great excitement, for I knew it must be; and he nodded and a tear splashed on the stone.

'Was it you that brought the boat, Gobchick?' I was amazed, for I did not think he had such strength in him.

He nodded again. 'From Paradise.'

'Paradise?'

'Now you will go,' he moaned. 'Leave Gobchick again.'

I could not speak for a moment. I understood why he'd hidden the key. Yet part of him wished to help: he had brought the boat for us. 'Come with us,' I said, saddened by his misery and worried for his state. 'You can't stay here.'

'Gobchick keeps Ambergate safe. Must say goodbye to his little Clem.'

'What did you call me?' I said, scarce breathing.

He looked at me with his bright eyes. 'Clemency. Gobchick's little Clemency. You are darling baby of the Lady.'

And at that self-same moment, as I gazed at him in shock, there came a clatter of boots down the steps outside the crypt and a voice shouted: 'Have you the girl singer there? She is under arrest by order of the Lord Protector!'

5

Gobchick must have vanished at once. Erland was the first of us to come to his senses. We were all too shocked to move. 'This is the Messenger,' he called back, his voice firm. 'She is under my guard. There is no need to concern yourself, whoever you are.'

'You are a traitor,' came the voice, boldly confident. 'The rebel Molde has confessed. We know everything. You, too, are under my arrest.'

It was Chance that burst into the crypt, brandishing his ceremonial sword. His face was smeared with smoke stains but triumphant as he eyed us all, not in the least taken aback to find himself outnumbered. He knew none of us was armed. His red-rimmed eyes glittered dangerously in the candlelight, and so did his sword.

'Quite a little catch!' he said, and he made a mock bow to Leah. 'Your uncle will be most pleased to find you safe and well, Miss Leah.'

'Safe, but distinctly unwell on seeing you, bodyguard,' she said, her lip curling.

'No thanks for someone who brought that ruddy great swanskin of yours all the way to the Cathedral today? Evil heavy it was, too.'

Leah said nothing, so Chance turned his attention to me. 'And you, Number 102,' he said slowly. 'Clemency Fane by your given name. You look so took back I see you'd no notion of your true identity. Yes, you've rebel blood in you, my sweet. You are the daughter of the late Lady Sophia and of her own true and secret love, Robert Fane. They carried on right under the Lord Protector's nose – until he found out, that is.'

I thought I might faint. I was dimly aware that everyone was staring at me, at Chance.

I am not a number. I am a name.

'The Protector tried to have you killed when she died,' mused Chance. 'Pity was, from his point of view, he didn't succeed. It wasn't till recent he was told by one of them very soldiers commanded to kill you all those years ago – on his death-bed, he was – that the little girl was still alive and not so little now.'

Erland's eyes, shadowed beneath their heavy brows, met mine. I couldn't tell his thoughts, but he reached out and pressed my hand as if in acknowledgement. Chance chortled. 'You don't know everything, see, Messenger!'

But I looked back at Erland and wondered. *Did you know all along?*

'How do *you* know this?' Nate said to Chance, frowning.

'Officer Mather told me the whole story on the way to

the Cathedral today. Like getting blood out of a stone to squeeze any confidences from that one.' He puffed out his chest. 'But he owed me. It was my sharp eye that spotted her, right back at Murkmere, see? Wanted to know what all the fuss was about, didn't I?' He looked at me impudently. 'Who knows, you might have made a leader yourself one day and we can't have that. They'd love you, the rebels. Daughter of Robert Fane? You're a dangerous girl, Number 102.'

'You said my name was Clemency,' I said tightly.

'Habit,' said Chance, shaking his head. 'It's the habit, see. Number 102 comes easier. That's what you'll be arrested under.'

Near me, Nate ground his teeth; I could hear him. 'Don't lay a finger on her. You'll have two strong men to fight if you do.'

Chance looked him up and down with a sneer, and then Erland. 'What, a Boy Musician, whose hands are better acquainted with a ratha than fisticuffs, and a silken sop of a courtier? Anyway, all I've got to do is guard you. I was clever. I knew you'd be down here. I've armed soldiers coming any minute.' He went up to Erland, watching us from the corner of his eye for any movement, and jabbed him under the chin with his sword hilt. 'What do you think of that, traitor-boy?'

'What makes you think I'm a traitor?' Erland said wearily.

'You spied on the Lord Protector, didn't you? Then you repeated all his doings to Molde and the other rebels.'

'Doesn't it rather depend on whose cause you support? I support the rebels' cause, I freely admit it.'

'Bit late for that, ain't it? You won't be doing any more spying for them.'

A strange little mutter came from the shadows beneath one of the arches where the dead men's caves were, then a breathy cough that might have been ghostly laughter echoed round and round the crypt.

Chance whirled around in fear. 'What's that? Who's there?'

A long thigh bone slid out over the stone almost to his feet and he drew back in horror.

The next moment Erland's arms were round his neck, squeezing, and he had dropped his sword with a ringing sound that went on and on, until the sword was picked up by Nate and pointed at his throat. Gobchick capered from the shadows in glee, his feathers bobbing, his little wizened face cracked by a grin.

Chance went limp. 'Now I've seen everything,' he moaned. 'A chicken man as well as a swan girl.'

In one movement Erland moved his hands from Chance's neck to his arms and grasped them behind him. 'All right, all right,' Chance muttered. 'I give up.'

I slipped off my underskirt and began to tear it swiftly into strips; it was not the best quality else it wouldn't have torn so easy. Then I bound the bodyguard's arms as quick as I could while Nate stood over him with the sword.

We made Chance sit on the floor against the wall. 'Worth a try, wasn't it?' he said sulkily.

'You mean all that about the soldiers coming was nonsense?' demanded Leah.

'No, they're coming all right. They're searching for bodies right through the Cathedral, hoping to find yours maybe. They'll be coming down here.' He looked up at us sideways. 'Suppose you'll kill me now, anyway. Might as well tell you there's no edge to that sword – it's just for show. You'll have to strangle me with your bare hands.'

'We're not going to kill you,' said Nate scornfully, but he laid the sword down out of Chance's reach. 'We'll have to take you with us, though. We don't want you staying here and telling the Militia about us.'

Chance looked amazed. 'Go with you? You think you can get out of this place? If you go up the steps you'll run slap bang into them.'

'We've a key to the Gate,' I blurted out most foolishly and then wished I hadn't, for the soldiers might arrive before we could use it.

I ran to the Amber Gate and Gobchick capered after me. 'Let Gobchick do for Clemmie,' he sang out, and so I gave him the key. He was the Gate's guardian and should unlock it, not I.

He looked at me with dreaming eyes, the key in his hands. 'Gobchick brought you here to play, long time ago.'

'I know, Gobchick.'

'Now Gobchick is alone again.'

'Are you sure you won't come with us?'

He shook his head. ' 'Tis goodbye at last for we two.'

I bent and kissed his wrinkled cheek. 'We'll meet again, I know it.'

He put his free hand to his face and cupped it there, as if he held the kiss. 'In the sky behind the sky.'

I had to watch while he fumbled the key into the lock with his old, bent fingers. Behind us I thought the others must be in a fever of impatience. Erland and Nate had heaved Chance to his feet; he was pinioned between them. He had a sardonic air about him.

'Is it that boat we're to go in? It'll sink, as sure as maybe.'

'You can be first in, then,' said Nate fiercely. 'You try it out for us.'

'You'll have to untie me first.'

'You'll come willingly?' said Nate, incredulous and suspicious.

'There's nothing for me here. I've disgraced myself today with that skin thing.' He glanced at the torn swanskin, heaped on the ground where we had been sitting. 'I'll be blamed. Mather will say I didn't fix it proper. I'm never going to prove myself to *him*, so I might as well throw in my lot with you.' He looked at me with strange humility. 'That is – if you don't mind.'

I looked back at him in surprise and found myself giving a tiny nod. Nate cast his eyes heavenwards, gave up on us both and darted back for his ratha.

Once Gobchick had managed to turn the key we all

pulled together, for the double gates were heavy, but at last there was a space wide enough for us to squeeze through on to the brick platform. Nate lifted the lantern and we saw that Gobchick had tethered the boat to the iron ring above the level of the black water.

'Goodbye, wise man,' said Nate to Gobchick, and pressed his shoulder. Then he lowered the lantern gingerly, so that it rested in the bows of the boat.

Chance seemed surprising happy to be first to climb in. The boat bobbed on the gently moving surface, but didn't sink. 'Who's next?' he said, with a cheeky grin, and crouched down in the stern.

Nate climbed in, giving him a disgruntled look, and stored his ratha case by his feet in the bows. He held out his hand for me. I stepped from the platform on to the edge above the channel. 'Erland?' I said. He was still the other side of the Gate.

Leah whirled around on the platform and saw him hesitating. 'Erland! Why are you waiting? Hurry, for God's sake!'

'I can't come, Leah.'

She stared back at him, her eyes wide and frightened. 'What do you mean? You must come!'

He looked over at the two youths. 'There's not enough room in the boat. It will sink with a grown man's weight. I'll make my own way out of the Cathedral. I'll find you later, never fear.'

If my heart sank, so must hers have done. Her face

crumpled; she looked so taken aback and forlorn. If she had not been my rival, I might have wished to comfort her. At once she ran back through to him. 'Then I will stay with you!'

He held her hands, murmuring to her. I saw him shake his head.

'Climb into the boat, Scuff,' said Nate, exasperated, since I still hovered on the edge, looking back. 'Leah will come. Take my hand.'

'I need no help,' I said stiffly. 'And my name is Clemency.'

'I'll settle for Clemmie,' said Chance.

Nate looked furious. 'What's it to do with you?'

Erland looked over at me. 'Goodbye, Clemency . . .' he said, so gravely that I felt my name did have a meaning, as Gobchick had told me only yesterday if only I'd understood him '. . . Goodbye, Clemency. Your shoes will fit you now.'

I couldn't say goodbye. Lifting my skirts, I climbed awkwardly into the boat without looking either at him or Leah again; and sat on the middle seat with my back to them both, I was so choked. Leah would have the private goodbye I so desired, for Leah was his true soul's love, as well I knew. His love for me had been care and kindness and responsibility, no lesser love but not the same.

So I did not turn around. I feared they might be kissing, and that would send the last bitter pang through me. I gazed at my hands, clenched together, and when I looked up it was to see Nate on the plank seat in the bows opposite, staring at me, his back to the lantern, his face in shadow. He dropped his gaze at once, and reached for the oars that were stowed in the bottom of the boat.

'Leah!' he called, sharply for him, forgetting his usual 'Miss'. 'We must leave!'

I only hoped he knew how to row, for though the oars looked serviceable enough, I, for one, had no notion what to do with them. But already he was fitting them into a sort of clasp, one each side of the boat.

'Here's my bag,' I heard Erland say to Leah. 'There's the water bottle and spare candles inside.'

'But won't you need them? Let me take them out . . .'

'No,' he said.

She climbed into the boat with the bag and sat next to me on the middle seat, resting its bulkiness against her skirts. She was so close I could see the glitter of tears standing in her eyes. Then she started and turned around, and I did too.

It was the sound we dreaded: the hard ring of boots on the steps. Soldiers! How many were coming? Leah's hand went to her mouth. 'Erland!' she whispered.

The boots clattered on the stone, then stopped. We could hear their raised voices arguing about whether to venture all the way down. They must know it was a crypt, full of dead people. Then a louder voice, in command, ordering them on.

I thought Erland must join us now, for he was on the wrong side of the Gate; but he still did not leave the crypt.

For a second he was motionless, then he began to push both sides of the Gate together with all his might, while Gobchick struggled to help him. Beside me on the plank seat, Leah was white-faced and helpless.

'Undo the knot!' Nate hissed at me, and I leant over to the side where the ring was and tried to loosen the rope, for I must not let him down now. My hands trembled so much, it was hard to do. Then at last I'd done it, and I gathered the painter into the boat.

Leah's gaze hadn't left Erland. Tears ran down her face that she did not brush away; she made no sound.

'You can't lock the Gate from this side,' Nate whispered to me.

Erland slipped the key into the lock and turned it, then stood with his back to the Amber Gate, waiting. He made no move to hide, but Gobchick slipped away into the shadows. I did not see him again.

The soldiers burst into the crypt, too many to count, the leading figure clearly in command. They took a moment to gather their wits, blinking at the unexpected candlelight, staring about them, kicking the mahogany box to one side, trampling over the ruined swanskin where it lay on the stone floor. I saw Mather, still in his ceremonial uniform, soot-blackened, dishevelled, scarce recognizable, his control of things run amok.

In the boat Chance looked sick with fear.

Erland remained where he was; I could see the key clenched in his fingers.

At once Nate pulled on the oars, tentative, not a strong pull. Even so, there was a splash, a ripple of yellow lamplight on the black water.

They looked over. They saw Erland. And they saw us. 'Open the Gate!' shouted Mather.

The crypt suddenly rang with sharp, harsh echoes as they rushed over, Mather in the lead, athletic, determined. There were six of them. Two soldiers pointed their pistols direct at Erland's heart as he faced them calmly, his hands behind his back, standing against the Gate.

In the boat Nate seemed transfixed, his face aghast. He had stopped rowing at once. I believe he hated to see Erland left behind and defenceless when he himself had the means to escape. But we were trapped the longer we stayed there, exposed by the lamplight. Soon they would wrench the key from Erland's fingers even if they had to break them to do it.

'You're under arrest for treachery, Messenger!' Mather said brusquely. He glared through the Gate, saw Chance with us and looked even grimmer. His eyes were still the same as ever, cold, inhuman and now gleaming with an obsessive light. 'You're all to be taken in for questioning. That includes you, Miss Leah Tunstall.' He jerked his head at the Gate. 'Get it open!' he ordered his men.

They grunted as they struggled with it, pulling and pushing. Mather waited, his face unreadable. 'Must be locked, Sir,' said one, giving up at last.

I saw Erland's fingers feel the twining branches behind him, the curving bars of the Amber Gate: a tiny searching movement, undetected by the soldiers.

'Have you the key, Messenger?' hissed Mather viciously. He turned on his men. 'Search him!'

With a sudden twist of his fingers, Erland flicked the key through a gap between the branches. There was a brief glint of gold, then a deep *plop* as the key fell into the water. 'Row, Nate!' he shouted hoarsely.

Nate came out of his trance. He dipped the oars in, then out, pulled strongly. The boat lurched, then began to move more smoothly. We scarce breathed lest it should sink. We felt the water slide away beneath the wood. Above us, the curved roof dripped.

We gazed at each other wide-eyed with sudden hope, then back at Erland.

Our last glimpse of him, as we rounded the bend of the tunnel into darkness, was of a dusty white silk jacket pressed against the glory of the golden birds and amber fruit.

That was when we heard the shot fired.

6

The blast reverberated down the tunnel, hitting the walls around us so that I thought they would collapse. In that contained space it was the most terrifying, ugly sound. I slammed my hands to my head and ducked. My ears rang; I felt sick with terror.

As the echoes went on and on, Leah jerked forward so that the boat rocked. 'What have they done?'

There were no more shots, but the silence that finally came was uneasy, full of horror. We stared at each other. 'Erland?' I whispered.

'Mather has his ways with traitors,' muttered Chance. 'Sometimes slow, sometimes quick.'

'And you have learnt them, no doubt!' Leah snarled, but was not diverted long. She gazed back the way we'd come with such a savage look in the lamplight that I think she would have attacked Mather herself if she'd been able.

'Surely they have not killed him?' I said, pleading.

Chance shrugged. 'He dropped the key.'

Nate had paused on his oars as soon as the shot sounded.

He looked at me so apprehensive I knew he thought Erland was dead. We gazed at each other for a few agonized heartbeats, waiting – I don't know for what, exactly. Perhaps for some further sound from the other end.

What we heard next was so unexpected I don't believe either of us could have dreamed of it, ever.

Someone was singing by the Amber Gate.

A clear, pure sound curled along the tunnel towards us, so beautiful it made tears prick in my eyes, as if the singer had been waiting all his life to sing and was putting his whole self into the song. It filled my ears; it filled my very soul. It echoed all around us. Ethereal, it was – unearthly. I'd never heard singing like it before, nor since. It was so sweet, it reminded you of all the joy there is in life, yet it sang of sad things, too, for you cannot have one without the other.

At first it was notes alone, like a high sweet carolling, then it seemed to steady itself into a song – a song I knew.

> *'I left my love by the Amber Gate*
> *Where swans with crowns shall reign.'*

The song came to its end, the voice hung on the last dying note and faded. There was silence, but for the soft slip of water against the sides of the boat.

Nate clenched his jaw and took up the oars. He began to row again, saying nothing.

'What's happened to Erland?' I cried, as the brick walls skimmed past on either side. 'What does it mean? Should we go back?'

Chance shook his head in fear. 'Mather will kill me.'

'We can't go back,' said Leah stonily. She did not look at us but straight ahead at the darkness. 'There's no point. Erland is dead.'

'How do you know?' I whispered. I knew he must be, but I could not say so. The dreadful sorrow of it swept over me. I could not be like Leah and suffer in silence. I put my hands to my face and wept, and the sound of my dreadful, shocked weeping echoed all around us, until I saw the pain that Nate suffered too and was ashamed at my lack of courage.

As I pulled myself together, Leah said quietly to me, 'He did it for us, for all of us. And for the future.'

We were silent for a while as the boat eased its way through the suffocating darkness, a tiny floating light on the black water. The lichen on the dripping walls made a mosaic of rust and emerald green, touched by a faint glitter. Frail, leggy insects, caught in the lamplight, flickered away to hide beneath it. Delicate ferns grew from cracks in the brickwork; they brushed us wetly as we moved along the narrow channel. The damp air had a sour, salt smell to it, thick to breathe, as if imprisoning it for so long underground had changed its nature.

We were all damp, and chill to the bone. I thought of

Gobchick making this self-same journey for our sake, his bent little arms wielding the oars.

Then I thought of Erland.

'Which of us did he love?' I must have spoken my thought out aloud.

'He loved both of us,' said Leah.

I shook my head. 'You were his soul's love.'

There is no one to love me, I thought. I had lost Erland, my guardian; I had left Gobchick behind. I did not mean to think such selfish thoughts, but in the strange, drifting darkness, somehow I was full of melancholy when I should be happy at the thought of my return to Murkmere.

Leah goes back to Aggie, who is her great friend and loves her like a sister. I have no one.

Yet I knew that in the past I had not understood about love at all: that there are many kinds, and that it also embraces forgiveness and compassion and mercy. And thinking of Gobchick, I remembered how he had said that to receive love you must also give it; and perhaps I had not ever done so in my life, perhaps I had never had the chance.

And now I had.

'You have a family now, Clemency Scuff,' said Leah, as if she read my thoughts.

'A family?' I said, in amazement.

She gave a tiny crooked smile. 'Only a small one, I'm afraid – only me. I am your cousin. Your mother – the Lady Sophia – her maiden name was Tunstall. She was my aunt. So we are cousins, and I hope shall be friends.' And she held out her hand and I took it, and we shook hands on it. And she was my enemy no longer.

I looked from Leah, my new cousin, across to Nate. I saw the eagerness and warmth with which he gazed at me. I did have a friend, of course I did, and he had been one to me since the day we met.

And I had had other friends since I left Murkmere: Becca, Shadow, even Dog.

'You have the blood of the bravest rebel of all in your veins,' Nate said. 'The whole country knew the name of Robert Fane.'

I bowed my head. Most of my courage had come from him, my father, but perhaps a little bit of it I had made myself.

I had a half-brother, Caleb, but though I'd never love him, I had shown him clemency.

'I am sorry about your swanskin,' I said to Leah, and I truly meant it.

She touched the bag against her legs and smiled, a sad, strange smile. 'It's in here,' she said. We all stared at her in astonishment, for we had seen the ruined skin in the crypt, trodden over by the soldiers' careless feet, kicked aside with the mahogany box. 'It's true,' she said. 'The other swanskin belonged to Erland's grandmother. He swapped the two of them over when mine was still in the Palace showcase. It was his swanskin hanging in the Cathedral.

He gave my swanskin back to me when we said goodbye, and it's in here, unharmed, whole and beautiful.'

'Crafty blighter,' said Chance, with a touch of admiration. 'So he must have tricked his way into that room, unlocked the case and all.' Then he sounded the same as always, a sneer in his voice. 'But what does it matter, anyway? Isn't one swanskin like another?'

Leah picked up the bag and hugged it to her chest. She turned for the last time and stared at the darkness behind the boat; I saw her pale, proud profile. She murmured to herself, or whoever was listening, 'When I get back to Murkmere, I think I'll bury it again, at least for a while.'

Then she turned back, looked at us in the shifting lamplight and said in her most challenging voice, 'First to Murkmere, but then the rebels in the Eastern Edge will need a new leader. Which of us is it to be?'

After a while Nate lost all track of time. They had fallen silent in the boat, the two girls slumped against each other; Chance, in the stern, hidden in darkness.

Nate felt as if he had been beneath the city a lifetime. His shoulders and arms ached; he felt bruised from the waist up. Like a clockwork toy, he moved the oars automatically, dip and pull, dip and pull. Yet he dared not hand them over to Chance, for he could not trust him yet.

We are a motley crew, he thought. *A swan girl, a knave,*

a boy musician and a girl singer – yet who knows what we may achieve?

The air was growing fresher, warmer; his clothes were drying. His gaze lingered on Scuff. He was sure that her dear, sleeping face was clearer to him now; he could trace the fall of her hair, her closed eyelids, the shape of her half-open mouth. He saw the head of a swimming rat, its eyes shining red in the lamplight. Soon slats in the brickwork began to appear, lighter squares, as if behind them there might be twilit sky. Through one gap he thought he saw a star.

And then there was a widening in the channel, an expanse of water on either side, a great space around them, sudden heat. They were outside and the curve above their heads was the curve of the evening sky. Behind the boat he could see the black circle of the tunnel mouth below the grassy mound of an island.

Nate rested his oars and let the boat drift. He wanted to tell the girls, but they were asleep, their faces stilled of all emotion. But in the bows Chance raised his head and gazed, silent, his face transfigured by wonder.

This was Paradise – Paradise Park – the old ruined cemetery to the west of the Capital. Nate had heard his father mention it, but he had never been here. No bodies were brought here nowadays: the cemetery was forgotten. Around the wide black lake on which they floated were sloping banks on which hundreds of pale gravestones toppled and leaned amongst the weeds and overgrown grass. No birds sang their last evening trills here: it was an eerie, mysterious place, where spirits moved without a sound.

Towards the east the sky was a fiery red over the Capital, as if the whole city was ablaze. But it was only the last rays of the dying sun. He could see a black plume of smoke rising and drifting against the red, as if the Cathedral scaffolding still burned. But perhaps it was another fire altogether: in the summer, somewhere in the city was always burning. Far off he heard a dog howl, but the tumult of the people had died away.

When he turned his head the sky behind him was a deep, rich blue and there was the glimmer of the first star. The storm that had lurked earlier had passed away.

A wind arose, rocking the boat gently. On the banks the grasses rustled amongst the gravestones. Nate licked his finger and raised it in the air. The wind had changed direction, was blowing from the west. Soon the days of heat would be over.

He took up the oars again and began to row across the lake. He could see where a stream meandered away through a dip. If they followed the stream on foot, they would come to Gravendyke, the great river, and find a boat to take them up the coast to the Eastern Edge.

Out of the corner of his eye he saw a white shape gliding on the black water. With a jump of his heart he thought for a moment it had come out of the tunnel mouth. But that was not possible. Although it did not come close to the boat, he could see now it was a swan. In the dusk it seemed almost translucent, as if he could see through it, like a ghost or spirit.

But that was hardly surprising. This was the place of such things, after all.

MURKMERE

Patricia Elliott

'Yours is an unblemished soul, Aggie,' he whispered, *'a sweet, pure delicacy of a soul – and we must keep it that way, mustn't we?'*

Born and brought up in a small village, Aggie knows that she must never question the power of the divine beings – the birds – nor the omens in the Table of Significance. But when the Master of Murkmere Hall summons her to be companion to his ward, Leah, she enters a new and disturbing world. Leah is headstrong, spoilt and unhappy, and challenges everything Aggie has ever known to be true.

Secrets and betrayals lurk within the old house, and when the shadowy but all-powerful Ministration arrives for a grand ball, questioning becomes a dangerous game . . .

Longlisted for the Guardian Award 2004

THE ICE BOY

Patricia Elliott

There on the horizon were the unmistakable shapes of mountains, of snow-capped peaks, glaciers. He could see glittering towers and palaces of ice. On his lips was the powdery numbness of frost.

Could there really be a distant land far across the sea?

Edward's vision brings him hope that his father is alive and well, and didn't perish in the storm. If only he could reach the island and look for Dad.

When he rescues a mysterious stranger from the waves, Edward is given the chance to attempt this perilous quest, but time is fast running out . . .

Winner of the 2001 Fidler Award